SHE HAD TO STOP DWELLING ON THE NEGATIVE.

She had to put all the day's problems from her mind and think instead of her beautiful, secure home—an inviting image, even if the house would be empty and she'd have to spend the evening alone.

That was the only thing that made her home less than perfect. Molly wouldn't be there. Her daughter was the only person who truly mattered—which was exactly why she'd sent her to David's. Molly was better off with her father, at least until things calmed down.

As she neared the crest of the hill, she slowed the Mercedes. The rain intensified, obscuring her home perched at the summit, overlooking Marin and the lights across the bay. She entered the drive that rose steeply to the house. The floodlights came on automatically as she approached, illuminating the entire front of the structure. She stopped fifty feet from the house to look it over more carefully. Lights shone from nearly every window.

Satisfied everything was in order, she reached for the remote control to the garage. As she did, she saw them—two armless dolls dangling from the frame of the garage door, rope nooses around their necks. The larger, dark-haired doll was spattered with red. A butcher knife skewered a piece of paper to the front of it. The other doll, the smaller one, could represent only one thing—Molly.

Also available from MIRA Books and
JANICE KAISER

PRIVATE SINS

Coming soon

LAST NIGHT IN RIO

This
Best
of the
Best™
Collector's Edition
belongs in the
personal library of

JANICE KAISER

FAIR GAME

MIRA BOOKS

ISBN 1-55166-065-2

FAIR GAME

Copyright © 1996 by Belles-Lettres, Inc.

MIRA and the star colophon are trademarks of MIRA Books.

Printed in U.S.A.

For Sherie Posesorski

One

Ross, California
Wednesday, February 25

She drove along Sir Francis Drake Boulevard, unable to shake the feeling that something ominous was about to happen. The surrounding hills were shrouded in mist, the darkness was menacing—or was it only her mood? She didn't like the dank or the cold or the long winter nights. She was looking forward to the warmth and security of home.

The wipers on her pale blue 560 SEL Mercedes brushed away the moisture gathering on the windshield. A melancholy jazz piece played on the radio. She tried to listen, but her mind kept drifting back to the dinner meeting she'd just had with Bev O'Connell.

"I'll let you know soon," Bev promised as they said goodbye in the parking lot. "I won't keep you waiting long."

"Take your time," she'd replied. "It's an important decision. Nothing you want to rush."

"I need to talk to Ted," Bev said. "He takes a big interest in my career, you know."

Dana Kirk understood exactly what Bev was saying. Everybody who knew the O'Connells was well aware that Ted was a domineering bastard. He was a born loser, hav-

ing failed at everything he'd ever tried. Yet he resented his
wife's success and frequently belittled and humiliated her
in public. Dana couldn't forgive that, though of course it
was none of her business—it was Bev's life.

The chances were good Bev would leave Cedrick &
Betts—unless Ted mucked things up, that is. Unfortunately she hadn't given any indication as to what his attitude might be. And Dana didn't know him well enough to
say. She'd only had limited contact with the man. Their
most memorable encounter had been at a Cedrick & Betts
Christmas party a few years earlier. Ted had gotten drunk
and propositioned her. She'd shrugged the incident off to
booze, and the fact that the guy was basically a jerk. But
there was no way of knowing whether he'd hold that incident against her now.

She stopped at a light as the rain started coming down
harder. The windshield blurred, so she turned the wipers to
a higher speed. Waiting, she absently glanced at the car
beside her. She had been doing that more and more these
days. Being wary. Always wary of those around her.

The light changed and she started up again, checking the
side street. The weather slowed everything down, though
this storm was nothing compared with what they were
forecasting for the weekend. Rain always put her in an uneasy mood—not that she wasn't already tense enough. No
matter how hard she tried to stay up, the last few weeks had
gotten to her. Maybe that was why signing up Bev had become such an emotionally charged issue. She couldn't afford any more failures.

Just the same, it upset Dana that her battle with C&B
had gotten down and dirty. For all her competitiveness, she
had never thought of herself as cutthroat, and she hated it
that running her own company called for a new kind of
toughness.

Months earlier, when she'd told Frank Betts she was leaving C&B to start Kirk & Company, he'd said, "Don't even think about getting in the game with the big boys unless you're willing to play by their rules." It was as though he had dared her to take a swing at him, maybe thinking she didn't have the guts. Frank, of all people, should have known better.

But she didn't want to think about old lovers and her days at C&B. Both had become a source of guilt. She suspected that went back to something her father had once said in a rare moment of sobriety—"Profit's not profit if it comes at another's expense." Maybe that was the source of her unhappiness. These days, winning meant hurting people who'd once been her friends.

Dana started to turn off the boulevard onto a side street. A figure suddenly darted in front of the car. She slammed on her brakes, skidded on the wet pavement and barely stopped before hitting him. The man, a jogger, lost his balance and toppled over the fender, catching himself with his hands. Dazed, he stared at her from under the hood of his slicker, his eyes round with fright.

Dana was stunned. The man righted himself and stood in the glare of her headlights, appearing unsure whether to be angry or apologetic. She lowered her window, but he had gathered himself and began to move away.

"Are you all right?" she called after him.

He glanced back, but like a frightened animal simply fled into the darkness. Dana stared off in the direction he'd gone. She was too dazed to move until the rain blowing against her face brought her back. She started to run the window up, not realizing until then that the engine was dead.

She got the motor started again, wondering if it was really all right to drive away. What if the jogger had been hurt and hadn't said anything? She proceeded up the street, deciding since he left the scene first, he must have been okay. It could easily have been a disaster, though. She was lucky. She might have killed him.

At the next intersection she slowed, making the turn with extra caution. Trembling, she drove up the dark twisting road toward her home, the headlights of the car raking the towering eucalyptus trees that lined the pavement. She glanced at the homes of her neighbors. Some were lit like jewel boxes against the night sky. Others were hidden behind walls or wrought-iron fences. Vigilance, she'd come to realize, was a way of life for everyone, not just her.

She had to stop dwelling on the negative. She had to put the jogger, Bev O'Connell, Cedrick & Betts and all the rest of the day's problems from her mind and think instead of her beautiful, warm, secure home. It was an inviting image, even if the house would be empty and she'd have to spend the evening alone.

That was the only thing that made her home less than perfect. Molly wouldn't be there. Her daughter was the emotional focus of her life, the only person who truly mattered—which, of course, was exactly why she'd sent her to David's. Molly was better off with her father—at least until things calmed down. Still, a part of her feared that he might somehow take advantage of the situation.

Dana gripped the wheel, knowing that particular train of thought was the most dangerous of all. She was suspicious of everyone and everything, and that would only work against her in the end. She had to take control, think of something positive—like the hot bath that was waiting for her. Afterward she'd pour herself a glass of wine, put on some music and unwind. Pamper herself. Yes, that was what she needed to do; get her mind off her troubles.

As she neared the crest of the hill, she slowed the Mercedes. The rain intensified, obscuring her palatial home perched at the summit, overlooking Marin and the glittering lights across the bay.

She entered the drive that rose steeply to the house. The floodlights came on automatically as she approached, illuminating the entire front of the structure. She'd already had the largest shrubs removed so that a prowler wouldn't have a place to hide. She wanted to be able to see everything when she came home late—to be able to enter the garage without the fear that someone would slip in behind her before the door went down. In this instance, it wasn't paranoia. It was common sense.

The steady rain blurred her view, so she stopped fifty feet from the house to be able to look it over more carefully. Lights shone from nearly every window.

Satisfied everything was in order, she reached for the remote control. As she did, she saw them—two armless dolls dangling from the frame of the garage door, rope nooses around their necks. The larger, dark-headed doll was spattered with red. A butcher knife skewered a piece of paper to the front of it. The other doll, the smaller one, could represent only one thing—Molly. It was all Dana could do to fight the rising panic. Her hand trembling, she reached for the car phone. It would not be the first time the police had heard from her at night. Nor, judging by the way things were going, would it be the last.

Two

San Rafael
Friday, February 27

Mitchell Cross sat at his desk, staring at a two-year-old burglary file. He'd been at it for fifteen minutes and hadn't digested a word. The problem was easy to diagnose. Apathy. An early sign of burnout. At least, that was what he'd heard from the old-timers. Damn.

Cross got up and went to the window of his cramped basement office. He looked up the window well at the gray misty sky. It was nearly dusk, but it wasn't raining hard. It was just dreary. He didn't mind the weather. It kind of went with the work.

Cross hoped this feeling was temporary. He'd always enjoyed being a cop, and at thirty-nine he was too young to hang it up. Besides, what could he do that wouldn't be twice as boring, even on the good days?

Things had been routine lately. That was the problem. Some guys liked a nice, slow, steady pace. He wasn't one. He thrived on challenge—something new and different. The thing he liked best about police work was the thrill of the hunt. The thing he liked least was routine. Unfortunately, that was a big part of the job. What he needed was a hot case that got his juices flowing.

Cross watched the drizzle, yawning. He still had an hour to go on his shift and nothing special to look forward to that night. He considered giving Carole a call, have her fix him dinner, get drunk, then get laid—a nice domestic evening with the lady of the month. Trouble was, she didn't appreciate last-minute calls on a Friday or Saturday night, and had told him so in no uncertain terms. "Makes me feel like you couldn't find anything better to do," she'd say. And she had a point.

So scratch Carole. Maybe he'd drive up to Santa Rosa, have a steak and a few beers, then go over to Hogg's and watch the girls dance, maybe shake his own boots a time or two.

Cross's reverie was broken by a rap on the door. He turned around. Lieutenant Bensen, his portly supervisor, was standing there, his ever-present service revolver perched on his hip. He had a file in his hand.

"Hope I'm not interrupting anything important," Bensen said.

"No, Al, I'm just bored. Can't decide if it's worth trying to get laid tonight or not."

The lieutenant smiled sardonically. "Things are that bad, huh?"

"Figure of speech."

Bensen chuckled. "Yeah, sure."

"What you got?" Cross asked, glancing at the file in Bensen's hand.

"Don't have a homicide to send you out on, unfortunately—or fortunately, depending on how you look at it— but I do have a question. Do you recall any cases involving harassment of a real-estate broker?"

"A real-estate broker? You kidding?"

"I know it's hard to believe anybody would want to harass one, but I thought you might remember seeing something."

"Not anything active in the department. Why?"

Al Bensen sat down on the wooden visitor's chair and crossed his ankles. "Late yesterday afternoon I got a call from Walt Applegate, the chief over in Ross. He wanted to know if there was any way he could palm off a case to the Hate Crimes Task Force. Some froufrou lady broker by the name of Dana Kirk has been getting death threats. They figure it could be somebody who hates real-estate agents and thought other jurisdictions might be getting more of the same."

Cross returned to his chair. "Sounds like a fascinating case, Al." His sarcasm wasn't lost on Bensen.

"Naturally, when this came in, you were the first person I thought of, Mitch."

"Must be my Yuppie mentality. I guess I look like someone who could relate to a—what did you call her?—froufrou real-estate broker?"

"Yeah."

Cross folded his hands over his stomach and smiled. "But let me get this straight. The guys in Ross seriously think death threats against a Realtor constitute a hate crime?"

"Walt was serious enough to send over the file," Bensen said, holding up the folder before putting it on the desk. "He really wants to unload it."

"Can hardly say I blame him."

"This might be more interesting than you think. Not that 'interesting' is a requirement when there's work that needs doing, if you get my drift."

Cross sighed with resignation. "Yes, sir."

Bensen grinned. "I like your attitude, Cross."

"Anything for a pal."

"To be honest, this is one of those obligation things. I owe Walt a favor." He scratched his head. "Anyway, the task force could use something to do. We wouldn't want to lose our funding."

"I'm understanding the case better and better." Cross leaned across the desk and picked up the folder, briefly paging through it. He found the four notes, each written in pencil in block letters. The language was full of invective. He closed the folder and put it down on the desk. "Well, the words seem hateful enough," he said, repressing a smile. "I guess that officially makes it a hate crime."

"Before we get too glib, you might like to know that the victim has a friend over in the D.A.'s office. One of the assistants. Liz Rogers. I think you know her."

"Yeah, Liz and I did a big drug case together a few years ago. Nice lady."

"Ms. Rogers already gave me a jingle. Asked that I have whoever works the case give her a call. She seems to think she can give a little perspective on the victim since they're friends."

"Great. A case with an interdepartmental political angle. Exactly what I need."

"There's not much background information about the victim in the file," Bensen said. "Liz Rogers could be helpful. And since when has it hurt to make the D.A.'s office happy?"

"Politics stinks. But that's a personal opinion," Cross said, opening the file again. He looked at the data sheet. "Dana Kirk, huh?"

"Yeah. Walt Applegate said she's not a bad-looking piece. That ought to appeal to you."

"Think so?"

"Weren't you the guy complaining about not getting laid a couple of minutes ago?"

"You're going to hold that against me, Al?"

Bensen got to his feet. He pointed at the file. "There's your chance, Mitch."

"Thanks, but she's not my type."

"You haven't even seen the lady."

"Believe me, I know."

"Well, far be it from me to tell you what to do with your cock." He went to the door and stopped. "But let's not forget it's the taxpayers who pay our salaries."

"Especially the froufrou lady real-estate brokers with political connections. Right?"

"Yeah, that about sums it up."

"I'll get on it first thing in the morning."

"Handle it any way you want, but do us both a favor and schmooze Liz Rogers a little. Politics, you know," Bensen said, clucking his tongue.

"You owe me, Lieutenant," Cross said.

Bensen put his hands on his hips. "In one fell swoop I cure your boredom and give you a chance to enhance your sex life, and you say I owe you?"

"I'd prefer a nice juicy murder case—not that I wish anybody dead or anything."

Al Bensen grinned. "Catch the sonovabitch who's writing the threatening letters, and maybe you can prevent a murder. Not to mention saving a damsel in distress." He playfully pointed his finger at him like a gun. "And who knows, maybe the lady will be so foxy she'll sell you a house." He winked and left the office.

"Mitchell Cross," Liz Rogers said when she came on the line. "What's it been, two years?"

"Something like that. How've you been, counselor?"

"I'm eight months pregnant, if that tells you anything."

"Probably more than I need to know," he said with a laugh.

"You've got that right."

"Congratulations."

"Thanks, but consolation would be just as appropriate."

Cross smiled. He'd forgotten how quippy the cute little blond attorney was. But he hadn't forgotten she was Stanford and Berkeley Law. Nor had he forgotten that prick of a husband of hers.

Cross had met the guy just once—at an open house Liz had invited him to shortly after they'd wrapped up their drug case. He figured the only reason Martin Rogers had deigned to talk to him was out of curiosity about the man his wife had been spending so much time with. Satisfied that he was sufficiently plebeian, the bastard had gone off swirling his martini, his Harvard-and-Yale nose up in the air.

"Then you have my condolences, counselor," Cross said.

"I take it Lieutenant Bensen put you on the Dana Kirk case."

"Yes. He said you wanted a call."

"I thought it might be helpful to chat since I know her. I can give you some insights."

Cross couldn't imagine what Liz Rogers could tell him that he couldn't get from Dana Kirk herself but he'd listen—hell, he was paid to listen. "Fine. I understand you and she are friends."

"Not close friends. She sold us our house several years ago and we've stayed in touch. Dana called me when she got the first letter."

"I see. So tell me about Ms. Kirk."

"Well, how do I describe her? Dana's about thirty-five. A lovely person. Quite attractive. She's been divorced several years. Her daughter is living with the ex now because of this business with the death threats. He's a local shrink. Actually, Dana's as concerned about Molly as she is about herself."

"Does she get along with her ex?"

"I don't know. She never spoke much about him until the other day. I think David's been wanting Molly to live with him for some time, and with Dana getting death threats it's become an issue. I'm not sure how heated."

"So you're saying Ms. Kirk has problems in her personal life."

"Nothing compared to her professional problems."

"I'm listening."

"Dana was the top producer at Cedrick & Betts."

"The big firm here in Marin."

"Yes. She left them to start her own company and took some people with her."

"So her old bosses have an axe to grind."

"We discussed the possibility that somebody at C&B was upset enough with her to send threatening letters, but Dana told me it wasn't likely. Brokers are always trying to lure the best people from the competition. It's a reason to get pissed off but not a reason to kill somebody. At least, that's what she says."

"In other words, she doesn't suspect them."

"That's right, Mitch."

Cross thought for a moment. "What about disgruntled clients?"

"I discussed that with her, too. She said she can't name a single person who's truly angry with her. Not to this extent."

Cross flipped through the file as he listened. "Sounds like she's underestimating someone. Either that or we're dealing with a nut."

"That's what Dana's afraid of, Mitch. If the guy's crazy enough, he just might try to hurt her daughter."

"I haven't studied the file carefully, but offhand I'd say Ms. Kirk is going to have to come up with the key to this thing. I'll talk with her and see if there's anything, or anyone, she's overlooked."

"I'm glad Lieutenant Bensen put you on the case," Liz said with surprising candor.

"Oh?"

"Yes. To be honest, I always liked your bedside manner, Detective Cross."

"If you weren't eight months pregnant I'd read something into that," he said with a laugh.

"If I weren't eight months pregnant, I wouldn't have said it."

"Touché."

"Keep me informed, would you?" Liz Rogers said. "I feel a certain amount of responsibility."

"You got it, counselor."

Mitchell Cross hung up, a big smile on his face. Liz Rogers was cute and quippy, but she was still a rich Yuppie. She drove the most expensive BMW made, did her skinny-dipping in a hot tub, and rooted for Stanford at the Big Game each year. Some guys wanted that. He didn't. A long time ago he decided the best women were corn-fed. No pretensions that way. And no phony Yuppiness, either.

Ross

"Come to the party with me. It would do you good to be out among people."

Dana smiled, moving the phone to her other ear. "Robin, I just got all the doors bolted and the curtains closed. I've got my clothes off and I'm about to run a bath. The party would be half over before I was ready."

"So come late. Laurel wouldn't mind. We'll go someplace afterward. Dancing or something."

Dana laughed. "You're too much! I can't believe you'd want to be seen in public with me."

"Why? You don't think the guy would spray a nightclub with machine-gun fire, do you?"

"No, he'd just bomb my car. Why kill innocent people?"

"At least you can laugh about it," Robin said. "That's good."

"I'm not laughing, Robin. I'm scared shitless, if you want to know the truth. All I want to do is get in bed and pull the covers over my head."

"Oh, poor baby." Robin had been genuinely concerned ever since Dana had gotten the first letter. "I guess that means you definitely won't be coming to the party."

"No, I don't think so. I put in a long day at the office. Judy Povich sold a condo in Tiburon. I was helping her iron out the wrinkles until after six. At least we made some money. I'm trying to keep my mind on positive things."

"That's why I thought the party would be good for you."

"Next time."

"Want me to drop by after I leave Laurel's?" Robin asked. "I can bring you some food."

Dana had to smile. Though single and childless, Robin Cohen was a classic Jewish mother. For her, food somehow figured into the solution of almost every problem.

They'd been close for five years. Dana had started out as her mentor and they'd become best friends. Robin very nearly left C&B to join Kirk & Company but ultimately they decided it was in the best interests of their friendship to avoid a boss-employee relationship.

Dana was glad it had worked out that way. With Robin on the outside, she could let down her hair more easily. With her sales force, as with her daughter, she had to be a rock—the strong one the others could rely on.

The portable phone cocked to her ear, Dana walked into the bathroom. "I'd love to see you tonight, Robin," she said, "and if you think some party food will help keep the bogeyman at bay, then bring whatever you can scrounge."

"Are you kidding? Laurel will tell me to load up. She overdoes every party by fifty percent but then she knows I'm always good for half the excess." Robin sighed. "Well, if you're going to be a stick-in-the-mud, I guess I go man-watching alone."

"Good luck," Dana said, heading for the tub. "And thanks for thinking of me."

"Hey, what are little sisters for?"

Dana locked the bathroom door behind her. "Little in what sense, hotshot?"

"Bitch."

"I love you too, Robin."

"See you in a couple of hours."

"Okay. Come by whenever you feel like it. And if you meet Mr. Wonderful, do what you have to do. I'll assume you've gone off with him to his swinging bachelor pad if I don't hear from you."

"Ha! With the hair day I'm having, the apocalypse is more likely. Keep your head down, Kirk."

"Bye." Dana turned the phone off and set it on the green marble vanity. There was a big smile on her face because she felt much better for having talked to her friend.

She started running water into the whirlpool tub, adding bubble bath. As she waited for it to fill she glanced around. The adjoining dressing room was about the size of the bedroom she'd had as a girl. In fact her bedroom suite was larger than the tiny house in Napa she'd shared with her father as a child.

But Dana took special pride in the bathroom. It was both luxurious and beautiful. Still, at the moment, it offered little solace. Her business was on the line, her child gone. And her life was in danger.

When the tub was full she turned off the water and climbed in. She did not turn on the jets, contenting herself with lying in the warm, still water. It felt wonderful on her taut muscles. These moments of peace came so infrequently. She had to savor them.

As a child she'd felt secure in her warm bed. Now, as an adult, a hot bath behind a securely locked door did the same.

Dana closed her eyes, telling herself for the hundredth time that dwelling on her problems was exactly what *he* wanted. She couldn't let him beat her. She had to stay in control. It was time for a "gut check." That's what Frank used to say whenever anybody went through a rough patch. Gut check.

Dana searched her memory for the most pleasant recollection she could find. It was the best way she knew to change her mood. One of her earliest annual-awards breakfasts at C&B came to mind—the one where she'd first received the award for being the company's top producer. When Frank called out her name, she'd jumped up on the stage. Everyone had cheered. It had been wonderful. Life was simpler back then. Or at least, her problems had been simpler.

The water started getting tepid and she knew she had to get out. She stood, the filmy water dripping from her body. She quickly dried herself with a bath sheet, then rubbed body lotion over her skin.

As she was drying her hair, her mind flashed on the armless dolls again. The one with the chin-length black hair and bangs had represented her. She shivered at her recollection of the way it had been covered with fake blood. She turned off the hair dryer and stood listening to the silence in the house. Outside she could hear the wind picking up. Inexplicably, she had a feeling that she wasn't alone.

Her mind had been playing tricks on her recently. She was always getting creepy feelings, hearing sounds, imagining that people were following her. Paranoia. But she had good cause. She wasn't sure whether to take comfort in that or not. Was it better to be nuts or in real danger?

She dressed, putting on a black velour jogging suit. Then she went to the door. As she reached for the knob, her hand froze. She had to tell herself there wasn't anyone standing on the other side, ready to grab her.

It took an effort of will to turn the knob and release the lock but she did it. Slowly pushing the door open, she found the bedroom suite as she left it, the curtains closed, every light on.

Dana walked around the room to satisfy herself that she was alone. She looked behind the heavy wicker chaise longue and the matching upholstered armchairs in the sitting area. She glanced under the antique writing desk, behind the Indian-style paisley-print draperies and even under the bed, still only half convinced it was safe. It would have been embarrassing to behave this way if her fear wasn't so real. Then, she sat on the bed, emotionally exhausted.

Glancing at the Waterford clock on the bedstand, she calculated it would be an hour, maybe two, before Robin arrived. She wished it were sooner. Robin was a little island of sanity. Her salvation. God knows, the police hadn't done much. They'd been sympathetic, but they were as baffled by the death threats as she. And now it seemed the case was being taken over by somebody new.

Dana was glad. Ray Brockmeyer, the detective she'd dealt with thus far, hadn't given her a lot of reason to hope. He'd been sympathetic, of course, but she still felt as though she'd been left twisting in the wind, alone.

At first it hadn't seemed all that serious. The initial letter had struck her as a childish prank, though the language had been strong. "You're a stupid bitch and you deserve to die," he had written. But why did she *deserve* it? He hadn't even cited a crime. It had to be a joke.

Robin had been worried. She'd persuaded her to call Liz Rogers, which led to the police getting involved. Even then, Dana still wasn't certain it was serious. She had remained skeptical until the second letter came: "You're too fucking arrogant and stupid to believe I'm going to kill you, aren't you, bitch? But I am. When the time's right."

The third letter had been taped to her front door in the middle of the night. Knowing the perpetrator had dared to enter her property had scared Dana to death. And the words in that note had been much stronger: "Think how close I came, cunt. Would you rather die in your sleep, or see my face?"

Every word the bastard had written was burned into her brain, the last one—the one he had pinned to the garage door with the butcher knife—more than the others: "You don't get the message, do you, you stupid-ass bitch? Maybe if I pull off your little girl's arms before I pull off yours, you'll see I mean business."

That night she'd sat trembling on the sofa in her front room while the police officers had looked on sympathetically. "What's the damn message?" she'd asked tearfully. "He never says what he wants me to do!"

"Maybe that's the point, ma'am," the patrolman had said. "This jerk's trying to drive you bananas, in my opinion."

"He's doing a damn good job. I'll tell you that!" And then she had cried.

Once the police had become involved she'd had no choice but to tell David what was going on. He'd insisted that Molly move out, and she couldn't blame him, even though the past couple of weeks without her had been pure hell. But she couldn't be sure the son of a bitch wasn't crazy enough to harm an innocent girl. If there'd been any doubt before, the last incident with the two dolls had proved to her she'd been right not to take the risk.

On top of everything else, she'd been getting strange calls the past week or so. The phone would ring but when she answered, nobody would be there. No heavy breathing. Nothing. It happened once or twice each evening.

The police said it might be coincidental—a kid from Molly's school, maybe. They hadn't taken it too seriously since no verbal threats had been made. But Dana was positive her tormentor had found a new way to terrify her. Ray Brockmeyer had mentioned the possibility of having the phone company put a tap on the line, but she figured he'd only said it to appease her.

When she happened to mention the calls to Stu Lindstrom, the guy who'd installed the computer system at her office, he offered to help. He had come by her house with a caller ID device that gave a readout on a display screen of the telephone number of the incoming caller.

"This baby is illegal in California," he'd said when he'd hooked it to her phone, "but mighty handy if you've gotta know who's calling. Don't tell anybody where you got it."

Stu's gizmo had worked nicely. When her receptionist, Chiara Fiolli, had called from the office, Kirk & Co.'s number had popped up on the display. The same when Laurel Easterbrook had returned her call that morning. She'd known it was Laurel even before she picked up the phone.

Dana gazed over at the clock on the nightstand, realizing it would be a long time still before Robin showed up. She hadn't eaten yet. Maybe that was what she ought to do—fix herself some dinner. She headed for the kitchen, though she wasn't particularly hungry. But she had to keep up her strength. That's what Robin had said in one of her lectures.

As Dana stepped into the family room, she paused to listen. She could hear the rain blowing against the double sliding-glass doors that led onto the deck, but she couldn't see anything because she'd closed the plantation shutters. She shivered at the thought that somebody might be on the deck, but she couldn't call the police every time a floorboard creaked.

She went into the kitchen to fix herself something to eat. The hardwood floors, green granite countertops and white cabinets were immaculate. The cleaning lady had been there that morning, arriving as Dana had left for the office. This was the third house Anita Gomez had done for her. Anita had six women working for her nowadays, but Dana paid extra for her to do the house herself. Now more than ever, she needed people she could trust.

Only then did she notice that the message light was blinking on the answering machine. Apparently the call had come in while she was in the bath. Taking a deep breath, Dana hit the Replay button. The tape rewound, clicked, then a man's voice came from the machine.

"Mrs. Kirk, this is Detective Mitchell Cross from the San Rafael P.D.," he said. "I'd like to meet with you at your earliest convenience to discuss your situation. Please give me a buzz at my office. I have the morning shift tomorrow and should be at my desk early. The number of my direct line is 555-4242."

The message ended, but the sound of the man's voice stayed with her. He'd referred to her "situation." Was that police jargon, or simply a euphemism? "Detective Mitchell Cross," she said, repeating the name to herself. Her new guardian angel. She wondered if he'd be any better than Ray Brockmeyer.

Dana had rinsed out her soup bowl and was cleaning the countertop when the phone rang. A chill went through her. She glanced at the number on Stu's gizmo. It wasn't familiar. She swallowed hard, reminding herself that didn't automatically mean it was *him*. She jotted down the number, then warily picked up the receiver.

"Hello?" she said softly.

There was no reply.

"Hello?"

Still no reply.

It *was* him. She listened with the phone pressed to her ear, her body becoming more and more tense. She could hear some faint background noise. A low roar, like the sound of traffic. Was he outside, at a pay phone, maybe?

Dana closed her eyes. Her heart was pounding so hard she began to hear her pulse. Or did she feel it? He was silent. The same cat-and-mouse game as before. The police had told her to wait him out, not to speak if he didn't. After a minute the phone clicked and there was a dial tone. He'd hung up. But she had his number!

Dana immediately dialed it. It rang seven or eight times but there was no answer. She was about to hang up when somebody picked up the receiver.

"Yeah?" It was a man's voice.

It took her a second to gather herself. "Who's this?"

"Billy."

"Billy who?"

"Who do you want?"

"Did you just call me?" she asked.

"Look, the phone here was ringing and I answered it. What do you want?"

"Someone called me from that telephone a minute ago. Where is it? Where am I calling?"

"This is the Chevron station on Center. The pay phone."

"In San Anselmo?"

"Yeah."

"Did you see who used it a minute ago?"

"No, I just heard it ringing. Sometimes my girlfriend calls on this phone 'cause the boss doesn't like havin' the station phone tied up for personal calls."

"Listen, I've got to know who just used that phone. Don't you see anybody around? Walking up the street, maybe? It's very, very important."

"Look, lady, there's a million people around here. I don't know who used the phone but I got to get back to work. I'm not the answering service. Sorry."

The phone went dead. Dana groaned. Why couldn't he have seen who'd called? Whoever *he* was, *he* was either very lucky or very smart. Too damned bad *he* didn't call from home. A slip like that and they could nail him.

She stared at Stu Lindstrom's caller ID device. At any time the phone could ring and another unfamiliar number could appear on the display. Her nemesis usually called at least twice in an evening. If he held to the pattern, he'd likely strike again. And there wasn't a damn thing she could do about it but wait.

San Anselmo

He finished the last of his drink and put the glass down, feeling more nervous than usual. Then he looked at his watch. He didn't have much time and he had his second call to make. He started to get up from the stool, leaving the bills on the bar, but then he thought better of it. There was no point in drawing attention to himself by overtipping. Removing all but the coins, he made his way toward the rest room.

The pay phone was in the back corner of the hallway. It was free. A skinny woman with big red hair came out of the ladies' rest room. She had that look of a cheap broad on the make. A momentary feeling of revulsion coursed through him. He stepped over to the phone, looking back toward the barroom to make sure no one was coming.

This routine was getting to be a drain but it had to be much harder on her. Had to be. She'd crack eventually. She *had* to, by God.

Slipping a quarter into the slot, he dialed her number for the second time that evening and waited, shifting uneasily. She answered on the third ring.

"Hello?"

He slipped his hand over the mouthpiece so that the noise coming from the bar wouldn't be heard. He waited.

"Hello?" she said again.

He said nothing.

"Damn it!" she cried hysterically. "What do you want? Tell me!"

He smiled, hearing the panic in her voice. Finally! The bitch was losing her cool. It had taken long enough. After a long desperate minute that ended with a sob, the receiver slammed down. Feeling a burden had been lifted, he hung up and stepped into the men's room to relieve himself.

There were two other men there, one washing his hands, the other combing his hair. He went to the urinal. As he began to pee, he heard the telephone ring outside in the hallway.

The man who'd been combing his hair left. The telephone continued to ring. The man who'd been at the basin was drying his hands on a paper towel while examining his face for pimples in the mirror. The ringing continued.

"Jesus," the guy mumbled as he tossed a towel into the wastepaper basket, "some poor bastard's wife must be trying to track him down." Chuckling, he walked out.

The ringing was beginning to bother him. The rest room door opened again and a young fellow with long hair entered, going directly to the urinal. The phone stopped ringing abruptly.

"Hello?" an irritated female voice said out in the hall. "What do you want?"

He lingered near the door, fiddling with a paper towel while he listened.

"Look, how should I know who's been using this phone? You calling for somebody in particular or what?"

His brow furrowed. What the hell was going on?

"No, I didn't see anybody," the woman said. "I answered to stop the damn ringing. Look, I got to get back to work."

Apparently one of the cocktail waitresses had picked up the phone. Surely she wasn't talking to Dana. How could she have known where to call?

"No, this is not a service station, it's a tavern," the barmaid said. "You called the wrong number."

An icy pain went through him. My God, she did know! Dana must have gotten hold of one of those gadgets that gave a readout of the caller's number. His heart started tripping. He hadn't expected this. Shit, this meant he had to be damned careful. If that waitress had seen him on the phone, he'd be a dead man.

"Well, sounds like you better take your problem to the cops," the barmaid said. "I sure as heck don't have time to describe everybody who's been in here the last ten minutes. I don't look at their faces anyway. Just their money."

He heard the sound of her heels as she walked away. The young guy with the long hair brushed past him and he followed him back into the barroom.

The place was crowded. He'd be inconspicuous. Still, his hand trembled. He'd gotten a good lesson. But he couldn't be deterred. He had to keep the pressure on.

Zipping his jacket, he went to the front door. Before going into the rain he glanced around. Both cocktail waitresses were busy. Nobody seemed to be paying attention to him. That was good. Just the way he wanted it. Anonymous. Seemingly innocent.

Ross

Dana stared at the phone numbers scribbled on the pad. A service station and a bar. Her tormentor had been at each place, but the information was useless. He was like a ghost—invisible even in public.

She fought back a sob. She didn't know what to do and there was no one she could to turn to. Her friends—Robin especially—could offer sympathy and understanding but they couldn't reverse the awful course her life had taken. No one could.

In a fit of desperation Dana picked up the phone and dialed David's number. Maybe if she talked to Molly she'd feel better. It rang four times and then the answering machine came on. Dana groaned. They couldn't be out! After the recorded message the machine beeped.

Dana sighed. "It's me," she said. "If either of you are there, please pick up the phone. If not, Molly, could you give me a call later?" She waited a moment. "Thanks."

She was about to hang up when she heard a click, then Molly's voice. "Mom?"

"Good, you *are* there. I'm glad you're using the answering machine to screen calls. It's important to be careful."

"Dad told me to, especially when he's not here."

"Isn't he there now?"

"No, he had some errands to run."

"You're alone?" Dana couldn't help the alarm in her voice.

"Yes, Mom. I'm not a child, you know."

"I know that, Molly," she said, looking at her watch. "I'm surprised, that's all, especially considering it's nearly eight on a Friday night. What's he doing, anyway?"

"I don't know," the girl returned, "I didn't ask. He doesn't cross-examine me, so I don't cross-examine him."

The implied criticism was obvious. "I wasn't suggesting that you should. I just thought your father might have said where he's going."

"Maybe it was the grocery store. He asked if I was hungry for anything special."

"Well, that makes sense. Guess you haven't had dinner yet."

"No, Mom."

"I hope you've been eating properly."

"Actually, Dad's been starving me. I'm lucky if I get a scrap of bread around here."

"Is the sarcasm necessary?"

"I was only kidding. Since you're so interested in my diet, last night Dad made his tuna casserole," Molly said blandly. "It was nice to get something that wasn't frozen for a change."

Another shot! A good percentage of the meals Dana made came straight from the freezer. It had been a sore point, especially since David had always been domestic, working hard to create a homey atmosphere. But what could she do? She'd never given a damn about cooking, and putting in long days did not make it easy to play Holly Homemaker at night.

The real problem, of course, was the divorce. Molly had blamed her. And if anyone had been at fault, then it probably was her. On the surface her marriage hadn't appeared that bad, but she'd been dissatisfied and unhappy. For several years she'd tried to make it work, mainly because of Molly, but eventually she'd yielded to the sad fact that she and David simply didn't belong together.

She'd tried to explain to Molly once what had happened, but it had been a mistake. To a teenager, anything parents did that wasn't in the kid's interest, was hostile and selfish. And since there always had to be a good guy and a bad guy, David became the martyr and she the villain.

Dana had discussed Molly's attitude with David on several occasions. His comments were lengthy, as always, but what it boiled down to was that Molly was a teenager and she liked to push people's buttons. Of course, that didn't make it any easier, especially coming on the heels of her struggle to get Kirk & Company going, paying for the new house, and dealing with the death threats.

"It's good you're spending some time with your father," Dana finally said, trying to sound as upbeat as she could. "Weekends haven't been enough for you to get to know each other the way you can living together."

"Yeah, I guess."

"Still, I'm eager for you to come home. I miss you."

"Do you?" Molly's tone fell midway between surprise and accusation.

"Of course. Don't you believe that?"

"I don't know. I figured you were glad to get rid of me. It gives you a chance to screw Frank any time you want."

"Molly!" Dana was shocked.

"Well, it's true, isn't it?"

"No, it's *not* true. I haven't seen Frank in months. And you're completely out of line talking to me that way. It's impertinent. What's more, I'm sure your father would agree."

"He doesn't care who you sleep with, either."

"I was referring to your language. And you damned well know it."

"Give me a break, Mom. You and Robin say things like that all the time. Besides, you're wrong about Dad. He's not uptight about everything like you are."

Still another blow. Dana's instinct was to defend herself, but she told herself it would just fuel Molly's hostility. It wasn't easy. Nothing, absolutely nothing, seemed to be going right.

"Listen, Molly, I'm going through a rough time right now, and I know you are, too. Moving in with your Dad has been a big change and it takes some adjusting. My problems will blow over soon, everything will get back to normal, and you can come home."

The girl said nothing.

"Assuming you want to," Dana said.

"I guess I do."

"I won't twist your arm."

Molly remained silent.

"Look," Dana said, "are you upset about something I've done? Is it Frank? Do you really—"

"No, Mom, I didn't mean anything by that. I really don't care who you date."

"Well, I'm not dating anyone. The way my life is at the moment, it's impossible. But—"

"You don't have to explain," Molly said, cutting her off. "Just forget it."

Dana sighed wearily. "You're right. We do need to forget. A lot of things. Maybe if we tried to do something fun together, something to get our minds off our troubles, it would help."

"Like what?"

"How about if we went shopping in the city, made a day of it?"

"When?"

Dana saw she'd made a crack in Molly's veneer of hostility. "Why not tomorrow?"

"On a Saturday? That's one of your biggest days."

"I can take the day off. After all, I'm the boss."

"You always said that meant you had to work harder than everybody else," Molly returned.

"That's true, but it also means I get to choose when I get away for a few hours. Anyway, I'd rather be with you. What do you say?"

Molly didn't reply immediately. Finally she said, "I've got a lot of homework. Tiffany and I were going to do our biology project together. But I guess we could work on it tomorrow night."

"If you'd rather not spend the time shopping, I understand."

"No, I'd like to go to the city."

Dana felt a glint of hope. "How about if I pick you up at ten?"

"Okay."

"See you tomorrow, Mol."

"Okay, Mom. Goodbye."

Dana hung up the phone feeling better in one way, worse in another. It was good hearing Molly's voice even if it wasn't the most pleasant conversation. She was glad they'd be going to the city together, too. But Molly's comments about Frank proved that the past weighed heavily on all aspects of her life.

Dana went to the refrigerator to get a glass of wine. She'd intended to have one with her bath and had forgotten. Between the conversation with Molly and the calls from her nemesis, she needed a drink.

As Dana lifted the jug of chilled Chenin Blanc from the lower shelf, it slipped from her fingers and shattered on the hardwood floor. "Oh, damn!" she said, looking down at the mess.

There was glass and wine everywhere. If she hadn't been so annoyed with herself, she'd have burst into tears.

Dana got to work. After picking up the glass, she mopped the floor. Once the kitchen was cleaned up she went into the pantry for another jug of wine, but discovered there wasn't one. She had a few bottles of good Bordeaux but they were for dinner parties. Anyway, she preferred white. And so did Robin.

Dana looked at the clock. It would be a while before her friend showed up. Dana wondered if she ought to run down to the store. She could use some milk and bread, as well. The thought of going out in the storm—going out, period—sent a shiver down her spine. Then, she figured what the hell, she wasn't going to be a prisoner in her own house.

Seizing the burst of courage, she got her purse from the bedroom and her ski parka from the hall closet. There was a market down on Sir Francis Drake Boulevard where she usually shopped. She'd be safe in her car, except to run into the store, which would be lit and full of people. Besides, doing something other than sitting and waiting would be good for her.

She left the lights on, reset the alarm and went downstairs to the garage. She got in the Mercedes, her adrenaline carrying her. She locked the doors, pushed the remote control, started the engine and waited for the door to roll up. She backed out of the garage and into the pounding rain. Then, as she turned the car around to head down the drive, she saw another car sitting in the road. Its lights came on, the engine roared to life and it took off down the hill.

For a second Dana froze. Was it *him?* Had he been watching her house?

If she could get a license number, she could identify the guy. More adrenaline shot into her veins and she jammed the gearshift into Drive and sped down the driveway. She hit the road just as the taillights of the other car disappeared around the first bend.

The windshield wipers flying at top speed, Dana pressed the accelerator to the floor. The Mercedes lurched ahead, its tires spinning, then grabbing the wet pavement. She took the curve at twice the normal speed, her hands clenching the wheel. There was another sharp turn ahead. No taillights were in sight. She skidded around it, fishtailing on down the street. There were hardly ever any cars parked in the road, so she could speed. Ahead she had another glimpse of the taillights. She was closing in on him some. Only a few hundred feet separated them now.

Because of the rain she wasn't able to get a good look at the car. Dana pressed down on the accelerator, knowing she was already going as fast as she dared. The road was very slippery.

She wasn't at all sure what would happen if she caught up with him. What if he stopped? What if he was luring her out of her house? Maybe this was exactly what he wanted. No, she decided, he was fleeing. Anyway, she wasn't trying to catch him. All she wanted was to get a license number, identify the make of the car.

After a few more turns she'd closed in on him. It looked like a sports car. Maybe a dark-colored sports car. He must have realized she was catching up, because he increased his speed.

Coming out of a turn, she almost skidded into a rare parked car, nearly spinning out when she braked. She had to be careful. There was no point in getting herself killed.

There was a Stop sign at the bottom of the hill. If he respected it, Dana figured she might get close enough for a good look. But the sports car roared right past the Stop sign. Dana only slowed enough to make sure the intersection was clear.

He was pulling away again. He went around the next corner and by the time Sir Francis Drake Boulevard was in sight, he was making the turn onto it. But in the bright lights of the intersection she got her best view of the car yet. It was a black sports car, all right. It looked like a Ferrari Testarossa.

Dana's heart practically stopped. She'd been in one many times. Frank Betts had a Testarossa. A black one. Jesus.

Belvedere

Robin Cohen spotted Nola Betts standing between Laurel Easterbrook's matching pair of 18th-century Chinese wedding cabinets, talking to the young lawyer in Alvin's firm who supposedly had been invited for *her* benefit, not Nola's. Laurel was fastidious about mixing and matching her guests, making sure there was at least one Jewish bachelor around whenever Robin was a guest. But Nola, damn her hide, was equally fastidious about claiming every man she could lay her hands on for herself.

A smile pasted on her face, Robin continued to observe Frank Betts's ex. She was working overtime to get Morton Feldman to proposition her. Hardly surprising. Nola had a reputation for taking on all comers. A story had been circulating that she'd taken on an entire motorcycle gang at her place in Sausalito the week after her divorce from Frank was final. Robin assumed it was a gross exaggeration. Dana had said whether it was true or not, Nola was more pathetic than venal. The whole thing was sad, really.

At the moment Nola was rubbing her bosom against Morton as she fiddled with his tie. He was grinning like a Cheshire cat. Robin wondered if she wanted to go out with the guy, after all. He'd gotten her phone number earlier in the evening, during their obligatory show-and-tell of schools, jobs and toys. He'd seemed decent enough at the time, but now she wasn't so sure. When she thought about it, she hated that about the singles game. In essence it was humiliating. Showing your underwear in kindergarten had at least been more honest.

Tired of the whole scene, she went over to the big picture window offering a perspective on Richardson Bay. She stared out at the lights of Sausalito. It was difficult to see much. The rain was coming down so hard it sheeted the glass.

Robin decided that the party, while not a dud, offered no real promise. She'd met the only man there was to meet. He had her phone number. The future was in the hands of fate. Rather than standing around making small talk, she might as well go on over to Dana's. First, she'd find Laurel and tell her goodbye.

Robin put her glass down on a nearby table and, as she turned, saw Nola making her way toward her. The redhead had a large wineglass in her hand. It was three-quarters full. She was wearing an emerald green satin cocktail dress that showcased her ample bosom. It was dynamite with her hair.

"So, how's Robin Redbreast this evening?" she said, her boozy, perfumed essence filling the air.

Robin was in a red knit St. John sheath with a matching beaded jacket, which probably accounted for the remark. Red went well with her raven hair and had long been a favorite color. Maybe she wore it too much.

"Chirpy as ever," she replied, smiling faintly.

"So where's your little friend tonight?"

"If you mean Dana, she's not feeling well."

"Oh, really?" Nola arched a brow. "Hope it's serious."

Robin gave her a look.

"Do you blame me?" Nola asked.

"It's none of my business. I'd just as soon leave it at that."

Nola took a slug of wine. "Okay, let's talk about you instead," she said.

"Me?"

"Sure, why not?"

"I'm surprised you'd want to."

"To be honest, I've been wondering something."

"Oh? What's that?"

"Whether Frank's ever gotten into your pants."

Robin shook her head in disgust. "How delicately you inquire."

Nola shrugged. "I'm curious. Not that it particularly matters. I'm aware Frank's cock is considered one of the fringe benefits of working at dear old Cunts & Betts." Nola gave her a sober look. "Or don't you agree?"

"Some of us get our rocks off selling houses, Nola. Believe it or not."

"I really wouldn't care if you'd balled him. Honest. I know the difference between business fucking and serious fucking." She gulped more wine. "So tell me—just between us chickens—ever fucked him?"

"No."

"Really?"

Robin nodded. "Somehow he's managed to overlook me."

"Well, I'll be damned." Nola sloshed the wine around in her glass. "I figured with you it was more likely than not." She looked pointedly at Robin's bustline. "You've got what Frank likes." Then she drew a long breath, a far-off look in her eye. "He married me for my tits, you know. That and the blow jobs."

Robin blinked. Even if half drunk, she couldn't believe Nola had said that. "I don't mean to offend you, but I'd prefer not to hear about your sex life, Nola."

"Why so squeamish, dearie? My impression was that sport fucking was part of the business—along with getting the Mercedes and the face-lift."

"Maybe I have a lower retch threshold than most people," Robin said dryly. "But if I offend you, maybe it's better if I leave."

Nola reached out and took her arm, stopping her. "Please, Robin. I apologize. I'm drunk. Anyway, I'm not even thinking of you."

Robin wanted to go but took compassion on the woman—even though Nola hardly deserved it. It was widely accepted that Frank had been a real bastard. Maybe she was entitled to a little slack.

Nola took another slug of wine. "No point in talking about Frank. It only makes me bitchy. You're an innocent bystander. It's your little home-wrecking sidekick I should be talking to." Nola was slurring her words badly.

"I'm not Dana's keeper."

Nola's expression hardened. "Well, somebody should have been. The bitch."

"I don't mean to tell you your business," Robin said, "but you really ought to let go of that. For your own sake."

Nola gave a derisive laugh. "What goes around, comes around. Little Miss Prom Queen will get hers. You can bet on it." She stared off, glassy eyed. "Somebody needs to knock her down to size. She ruined his life, you know. Frank's not the man he was. Not after she finished with him."

Nola had a point. People in the company were saying Frank had lost a lot of the old fire—and not just the fire in his loins. But more than a few of his former playthings were glad to see him stub his toe.

"Nothing is forever," Robin said, glancing around the room.

"Yes, Robin Redbreast, you're right about that. Nothing lasts forever." Nola gave her a final drunken smile and slunk away.

* * *

Kentfield

Frank Betts pulled his Testarossa through the gate of his condominium complex, then made his way along the curving drive to his garage. The automatic door opened. He drove in and turned off the ignition. Before he shut off the lights, he removed the CD he'd been listening to. Marian McPartland's *Willow Creek* went into the CD box, then he slipped it into his pocket.

For a minute he sat in the darkness, motionless. His brow was covered with perspiration. He felt like a goddamn criminal. If not that, he certainly was a fool. He couldn't believe he'd done that—driven up to Dana's house. He might as well have tried to peep into her windows.

He had no idea whether she'd gotten a good enough look to recognize the car. She'd chased him, though; there was no doubt about that. Why? he wondered. Did she think he was a burglar?

He'd made his mistake in running. It was like an admission of guilt. But when her garage door had opened, he'd panicked. The last goddamn thing he'd wanted was to be caught spying on her like a fucking teenager. Christ.

Shaking his head with disgust, he got out of the car. He shut the garage door and headed off in the light drizzle. He pulled up the collar of his windbreaker, glad the rain had let up.

Why he'd gone up there tonight, he didn't know. When he'd left to pick up a few odds and ends at Safeway, Dana was the last thing on his mind. Then Marian McPartland had gotten him to thinking about her and the next thing he knew he was in Ross, driving up that hill to her place. When she'd planned the house, they'd been intending to live in it together. She hadn't said it in so many words, but they'd been definitely moving in that direction. Then, without warning, everything had blown up in his face. He still didn't know why. Dana hadn't explained it. Not in a way that made sense. And so he'd found himself out in the cold, dropped like a hot potato.

Frank took out his key and opened the door to his unit. The goddamn bitch. One minute he felt like killing her, the next he saw himself kissing her feet, begging her to come back.

He sighed wearily and unzipped his jacket. No sooner had he hung it in the closet than he realized he hadn't even gotten his goddamn groceries. That woman was destroying his mind!

Frank took his keys and flung them as hard as he could against the wall, barely missing the oil painting Dana had helped him pick out. "Bitch!" he yelled at the top of his lungs. Then he stared at the dent in the wall where the keys had struck. "Fuck!"

Frank went and got himself a Scotch. He needed one. He poured the booze into a glass and gulped down half of it without blinking. Then he poured some more. Glass in hand, he retreated to the front room and dropped wearily onto the couch. He rubbed his temples, hoping to soothe the pounding in his head.

A profound yearning for her went through him. Why had she done this to him? It could have worked out so beautifully, if she had let it—the perfect ending to a poignant love story. He took another long pull on his Scotch and leaned back. When he closed his eyes he saw Dana as she'd looked the first time he'd laid eyes on her.

She'd come to his office, inquiring about a job. Normally office managers hired new agents, but Dana had insisted on talking to the top man. She was only twenty-two, had a baby and a brand-new real-estate license. She'd sat across the desk from him, her eyes shining, her pert breasts rising under her cashmere sweater. God, she was a pistol.

His first thought had been to offer her a clerical job so he could boff her. He was thirty-five and had been married a few years, enough that the tingle in his balls was more important than his marriage vows.

"I admire your ambition," he'd told her as he'd leaned back in his desk chair, his hands behind his head to show off his chest. "But you'll never make it in this business—at least not until you're older."

"Why is that, Mr. Betts?"

He'd explained how instilling trust was key—and the fact that clients were reluctant to trust someone who was too young to have shared the same life experiences. There weren't many twenty-two-year-old buyers, especially in Marin.

Dana had sat back and crossed her legs, looking him dead in the eye. "If you want to reject me because of my age, that's your privilege," she'd said. "But I'll tell you right now I'll go to work for one of your competitors. I don't know who, but I'll make more money for him than anybody here is making for you. On the other hand, if you're smart enough to hire me, I'll make you a richer man than you are now."

God, did she have spunk. He'd sent her to talk to Adrianne Stevens, manager of his flagship office in Kentfield. Adrianne had promptly taken her under her wing, polishing the rough stone into a fine gem.

Frank had followed Dana's progress carefully. When she'd sold her first house he took her to lunch at Dominick's.

"I don't want you to be disappointed if you aren't our top producer your first year," he'd teased. "Anyway, we wouldn't want to demoralize the rest of the staff."

"If they aren't tough enough to take it, they don't belong in the business," she'd replied.

Frank had taken a long, languorous look at her breasts. The combination of sex appeal, true beauty, brains and toughness had been too much. Dana had nursed her one martini through three of his. By the end of their two-hour lunch he was flirting outrageously. She deflected him like a seasoned pro, telling him he'd learn to value her money-making ability more than anything he'd get in a motel room.

Her prophesy had set the tone for the next ten years. Dana never let him get in her pants. Frank figured he'd screwed just about every woman in the company who wasn't a lesbian, a dog, a misanthrope, or a born-again Christian. But never Dana.

Dana didn't make top producer her first year, but she was top rookie. By her second year she was third out of seventy-five agents. She eclipsed the longtime company title-holder in her third year—when the sales force stood at a hundred and forty. And the more her income went up, the more painful Frank's hard-on became.

In her ninth year in the business, Dana had made a million dollars selling homes—the first time to his knowledge someone not hawking French châteaus, Beverly Hills estates, or entire subdivisions had accomplished such a feat. It was also the year before she divorced her husband.

Frank hadn't been sure how the breakup would impact on her—it destroyed some people and made others even better. Most of all he'd been curious what effect it would have on her attitude toward him.

He'd played his hand well, pulling back, making her come to him. For a year nothing happened. Then one evening they had a long talk. He and Nola were separated at the time, so they were both free. Dana hinted she was at a crossroads. Selling real estate wasn't enough anymore.

That hadn't come as a surprise. Shooting stars had a way of burning out. Some learned to adjust. Dana wasn't like most—she needed a new challenge, a different sort of acclaim to validate herself.

When she admitted she was thinking of opening her own shop, Frank had been wounded. It was worse than a kick in the balls. He couldn't imagine waiting all this time only to see her slip away. The truth was he would have traded the company end of all the business she brought in, just to take her to bed one time.

They'd been at his place the night she'd first talked about leaving. It was after the annual Christmas party and she'd come by for a drink. He had a fire going. Dana had kicked off her shoes and was lying before the fireplace, staring at the flames. He was in a chair to the side, a glass of champagne in his hand, his eyes sliding back and forth between her face and her ass.

They didn't screw that night. For a couple of months afterward they met regularly for lunch or whatever, but mainly to talk about her future. He'd tried to convince her to take over an office—a suggestion she rejected, saying if she was going to manage for anyone, it would be for herself.

Their conversations became an agonizing dance. Would she stay, would she go, would she finally give in to the horrendous sexual tension that all but had him foaming at the mouth?

When Dana finally succumbed it had been sudden and unexpected. One night she showed up at his house looking frazzled. She'd sold a place in Ross for a million-two and complained that she wasn't happy. She almost dreaded the thought of the escrow.

"Maybe, if I let you do what you've been wanting to do, I'll feel something," she'd said. Then she'd started crying. "I want to feel something, Frank. I want to feel something badly."

They'd made love then. He wasn't great. He'd been clumsy, but getting his rocks off had never felt better. Ten years. Ten long, agonizing years of wanting her.

In retrospect, that night was the high point of their affair. They saw each other for a few months but Dana wasn't happy. When she left, Frank's partner, Lane Cedrick, was livid. He swore Frank deserved to have his cock surgically removed.

No doubt about it, her departure had devastated him. He had begun doubting himself. There were times he couldn't get it up, didn't even want to get it up. He couldn't concentrate anymore. Some days he'd be sitting at his desk and he'd just walk out, go someplace to get drunk.

Frank took another gulp of Scotch and squeezed the bridge of his nose. His head was pounding, but his balls were tingling and he had a hard-on. Even now, while he and Lane were being fucked by her, the thought of Dana Kirk could turn him on.

He finished off his drink and sat there, undecided whether he should fix himself another. A hangover wouldn't serve him well, but if he got drunk, he'd sleep. His eyes were drawn again to the dent in his wall. He shook his head. He felt like shit. But the worst thing was driving up to her house and nearly getting caught.

Christ Almighty. What if she'd recognized the car? What would he do then? His life was rapidly going to hell, and he felt like there wasn't a goddamned thing he could do about it.

Ross

It was between Michael Bolton and Luciano Pavarotti. Dana decided that with the storm raging, and her blue mood, *Aïda* was more in keeping with the spirit of things. Besides, she often listened to opera when she worked out.

The time was nine forty-five and there was still no sign of Robin. Dana had been on the NordicTrack for twenty minutes and was working hard enough that a fine patina of perspiration had formed on her brow. When she'd first gotten on the fast track to sales stardom she'd been a jogger. David's idea of exercise was to bring in the groceries from the car, so running had been a solitary occupation.

For a while she'd had a personal trainer, but when she'd built her house she'd opted to make one of the extra bedrooms into an exercise room. She'd put in floor-to-ceiling mirrors and filled it with a NordicTrack, a treadmill, a rowing machine, and some free weights. She'd had the best intentions, but hadn't used the room half a dozen times in the two months they'd been in the house.

Why the sudden urge to exercise had struck her, Dana wasn't sure. After she'd gotten back from the market, she'd put the wine in the refrigerator, changed into her exercise clothes and gone in to work out with a vengeance. It felt good to sweat a little, to move those muscles, but mostly she wanted to burn off some of the adrenaline from the car chase.

She still couldn't decide what it meant that Frank Betts had been sitting outside her house in the dark and that he'd raced off when she came out. Of course, she couldn't prove that it was Frank, but how many black Testarossas were around? And how many were likely to be at her place on a rainy night?

She considered calling the police, but to what end? He hadn't actually done anything except speed and run a Stop sign. So had she, for that matter. And though it could have been a chance thing, she doubted it. A chill went down her spine at the thought Frank might somehow be behind the death threats. Could he hate her that much? She never would have thought so.

The storm had intensified and, despite Luciano, she could hear rain pummeling the side of the house. At the moment Ghena Dimitrova was singing an aria and Dana was puffing away, wishing she was up in the Sierra Nevada, cross-country skiing, with a blue sky overhead and a cold wind in her face.

No sooner had Dimitrova hit the last note when the portable phone began to ring. She stopped and stared at it as her chest continued to heave.

"Damn," she said, wiping her forehead with the back of her hand. Stu's gizmo was connected to the phone in the kitchen. She'd have to run to the other end of the house to see who was calling. Or she could take her chances. The car chase had given her a shot of courage, so she decided to throw caution to the wind a second time. She picked up the receiver.

"Hello," she said, breathing hard from the exercise.

There was a laugh, then, "Are you getting laid or running from an ax-wielding murderer?" It was Robin.

"I was skiing in a snowy field...with Luciano Pavarotti, if you must know."

"Should I inquire further, or let it drop?" Robin sounded like she was on her car phone.

"I was exercising, Robin. Where are you, anyway?"

"Crossing a lake in the middle of Sir Francis Drake Boulevard. Thought I'd warn you that I'm on my way, so you wouldn't think that the car pulling into your drive in a few minutes was Jack the Ripper."

"Very thoughtful."

"No, just self-interest. I don't want to get shot."

"The gun I got a few years ago is at the bottom of my desk drawer at the office. And I haven't even looked at it since I bought it."

"Maybe you should rethink that."

"I thought you were the one who's always marching for gun control, against capital punishment, et cetera, et cetera."

"I make exceptions for my friends," Robin said with a laugh.

Dana smiled. Robin always cheered her. "Do I have time to jump into the shower?"

"If you want to drink with me, you do."

"Ten minutes?"

"No sweat—pardon the expression. If these puddles get any bigger I may be needing the Coast Guard to get there. Call you again from your driveway."

"Be careful."

"You, too."

Dana got cleaned up quickly, put on a pale blue jogging suit and was already at the front window, portable phone in hand, when it rang. At almost the same moment she saw headlights coming up the road. She pushed the button. "Hello?"

"I'm turning into your drive," Robin said.

"I see you. I'll be at the door."

"Ten-four."

Dana chuckled as she hung up. She waited at the window a moment to make sure Robin got up the drive all right. The rain was really coming down, even harder than when she'd been out.

After Robin's Lexus had come to a stop and the lights went out, the door opened and an umbrella protruded from the vehicle like a periscope. Dana skipped to the entry, opening the door just as Robin arrived on the porch, accompanied by a gust of rain and wind. She had a cellophane-covered plate in one hand, her umbrella in the other.

"Gotta towel?"

"You poor baby," Dana said, beckoning her in.

Robin was wet despite the umbrella and trench coat. She stepped in and Dana put the plate on the hall table with one hand and helped Robin off with her coat with the other. Robin looked down at her feet and the puddle on the granite tile entry.

"Well, it looks like it's off to Nordstrom in the morning. These are my only decent pair of black shoes." She gave Dana a smile. "How are you doing?"

Dana, feeling a rush of emotion, hugged her, squeezing her tight. "Better, now that you're here. It hasn't been a very pleasant evening."

Robin patted her back as they continued to embrace. "You should have come with me."

"Oh, no. I'd have missed the excitement here. You'll never guess what happened, Robin."

Her friend looked at her, searching her eyes. "What?"

Dana told her about Frank and their car chase through the rain.

Robin's jaw went slack. "Jesus."

"The trouble is, I don't know what to do about it. Do I confront him? Do I call the police?"

"You can't let it pass. It could be significant. I wouldn't have thought so, but maybe he's involved in the threats."

Dana took Robin by the arm and, picking up the plate of goodies, led her back toward the kitchen. "I've been thinking the same thing."

"It doesn't seem like Frank," Robin said. "He's been a bit strange recently but not in this way. It's not Frank's style. He's more up-front. If he was going to threaten you, he'd do it to your face."

"Yes, I know. And there's a big difference between hanging around someone's house and threatening their life."

"But you *are* going to inform the police, I hope."

"There's a new detective on the case. I'm supposed to talk to him tomorrow. I guess I'll mention seeing the Testarossa and let him decide what to do."

"Well, he'll talk to Frank, I imagine."

They'd come to the family room. Robin went to the big beige-and-black plaid sofa and plopped down. Dana carried the plate into the kitchen. She returned with a hand towel and tossed it to Robin.

"Your face is wet."

Robin dabbed herself. "It's really awful out there. Phew, what a night, huh?"

"Yeah. As if that business with Frank wasn't enough, I had a few calls from my secret admirer, too."

"Before or after Frank?"

"Before."

"Long enough that it could have been him?"

"Yes, I guess so. One was from a service station in San Anselmo, the other a tavern. I guess it could have been him."

Robin shook her head. "Well, if it is Frank, the threats might stop now that you've seen him. It sounds like he knew you were following him."

"Oh, he knew, all right."

Dana sat in one of the beige-and-black plaid chairs that matched the sofa. She gazed at the sand-colored grass cloth wall. It was mostly bare, awaiting the discovery of the right paintings. The emptiness of that struck her. It was sort of like her life right now—on hold, waiting for something better.

"Well, let's change the subject. How was the party?"

"Food was good."

"Did Laurel's usual caterer do it?"

"Yeah. I picked out all the best stuff for you."

"Yum. I'm actually a little hungry. So... any men there?"

"Laurel's offering of the evening was a mensch by the name of Morton."

"Ugh. Terrible name."

Robin picked up the copy of *Vogue* lying on the cushion beside her and absently began paging through it. "He wasn't as bad as he sounds, actually. He's a lawyer. Average sense of humor. Average looks. Sort of on the short side. Smart, of course. Overall, he was okay, but not great."

"Is Morton Jewish?"

"Yes, Jewish and into tits."

"You must have seemed like manna from heaven."

Robin gave her a slightly bemused look. Though pretty, Robin had trouble attracting the sort of man she wanted. She was the youngest of four daughters and the Cohen family beauty. Her complexion was smooth as porcelain, and her hair was nearly the same shade as Dana's. In fact their coloring was similar, except that Robin's eyes were the color of a walnut, whereas Dana's were blue green. Robin joked that she lusted after them. "Will me your eyes when you die," she'd said once. The remark had been endearing at the time, but under present circumstances it had macabre overtones.

They were close in height, too, though Robin was a stubborn ten pounds heavier. Her weight had become a preoccupation and Dana felt Robin was much too critical of herself. Dana had taken to teasing her about it, just to lighten things up.

Robin put the magazine aside. "Morton ogled, all right, but he also ogled every other pair of tits in the room, especially Nola Betts's."

"Oh, *she* was there."

"Yeah. Said to give you her best, by the way."

Dana folded her arms. "I bet. Did she make a scene? I imagine she was drunk. She usually is."

"Except for a few very choice words about a dear friend of mine who'll go unnamed, she wasn't too bad. God knows what she did after I left, though. She was guzzling the wine like it was Kool-Aid."

Dana rolled her eyes. "I'm glad I wasn't there. A tête-à-tête with Nola would have been all I needed. I wonder if she's ever going to get on with her life."

"Who knows? I have to admit, though, her act is getting a little old."

Dana was ready to change subjects. Her feelings toward Nola had always been mixed. She knew in her heart she wasn't to blame for the breakup of Nola and Frank's marriage, but at the same time she knew Frank had been in love with her for years.

"So, did you pick up any business?" Dana asked.

"Nope. You didn't miss a thing. Not that you need more clients. It's a miracle you can service the ones you've got."

"Believe me, it's almost impossible to do a good job and try to run the company at the same time. I had no idea it'd be this tough. It takes a lot of bread to keep the doors open and make mortgage payments, too."

Robin crossed her legs and rotated her bare foot. "You aren't the only one under the gun, so to speak. As one of the last Mohicans at Cedrick & Betts, I can assure you that they're squirming, too. Personally, I think it's quite possible Frank and Lane are behind this campaign of terror that's being waged against you."

Dana scoffed. "I can't believe a little competition, even fierce competition, would drive them to this. True, they've had it easy in recent years. Maybe they've gotten complacent. But I can assure you, they're not hanging on by their fingernails the way I am. Even if I've put a big dent in the Kentfield office, they're a long way from going under."

Robin playfully tossed the towel at Dana. "You know what the latest rumor is, don't you?"

"What?"

"People are saying Bev O'Connell is about to jump ship."

"Really?"

Robin saw Dana's smile. "Don't be coy with me, Dana Kirk. You've been hustling Bev for weeks and there's not a Realtor in Marin who doesn't know it."

"Any broker would give her eyeteeth to sign Bev. I'm not the only one who's wined and dined her. Besides, what do Frank and Lane have to complain about? They've been raping and pillaging the competition for years."

"Believe me, girl, you are not a popular lady at C&B. I don't care what you say."

Dana tried to picture her last conversation with Frank. It had been a month or so earlier at a Board of Realtors breakfast meeting. He'd joked that he might be willing to move his license, if she'd have him. There had been false hardiness in his tone, but no deep hatred or bitterness. If anything, he'd looked at her a bit wistfully.

"They may be pissed at me, but I have trouble believing they're *that* pissed. They've been through wars like this before, Robin. I'm not their first defector, nor will I be the last."

"What about Marin Pacific Savings? You're still on their board of directors, aren't you? That must gall Frank and Lane. Maybe the threats have something to do with that."

"I don't see how. If they didn't want me on the board, they'd buy me out. And to tell you the truth, I expect them to be making me an offer. I'm biding my time, waiting for them to make the first move."

"Well, if it's not the recruiting war and it's not the bank, that leaves only one thing," Robin reflected. "Maybe Frank can't live without you. Have you considered that?"

"Robin, if that's what's behind this, Frank has chosen a strange way to demonstrate his love. If you care about somebody you don't threaten to kill them."

"Maybe he's nuts. Maybe he went off the deep end."

"Possible, but it could also be some other nut. I've thought that all along. Hell, maybe it wasn't Frank in that car tonight." She shivered violently and shook her head. "Let's change the subject. This conversation's not doing a lot of good."

Robin gave her a sympathetic look. There wasn't much that could be said that hadn't been said already—a dozen times. "I've got an idea, Kirk," she said. "Why don't we open a bottle of wine, eat the goodies I brought, and get good and drunk? It's been ages since we've tied one on."

Dana thought for a moment. "I hate to say it, but I'm tempted. Come to think of it, that's probably why I went all the way down to Safeway to buy a new jug."

"You'll have to let me sleep over," Robin said with a diabolical grin. "Last thing I need is a DUI."

"You sure you want to spend the night under my roof, Robin? You'd probably be safer bunking with Salman Rushdie."

Robin shook her head. "Whoever's harassing you writes letters and makes phone calls. He doesn't murder people in their beds."

"Not yet, anyway."

Robin stood, offering Dana her hand. "Come on, it's time to eat, drink and be merry."

"For tomorrow we must die?"

"I meant to leave that part off."

Dana smiled sadly, took Robin's hand, and stood. They embraced. Tears filled Dana's eyes, but she didn't cry. "I hope jug wine's okay," she said over her friend's shoulder.

"At a time like this, quantity is more important than quality."

They went off to the kitchen together. Dana got the wine out of the refrigerator, but it had barely had time to chill. Robin removed the cellophane from the plate of goodies. She popped a crab puff into her mouth while Dana filled two big wineglasses almost to the brim. Dana handed her one of the glasses.

They looked into each other's eyes. Dana felt hers tear up again. Robin touched her glass to Dana's. "May the Mounties get their man. May Molly come home. May you live happily ever after. And may Morton turn out to be a veritable stallion."

Dana grinned and wiped away a tear. "And may God find it in his heart to send me both ends of a half-million-dollar deal this month."

"What the hell," Robin said, "let's make it a million. If we're going for the brass ring, we might as well go for it all."

Kentfield

After the local news ended, Frank Betts stayed cemented to his chair. He stared at the commercials, mesmerized, yet hating them at the same time. In a minute he'd summon the strength to turn the damned thing off. For the moment, inertia had the best of him.

When the phone rang, he groaned. For over twenty years he'd gotten calls at all hours of the night from desperate salespeople. Running a real-estate company was like mothering a sick child, though nowadays office managers dealt with most of the problems. But some old-timers considered it their God-given right to get their advice from the top.

Frank roused himself from his recliner and made his way to the telephone. "Hello?"

"Home on a Friday night, Frankie? Get tired of the pickup bars, or did you call one of your salesgirls over to give you a blow job?"

It was Nola. "What do you want at this time of night?"

"Glad you're so thrilled to hear my voice. Makes a gal really feel wanted."

"How can you expect to feel wanted when you call up and insult me?"

"I thought I was being funny. What happened to your sense of humor? Too much pussy, Frankie, or not enough?"

He heard the unmistakable slur. "You're loaded, Nola. I'm not going to listen to you run off at the mouth when you're drunk. I don't need this. Goodbye."

"No, Frankie, don't hang up. I'm sorry. I . . . have been drinking, it's true. But I don't mean to give you a bad time. Honest. I'm calling to see—"

"To see what?"

"If you're alone."

"Nola, for chrissake." He shifted uncomfortably. He was bone weary and his head was pounding something awful. Picking up the phone, he pulled the coiled wire from behind the stand and returned to his chair, setting the phone down on the end table.

Nola was lamenting. "Don't get mad at me. Please. I'm calling because I want to know if that bitch is there."

"Bitch?"

"Don't be coy, Frank. You know who I'm talking about. She wasn't at the Easterbrooks' tonight. I figured she had to be there with you."

"Well, if you're talking about Dana, you figured wrong."

"You're lying."

"Will you give it up," he said through his teeth, his anger building. "I haven't seen her in months. As a matter of fact, she's in the process of screwing us over."

"What?"

"She's raiding our Kentfield office, eating us alive. So, don't talk to me about Dana Kirk."

Nola laughed drunkenly. "You see, Frankie, some women just can't be trusted."

He thought again of racing down that hill with Dana in pursuit, and it made him sick. All evening he'd been agonizing over it, feeling like a blithering idiot. "Don't gloat, Nola," he warned, tilting the recliner as far back as it would go. "Those real-estate offices provide the money for your goddamned alimony. Unless you want to go down the tube with Lane and me, you'd better hope Dana falls flat on her face."

There was a long, sobering silence on the line.

"Well, if you don't want to fuck her, Frankie, why don't you come over here and do me? There was a time when you thought I wasn't such a bad lay."

"Thanks for the offer," he said, "but our time has passed. The sooner you accept that, the better off you'll be."

There was another silence, then he heard crying. It wasn't the first time this had happened, but it had been a while since she'd let him hear her misery. He wondered if something had gotten into her besides too much booze.

"Go to bed, Nola," he said. "Sleep it off."

"Oh, Frank," she sobbed, "how did we let this happen?"

There was nothing he could say to that. He listened to her cry, his insides churning. Nola found any way she could to exact her revenge.

After a few seconds of more crying, Nola murmured a little-girl goodbye, then hung up. He sighed, put the receiver in the cradle, then pressed his index fingers into his throbbing temples, trying to relieve the pain. His headache was getting worse.

He lay there in his recliner wondering why, after so many good years, his life was going to hell. Maybe God—if there was one—was exacting His revenge. They say the good life has its price. Maybe this was it. Maybe the time had come to pay up.

It was hard to say when the turning point had come. Perhaps when he'd dumped his wife of sixteen years. According to some, bad karma grew out of things like that, but Frank didn't believe in that sort of crap. He believed in living life to the fullest and that was exactly what he'd always tried to do.

There had been a time when a full life involved Nola. In those early days she'd really been special. He was a young hotshot when they met, screwing everything in sight. And Nola, with those luscious knockers and a mouth that couldn't get enough of him, was too much to handle. She'd been a flight attendant and had had a year and a half of college. But what the hell, he'd started out as a copy-machine salesman with a high school diploma. He didn't have to marry royalty. They were in love and in lust, and nothing else mattered.

For the first five years they'd fucked their brains out. The only pieces he'd knocked off on the side were purely for ego gratification—that and office politics. For a man who managed a sales force made up mostly of women, his cock could be his most valuable management tool.

In the last few years he'd been slowing down, though. At forty-eight, he wasn't as hungry or as willing as he used to be. Now the congratulatory hugs and kisses didn't lead ineluctably to afternoon trysts. The validation fucks were less common. The girls were having to make do with a pat on the butt.

It hadn't been an evolving thing. His transformation had come suddenly—at the time of his fling with Dana. That had changed everything. At times he felt he was living a goddamn soap opera. All he could think about was Dana Kirk. Christ, he was acting like an idiot. He hated himself for that. He hated his stupidity.

Frank sat upright in his chair. He couldn't remember if he'd had any aspirin since he'd gotten home. There was a period there when he'd been pretty fuzzy from the Scotch. What the hell, a couple more aspirin couldn't hurt, even if he had taken some.

Getting up, he went to the bathroom and got some aspirin out of the bottle in the medicine cabinet. He put them in his mouth and, using his cupped hand for a glass, got some water from the faucet. The tablets momentarily stuck in his throat, making him wince.

"Damn," he said, glancing at the haggard face in the mirror. Life just wasn't fun anymore. Not the selling. Not the recruiting. Not counting his bloody money. Even the screwing had worn thin. He was feeling defeated. And that wasn't like him.

Dana was the problem. She had double-crossed him—screwed him after he'd put himself on the line for her with Lane. What a fool he'd been to give her a piece of the bank. He'd thought it would keep her from leaving, but what had she done? Picked up her marbles and taken off anyway. It was because of her that C&B was hemorrhaging like a buck with a round in its belly. They could still recover, of course. With effort and a little luck they could even turn the tables. But it was going to be bloody. Real bloody.

God, he hated her. Almost as much as he loved her. She was a bitch, but that didn't stop him from loving her. Truth be known, he'd go to her this minute if she'd have him. All she'd have to do was say the word. But love her or not, he had to survive. A man had to do what a man had to do—

even if it meant getting rough. Even if he was nothing but a piece of shit without her. His pride was worth something. Not much, maybe, but enough to fight her. And he'd win—whatever it took. Whatever it took.

Forestville, Sonoma County

It was raining lightly as Mitchell Cross drove along the dark country road in his Bronco, listening to Crystal Gayle and idly wondering what kind of woman she was in real life. The voice really did something for him.

He passed orchards, chicken ranches and the estates of the Yuppie farmers, as he called the commuters who chose to move out into the country, but brought their swimming pools and tennis courts and golf clubs with them. Sonoma County was getting more gentrified by the day and he didn't much like that. Neighbors who lived in ramshackle houses and drove fifteen-year-old pickups were more to his liking. The carpetbaggers still reeked of Union Street or Montgomery Street or the Peacock Gap Golf and Country Club. It wasn't his kind of smell.

The pungent aroma of beer that filled the car was better, but it wasn't exactly an appropriate odor on the clothes of a cop who was driving—even an off-duty cop. But he was innocent. A giddy broad at Hogg's had accidentally spilled a glass of the stuff right down the front of him. She'd apologized profusely and said she'd buy him another beer. He'd offered to settle for a dance instead but she'd told him she was with her fiancé, so he'd have to make do with the beer.

He'd only danced a few times—once with a twenty-three-year-old redhead in tight jeans who was friendly until she found out he was a cop, once with her girlfriend, to make a point, and once with a forty-five-year-old divorcée who'd asked him. She was out looking to do a little revenge fucking. He wasn't in the mood for revenge, so after that, he'd decided to call it a night.

There'd been a time when an evening was a failure if he dragged himself home without getting laid. Nowadays it was a failure if he didn't at least meet someone he'd have liked to go home with. The redhead qualified. She'd have been a good lay—she had the body and she was pretty—but she was totally self-possessed. In his old age he could no longer overlook that in a woman. A degree of subtlety was essential.

He was coming to Collier Lane, the side road where he lived, so he slowed down. Near the intersection he came across a fresh roadkill—a skunk and it smelled to high heaven. Fortunately his place lay to the west, upwind. There was nothing like trying to sleep under an open window with the smell of skunk wafting in all night.

He made the turn and drove through an eighth of a mile of apples and almonds, none of which was his. He had a few odd fruit trees on his parcel—citrus and a couple of apricot—but no real orchard. His place lay in the flat along a seasonal creek and against the flank of a low hill, eleven acres in all. Enough to graze his horse and keep the neighbors out of sight.

The house was a modest wood-frame structure that had been built by a previous owner thirty years ago. Two bedrooms, one bath. There was a small barn, a hay shed, a carport, irrigation lines, top-quality fencing and a fat mortgage. He was set for life.

Entering the long gravel drive that led to the house, Cross saw a vehicle sitting out front. That gave him a start. Rural burglaries were commonplace these days so he immediately reached for his service revolver in the door compartment. But then he recognized the car. It was Carole Dixon's old boat, a '74 Oldsmobile. He wondered what the hell she was doing there.

He pulled into the carport, got out of the Bronco, locked it, turned up the collar of his Levi's jacket, and ambled over to the Olds. Carole was slouched behind the wheel. She rolled down the window and looked up at him, embarrassed.

"You alone, Mitch?" she asked uncertainly.

"Yes, I'm alone. What are you doing here, Carole?"

She sighed, as if that ought to tell the story. He could barely make out her features in the shadows. Garth Brooks was warbling softly on the car radio. She was smoking a cigarette. "I guess the honest truth is I'm lonely," she finally said. "I tried calling you, but all I got was the machine. On an impulse I decided to drive over."

"So when did you start smoking?"

Carole looked at the cigarette in her hand as though she was surprised it was there. "I haven't. Kay or somebody left one in the car. I don't know why I lit up. Haven't had a cigarette in my mouth since I was twenty." She flicked it out the window onto the wet ground. "Guess it was the music and the rain."

He wasn't sure what to make of her. This wasn't like Carole. Everyone had a little desperation of one sort or another in them, but Carole usually guarded hers pretty well. When she was interested in sex, she was normally a lot more subtle in letting him know.

"You know what I was afraid of?" Carole said, interrupting his thoughts. "I was afraid you'd bring somebody home with you and I'd be sitting here feeling like a fool."

"Well, I didn't, so you don't have to worry."

She looked up at him. There was just enough light to see the doleful expression on her face. "Where..." But her voice trailed off.

"Where, what?" he asked.

"Oh, never mind. Do you want me to go, Mitch?"

"No, you're here. You might as well come in."

"Well, I don't want you to have to grit your teeth at the thought," she groused.

"I didn't mean it that way and you know it, Carole."

"What *did* you mean, then?"

"I didn't mean anything except that I'm getting wet standing here and I'd rather have this conversation inside."

"No, I'm going," she said. "I shouldn't have come in the first place. It was stupid."

"I thought you wanted company."

"Well, Jesus, Mitch." She shook her head. "Is a little consideration too much to ask for?"

"Look," he said, "we're getting nowhere fast. I'm glad you're here. I want you to come in, and I want to get out of the goddamned rain."

Carole gave him a look of disgust and rolled up her window. For a moment he thought she was going to start the engine and drive away, but she opened the car door instead.

"Honestly," she mumbled, as she felt around the floor under her feet, "sometimes I wish I was a lesbian. Men are such a goddamned pain."

"What are you doing?"

"Trying to find my shoes."

She located them and, while he held the door, slipped them on. He took her hand, helping her out.

She brushed her body against him, another not-too-subtle signal of her desire. In the damp air her perfume smelled lush and womanly. He looked down at her body. She had on jeans and a man's flannel shirt with the tail hanging out. He could see the rise of her breasts in the light coming from the porch.

She had light brown hair and wasn't pretty so much as she was sexy. Her features were a bit coarse, but they were even. She had a good mouth and she knew how to use it.

She was on the tall side and had a wasplike figure—a small waist and well-rounded hips, though a trifle large.

Carole Dixon was thirty-seven and had been divorced for ten years, no children. She worked as a lab technician in Santa Rosa, but her real love was country-and-western music. After her divorce she'd tried to make it as a singer, but by her own account she was "good enough to get gigs by sweet-talking club managers, but not good enough to go any further without sleeping with the bastards." She'd told Cross that she'd gotten tired of being hit on and finally gave it up.

They'd met at a livestock auction up near Cloverdale. He had gone to look at the cattle, Carole to look at the cowboys. They'd had a cup of coffee. The next weekend they'd driven over to Bodega Bay for lunch and come back to his place and made love.

They both knew it would never lead further than the bedroom. Carole was, by her reckoning, even more averse to marriage than he, which suited him just fine. He knew there was a good chance it wasn't true, but believing it was convenient, so he did.

"Don't you have a jacket?" he asked.

"Mitch, I don't even have on underwear."

He smiled, taking her arm. "You *are* horny, aren't you?"

"It was one of those crazy days," she said as they walked toward the house. "All afternoon at work I couldn't think about anything but sex. By the time I got home I wanted to get laid so bad I could scream."

"I'm flattered you chose me. Or was I your second or third choice?"

"Lord, give me a little credit. You know I don't sleep with more than one guy at a time."

"That's what you say, anyway," he teased.

"You don't even bother saying it."

"I don't screw around," he said. "Not in this day and age."

Basically that was true, though under the right circumstances he was capable of ranging a bit. But he never did anything stupid—for his partner's sake as well as his own. People didn't anymore. Not if they used their heads. And he preferred to use his head first and his cock second.

They'd come to the porch and he took out his key and unlocked the door. Carole stepped into the cool, dark house. He flipped on the wall switch, illuminating a lamp across the small, sparely furnished living room. One brown leather couch. One black leather armchair. An oak side table, a lamp. TV and stereo equipment. No pictures on the walls, just a framed map of Nevada, his home state. Carole gave the place a cursory glance as though she might be able to divine what had transpired there since her last visit. Then she turned and put her arms around him, bumping her body up against his.

"Jesus, you smell like a brewery," she said, shimmying against his chest.

"I got some beer spilled on me at Hogg's."

Carole looked up at him, her eyes on his mouth and chin as she ground her pelvis against him. "So, how is it you didn't score?"

"I didn't try."

"You just went to Hogg's to look at T&A?"

"Something like that."

She slid her hand down between them and began rubbing his crotch, making him hard almost instantly. "Guess I can consider myself lucky you're just a voyeur."

He was surprised as hell at her aggressiveness. Once Carole got turned on she could be as wild as any woman he'd ever known, but he'd never seen her like this before. She was different tonight and, not surprisingly, it turned him on.

He lowered his mouth to kiss her and she kissed him back, biting at his lips as she squeezed the ridge in his pants.

"Jesus, oh, Jesus," she mumbled, as she swirled her tongue around his. "You know, Mitch, I got wet sitting in the car, just thinking about this."

He started getting a sense of just how hot she was. And he was getting so hard it was beginning to hurt. "I don't...know what you...had for dinner, honey, but...I ought to lay in a supply."

Carole wasn't paying any attention to him. She was digging her nails into his back. He was damn glad he had on his jean jacket.

"Oh, baby," she groaned.

With that she stepped back and started unbuckling his belt. Once she had the top button of his Levi's undone, she unzipped the fly and peeled his pants right down to his boots, dropping to her knees to do it. Then she pulled down his underpants.

His penis protruded through the opening of his shirt. Carole began stroking it. As he stood looking down at her, she put his cock in her mouth and began sucking.

He swallowed hard, surprised by the suddenness of what she'd done. He took a deep breath, closing his eyes. Carole started working him hard. Within seconds he felt like he was going to come.

"Hey, babe," he said, stroking her hair with his free hand, "you better stop if you want anything left for you."

Carole looked up at him, not smiling, but not frowning, either. Then she stood and unbuttoned her shirt. Her nipples were taut and hard in the cool air. He lightly stroked the tip of one with his thumb. After a minute, she gently pushed his hand away.

"Let's get in bed, Mitch," she said. "I want you to make love with me."

"Go on into the bedroom," he said. "I'll be right in."

She touched his chin with her fingertip, then turned and went off, unbuttoning her jeans as she went. Mitch gazed down at himself. He looked foolish with his pants down. He lifted them up enough to get to the chair, where he sat and pulled off his boots. Then he finished stripping.

By the time he got to the bedroom door, she'd turned down the bed, had a candle lit, and was lying naked on the sheets.

"Come, lie next to me, Mitch," she said, her voice husky now.

He climbed on the bed, moving between her legs. She took him in her hand, guiding him into her. "Oh, God," she moaned.

Her body trembled under him. He kissed her temple and she grabbed hold of his buttocks, forcing him hard against her. Mitch began humping, driving himself into her with greater and greater force. At first she urged him on, groaning and grunting with each thrust, but after a while her body relaxed and she grew compliant, giving herself to him.

He held on for as long as he could, knowing she was close. And when she started to come, he did, too. For a long minute or two afterward they lay together, trying to catch their breath.

Finally, he rolled off her. She lay motionless and he sensed there was something wrong. He put his hand on hers.

"Damn," she said, her voice scarcely a whisper.

"What's the matter, babe?"

"Sometimes I really hate my life," she said.

"Oh, it was that good, huh?"

"I'm not talking about the sex."

"That's a relief."

She said nothing.

"What's the matter, Carole?"

"I don't want to talk about it and you don't want to hear."

Somehow he knew he should leave it there. At times, when someone said they wanted to let something go, they really meant it. This, he judged, was one of those occasions.

Sausalito

Nola Betts stared blindly at the television as she plucked tissue after tissue from the box, alternately wiping her eyes and blowing her nose. She couldn't stop crying.

She was sitting on the chaise longue in her bedroom, the TV from the den of the house she'd shared with Frank was in the armoire on the opposite wall. It was not a large room, but the decorator had squeezed as much Victoriana into it as possible. Nola loved Laura Ashley—her chintzes, flowery fabrics and lace pillows. She considered it sexy and sensuous, a real boudoir. And she loved scents, strong scents. There were bowls of potpourri everywhere.

Frank hadn't let her have a bedroom like this, vetoing the proposal when they'd redecorated about six years ago. "I'd feel like I was sleeping in a goddamn whorehouse!" he'd said. "Save it for when you're a widow." He hadn't said, "Or a divorcée," but he'd probably thought it. Even then.

The thought of him sent her into a paroxysm of sobs. "Damn you, Frankie," she mumbled drunkenly through her tears, "why have you fucking done this to me?" She shook her head, lamenting, "It just goes to fucking show you're a goddamn ungrateful bastard." She sniffled and blew her nose, tossing the tissue on the pile forming next to the chair.

"What did I do wrong, for chrissake?" She waited a moment before answering the question herself. "Nothing, that's what! Just worshiped your cock, gave you what you wanted anytime you wanted it!''

Nola threw her head against the back of the chair and sobbed for a moment or two. Then, pulling herself together, she looked down at the creamy white legs protruding from her caftan. She raised one toward the ceiling for a better look.

''I still look great, you sonovabitch. My legs are as good as ever. My tits don't sag much. You spent ten thousand goddamn dollars on my face so I'd be beautiful, you stinking bastard! So why do you hate me?''

She wiped her eyes and hurled the tissue toward the wall.

''If it's because I'm a drunk, then maybe you're right. But I'm still the best goddamn lay you ever had, Frankie, I don't care what you say!'' She sniffled. ''So why didn't you come over and screw me tonight? You wanted to. I know you did. Instead I'm here alone. Damn you to hell anyway, Frank!'' she screamed at the top of her lungs.

Nola got to her feet and lurched toward the door. She staggered down the hallway, grazing her shoulder against the wall as she went.

The house was one of the refurbished little gems that dotted the Sausalito hillside. It had two bedrooms, one and a half baths. The master bath was redone in marble with gold fixtures. The previous owner was a celebrity chef, so the kitchen was incredible—more than a gal whose best dish was meat loaf could possibly need, but she loved it for its exclusivity.

The best view was from the front room. Through the telescope standing next to the sliding-glass doors, Coit Tower seemed like it was across the street. The room itself wasn't as big as the master suite she'd had with Frank, but it was as cozy and plush as the bedroom. More Laura Ashley. Big fat sofas and pillows the size of bushel baskets.

The whole damn place was only twelve-hundred square feet, but the location and the view were primo. Six-hundred-and-twenty thousand dollars. Frank took the commission, but had to settle for a three-hundred-thousand dollar condo for himself. To Nola that had seemed fair enough. The bastard.

Once in the kitchen, she opened the refrigerator and pulled out a jug of Gallo burgundy. "You say I'm a drunk, Frank, then I'll drink."

Taking a water glass from the cupboard, she began pouring wine until the glass was full. When she looked up, she saw her reflection in the dark windowpane over the sink.

The woman she saw was startlingly beautiful. For a moment she stared at herself. The words *tragic beauty* came to mind. She didn't know from where, they were just in her head. And the longer she looked, the more tragic her image seemed. Her lip trembled as she remembered something Dr. Silverstein had said to her in therapy: "When you decide you want to stop, Nola, you will." Those words kept going around and around in her head. "Maybe now," she whispered. "Yeah, why not now?"

Holding the glass of wine over the sink, she turned it upside down. Then, on an impulse, she poured the rest of the jug down the drain. Staggering to the cupboard, she took down all the booze in her stash, pouring the contents of each bottle into the sink, one after another.

"There!" she cried triumphantly when her liquor was gone. "This is only the beginning, but you'll see, you'll see."

The tears continued rolling down her cheeks, but they weren't as bitter as before. Wasn't that choice! Dr. Silverstein would be proud. But what about Frank? He was the only one who really mattered, the only one who *ever* mattered.

* * *

Forestville, Sonoma County

Mitch Cross lay listening to Carole's heavy breathing. She'd gone out like a light and that sort of amused him. Usually he was the one who nodded off first. Sex was the best damn soporific known to man. That spent feeling as you lay there with sleep tugging at your brain—there was no better feeling in the world. But for some reason, this time sex had him energized rather than enervated.

Maybe it was Carole. He'd been so aware of her excitement that he hadn't gotten as lost in his own pleasure as he usually did. And so maybe, even though he'd gotten his rocks off, there was still an edge left. It could also have something to do with that little fit of moodiness she'd had afterward.

There was no great mystery as to what that was about. Women might say they wanted sex and nothing more, but it was never all they really wanted, no matter what they told themselves. Being loved was more important, no matter how jaded or cynical a woman was. Of course, nobody wanted to be just a piece of ass, but men seemed better able to rationalize things.

Over the years he'd speculated on why that should be, but he'd never really figured it out. He knew it had something to do with the difference between submitting to something and taking something. Beyond that, it was a mystery.

It was raining again. He was aware of the patter of drops against the aluminum sash window. He lay still, wondering how long it would take him to get to sleep.

After a while he flipped over on his side and stared at the luminous dial of the clock on his bedstand. Shit, it was nearly midnight and he had to be at his desk by seven. It was a cinch Carole would be staying the night, which was fine. It wouldn't be the first time. But fortunately for her, she didn't have to get up and go to work. He'd let her sleep in. She could go on home when she felt like it.

When he got home tomorrow night he'd find the place all cleaned up. Carole claimed she did housework for him because it satisfied whatever limited need she had to pick up after a man. Once a week, she'd told him, was about right. Once a week was about right for most of what they did together—from his standpoint, as well as hers. They kept the interest level up that way, by judicious self-denial—his term, not Carole's.

"You know what you are, Mitch?" she'd told him one night after he'd gone to her place to install a new dryer, eat her spaghetti and get laid. "You're a sex machine who happens to be a nice guy."

He'd swallowed a mouthful of spaghetti. "Can't remember a woman ever saying anything so sweet to me before," he'd replied.

They'd been sitting at her kitchen table. She'd sipped her wine and stared off a long time before saying, "You know, except for worrying sometimes about what I'm going to do when I'm old, I could go on like this forever, screwing when the urge strikes and leaving it at that—no demands, no obligations."

"Forever?"

"Not with you, necessarily, lover boy, but with whoever."

That had been a couple of months ago. At the time he'd believed her. She might even have meant it. But he'd had a feeling that some kind of emotional corner had been turned. They'd been together quite a while by his standards, and relationships did have a way of dying under their own weight. Tonight might have been the apogee of their affair. Funny, but the best lays with a given woman were often among the last. When it really got good, that meant it was nearly over.

He focused on the clock again and groaned. An hour or two of tossing and turning and he might as well get up and listen to the farm news. It was a shame tomorrow wasn't his day off. If he had his druthers, he'd saddle up Jake in the morning instead of drive down to Marin. Not that he didn't like his work, he did. But the issues weren't quite as obvious as they'd once been. Lately he wasn't sure the line separating good from evil was all that clear. Life had started throwing him curves. And so he had to adjust. That, he'd learned over the years, was the name of the game—adapting to changing circumstances.

Mitch decided to get out of bed. He found his tattered old robe in the closet and silently made his way to the front room. At the window he looked out at the yard light to see how hard the rain was coming down. The wind had picked up and it was gusting, blowing rain against the side of the house.

For some reason, his father came to mind. Maybe because as a kid he'd spent so much time staring out the window, wondering if his dad would ever come home. Bill Cross had abandoned his wife and son when Mitch was eight. His mom couldn't take care of him and work at the same time, so they'd left Portland and moved to Reno to live with his grandmother. Four years later his mother died of cancer, leaving his grandmother to raise him.

At the time of his mother's death, he'd been so sure his father would come back for him, but he didn't. Granted, Bill Cross sent money, a fair amount over the years, but he didn't come to visit until Mitch was fifteen. Instead, he'd spent his time and energy building an airplane charter service into a small commuter line. Eventually he and his partner had bought out an ailing scheduled carrier and turned it around, making a fortune in the process.

Mitch didn't discover how rich his old man had become until his twenty-first birthday, when he visited him in Dallas. As it turned out, Bill Cross was a millionaire, living on a big ranch and pretending he was J. R. Ewing. He'd married a blond bimbo with social pretensions who had a five-year-old son. His father had adopted the kid—Mitch's "little brother." The whole thing had made him sick. Fifteen minutes after he arrived, he realized it had been a mistake to come.

After dinner the night before Mitch was scheduled to fly back, his father took him into the den for a man-to-man talk. He began pouring the bourbon, and then, when they were both good and drunk, his father handed him a check for twenty thousand dollars. Mitch looked at it, then at his father, realizing it was nothing but conscience money. Suddenly all the resentment and anger that had built over the years came boiling out. He threw the check in Bill Cross's face and told him he could wipe his ass with it, for all he cared. And then he walked out. He'd spent the night at the airport and had never seen his father again.

Mitch never regretted what he'd done. Sure, he could have taken the check, and probably a lot more over the years, but he wanted no part of it. His father had taught him an important lesson. It took a certain kind of person to accumulate wealth—the kind who put making money above everything else, even his own child. That was Bill Cross.

Mitch stared out at the puddles in the parking area. They glistened like mirrors, their surfaces shattered by rivulets of raindrops. He closed his robe over his chest, shaking his head at the irony that he should be thinking of his father with such bitterness after all these years.

Mitch liked to think his father was irrelevant to his life and always had been. Maybe some of his childhood problems could be traced back to the fact that his father had abandoned them, but if Bill Cross was to be blamed for the bad, he'd have to get some credit for the good, and Mitch wasn't willing to do that.

His whole life he'd considered himself his own man. He made his own choices and his own mistakes. And a few of them had been real doozies. He'd gotten into more than the usual bit of trouble when he was young, putting in some time at juvie hall, and nearly breaking his grandmother's heart in the process.

As it turned out, the person who put him on the straight and narrow was the most unlikely candidate imaginable. At sixteen he'd met a young woman named Sydney. She'd moved into the little house across the street from them. Sydney wasn't like the other residents in their modest neighborhood. She was in her early twenties and the most beautiful woman he'd ever seen. Mitch instantly fell in love with her. He would wait by his window hour after hour, hoping for a glimpse of her.

Sydney was a total mystery to him. She didn't work during the day and when she left the house, it was usually at night. A cab would pick her up. She was always dressed beautifully, very sexily. Occasionally Mitch would see her arrive home in the morning, still dressed up. He decided that she must work at one of the casinos, maybe as an entertainer or something. Her mysterious life really intrigued him.

Then one summer afternoon he saw her pull up in front of her house in a Mustang convertible. Mitch couldn't believe his eyes. She had on a pair of shorts and a tank top. Climbing out of that car was the foxiest creature he'd ever seen.

She got a hose and a bucket and started washing the thing, right there in the driveway. Every time she bent over, he groaned. Finally he couldn't stand it anymore. He went out and sat on the front steps, unable to take his eyes off her.

After a while she saw him and called him over, asking him if he wanted to help. "It's better than sitting there looking like you'd never seen a girl in shorts before."

Mitch was so embarrassed he could have died, but he went over. She didn't have a bra on under the tank top and it was all he could do to keep from gawking.

"You wash the tires for me and I'll take you for a ride," she told him.

Mitch didn't have to be asked twice. He scrubbed the tires within an inch of their lives. And he did all the windows, too. And chamoised down the entire car. True to her word, Sydney took him for a ride. They headed down toward Carson City. Sydney opened the Mustang up to about eighty-five. She had on sunglasses and a big smile. He watched her hair blowing in the wind and had the biggest hard-on he'd ever had in his life. God, she was incredible.

On the way back to Reno she let him drive. She asked him about school and what he liked to do. Mitch talked about sports because that was all he had to talk about. Sydney rested her hand on the back of his seat and she gave his ear a tug once when she made a joke. He thought he'd die.

When he got up the courage, he asked if she was an entertainer. She told him she was but didn't elaborate. The following week he helped her wash her car again. And she paid him to clean the trash out of her backyard. They talked some. She told him the thing she regretted most was that she hadn't gone to college like her parents wanted. She advised him to go on and get a degree.

In September, soon after school started, Mitch came home one afternoon to find half-a-dozen cops over at Sydney's. A few of the neighbors were standing around and one of the women told him Sydney had been murdered. They'd found her body in the Mustang, out in the desert. She'd been shot. The news devastated him.

Just as painful was reading the write-up in the paper the next day. Sydney was identified as a call girl who had worked the casinos. The thought of her renting out her body to a bunch of rich bastards had made him want to vomit.

Sydney's murder became a celebrated criminal case and the papers were full of it for weeks. Every day he would read the accounts with tears in his eyes. Gradually the whole story came out. She was from a little town in Minnesota. A cheerleader, businessman's daughter and local beauty queen, with a lifelong dream of making it in show business. What a tragedy.

Mitch hadn't known her well enough to understand her, but to him she'd been a sweet person. There was nothing about her that was hard or mean. He idolized her even after he learned what she did for a living. He hated the fact that he'd been so young and unable to do anything to help her.

They never solved the crime. Mitch figured it was some jerk who thought his money entitled him to more than Sydney wanted to give. The experience made him hate the money-grubbing world that had destroyed her. And from his bitterness came the first seeds of his desire to become a cop.

Though it had happened over twenty years ago, he still thought of Sydney on occasion. He had a vivid recollection of her pretty face. In a way, he'd lost his virginity to her. And even though she'd been a hooker, she was still the most beautiful woman he'd ever laid eyes on.

"Mitch," Carole said from the doorway behind him, "what are you doing? Is something wrong?"

He turned and saw her in the muted light. She was naked. He could see the curve of her hips, the dark patch between her legs. He thought again of Sydney and his heart tripped.

"No, babe," he said. "I couldn't sleep, that's all. Just watching the rain."

She padded across the bare floor and slipped up beside him, putting her arms around his waist. Her skin felt cool and she shivered. Mitch opened his robe and put it around her. She hugged him for warmth. Her hair smelled vaguely of cigarette smoke, which he didn't particularly like, but she smelled of sex, too—their sex.

Carole ran her fingers over his buttocks. "You won't believe this," she said softly, "but I'm horny again."

"Oh, yeah?" He squeezed her body against his.

Pressing her face against his neck, she inhaled his scent. Then she slipped her hand down between his legs, lightly stroking his penis.

"You're serious, aren't you?" he said.

"We don't have to make love again, if you don't want to. I know you're tired."

"That sounds more like a challenge than sympathy."

She pulled his face down and kissed him.

"How can I pass up an offer like that?" he said.

Carole took his hand and led him toward the bedroom.

Three

Ross
Saturday, February 28

Dana shuffled into the kitchen in her robe and slippers. Robin was standing at the sink, cleaning up the mess from the night before. She was dressed, looking a bit odd in her party clothes. It might have been the puffiness of her eyes, the less-than-perfect hair, or maybe just the harshness of the light, but she definitely had that "morning after" look.

Dana had a throbbing head. She'd run a comb through her hair, washed her face and brushed her teeth, but that was it. She leaned on the counter, the smell of the coffee making her stomach queasy. She stared woefully at Robin.

"Well, if it isn't Venus, risen from the dead," Robin said, using Frank Betts's pet name for her. "Do you feel as bad as you look?" She sounded annoyingly chipper.

"Do I look like shit?"

"I wouldn't go *that* far."

"I would," Dana said, slumping onto a stool. She put her head into her hands. "Did we both make fools of ourselves last night, or was it only me?"

"I think you had one glass of wine more than I did, but I'm not sure. We were both pretty far gone by the time we staggered off to bed."

"Oh, Robin," Dana lamented, "what could make two grown women act like a couple of college girls on spring break?"

"I think we were venting, blowing out the pipes. Every once in a while a person has to be totally irresponsible, forget who they are and let down their hair. Want some coffee?"

"I'm not sure."

"Well, while you think it over, I'll make some juice." She went to the freezer and removed a can of frozen orange juice from the door. "How is it you've got a million frozen juices in the freezer, but not a single one mixed?"

"It's Molly's job. I don't do juice."

"Now that you're on your own, Kirk, you may have to learn to do a few of these domestic tasks yourself."

"Don't give me a hard time about my lack of domesticity, Robin. I've got all I can do to cope with my pounding head."

Robin stood looking at her with her hands on her hips. "You know, the saddest thing about this is that we've paid a terrible price and didn't even get laid for our trouble."

"Please. Sex is about as appealing right now as the thought of a glass of wine."

Robin looked at her contemplatively. "Is that really true?"

"Yes."

"You must have anesthetized yourself."

Dana grinned, despite the throbbing head. "No, it's just that old thing about losing it if you don't use it. After a while you don't think about it and you don't even notice that you're not getting it."

Robin stroked her chin thoughtfully. "You think so?"

Dana nodded.

"I wonder how long before that kicks in?"

Dana laughed. "Well, if you spend all your time thinking about it, I suppose you'll never get it out of your mind."

Robin got a couple of mugs from the cupboard. "What I don't understand is, *why* you'd not want to think about it. I mean, sometimes my fantasies are the high point of my day."

"Well, you've never been married, so by definition you can't have soured on men."

"Spinsters can be soured on men as easily as divorcées," Robin argued, pouring coffee into the mugs. "Anyway, you're not soured on men. You're just off them for a while. In a week or two you'll have a glass of wine and who knows, maybe a man as well."

"I've learned never to say never," Dana said. "So I content myself by thinking about more important things."

Robin carried Dana's mug of coffee to her. "Let me ask you a totally inappropriate question that's none of my business. Was Frank the last man you had?"

"I make it a rule not to answer personal questions about my sex life. But given the low level of my resistance, I will tell you. Yes, he was the last."

"Heavens," Robin said, leaning on the counter across from her, "you're practically a nun."

"You've had your dry spells like everybody else."

"Yes, but not happily. A weekend without a date is painful, a month without a date is grounds for suicide. I readily admit to being obsessed."

"Nonsense. It's not men or sex you're obsessed with. It's with finding Mr. Wonderful. That's a different phenomenon altogether."

"I suppose even my mother would agree with that," Robin said listlessly. She shook her head. "Dear old Mom insists that if I didn't give it away, some guy would marry me to get it. Can you believe that? Who buys a car without giving it a test drive? But when I tell Mom that, she just doesn't get it."

"A different generation," Dana said. "Still, I have to admit, the day you get married will be the happiest day of my life."

"Why? So you won't have to hear me whine anymore?"

Dana chuckled. "Maybe you should give that fellow from last night a call. What was his name? Marvin?"

"Morton."

The telephone rang and they both looked over at it. Neither of them moved.

"It's not Morton, that much is certain," Robin said.

Dana got up from the stool and went to check the number of the caller. It wasn't familiar. She glanced at Robin, who also looked at the number. "I don't know who it is, either."

The phone continued to ring.

"There's only one way to find out."

Dana jotted down the number on the pad, drew a fortifying breath, then picked up the receiver. But she hesitated, taking a moment to find her courage. Finally she spoke. "Hello?"

"Dana?" It was a woman's voice.

"Yes..."

"Sorry to bother you so early," she said, sounding anxious. "This is Bev O'Connell."

"Bev," Dana said, relieved.

"I'm calling because I need to talk to you." She seemed upset.

"What's wrong, Bev?"

"I decided this morning. I'm moving my license, if you'll still have me, that is."

Dana was delighted. "That's wonderful! Of course, I'll have you! I've been polishing that desk I've been saving for you, getting it ready."

Bev laughed joylessly. "This has been a very difficult decision."

"It's never easy to leave a place that's been home. It wasn't for me. But I'm glad you decided to join me."

"I had dinner with Lane Cedrick last night," Bev said. "I figured I owed it to him and Frank to give them my reasons. Lane wasn't pleased when I told him I was going, especially when I made him sign off on my license right then. He had to open up the office to do it. God, was he pissed. You're not a very popular alumna at C&B, Dana. But I don't suppose I have to tell you that."

"No."

There was a pause. Dana could tell Bev's emotions were running high. She even thought she heard a muffled sob.

"Honey, you all right?"

Bev sniffled. "Yes. This is a bad time for me. All kinds of things are happening." She blew her nose. "Ted and I have been having problems again."

There were rumors, unconfirmed, that Ted O'Connell had physically abused Bev. When her income moved up around the two-hundred-thousand mark, the rumors died back. Dana had no idea if there was any basis to the gossip.

"You don't need that right now, you poor thing," Dana said.

"Would you mind if I moved into the office today? I hate feeling homeless. Besides, I need someplace where I can sit down. I slept in my car last night."

"Bev, what happened?"

"It's okay. Things just got a little heated with Ted. I think he's probably calmed down by now, but I'm not sure I can take any more. I'm not going home. At least not tonight."

"Where are you now?"

"In a coffee shop. I just had breakfast. On my way out I decided to call you."

"I'm so sorry."

"It's not your problem. When can I meet you to do the paperwork? Are you tied up this morning?"

"No, I'm just sitting here having a cup of coffee," Dana said, glancing at Robin. "Slept in a little later than usual."

"I suppose it could wait until Monday."

"No, if you're ready, let's do it." Dana knew there was nothing so skittish as a salesperson with personal problems, especially if they were contemplating changing companies. More than once she'd seen someone sit down to present their license to a new broker, only to get up and walk out.

"Sure you don't mind?" Bev said.

"Not at all. Shall we meet at the office in, say, an hour?"

"I'd really appreciate it, Dana." Bev's voice cracked. "I want to get it over with."

Dana heard more than urgency in her voice. She also heard fear. "Bev, what's wrong? Has something happened you haven't told me about?"

"Oh, God," she said, stifling a sob.

"Bev?"

"Last night was just horrible," she croaked. "For a while...I thought Ted was going to..."

Dana swallowed hard. "Going to what?"

Bev did sob then. "Kill me."

"Lord," Robin said, after Dana told her about the call.

"That woman's no cream puff, but she was scared. *Really* scared." Dana took a gulp of coffee. Her stomach wasn't happy with the result, but the adrenaline was flowing and she was ready to shake off the hangover. "I'm going to meet her at the office in an hour, so I'd better get rolling."

"And I've got to go home and change," Robin said, moving around the counter and into the family room. She carried her coffee mug. "I want to preview some houses before I meet with the buyers I'm seeing this afternoon. But, if it's all right, I'll finish my coffee."

"Of course. Take your time." Dana got up from the barstool and faced Robin, who'd sat down in one of the plaid chairs. She cinched her robe and started to head for her room when she stopped dead in her tracks. "Oh, shit."

"What's the matter?"

Dana turned to her, a sick look on her face. "I'm supposed to take Molly shopping in the city this morning."

Robin read her anxiety. "Oh, Dana."

"A chance to sign up the hottest recruit in town, but to do it I have to stand up my daughter." She pressed her fingers to her temples. Her head was pounding, but it wasn't her hangover so much as it was Molly and all the things that had been going wrong in her life lately. "Well, I'm not going to stand her up. Even if I lose Bev, I'm taking Molly to the city."

"When are you supposed to pick her up?"

"At ten."

Robin looked at her watch. "You have over an hour. You could sign up Bev and still pick Molly up by eleven. An hour late wouldn't be the end of the world. Just call her and say you'll be delayed."

"I'm always doing things like that to her."

"This is hardly frivolous. Bev could make your company, Dana."

"But it's the principle of the thing. Molly always feels she gets short shrifted, and I just can't do it to her again."

"You're being overly sensitive. Molly would understand a short delay. It wouldn't hurt to call. Just be honest with her."

Dana felt torn. "Oh, God," she said, rubbing her head, "I can't even make a simple decision anymore."

Robin got up, went over and put her arm around her. "You're making too big a deal out of this. The past few weeks have been rough and you're extra emotional. Molly might be a teenager but she loves you. If she gets upset you can put Bev off."

"I don't even know how to get ahold of Bev." Dana shook her head. "How could I have forgotten my own daughter?"

"Come on, stop beating yourself. Give Molly a call and discuss it with her."

Dana gave her a teary smile. "Cohen, you're the best mother I've ever had."

"The only one, really."

"That's true. And that's why I hate being a failure as a mother myself."

Robin took her by the shoulders, turned her toward the phone, and pointed. "Call. Tell her you'd like to pick her up at eleven instead of ten."

Dana sighed, her heart aching. "Yes, Mother."

San Rafael

Frank Betts pulled his Testarossa into the parking lot of the Peacock Gap Golf and Country Club. Lane's Rolls wasn't in sight. That meant he wouldn't have to get out in the cold wind just yet.

He and Lane played golf at least half of the Sundays of the year. When they were building Cedrick & Betts from a little one-office real-estate company to the largest multi-office brokerage firm in Marin County, they'd promised each other a half day every week away from the phones. More creative ideas came out of eighteen holes of golf early on a Sunday morning than the whole rest of the week combined.

Lane had called him late last night, after he was already in bed, and asked if they could meet on Saturday instead. Frank had heard a vaguely ominous tone in his partner's voice. He knew it meant trouble. Things had been shitty the past few months, what with Dana fucking them over. Still, he couldn't imagine anything worse happening.

Especially after last night. When he'd awakened that morning he couldn't believe what he'd done. He'd considered giving Dana a call, but how in the hell did you explain something like that? "I felt like being near you, so I drove up to sit in front of your house." No, he'd just try to forget it and hope she'd do the same.

A few minutes later Lane Cedrick's Rolls-Royce entered the parking lot. Frank watched it approach and come to a stop next to him. It was raining now. Lane got out and opened the door of the Ferrari.

"Sorry to be late," he said, as he climbed in. The collar of his windbreaker was turned up. Lane rubbed his hands. "Not exactly golf weather, is it?"

Cedrick was fifty, medium height, trim. His blond hair was perpetually sun-bleached, and he was always tanned. He'd had some work done on his eyes. Lane pampered himself. He cared about his image. Frank had always found that ironic, though of course, seeking the favor of women was not the only reason to be concerned about one's appearance.

For several moments neither of them said anything. They were practically like a married couple when it came to unspoken communication.

"Bev O'Connell jumped ship last night," Lane finally said, as though announcing a death.

"To go with Dana?"

"Yep."

Frank groaned out loud. "Damn her to hell."

"She's raping us, Frank."

He closed his eyes and rubbed the bridge of his nose. He felt sick to his stomach. "Yes, and I'm more to blame than anyone. I realize that."

"I can take the loss of her production," Lane said. "I can even take the loss of the people she's stolen from us. But her involvement in the bank can put us in jail. One of these days the Oak Meadow Partners loan is going to up and bite us in the ass."

Frank was shocked. "I thought we were covered on that."

"I thought so, too. But Stan Bishop told me on Friday that he'd been through the loan portfolio. Said it might not be a bad idea if the loan committee took a look at several of the loans. If he opens up Oak Meadow Partners, we're as good as hung. With Wally and Viola dead, Dana and I are what's left of the loan committee."

"Christ."

"If Stan had let the sleeping dogs lie, we'd be all right. He's so goddamn conscientious. But how can I tell him to concentrate on new business?"

"Did he say which loans he wants to discuss?" Frank asked.

"No, and I didn't want to arouse any suspicion. I told him, fine. I don't think there's any danger from Stan. But if Dana sees a loan to Oak Meadow Partners for five-hundred thousand, she might wonder who the hell Oak Meadow Partners are, and why she's never seen anything on the deal. All she has to do is take a look at the minutes of that meeting, see that her signature was forged on the loan-approval forms, and we're up shit creek."

"Fuck!" Frank said, pounding his fist against the steering wheel. "That bitch will be the death of me."

"Let's hope not," Lane said dryly.

"What are we going to do?"

"We can try to lay the forgery on the Maplethorpes. Wally or Viola could have done it as easily as you, Frank." Lane's thin lips narrowed as he smiled. "And they sure as hell won't be able to deny it from the grave."

Frank felt his stomach clench. He thought for a moment he might get sick. He lowered the window, so that some cool air came in. He inhaled deeply.

"But if she does squawk, then Stan and everybody else will take a long hard look at the loan, and we're dead," he lamented. "How do we explain that we've drawn down four-hundred thousand and not much has happened out there except that some dirt was moved around?"

"We can't," Lane said. "That's why we've got to get Dana off the goddamned loan committee. Before it was desirable. Now it's essential—unless we want to spend the next ten years in San Quentin."

Frank lowered the window a bit more. He turned his face toward it and felt the spatter of raindrops on his cheeks and forehead. The coolness felt good, but he was still nauseous.

"We never should have used borrowed money on that stock deal, Lane," he said. "Buying that much on margin was insane. Why I listened to you, I'll never know."

"Don't try to make it my fault!" Lane snapped. "You were as hot for the deal as I was."

"Yeah, but it was supposed to be a sure thing. Good enough to risk forging loan documents and diverting all that money from Oak Meadow Partners to do it."

"We took a chance and we lost."

"And now we're paying for it."

"It's not the stock deal that's got us in the soup," Lane rejoined. "If you hadn't brought Dana into the bank, we wouldn't be worrying about getting nailed on that loan scam."

"So it's *my* fault!"

"Forget the fault shit, Frank. We're in this together. There's nothing to be gained by blaming each other."

Frank was glad of that. It had been his idea to give Dana the bank stock as a sort of bonus and an inducement to stay with the company. Then, within a few months of getting her the freebie, she left anyway. And now they were stuck with her on the board and looking over their shoulders.

Frank's gut was grinding. "Damn it to hell," he muttered.

"The immediate problem is the loan-committee meeting," Lane said. "If we can weather that, and get the goddamn brokerage operation back on track so we can pay back the money we borrowed from the Oak Meadow account, we'll be all right. The trouble is everything that's happened recently has compounded the problem."

"And it all goes back to Dana being a foe instead of a friend."

"Yeah, but in fairness she probably wouldn't have appreciated us forging her signature even if she was still our top producer and you were still boffing her every night."

Lane stared ahead as raindrops spattered the windshield. Frank watched, his jaw working. Lane was amazingly calm. That was his style—cerebral rather than emotional. But he could be a son of a bitch when necessary; the most icy bastard Frank had ever known.

As a man, Lane was neither effeminate nor particularly masculine. Frank had always thought of him as asexual, even though he'd known from the beginning that his partner was gay. To his credit, though, Lane had always been discreet. Frank had never witnessed anything overt, nor had he heard more than whispers around the company. Personally, he didn't care what Lane did. It simply meant he didn't have to compete with him for the women.

"So what do we do?" Frank asked. "You've obviously given it a lot of thought."

"I think we deal with Dana first," Lane replied. "Extraordinary measures are called for."

Frank saw cool hatred on Lane's smoothly tanned face. "What kind of measures?"

"It's time to fight back, Frank. I mean really fight back. We treated the bitch well, and now she's turned on us. I've got no compunction about wiping Kirk & Company off the map."

"But how?"

"I've already started things in motion," Lane said, a smile on his lips. "But we've got to kick into high gear. We've got to stop the hemorrhaging while we can. Above all, we've got to get her off the board of Marin Pacific, posthaste. We've got to buy her out."

"How? The Marin Pacific stock we gave her is worth more than we can comfortably pay."

"She'll have to give us terms, take a note, whatever."

"Why should she, Lane? She's got the leverage."

"You're going to have to find a way," Lane said irritably. "I see nothing wrong with gentle persuasion. At least the appearance of gentle persuasion. It's a good diversion at worst. Talk to her, Frank. Negotiate with her. Show her how reasonable we are, how we want to be fair and resolve our differences amicably. Who knows? Maybe she still worships your cock and will give you whatever you want."

"Don't count on it."

"I thought you were addictive, Frank. I thought once they got nailed by Betts they never went back."

"Save the sarcasm. I know I fucked up with Dana, you don't have to remind me."

"Such modesty is uncharacteristic, Frank. If you lose both your ego and your libido, they'll stop referring to C&B as Cunts & Betts."

"My cock's not the issue. It's Dana. I've got to have something to take to the negotiating table. What do I offer her?"

"Whatever you have to. If it's a little something extra out of your share of the pie, then offer her that. Or come up with another plan. You figure it out."

"And if I fail?"

"Then we go to step two."

"Which is?"

"Something harsher, and a bit more unpleasant." Lane turned to him, his eyes hardening. "We're not going to let this woman hang us, Frank. So we'll do whatever it takes. We don't have any other choice."

San Rafael

Mitchell Cross went into the coffee room, filled his mug, fished a dime out of his pocket, and dropped it in the can.

"Well, what do you know, an honest cop."

He turned around and saw Corinne Smith seated at the Formica table in the corner. She was the only black woman on the force and had seniority over Mitch by six months— a fact she never let him forget. At the moment she had a big grin on her face.

"Oh, hi, Corinne. Didn't see you when I came in."

"Congratulations on your honesty, Mitch."

"What do you mean? The coffee money? I wouldn't cheat my fellow officers."

She hooted. "Well, you're the first, honey. Five guys have come in since I've been sitting here. You're the only one who's paid."

"Maybe they put in a quarter last time."

"You shittin' me? Lordy, you gotta be smokin' somethin' to believe that."

Mitch shrugged. "So, I'm buying the office coffee." He gestured toward her mug. "Can I buy you a cup, Corinne?"

"Now if there's anything I like, it's a sweet-talkin' man. Yes, Detective Cross, I'll let you buy me a cup of coffee. Don't tell my man, though. He's always tellin' me to stay clear of you bachelors."

Mitch carried the pot over and filled Corinne's mug. Then he took it back and dropped another dime in the can. "Does that mean I can't join you?"

"Lord, no. What Ned don't know won't hurt him." She laughed and slapped the table. Mitch sat down. Corinne Smith was about his age, and pretty. She'd put on a little weight since he'd first gotten to know her, but she generally kept herself fit.

"Tell me the truth," he said in a conspiratorial tone, "are the bachelors on the force any worse than the married men?"

"Hell, no! The two or three worst lechers are married. Any woman can tell you that's the way it usually is. But my man don't know. I leave him clingin' to his illusions."

Mitch laughed and tapped his mug against hers. He took a big sip of coffee.

"I don't mean to rain on your parade or nothin', honey, but you're lookin' a little tired this morning. You have a rough night or what?"

"A late night."

Corinne grinned. "Was she worth it?"

Mitch had a mental image of Carole astride him.

"Is that a blush I see on you, Detective Cross?"

He turned bright red. "It's no accident they send you out on all the domestic disputes, is it?" he said. "You can look at a man's face and get the whole story."

"Honey, when it comes to men there's only one story. S-E-X. The only thing I have to figure out each time is what part of it's the problem. Usually it's not gettin' enough. Nine times out of ten, that is.''

"There may be a lesson in that for women," Mitch said.

"Yep, there is. Marry one that's enough older that he can't keep up."

Mitch chuckled.

Corinne fiddled with her coffee mug. "On another subject, I understand you're on that case with the real-estate lady who's getting the death threats."

"Yeah. Last night Al asked me to handle it. Why?"

"She in Larkspur, by any chance?"

"Her office is."

"What's her name?"

"Kirk. Dana Kirk," he said.

"Yeah, that's the one."

"What one?"

"Well, yesterday afternoon I went out on a domestic dispute, see. The wife called, afraid her drunk sonovabitch husband was going to beat the shit out of her. He was gone by the time I got there, but I talked to her some. She's a real-estate lady and she tells me she's changing companies. Her husband and her had a big fight about it. That's what brought me out. Seems he hates the lady broker at the new place."

"Dana Kirk."

"Yep. Seems the guy got pretty foul about her, and my lady—O'Connell's her name—was all upset, thinkin' he might take it out on this Kirk woman. She asks me what I think she ought to do. I said, 'Honey, you gotta worry 'bout your own butt first. If you got a man that beats on you, I'd say get out of here and worry about the rest later.'"

"So the husband's got a hard-on toward the broker, Dana Kirk."

"Yes," Corinne said. "I figured if you're working the case you might like to know."

"Thanks," Mitch said, "I appreciate it. I'm due to talk to her. Waiting for her to call, as a matter of fact." He looked at his watch. "Of course, it may not hurt to buzz her again." He got up, taking his coffee mug. "Maybe I'll do it now, while it's on my mind. Will you excuse me, Corinne?"

"Sure."

Mitch headed off.

"Thanks for the coffee, honey," she called after him. "Next time I'm buyin'."

He stopped and looked back at her. "You mean to say there are two honest cops in the department?"

"If I'm going to cheat on my man by hangin' out with a sexy bachelor, I'd best not cheat on my fellow officers, too, don't you think?"

He winked at her and left the room. Back in his office, he sat down at his desk and looked through his drawer until he found the paper with Dana Kirk's phone numbers. After glancing at his watch, he decided to try her office first. He dialed. A woman sounding like a receptionist answered. She had a slight accent.

"Dana Kirk, please," he said.

"I'm sorry, Dana's not in," the woman said. "May I take a message?"

He couldn't quite place the accent. It wasn't Spanish. Italian, maybe. "Do you expect her soon?"

"She's due in shortly, sir. She has an appointment in the office."

"This is Mitch Cross. Would you tell Ms. Kirk I'm going to be down that way and, if she's free, I'd like to talk to her?"

"Yes, I'll give her the message."

"Tell her not to worry, if it isn't convenient to see me. I'll catch her another time." He hung up, glad he hadn't been put off. He wanted the initial interview so he could get an idea of just what he faced.

He leaned back in his chair, his hands clasped behind his head. It was a funny thing. Last night, when Al Bensen brought him the file, he hadn't been all that excited about the case. Actually, he'd regarded it as a pain in the butt. But Dana Kirk's situation apparently had been percolating in the back of his mind, because just before he drifted off to sleep, he'd thought about the froufrou lady real-estate broker badly in need of a champion. It struck him as odd that he thought of her that way. Maybe it was because Bensen had referred to her as a damsel in distress.

Mitch had been told more than once that he had a savior complex. He wasn't exactly sure what that meant, but to his way of thinking, it couldn't be all bad. And now, after hearing about the Kirk woman, he'd gotten kind of curious what she looked like. Al had said she was good-looking, and so had Liz Rogers. The downside was that she was probably also a snooty bitch. Oh, well, he thought, things could be worse.

Larkspur

Kirk & Company was located in the Larkspur Landing shopping center, which overlooked the ferry terminal and San Francisco Bay. Dana drove down to the east end of the complex where she'd rented three thousand feet of prime office space. That was one of the more important lessons Frank and Adrianne had taught her—in sales, image was half the game, especially in a place like Marin.

There was already a small group of Mercedeses clustered in front of the office when she parked in her reserved slot. A light drizzle fell as she hurried to the door. Dana wiped her feet before stepping onto carpet that was thick as vanilla fudge and nearly the same color. She glanced at

Chiara who sat behind the reception desk, a dramatically lit Frank Stella painting behind her. Dana had bought it five years ago when she had her first six-figure month. She had wanted the customer's first sight of the office to be breathtaking, and it was. Between the Stella, a twenty-five-thousand-dollar custom-made reception desk, and Chiara, the effect was like opening a slick fashion magazine.

Chiara was Italian-born, pencil thin. She had an exotic face and dark hair that was the color of Dana's, though she wore it shoulder-length and invariably pulled back over one ear.

"*Ciao*, Dana," she said with a voice that could both laugh and seduce.

"Morning, Chiara." Dana slipped off her trench coat and hung it on the coatrack.

"Two calls for you," the girl said, handing her the message slips.

Dana looked at them. One was from David, indicating he was at his office and urgently needed to speak with her. She stared at Chiara's distinctive script, her eyes fixed on the word "urgent." She didn't like the term—especially not when he used it. And why, she wondered, was he working on a Saturday morning, anyway?

The other message slip indicated that Mitch Cross had called and would be dropping by later. "Oh, damn. I won't have time to talk to him," she muttered to Chiara. "Even if he comes while I'm still here, you'll have to tell him my morning and afternoon are both shot."

She glanced toward the bull pen where there were eight agent desks, each costing five thousand. Image. Three of her five salespeople were in. Sylvia Hansen, middle-aged, matronly, a librarian in pearls, occupied the nearest desk and was on the phone. She waved.

Sylvia's coming on board had put Kirk & Company on the map. Dana had to give her an extra five points in the split to induce her to leave C&B, but top agents could be loss leaders and still make money for you because of the momentum they created. Dana had done that for C&B for years.

When she turned back, Chiara was checking out her latest St. John knit. The dress was a rich cinnamon and was at once sexy and sophisticated. The two of them had a habit of looking each other over pretty closely each morning.

"No sign of Bev O'Connell?" Dana asked.

Chiara shook her head.

"She should be here at any time."

"A day like usual, eh?"

Chiara's accent was musical. Dana adored it. "I hope not. I want to get out of here in an hour, max."

"I don't think so," Chiara said. "Not you."

"I've reformed. Honest."

She entered her private office, situated opposite the reception area from the sales floor. There were a couple of good oils on the walls and a Waterford vase that was filled with fresh floral arrangements twice a week. Her desk would have made any Fortune 500 CEO proud, or at least, one with taste. The butter-soft leather chair accepted her body like a womb. The message slips were still clutched in her hand.

David's call worried her. He rarely telephoned her at the office. When he did, it almost always meant trouble. Molly had said nothing to indicate a problem was brewing when she'd spoken to her that morning, but they'd talked only briefly. As Robin predicted, Molly had not been upset by the delay in leaving for the city. In fact, she'd been surprisingly cool and unruffled about it.

Dana picked up the telephone and dialed David's number. Four rings and he answered.

"It's me," she said curtly. "You urgently wanted to talk?"

"Yes. I need to talk to you about Molly."

"I'm happy to discuss her, as always, but does it have to be now? A new agent is due any minute to sign up and I want to get out of here as fast as I can so I can pick up Molly."

"That's what I want to talk to you about. Do you really think it's such a good idea to take Molly shopping under the circumstances?"

She was taken aback. "What are you talking about, David? The threats?"

"Yes." He cleared his throat. "I'm wondering if it's wise for you to be taking her out in public."

"What do you think will happen?"

"I don't know. That's the point, it seems to me. There's a lot of uncertainty and a lot at stake. Why take the risk?"

She sat mute, trying to decide what was going on, what he was really saying. David was never blatant, preferring to draw things from people without having to say them himself. It was a trait that invariably infuriated her.

"Are you recommending that I not take her to the city, or are you trying to tell me that I can't?" Years earlier, she'd developed the habit of being direct with him almost to the point of being confrontational, as a countermeasure to his subtlety.

"I'm not trying to pick a fight," he said, betraying his annoyance. "I'm attempting to appeal to your common sense and good judgment."

"As defined by you," she retorted.

"For God's sake, Dana, I don't want to keep you from seeing her. If you want to see her today, go by my place and spend the afternoon with her. I'll be working most of the day anyway."

"Thanks, but I think I can figure out how to spend time with my daughter without your help. And if she's in such danger, why is it you've left her alone? Last night it was the same thing. When I called, you were out on errands. Is that your idea of protecting her? Or am I the only villain in the equation?''

"Dana, don't take this personally. I'm not criticizing you, nor am I trying to control your relationship with Molly.''

"Then why is it fine if you leave her alone, but if I do it, I'm a criminal?''

"I'm doing a seminar this afternoon for a community group. It's been scheduled for months, Dana. Otherwise I would be home with her.''

"Nice how you've carefully rationalized everything you do. I just wish you were as tolerant of the demands of my work.''

He fell silent and Dana seethed, partly because of his hypocrisy, partly because he was implying that she was being irresponsible. Actually, she hadn't thought of the danger in those terms. The evil, she'd assumed, lay in the night.

"I wish you wouldn't take this as an attack on you," he said, having regained his characteristic calm demeanor. "I'm trying to help. Neither of us wants anything to happen to Molly. You were courageous and selfless to send her to me in the first place.''

"Oh, David, stop patronizing me. I'm not a patient.''

"What do you want from me, then?" he returned.

"Oh, I don't know," she said, almost in tears.

"I suppose the danger is remote enough that one trip to the city won't be the end of the world. If it's really important to you, then take her." There was conciliation in his voice, but he wasn't very convincing.

"Thanks loads! You tell me it's fine to go, after putting the fear of God in me! Honestly, just once I wish we could have a conversation without you trying to manipulate me.''

"That wasn't my intent, and you know it. Molly's my child, too. I'm afraid for her, and I don't want anything to happen."

By now Dana was trembling with anger. "I have neither the time nor the desire to argue with you, David," she said firmly. "As a matter of fact, I'm up to my armpits in manure. To use a term you can relate to, I'm in crisis. Everything's coming down on me at once."

"I'm sorry, Dana. I truly didn't mean to add to your burdens."

"Since you felt strongly enough to intercede in my plans, maybe you would be good enough to help me resolve the problem."

"Sure. What do you want me to do?"

"Call Molly and explain that you vetoed our trip to the city. Tell her I've acceded to your wishes, but that I want to see her anyway. Tell her I'll be by your place with some deli sandwiches so that she and I can at least have lunch together."

"Dana, I don't want you to think—"

"Save your breath," she said, cutting him off. "Just do that for me and I'll try not to put Molly in any undue danger." With that she hung up, slamming down the receiver just in time to keep from crying.

She took a tissue from her drawer and blew her nose. As she did, she glanced out the window and saw Beverly O'Connell pulling up out front. Dana drew a ragged breath. Lord, from one fire to the next. Sometimes she wondered how she found the strength to go on.

The heavy mist had turned to rain. She noticed that Bev didn't immediately get out of her car. Was it the rain, or was she still anguishing over her decision? Dana watched her for a minute, her heart pounding from the emotional conversation with David.

Finally Bev opened the car door, got out and walked slowly toward the office. She didn't bother to open her umbrella. Her expression was grim. It was not a good sign.

Once inside, Bev stood in the outer office, anxiously looking at her through the glass partition. Dana got up and went to her door.

"Hi, Bev," she said as cheerfully as her acting ability would allow.

Bev was leaning with one hand on Chiara's desk. She looked distraught, anxious, ready to break into tears. "Oh, Dana," she murmured, shaking her head.

Dana walked over to her and took her by the shoulders. "What's the matter, honey?"

Bev swallowed hard, her body trembling. "I called Ted this morning to tell him I'm not coming back, ever. He was furious, and I'm scared to death. I know he's going to do something really terrible."

Mitchell Cross pulled into Larkspur Landing and drove to the east end of the complex. First he spotted the covey of Mercedeses huddled together in the rain, then he saw the big gold lettering: Kirk & Company. Al Bensen's description of Dana Kirk as a froufrou real-estate broker came to mind.

Judging by the looks of the place, this was no mom-and-pop operation. Beverly Hills North was more like it.

Mitch didn't pretend to know a lot about real-estate people. The only personal dealings he'd had with a broker was when he bought his place in Forestville. The guy handling it was a farm-and-ranch broker whom he'd seen a grand total of three or four times, mostly in his truck. Mitch had no doubt that Kirk & Company was a different kind of ball game altogether.

He parked his car and observed the office. The warm light inside seemed inviting. Half-a-dozen women were in the place and, while he couldn't see how they were dressed or what the office looked like, he could smell the money all the way from the parking lot. It wasn't his favorite smell, but he told himself that a victim was a victim, regardless.

Grabbing his trench coat, Mitch got out, slipped it on and walked to the fancy doors. Before going in, he dutifully wiped his shoes. Once inside, the beauty behind the reception desk caught his eye. What a face. He strode over to her, aware of the mélange of perfumes in the air.

"Good morning, sir," she said. "May I help you?"

She was the one he'd spoken to earlier. He recognized the melodic accent. Sexy.

"The name is Mitch Cross," he said amiably. "I'd like to see Mrs. Kirk, if she's available."

The girl glanced toward the glassed-in private office off to her left. Cross turned, following her eyes.

Through the miniblinds he saw two women, one behind a big fancy desk, the other in a visitor's chair. The one facing him was absolutely stunning. She had glossy black hair that came to her jaw, big beautiful eyes and lips that looked inviting from ten yards away. She was looking at him as he gazed in at her. Neither of them blinked. The staring continued as the receptionist spoke.

"Ms. Kirk is with somebody," she said. "She told me to tell you she's tied up today, but she'd like to meet with you another time, if you'd care to make an appointment. I have her calendar for the week."

He heard the words, but his attention was focused on Dana Kirk. She would be harder to dismiss than he'd imagined. He saw her break off her gaze and reach for the phone, saying something to her guest as she did. The intercom buzzed on the receptionist's console. The girl picked up the handset and listened.

"Yes," she said into the phone, "it's Mr. Cross."

Dana Kirk got up from her chair and stepped into the reception area. He watched her every move. The woman could walk. Sleek as a cat. Now that she was standing in plain sight, he could fully appreciate what she did for a knit dress. She was slender, but with all the desirable curves. He was embarrassed at being so taken aback.

"Detective Cross?" She affected a pleasantly cordial smile, not exactly phony, but not entirely honest, either.

"Yes," he said.

"I'm Dana Kirk." She walked toward him, her hand extended.

"I understand I've come at an inconvenient time."

"I'm sorry," she replied, "but this is a bad day."

He took her fingers in his hand. Her grip was business-like, no-nonsense. She used her eyes and body language effectively, projecting charm, yet with professional distance. He was reluctant to let go of her hand.

"I realize I'm dropping in uninvited," he said easily, returning her gaze, "but I thought we should talk sooner rather than later. Files mean more when I know the people behind the paper, if you know what I mean."

Dana glanced at the receptionist, signaling that discretion was appreciated. "Yes, I understand. Actually, I would like to talk to you, if at all possible. Something happened last night that could be important."

"Oh?"

"Yes." She looked at the clock and frowned. "The problem is, I've got a couple of balls in the air right now and little time to do everything that needs to be done. I'm really buried."

"The life of a busy executive."

She smiled faintly, as if she wasn't certain whether it was sarcasm or not. He wasn't entirely sure himself.

"I could wait awhile, I suppose, if that would help."

She glanced back toward her office, then at the clock again, calculating. He took the opportunity to discreetly look her over. She was dressed expensively. Between the gold watch, the ring and earrings, she was easily wearing the equivalent of a year's pay for a cop. Maybe more.

Engaging his eyes again, she said, "I hate to impose, but I really would like to speak with you. Could you give me fifteen or twenty minutes?"

"Sure. I'll go grab a cup of coffee. Just point me in the direction of a coffee shop."

"We have coffee here. Chiara would be happy to get you a cup."

"Thanks, but I'll get a doughnut to go with it. Civil servant's diet."

She smiled politely, then immediately looked away. She seemed awfully distracted. And her anxiety was beginning to show. Fissures in the rock.

The blonde in Dana Kirk's private office had come to the door. She was a large woman and she appeared to be upset. Her eyes were red, and she looked like she'd been crying.

"Dana," she said, her voice surprisingly childlike, "if you have something you have to do, I can wait."

"No, Bev. Thanks, but I'll be right there. This will only take a minute."

The woman went back to her chair. Dana Kirk turned to him.

"We're dealing with a volatile personal problem at the moment," she said, lowering her voice. "There's a lot more to this business than listing and selling property."

"So I see."

Dana Kirk looked torn, as if she didn't want him to go. Observing her closely, he saw the tension in her face. She held herself together well, but he knew stress when he saw it.

"There's a gourmet deli farther up that way," she said, pointing, "if you can make do with a French pastry instead of a doughnut."

"I suppose I can rough it."

"Thanks for staying," she said. "I really appreciate it."

"See you in a bit." Mitch Cross winked at the receptionist, who'd been taking everything in, her eyes on him the whole time. He went to the door, nodding at Dana before going out into the lightly falling rain.

Beverly O'Connell was dabbing her eyes when Dana returned to her desk. The poor thing had been virtually hysterical since she had arrived, though she'd turned weepy only in the last several minutes.

"This is so unprofessional," she said. "I hate myself for breaking down like this."

"Nonsense. I'm glad you turned to me, Bev."

"Was that a client? Am I keeping you from business?"

"No, he's a friend of a friend. You're what matters right now. We've got to figure out what we're going to do about Ted."

"Damn him," Bev said. "Why is he doing this to me? Why can't he leave me alone?"

Dana sighed. "It's rough, I know. I hate what he's doing to you. We women have to stick together at times like this."

"I'll make it up to you," Bev said. "I promise, I'll be your top producer."

Bev was thirty-eight, tall, thick-boned, a smidgen heavy. Her full blond hair was permed. She tended to wear tight skirts and sweaters, effecting a voluptuous air. But she had a natural warmth, an almost-maternal quality that was the key to her success. At the moment though, Dana was seeing a different Bev. Her face tear-streaked, she seemed small, vulnerable, like an overgrown little girl—one who had been abused.

"The important thing," Dana said, "is that you get yourself together so you can deal with Ted. Once the waters have calmed, you can worry about real estate. If you need a place to stay for a while, you're welcome at my house. I've got a big guest room. It'll give you time to see how things work out with Ted."

Bev forced a smile, though her lip quivered. "Thanks, Dana. I can't tell you how much I appreciate what you're doing. I feel so helpless."

Outside, the glimmer of a fast-moving car caught Dana's eye. Ted O'Connell's Porsche—the one Beverly had gotten him for Christmas—lurched to a halt. Dana felt herself tense, her heartbeat quickening. Bev was busy wiping her eyes and didn't notice. Dana drew a calming breath.

"Ted's arrived, Bev," she said, keeping her voice steady.

Bev whipped her head around. They watched as he stomped into the reception area. Dana could see his flushed face. She was sorry now that she'd sent that police detective away. He would have been handy.

Dana took a deep breath to fortify herself as Ted planted himself in front of Chiara's desk, his hands on his hips, waiting for her to get off the phone.

"Just stay calm," Dana said softly. "I'll deal with him."

Bev's knuckles turned white as she gripped the arms of her chair. Ted started looking around. Then he spotted them. He glared at Dana.

She stared back at him, looking as displeased and indignant as she could. His thinning reddish-blond hair, normally combed neatly over his freckled pate, was mussed from the wind. Despite the weather, he was in a yellow polo shirt and chinos, apparently having left in such a hurry that he didn't bother with a jacket.

When she saw him start for her office, Dana got to her feet. "You stay here," she said to Bev. "I'll talk to him." Her heart was pounding as she went to the door.

Ted O'Connell, onetime linebacker at San Jose State, onetime plumber, onetime would-be real-estate developer, waited. The sight of him took her back to that C&B Christmas party. They'd danced. She remembered his boozy breath spilling over her as he pressed against her breasts, asking how she managed to get it all—looks, money, the works.

She had a natural revulsion for men like that. Ted O'Connell was forty-three, a boy in a man's body, either perpetually euphoric or angry at the world. There was no place for him in between. Right then, he seemed as out of control as a three-year-old having a tantrum.

"What do you want, Ted?" she said as calmly as she could.

"I want my wife."

"Bev's upset. You are, too, Ted. Why don't you go on home? You can talk when everybody's had a chance to cool down."

"Listen, lady," he said, pointing at her, "you don't tell me when I can talk to my wife." He started to push past her.

Dana positioned herself in the middle of the doorway, making it clear she had no intention of stepping aside. Ted stopped inches from her, his six-foot-four frame so close she could feel the heat of his body. There was beer on his breath, despite the fact that it was still morning.

"Bev!" he roared. "Get your ass out here! We're going home."

"No, Ted," she replied, trying to sound resolute, "I'm not going with you."

Dana looked back. Bev was cringing in her chair, terrified. Dana turned to him. "Please, don't cause any trouble, it'll only make things worse."

"Bev," he shouted, ignoring her, "I'm giving you thirty seconds to come out of there, or so help me, God, I'll come in and drag you out by the hair if I have to!"

His anger sent a surge of adrenaline through Dana's veins. "You have no right to barge into my office!" she seethed. "Now leave, before there's trouble."

O'Connell shook his index finger in front of her. "Shut your fucking mouth, bitch. You caused this, so if you've got any brains at all, you'll butt out!"

"Chiara," Dana said, raising her trembling voice, "call the police."

Ted O'Connell was enraged. Shoving Dana hard against the doorframe, he pushed his way into the room. Bev rose from her chair, lifting her arms to deflect his blows, but Ted grabbed her wrist, giving her a yank and overturning the chair in the process. She screamed. Irate, Ted hit her on the side of the head, knocking her almost to her knees. She would have fallen if he hadn't had hold of her.

Dana ran past them to her desk. Opening the top drawer, she searched for her gun. She'd never pulled the weapon before. Her hand trembled as she lifted it from the drawer.

"Ted!" she screamed as ferociously as she could. "Let go of her!"

They were in the doorway, Bev half on the floor, sobbing, still trying to pull free. Ted looked back and saw the gun. His mouth dropped.

"I said, let go of her," Dana said through her teeth.

He did as he was told. Bev slid to the floor, her skirt riding up her thighs, her blond curls hanging over her face. Dana struggled to keep the gun from shaking.

"Leave, Ted," she commanded, "before the police come and arrest you."

He hesitated for a moment, looking as though he wasn't sure what to do. Behind him, in the reception area, Chiara was hanging up the phone. Across the way, in the bull pen, Sylvia Hansen and Helene Whitford stood at their desks, horrified.

Ted glared, his fists clenched. "For two cents I'd knock your head off, lady," he snarled. "Nobody tells me what to do. Nobody!"

"In my office, I'm in charge," she retorted.

"Your office! You're nobody. And buying a few fancy desks doesn't make you anybody, either. Why these idiots want to come here and sink with you, I don't know. You're all fools. But so help me, lady, you aren't taking Bev down with you."

"Ted, I'm not telling you again. *Get out of here!*"

His eyes narrowed. "You don't have the guts to pull the trigger."

Dana extended the gun with both hands, pointing it directly at his chest. "Don't make me shoot you," she said through her teeth. "Because I will."

He took a step toward her.

"No!" Bev screamed. "Don't do it! Please! Oh, God!"

The waitress, a girl of nineteen or twenty, brought over the coffeepot for the third time. In her frilly French-maid outfit she looked self-consciously cute.

"No more for me, thanks," he said. "You can bring my check, Brenda, if you would." He made a habit of addressing people wearing name tags by their names.

The girl gave him a coquettish smile and turned on her heel, briskly enough to make her skirts fly. Aw, the simplicity of youth, he thought. Suddenly he heard the roar of an automobile engine and the screech of tires. He turned toward the window just in time to see a red Porsche hurtling by.

"Look at that," a man said. "You'd think this was a freeway."

"Idiot," another man added.

Mitch shook his head and turned back to his coffee, taking another sip. He drew a reflective breath. While he'd had his pastry he'd been thinking about Dana Kirk, trying to decide how he felt about her; whether he should fall back on his prejudices or give her a chance. Cops who spent any time with victims formed opinions and developed feelings about them—regardless of whether they wanted to or not. He'd been analyzing what he saw in Dana Kirk, separating reflex from calculation. He took a last sip of his coffee and headed to the men's room.

Minutes later, as he was washing his hands, he listened to the sirens through the ventilation system, realizing they were probably somewhere in the complex. He wondered whether the guy in the Porsche had run someone down.

By the time he returned to the dining room the sound of the sirens had died down, but Brenda and two or three customers were peering out the front window. Coming up behind them, he could see a couple of black-and-whites, emergency lights flashing, sitting in front of Kirk & Company. His stomach dropped.

He flipped open his wallet and threw a five on the counter. As he headed for the door he heard a customer say, "Probably a heart attack over in the real-estate office." Somehow, Mitch didn't think so.

As he opened the door Brenda called to him, "Thanks. Come again."

He waved over his shoulder without looking back, his eyes on the real-estate office and the patrol cars. Al Bensen's comment about preventing a murder rang in his head. Christ, he'd been talking to the woman not twenty minutes ago. And he'd been sitting on his ass, less than a hundred yards away, when whatever happened had happened.

He picked up his pace to a slow jog. As he did he saw an officer come out the front door at Kirk & Company. He moved deliberately, giving no indication of urgency. Nor was there any sign of an ambulance. But that didn't necessarily mean anything. Mitch realized he was too late to make a difference. Most likely, Dana Kirk was either unhurt, or she was dead.

It had been half an hour since Ted had roared off, yet Dana's hands were still shaking. She walked through the bull pen, trying to look calm and confident. Her people's eyes were on her, wanting to believe she was all right.

Lucille Fernandez had come into the office a few minutes earlier and Dana had explained what all the excitement was about. It shook her up, just as it had the others. Lucille had gone to her desk at the back of the room where she'd been whispering with Judy Povich ever since.

Sylvia Hansen, bless her heart, had come through like a trooper, helping calm everyone until the police arrived. She'd already offered to take Bev to her place once the police were through talking to her. "My sister's husband was like that," she'd said. "Believe me, I'm experienced."

Dana glanced back across the entry toward her office where Bev was being questioned by Mitchell Cross. The detective had a nice manner and he'd shown a certain amount of sensitivity. He had spoken with her when he first arrived, making sure she was all right.

Finally, Bev and Mitchell Cross got up from their chairs and came out of Dana's office. Dana headed toward the reception area and Sylvia followed along. The detective looked her over as she approached, but she was scarcely aware of it. Men did that sort of thing out of reflex. He'd been businesslike and very much in charge. She liked that and took comfort in it.

Bev dabbed her eyes and Sylvia embraced her. Dana watched, but Mitchell Cross ignored them. His eyes were on her.

"I'd like to talk to you now, Mrs. Kirk," he said. "If I may."

"Certainly."

"I'll take care of Bev," Sylvia said, her arm around Bev's shoulder. "Don't worry."

"I'll call you at Sylvia's," Dana said to Bev.

Bev nodded but didn't speak.

"Let's get our coats," Sylvia said, adjusting her pearls.

Bev said goodbye and they went off. Dana turned to Mitchell Cross, who was waiting at the door to her office. His expression was sober.

There was something she liked about him beyond his good looks. He was tall—at least six-two—with sandy brown hair a bit on the long side, and pale blue eyes. He looked good in a sports coat and tie, but seemed like he might just as soon be dressed differently. He looked like he belonged outdoors.

Out of habit, Dana headed for her desk, but Mitchell Cross, whose manner was take-charge without being commanding, suggested she sit with him in the guest chairs.

"Sorry," she said. "Habit."

"Desks have a way of distancing," he explained. "I think our conversation should be friendly."

His grin was affable, but Dana detected an edge, possibly a touch of disdain. The man was polite without being warm.

"How are you feeling?" he asked, rediscovering his bedside manner.

"A little better, but I thought my hands would have stopped shaking by now."

"Once you stop pumping adrenaline, you'll calm down. If you aren't used to this kind of excitement, it can take a while."

"What scares me is what *could* have happened. I don't know what I'd have done if Ted hadn't backed down... If he'd come at me."

Mitchell Cross considered the question as though she sincerely wanted to know what he thought. He stared at her long and hard, like he was probing her soul. David used to do that, too, though always from behind a clinical mask, as if he were fitting her words into the chapter of a textbook. This man was trying to match what he saw against his experience.

"Don't tell me you actually have an opinion," she said, starting to feel uncomfortable with his scrutiny.

"The dynamics of confrontation are very complex."

"That's a cop-out, pardon the expression."

Cross grinned. It was a wide, handsome grin. "You'd have shot him."

"Oh? You sound rather sure."

"Nothing's certain. But I have a gut instinct you'd have pulled the trigger."

Dana wasn't sure if that was good or bad in his eyes. She wasn't sure if it was good or bad in her own. She must have had a quizzical look on her face because he responded as though he'd read her thoughts.

"And that's good," he said. "A person needs to be able to defend themselves in a time of crisis. Knowing you can and will shoot also has the benefit of making you feel a little more secure. Be glad you'd have shot the guy, Mrs. Kirk."

"Thank you. I feel so much better."

He smiled at the sarcasm, but seemed unaffected by it. He took a little notebook out of the inside pocket of his coat, but didn't open it. "We've got a bulletin out on Ted

O'Connell," he said, getting down to business. "We'll pick him up for assault. But that's not what I'm most concerned about at the moment. The question in my mind is if O'Connell might be behind the death threats. What do you think?"

"Ted? How could he be? This just happened."

"According to Mrs. O'Connell, her husband is not a big fan of yours."

"What do you mean by that?"

"Apparently he doesn't think much of you. He hates you, to put it bluntly."

Dana was shocked. "Why?"

"You tell me," he said. "You're the one involved."

"Hey, wait a minute," she said, her temper flaring, "You're making it sound like I have to justify myself. I'm the victim, here. It's *my* life that was threatened."

"Forgive me, Mrs. Kirk. I'm sometimes a little blunt. The more I know about your relationship with O'Connell, the easier it will be for me to evaluate the situation. I'm not here to make moral judgments. It doesn't matter to me whether you were lovers or mortal enemies. But the facts are important."

Dana leaned back in the chair and crossed her legs, uncertain whether her annoyance was justified. On the one hand Mitchell Cross seemed contentious; on the other, he had at least showed some enthusiasm for her case. Sympathy without action—which was all she'd gotten thus far—hadn't done much good.

"I guess this whole thing has caught me by surprise," she said, "because I don't have a relationship with Ted at all. I mean, I know him, but that's about it."

"How do you know him?"

"I've only spoken to Ted O'Connell half-a-dozen times in my life. Mostly at C&B functions."

"That's your former company."

"Yes, Cedrick & Betts. I was a sales agent there, along with Bev and almost everybody else who's in my company now."

"Okay, so you spoke with O'Connell just a few times. Tell me about it. Anything notable happen?"

"Our most significant encounter was maybe two years ago at the company Christmas party. Ted acted like a jerk. He came on to me."

"Could you be more specific?"

Her mouth tightened. "He propositioned me. He was drunk and asked me to dance. Then he asked me to go to bed with him."

Cross was studying her. Under his stoic veneer Dana thought she detected a hint of bemusement.

"Anything else?" he asked.

"No, that was it."

"You didn't have a relationship with Mr. O'Connell, then."

"No, of course not!" she snapped. "I told you, he was drunk and he got out of line. Basically, I told him to get lost. That was it." She sighed with exasperation. "Surely you aren't going to make something of that, Mr. Cross. This was a long time ago. I can't even remember the last time I saw Ted."

"So he propositioned you once a few years ago when he was drunk and that's it."

"Well, whenever I see Ted, he leers. That's the kind of person he is. I've given him no encouragement, so I'm sure he thinks I'm a bitch."

Cross flipped open his notepad as though he was going to make an entry, but he didn't. He didn't even take out a pen. He just stared down at the paper. "I see," he said.

"Well, what did Bev say?" Dana asked.

"I asked whether her husband was upset with you and she said he was opposed to her joining your firm."

"Yes," Dana said, "I know that, but I'm not sure why."

"She thought it was just a matter of her husband wanting to control her life—apparently he likes imposing his will—but then, in their last argument, Mr. O'Connell apparently leveled some accusations against you to bolster his case."

"What accusations?"

"He said you were always flirting with him and that at a Christmas party you propositioned him."

"*Oh!*" she exclaimed, enraged. "The *nerve!* That bastard!"

Cross's stoic veneer cracked and he smiled. Broadly.

"It's not funny!" she snapped. "That man is a damned liar. Bev didn't believe Ted, I hope. She couldn't have. She would have said something. And she wouldn't have come in here today with her license."

"Mrs. O'Connell assumed he was just stirring up trouble and brushed it off as desperation."

"Well, why did you say it so seriously then, like I was some sort of vamp running around seducing women's husbands?"

"I try not to prejudice people's answers, Mrs. Kirk. It doesn't matter to me what Mrs. O'Connell believes, only what really happened between you and O'Connell."

"Nothing happened!"

"Yes, you've said that. But I'm still perplexed why O'Connell feels such hostility toward you. Mrs. O'Connell said that they've been bickering for a few weeks over her leaving her old firm to join yours, and that Mr. O'Connell was hostile toward you from the start. The timing is interesting because of the letters. Their arguments coincide roughly with the start of the hate campaign against you."

Her eyes widened. "You think Ted wrote the letters and has been making the calls?"

"I didn't say that. I'm trying to evaluate the facts. What troubles me is why O'Connell would make death threats against you based on his not wanting his wife to work for you. It seems a bit extreme—unless there was more to it than Mrs. O'Connell was aware of. That was the reason for my blunt questions, Mrs. Kirk."

A horrible thought went through her mind. "Mr. Cross, you didn't tell Bev about the death threats, did you?"

"It came up. I had to ask if there was any reason for her to think her husband might threaten your life."

"Oh, shit."

He looked perplexed. "What's wrong?"

Dana bit her lip. "I haven't told anybody about the letters. Nobody but family and close friends. I was afraid if my salespeople were aware, they'd panic. Real-estate offices are very fragile."

"I'm sorry, but I can't investigate a crime without mentioning it to the people I question."

Dana sighed. "I suppose it was silly of me to try to hide something like this. It would have come out eventually. I was hoping the letters would stop or that you'd catch the person responsible before word got out."

"I see no reason to question the others in your office, but I had to ask Mrs. O'Connell about her husband."

"If Bev knows, she'll talk to Sylvia. I'm sure she already has. Everybody else will hear about it in a matter of hours. By tomorrow morning every office in the county will have heard."

"I'm sorry."

"I should have foreseen this. But I'm glad you told me. I'll talk to my people as soon as we're through here."

"Okay, I don't need to take a lot of your time, but I would like to ask a few more questions. Assuming O'Connell has nothing to do with the threats, then who else should I be talking to?"

"There is something that happened last night. In fact, when you came by earlier, I planned to tell you about it. Then with all the excitement over Ted, I didn't have a chance. Actually, it has me rather upset."

The detective did take out a pen from his inside pocket then. Dana proceeded to relate the incident with Frank— the chase down the hill.

"Are you certain it was Betts?" Cross asked, jotting the name down on his pad.

"Not absolutely sure. I mean, I didn't see the driver at all. But it was either Frank's car or one practically identical. There aren't a lot of black Ferraris around and even fewer that would be parked in front of my home late at night."

"Tell me about Frank Betts, Mrs. Kirk."

Dana looked at the pen poised in the detective's hand and had a sudden sick feeling. It was not a story she was eager to tell. She didn't know why she was suddenly so reticent, except that this man personalized things more. When she'd talked about Frank with Ray Brockmeyer, the conversation had seemed clinical. Circumstances were different now.

"I suppose you want all the personal details," she said.

He looked at her as though the remark were totally unexpected. "Anything that helps me understand the situation," he replied.

She took a deep breath, but found it hard to say the words. "Frank and I were ... We ... had a relationship."

"You had an affair."

"Yes."

Dana could feel herself turning red and looked away. Her liaison with Frank had been one of the less sterling moments in her life, but she had never felt shame over it the way she did now. Why she was so humiliated talking about it to this man, she didn't know.

"I'm not used to discussing my personal life with a stranger," she said.

"I don't need to know the intimate details, Mrs. Kirk."

She flushed an even brighter red. If Mitchell Cross repressed a smile, he did it so effectively she barely was able to tell. "What do you want to know?"

"Let's start with when."

"It was brief. It only lasted a few months. It definitively ended a year ago."

"Who ended it?"

"*I* did." She'd said it like she was claiming credit, only realizing after the fact how it sounded. "The whole thing was ill-advised," she went on. "I regretted getting involved with Frank almost as soon as I did."

"He took it hard?"

"I guess you could say that."

"So, from his standpoint it wasn't a casual affair."

"No."

"He loved you."

She sighed with exasperation. "Do the details matter, Mr. Cross?"

"Only in so far as they might explain his motive. But let me try it differently. Do you have any reason to think Betts would want you dead?"

"No. Frank has his faults. And God knows, we're less-than-friendly competitors at the moment. But this just isn't Frank's style. Not for personal or business reasons."

"You seem pretty certain."

"I've known Frank a long time. Our romantic involvement was brief, but we were friends and colleagues for many years. He was a mentor to me."

"But now you're former lovers and business competitors."

"Yes. I'm not defending Frank, by any means. It shook me up when I saw his car last night. It made me stop to think. I admit I'm concerned."

"I believe I should have a word with Mr. Betts."

"I'm not accusing him of anything."

"I understand, Mrs. Kirk, but this is a new development. I wouldn't be doing my job if I didn't follow it up. If you don't mind some friendly advice, I suggest you worry about yourself. Whoever has been sending you these letters is not playing around. And Ted O'Connell, whether he's our boy or not, is not likely to be joining your fan club. His wife painted a very ugly picture. He blames you for his problems. I recommend you be very careful until we've picked him up."

Dana glanced out toward the bull pen, then looked at her watch. "I'm supposed to have lunch with my daughter, but I've got to talk to my people before they hear about the death threats from somebody else."

"I'll get out of your hair," Cross said. "But I would like to talk to you in greater detail about your business dealings and Betts. I may turn up something when I talk to him."

She sighed wearily. "Okay."

Cross closed his notebook and returned it to his pocket. Then he handed her a business card. "Call if you need me, or if something comes to mind that might be helpful. But in any case, I'll be in touch."

"Thank you, Mr. Cross."

A wry smile touched his lips. "I don't mind formality, but if you must, it's Detective Cross."

"Sorry. I'm afraid I'm not familiar with police protocol."

"I don't stand on ceremony. My friends call me Detective. If you can stand the familiarity, feel free."

She laughed. "Thank you, *Detective*."

Cross got up and went to the door. "Do you know how to use that peashooter of yours, by the way?"

"I test-fired it a couple of times. It's *very* loud."

"Don't be afraid of pulling the trigger, if you have to, Mrs. Kirk."

"I don't mind formality, either, Detective. But Mrs. Kirk sounds so old."

"What do your friends call you?"

"Boss."

Mitchell Cross grinned. "I'll be in touch."

Dana watched him step out of her office. He went to the coatrack to get his trench coat. Passing Chiara's desk, he said something. The girl smiled and looked pleased. Dana could tell Chiara was taken by him. She had to admit he had a presence and a style that were different, a real in-your-face attitude.

The man's candor challenged and was unapologetic, yet he had a charm that lacked pretense. It was hard to say why she found him appealing, but it was evident that her receptionist did, as well. They both watched him leave the office and go out into the drizzle. Oddly, she and Chiara looked at each other at the same moment, then both looked away.

Dana went to her desk. She had to call her daughter.

San Rafael

Molly Kirk ran from the bathroom where she was fiddling with her hair to get the phone.

"Mol, I'm going to be a bit late," her mother said without introduction.

The girl rolled her eyes. "What else is new, Mom?"

"It's not my fault this time. Usually it is, I admit. There was an incident here at the office this morning. The police had to come."

"What happened?"

"I'll tell you later. First I've got to calm everybody down. If I walk out of here now, they might all be gone by the time I return."

"Was it the guy who's been sending the letters?" Molly asked. "Did he come to your office?"

"No, it was the husband of one of the new salespeople. Everything's all right now, don't worry. But I need about an hour. I know that makes for a late lunch, but I really want to see you."

"We can do it another time."

"No, Molly," her mother insisted, "it's really important to me. If you get hungry, go ahead and eat. No, wait…I have an idea. Why not order a pizza? Do you have enough money to pay for it? I'll reimburse you when I get there."

"I guess so."

"Wait fifteen minutes before you call. And if the pizza comes before I do, go ahead and eat. I'll be there in an hour. I promise."

"Mom, are you sure you want to bother?"

"*Very* sure."

Molly sighed. "All right."

She hung up the phone and plopped down on the front-room sofa. Sometimes it didn't seem worth getting mad at her mother anymore. Her dad said she should just accept that it was the way her mother was. He was probably right.

She was happy about the pizza, though. Her mom hadn't said what kind, which meant she could get anything she wanted. Cool.

She glanced around her father's tidy living room. It was the place they'd lived in when all of them were together. She was six when they split, and in a funny sort of way she still thought of this as home.

The house had bad associations because of the divorce, but good ones, too. The furniture was the same blue-and-brown print they'd had when she was a little girl. Her mother referred to it as her "country French period." Molly understood that to be a sort of backhanded put-down of her dad. She and her mother had lived in three different houses since the divorce, each one bigger and nicer than the last. And when they changed houses they changed half the furniture, as well. Her friend, Tiffany, had said something when they were eleven that had stuck with Molly—"Living with your mom must be like living with a movie star." It was true. Molly often thought of those words. Her mom definitely wasn't ordinary.

Slapping the arm of the couch she used to jump on when she was a kid, Molly got up and went into the kitchen. She hadn't washed the breakfast dishes and she knew she had to. Her dad was a stickler about keeping things cleaned up. Her mom wasn't as strict about things like that because she left dirty dishes for Anita herself. Especially breakfast dishes, because she was always in a hurry in the morning. Her father told Molly she had to clean up after herself because he wasn't going to. So she rinsed off the dishes and put them in the dishwasher.

Then she decided to clean up her room, as well. She hadn't the day before and her dad had talked to her about making her bed and keeping her room neat. He never yelled at her, just talked. In a way, that was worse.

Molly went to her room. She stepped over the pile of clothes on the floor to get to the window so she could open the curtains. To her surprise, there was a doll hanging outside the window from a string. Molly blinked. Where had that come from?

On closer inspection, she saw that the doll had no arms and the string was tied around its neck. There was a note pinned to the front of the doll, but she couldn't quite see it because it was turned. How weird. Who could have done that?

Molly decided it must have been one of the boys from school. They were always doing something stupid. The big oak tree in Carrie Natale's front yard had been tepeed two weekends in a row. And her dad was furious.

When Molly thought about it, maybe she had heard something outside her window in the night. But she didn't see anything especially funny or clever about the prank. And she wasn't so sure she wanted her father to know about it, either. She decided she'd go outside and take the doll down, even though her dad had told her not to leave the house under any circumstances.

Kentfield

Mitch Cross sat in the reception area, waiting for Frank Betts to arrive. The administrative offices of Cedrick & Betts were located on Sir Francis Drake Boulevard in a modern redwood building surrounded by mature landscaping. The architect had used lots of glass to take maximum advantage of the setting. Mitch was rather impressed with the way the outdoors had been brought inside.

He'd been paging through the company's annual report, which was lying on the coffee table along with some glossy decorating and architectural magazines. C&B, like Kirk & Company, was a slick operation. According to the report, the sales offices had spread into Sonoma County and there was also an affiliated development company and savings and loan, Marin Pacific Savings. Mitch could see who was David and who was Goliath in this battle. The realization gave him newfound respect for Dana Kirk.

Not that he'd been disdainful, exactly. In fact, he'd found himself liking the woman in an odd, begrudging sort of way. That surprised him. Dana Kirk was about as Yuppie as they came—even more so than Liz Rogers. He'd managed to forgive Liz for being self-indulgently materialistic because they'd connected. Now he was making excuses for Dana Kirk in the same way.

But there was a difference between the women. Liz had been a colleague and she was married. Dana was the victim of a crime and she was single. He'd bemused Liz Rogers. Dana Kirk, he'd irritated. The sadistic side of him liked that. "You know what, Mitch," Carole had said after the first time they'd made love, "you're the first asshole I've ever known that I could actually say was a nice guy." The characterization had endeared Carole to him. After all, what guy doesn't like being loved?

He tossed the Cedrick & Betts annual report on the table and glanced at the receptionist. She was an attractive brunette in her early thirties, more mature than Dana Kirk's girl, but not the beauty, not as exotic. He liked the Italian girl's accent. And he'd liked the way she looked at him. A woman betrayed loneliness much more readily than desire. Dana's girl was lonely.

"Mr. Cross," the receptionist said, "Mr. Betts just called from his car phone. He'll be here in a few minutes. I'm sorry you've had to wait."

"No problem."

The woman smiled graciously. She had a pleasant disposition. If he had to guess, he'd say she was married. The way women wore rings these days it was hard to tell unless you were sitting in their lap.

"Are you sure I can't get you a cup of coffee or a soft drink?" she asked.

"No, thanks. All I've done today is drink coffee. I have a feeling, though, I should have waited for yours. Smells good."

"It's quite good. Colombian."

"Does Cedrick & Betts sell coffee, too?"

"No," she said with a laugh, "we give it away."

Mitch chuckled. Score one for the receptionist.

She took a call and he got up to stretch. He was only halfway through his shift and he felt like it ought to be the end of a long hard day. Four hours' sleep wasn't nearly enough. That morning Corinne had told him he looked like shit; he couldn't imagine what he looked like now. One thing was certain—he was hitting the sack early tonight.

Mitch wandered over to the big floor-to-ceiling glass wall that looked out onto a flagstone patio and fern garden complete with an artificial waterfall. It appeared peaceful and relaxing despite the drizzle. He decided if his office was here, he might be willing to hang around more and read old files.

The front door opened and a fellow in his late forties swooped in and went to the reception desk. He was dressed casually in brown slacks and a blue windbreaker, although he had an officious, possessory air about him. He was just under six feet, dark-haired, with a certain natural affability. Good-looking without being handsome. Maybe a trifle paunchy. As Mitch watched, he went through a stack of messages, waiting for the receptionist to get off the phone.

Mitch could tell he was a man practiced in presenting a public face, yet there was something about him that suggested profound unhappiness. Deep pain. He had no doubt the guy was Dana Kirk's onetime lover, Frank Betts.

The woman finished with her call and gestured toward Mitch. "Mr. Cross with the San Rafael Police Department is here to see you," she said.

Betts looked over at him with that split second of alarm that the unexpected arrival of police seemed to evoke. It didn't necessarily suggest guilt—that tended to become evident, if at all, in the minutes that followed—but it did invite closer scrutiny.

Betts walked over to him with the air of a man who knew the best defense was a good offense. "Don't tell me one of our sign trucks knocked down somebody's mailbox again," he said, extending his hand.

The false hardiness fell flat.

"No, Mr. Betts," Mitch said. "I wanted to discuss a personal matter."

"I see. Why don't we go to my office?" He smiled like Mitch had just informed him he'd won a week's paid vacation in Hawaii. "Joan, hold my calls, will you, please?"

They went down the hall toward the rear of the building, which, it turned out, was built around the central garden.

"You'll have to excuse the way I'm dressed, Mr. Cross," Betts said. "My partner and I were disdainful enough of the weather that we thought we'd get in a round of golf this morning."

"I don't know about disdainful, but you were optimistic."

They entered a large office that was entirely glass on one side. The miniblinds were open enough to see a suggestion of the garden, yet provide a screen of privacy. Mitch could barely make out the reception area across the way. It was lit against the shadowed dreariness of the gray day.

Betts gestured for him to sit in one of the leather guest chairs, then he went around behind his large Danish-modern desk. Oddly he had not switched on the overhead lights, though he did turn on the lamp on the credenza behind him. It produced a warm, homey glow even though the decor was mostly of chrome and leather. It also kept the light behind Betts and in Mitch's face. The guy knew stagecraft.

Mitch looked around, noting the office was just tidy enough to be presentable. Files and books were stacked on the credenza and on a table nearby. The lithographs were of ducks. There was a large shelf crammed with trophies on one wall, but there were no photographs anywhere.

"I was looking through your annual report in the lobby," he said. "You do a lot more than sell houses, it seems."

"We're small, Mr. Cross, but working toward becoming a miniconglomerate." He beamed and leaned back in his chair.

Betts did not show any eagerness to find out the purpose of the visit, which Mitch took as a ploy. He decided to string him along. "How long have you been in business, Mr. Betts?"

"Lane Cedrick and I formed the company fifteen years ago. It's actually a successor company to a small brokerage firm I'd been managing that had belonged to Lane's aunt. When she died, Lane inherited the company and we formed a partnership, which has become what you see."

"Very impressive. You're the largest firm in the area, I understand."

"Easily the largest independent. Nobody in the industry counts the franchise shops as companies in the collective sense. They sell a logo, a manual and supplies to mom and pop. It's not the same as a multioffice firm like our own."

"I see."

"Should I conclude you're interested in selling or buying a property, Mr. Cross, or wasn't that the sort of personal business you were referring to?"

"No, this is official business, Mr. Betts. Excuse me for digressing."

"No problem. We at C&B are always happy to put our story out. Policemen have to live in houses, like everybody else."

"Ours tend to be a bit more modest than most of what you deal in, I'm sure."

"We handle everything," Betts said. "If a person has a need, we try to fill it. Service. That's what we sell."

Mitch was enjoying the repartee, knowing that Betts's stomach had to be grinding. As they talked, he kept trying to picture this guy as Dana Kirk's lover. The image wouldn't jibe, whether because it was incongruous, or because it was tainted by his own prejudices, he didn't know.

"We digress again," Betts said with a smile, though it was more pained than the earlier ones.

"Yes, sorry," Mitch said. "The reason I'm here is to ask for your help with a case."

"What sort of case?"

"I'm investigating a series of death threats that have been made against Dana Kirk."

"*Death* threats? Dana's had death threats?"

"Yes, I take it you weren't aware of them."

"No," Betts said, looking dutifully somber. "This is the first I've heard about it."

"Do you have any notion who might feel hostile enough toward Mrs. Kirk to threaten her life?"

Betts shook his head, his expression turning even darker. "This is a competitive business. You make enemies. Dana was once part of our family, Mr. Cross, and now she's in competition with us, but the same can be said of dozens of other people."

"As successful as Mrs. Kirk?"

"No, not as successful. Not at all."

Mitch watched him, waiting to see if he'd reveal himself. Betts stared back. His cool veneer was not without cracks, however.

"Let's be direct," Betts said, looking as if he might be on the verge of faltering. "Are you here to find out if I'm behind the threats?"

"I'm not here to accuse you, Mr. Betts. Certainly not. It's a fact-finding mission. I'm new to the case and trying to get to know all the players."

"How long has this been going on?" Betts asked cautiously.

"For a few weeks."

"Weeks?"

"Yes."

Betts reflected. "Well, I'm afraid I can't help you. Dana's problem is news to me, which is surprising, considering what a small community the real-estate business is. I'd expect to have heard about something like this."

"I'm sure the word will be getting around."

"Well, I certainly wish Dana no ill. Certainly nothing like that."

Mitch contemplated him again. "Could we discuss your personal relationship with Mrs. Kirk?"

"Our personal relationship?"

"I understand you and she were once lovers."

Betts hesitated, then smiled. "Nice to hear Dana would characterize it that way," he said, self-deprecatingly.

"Not true?"

"Oh, it's true, Mr. Cross. But not true enough. I was a lot more in love with Dana than she was with me. It ended too soon as far as I'm concerned. No, that's not right. I wish it hadn't ended at all."

Mitch heard the surrender in his voice and decided to pounce. "What did you do last night, Mr. Betts?"

Frank Betts looked at him blankly, unblinking. He didn't say anything for a moment. Finally he sighed. "She recognized me."

"Apparently you have a distinctive car."

Betts lowered his eyes. He shook his head. "I feel like an idiot."

His eyes turned glossy and Mitch wondered if the guy was also an actor. He waited, giving him all the rope he needed to hang himself.

"I'd better call Dana and apologize," Betts said. "I should have done it last night."

Mitch continued to wait.

"I was so embarrassed when she backed out of her garage that I just took off like a silly moonstruck kid."

"Let's back up a minute," Mitch said. "What, exactly, were you doing out in front of Mrs. Kirk's house in a rainstorm?"

"I was just sitting there, thinking about her. I wanted to go up and ring the bell, but I didn't have the nerve." Betts looked up at him, embarrassed. "I can't tell you how humiliated I am. I didn't intend to go up there. I was out on an errand, listening to a song I associated with Dana, and the next thing I knew I was driving up the hill to her place."

Mitch watched him, looking as though he didn't buy it. Betts fumbled self-consciously. Finally he became aware of the accusation in Mitch's eyes.

"You aren't suggesting because I was up at Dana's place last night that I'm behind the death threats?"

"Are you?"

"No, of course not! I'm guilty of being a sap, an idiot, but that's it."

Mitch stared.

"Look, it might be stupid to sit in front of somebody's house, but it's not a crime. I didn't do anything illegal except run a Stop sign. If you want to arrest me for that, go ahead."

Betts had gotten irritated and Mitch realized he wasn't going to get a tearful confession.

"I didn't come here to arrest you, Mr. Betts," he said, "I came to see if you might be able to shed some light on our investigation."

"I'm guilty of being in love with Dana Kirk," he said calmly, "but that's it. Under the circumstances, it's not easy to make that confession. And I was telling you the truth when I said I wasn't aware of any death threats. I'm pissed at Dana, pissed as hell, but I don't wish any harm on her."

"Do you know anybody who would?"

"Not to do something like that."

Mitch steepled his fingers and stared at Betts. The man was unflinching, but not exactly at ease. "My investigation is just beginning, Mr. Betts. As I get into the case, I may wish to talk to you again. Presumably I'll have your cooperation."

Betts shrugged. "Sure. I have nothing to hide. But I don't have anything that would be helpful, either."

"Maybe something will come up." Mitch took his business card from his pocket and handed it over. "If you hear anything that might be of interest, give me a call."

Betts got to his feet. "Sure."

They shook hands and Mitch headed for the door.

"Oh, Mr. Cross," he said, stopping him.

Mitch turned.

"Does Dana think I'm behind the threats?"

He took a second to reflect, then said, "Maybe that's something you should ask *her*, Mr. Betts."

San Rafael

Nola Betts felt her first twinges of doubt when she pulled into the parking lot of Dominican College and turned off the engine of her red BMW convertible. The top was up. She'd used the windshield wipers some during the drive up from Sausalito, and the heater as well. But, considering her state of mind, it might just as easily have been a beautiful spring day. That is, until now.

"Don't blow it, honey," she said, rapping her fist against the steering wheel. "Courage."

She had awakened with a determination to do something with her life—something besides hunt for men at parties and bars and drink herself into a state of numbness. The previous fall she'd tried joining an amateur theatrical group and that had worked out fine until she'd boffed the director's husband and created a miniscandal in the troop. It had been easier to drop out than to try to make amends. Besides, she'd become unwelcome.

This time it would be different. She'd sworn off booze. And attending this seminar was different, too. It wasn't only something to do, it was an opportunity to change. Dr. Silverstein had counseled involvement. They'd talked in session after session about self-image. What could be better than a seminar on "Managing Your Self-Image"?

She'd seen an ad in the newspaper a few days earlier. Two things had caught her eye—the reference to self-image and the name of the seminar leader, David Kirk, M.F.C.C. The bitch's ex. Nola knew that she'd met him at some C&B function, but for the life of her she couldn't remember what he looked like.

And so, that morning, while pouring a glass of orange juice—straight, without a kicker—she'd noticed the clipping under a refrigerator magnet. Admissions would be accepted at the door on a space-available basis, the ad said. Working on her self-image seemed a suitable thing to do on her first day of sobriety, and so she'd gussied herself up and headed up the freeway for San Rafael.

Nola had arrived early in case the available spaces were limited, but now that she was there she was suffering a crisis of confidence. "You've got nothing to lose," she told herself. "It might even be fun. Buck up!"

Taking her purse, Nola climbed out of the car and locked the door. She'd worn tight leather pants and a sweater, both purple, under her Burberrys. She'd be dressed more flamboyantly than the rest of the people, there was no doubt about that, but that was fine. Flamboyance was her trademark. Dr. Silverstein said what a person did was not as important as why they did it. The remark came after a discussion about her insistence on dressing sexily for their sessions. "Whether you do it or not isn't the issue," he'd said. "We must ask why."

The answer that came out of months of therapy was—not surprisingly—that she wanted to be loved. Dr. Silverstein tried to convince her that she was wrong to assume that the only way to win a man's love was through sex. Accepting that, he said, would be the first step toward moving beyond it. That was where she was now—aware, but trapped in a habitual pattern of behavior.

Still, she'd made progress. Random, impersonal fucking had lost its appeal. "I'm down to personal fucking," she'd said in one of their last sessions." That, it seemed to her, was progress. And Dr. Silverstein agreed.

Two months earlier he'd left for a six-month sabbatical in Europe. He'd given her the card of a colleague who was willing to see her in his absence, but Nola hadn't availed herself of the opportunity. She'd wanted to use the six months he was gone to test her wings. A seminar with David Kirk seemed like a step in the right direction.

Entering the main building, she followed the signs to the seminar room. An older woman was seated at a table outside the door. She greeted Nola cordially.

"Any places left?" Nola asked, unbuttoning her raincoat.

"Half a dozen. We picked up a number of additional registrations the past few days, but there's space for you."

"The luck of the Irish."

Nola signed up and paid her fee. She went into the room, which was set up with tables in a rectangle and places for about thirty. Seven or eight people were already there. Nola went to the table opposite the lectern. She took off her coat and put it on the back of her chair. The three men present checked her out closely and a couple of the women looked her way.

Nola pulled down her sweater and slipped gracefully into the chair. She glanced around, confirming that none of those present was David Kirk. He evidently hadn't arrived.

She turned her attention to the seminar materials. Included in the packet was a brochure on David Kirk. Seeing his picture, she remembered him. In fact she recalled one time in particular when she'd been drunk and had sidled up to him at a party and said, "I have the distinct impression my husband wants to fuck your wife. How do you feel about that, Mr. Kirk?"

Nola couldn't remember his reply. People tended not to say memorable things in response to outrageous drunks. But the fact that she remembered the incident made her blush. She wondered if David Kirk would recall it, and decided he probably would.

Oddly enough, she had an image of Dr. Silverstein—cute, cuddly little Dr. Silverstein—grinning at her with his thin lips that he could stretch from ear to ear, and saying, "This could be good, Nola. This could be good."

San Rafael

Dana pulled up in front of the ranch-style house that had once been her home. She avoided going to David's place as much as possible. In the past he'd carried the burden of picking up Molly for their weekend visits and dropping her back home again. His benefit, his burden—that was the way Dana had looked at it. Occasionally, though, she'd come by for one reason or another, and it never failed to make her clutch a little at the sight of the place.

Ivy still grew on the overhanging porch, though it was much more dense and mature now, as were the two evergreens out front. The ivy had been her idea. She'd thought it gave the house a cottagey feel. Now she saw the place for what it truly was—a tired thirty-year-old ranch-style that harkened back to a different time in her life. That era was over, but it was still imbedded in her soul.

She looked in her rearview mirror before opening the door to her car. Since the incident that morning with Ted, she'd been even more leery of her surroundings, if that was possible. Had Mitchell Cross not said anything about Ted having it in for her, she'd never have considered the possibility that he was the one behind the letters and the calls. It still seemed unlikely, but she'd begun to understand that you couldn't assume anything.

Truth be known, she almost hoped it was Ted. A known enemy was easier to deal with—even one as vicious as Ted O'Connell.

Getting out of the car, Dana went up the walk to the front porch. She remembered so clearly the day she and Molly had left for good. It was eight years ago, but it could have been last month, considering how distinctly the memory was etched in her mind. David had carried their bags to the car and he'd kissed Molly goodbye. Dana had sat behind the wheel of her BMW, tears running down her cheeks, knowing she was wrenching her family apart, yet aware that the failure to take the step required the basest dishonesty. To stay in a marriage that was wrong would inevitably fuel resentment. At some point a person had the right to put themselves first, but where was that point? How much unhappiness did you have to endure before it was okay to be a little selfish? She'd struggled with that question for months before the divorce, and for years afterward.

She was about to push the doorbell when she heard a vehicle pull up behind her. It was the pizza-delivery truck. She was surprised it was just now arriving. She was ten minutes later than she'd said she'd be.

The delivery boy came up the walk with the carton in his hand.

"Perfect timing," Dana said, opening her purse.

The boy, lanky and long-haired, handed her the pizza box. Dana gave him a twenty and told him to keep the change.

"Thank *you!*" he said, turning on his heel and jogging back down the walk. Dana pushed the doorbell and Molly came bouncing to the door.

"Pizza lady," Dana announced.

Molly looked surprised, then, seeing the truck, realized what had happened. She took the box. "Thank goodness. I'm starved." She kissed Dana on the cheek and offered her own. "Pretty good timing though, huh?"

"You assumed I'd be late," Dana said, entering. She glanced around the room, seeing the past it represented, feeling twinges in her stomach.

"I always double whatever time you say, Mom." Molly kicked the door closed and went off toward the kitchen.

"Hey, I'm only five minutes late," Dana said, putting her purse down on the entry table she'd gotten in a used-furniture store years ago.

"Almost fifteen," Molly called over her shoulder, "but that's better than usual."

Dana looked at the furniture like she was looking at old family photos. It had been a couple of years since she'd been inside the house. When she did come by to pick up Molly, she usually tooted the horn out front, or maybe came to the porch to ring the bell.

"Come on," Molly called. "Let's eat."

Dana went into the kitchen. Molly had the table set and was at the counter, opening the pizza box. Dana remembered making dozens of meat loaves in this very room, eating countless meals with her husband and child, all the while feeling like an alien in her own home.

"I see your father got a new dinette set."

Molly looked over. "That was a couple of years ago."

Dana sat down, knowing she was a different person than she'd been when she was mistress of this house, yet she felt haunted by the past. The sensation was more poignant than disturbing.

She observed her daughter, thinking how much she missed her. Molly was beginning to get a figure. They were almost the same height, though Molly was fifteen pounds lighter. She had Dana's eyes, the same-shaped face, and the same long legs. Her fairer coloring, and her nose and mouth and hands, were more David's.

Molly brought them each a plate with two pieces of pizza. She'd ordered a combination with what looked like every available topping—not the most appetizing-looking dish. Dana refrained from comment.

"Do you want milk or a cola?" Molly asked.

"Cola, please."

Molly got them each a can of diet cola from the refrigerator. "Want a glass?"

"No, the can's fine."

Molly sat down and tore into the pizza. "It's not very hot," she said, after the first big bite. "Should I stick it in the microwave?"

"Whatever you want."

Molly took another quick bite and got up to put the carton in the microwave. "Want me to put your plate in the oven to warm?"

"No, this is fine."

Molly returned to the table. She saw Dana struggling to open the soft-drink can without ruining her nails and, taking compassion on her, removed it from her mother's hand and popped it open.

"I can't tell you how handicapped I've felt not having you around the house," Dana said. "No soft drinks since you left and it's been two weeks since I've made any orange juice."

"Mom, you need a wife."

"You're right, Mol, but that's not a very enlightened way to put it. Housework shouldn't be gender specific any more than being a doctor or businessperson."

Molly was too busy stuffing pizza into her mouth to reply. Dana was hungry, but there was a day's quota of calories lying on her plate.

"So, what was the big crisis at the office?" Molly asked.

Dana told her about Ted making a scene, but played down her role. There was no need to worry her unnecessarily.

"Bummer," Molly said. She took a long drink of cola. "So, have you gotten any more letters?" She said it casually, as though she were asking if the latest issue of *Vogue* had arrived.

"Actually there's been another one. And I want to talk to you about it."

Molly looked mildly quizzical. "Why?"

"Because you were drawn into it for the first time, Molly, and I think you need to know about it. I want you to be aware just how serious this business is."

Molly took another long sip from her can. "What do you mean, I'm drawn into it?"

Dana explained about the armless dolls, and how one of them had represented Molly. Molly looked stunned.

"I know it's upsetting," Dana said, "but there's no reason to panic. This nut is trying to hurt me any way he can, including bringing you into it. I'm sure you're safe here with your father, but it does mean that you have to be very careful."

Molly shook her head. "No, Mom, that's not it. There's something you don't know." She sprinted out of the kitchen and returned a minute later, an armless doll suspended from the string in her hand. It was identical to the one Dana had found hanging from the garage door. Dana got to her feet, her heart starting to race.

"Where did that come from?" Dana said, hearing the panic in her voice.

"It was hanging outside my bedroom window. I found it this morning when I opened the curtains."

"Oh, my God!" Dana backed away, feeling an uncontrollable horror. In the process she nearly knocked over her chair.

"Mom?"

"It's all right, honey, it's all right," Dana said, pulling herself together. Without hesitating, she hurried over to the wall phone, snatched the receiver and nervously dialed 9-1-1.

Kentfield

There was a knock on Frank's door, but it opened before he could say anything. Lane Cedrick, dapper in a tan Harris-tweed sports coat, brown Italian silk tie and matching handkerchief, peered into the semidarkness of the room.

"What the hell are you doing, Frank, having a séance?"

"Sort of."

Lane stepped in and closed the door. He flipped on the light switch without asking if Frank minded. "Gayle said you wanted to see me."

"Yes," Frank said, righting himself in his chair, "I've got news."

"So do I," Lane said, slipping into the visitor's chair and crossing his legs in one motion.

It was the one mannerism of Lane's that struck Frank as undeniably gay. Occasionally his hands gave him away, as well, but Frank was so accustomed to Lane's foibles that he rarely noticed them anymore. This time, for some reason, it jumped out. He also noticed that Lane was sitting in the very chair that Mitchell Cross had occupied an hour earlier.

"If yours is good," Frank said wearily, "let's hear it first. I need a lift."

"Your little friend, Dana Kirk, seems to have run into some bad luck," Lane began. "I've just come from the Corte Madera office. The word going around is that Bev O'Connell's husband tore up Dana's office this morning, beat Bev and threatened to kill Dana. She ran him off with a gun."

"Oh, Jesus," Frank said.

"That's not all. Apparently Dana's been getting threatening letters. She didn't tell anybody until today. But it's all over Marin." Lane smiled.

Frank did not share his partner's joy at the news and he let it show.

"Why so glum, Frank? Dana might be an old girlfriend, but she's not exactly giving you blow jobs these days. Do I have to remind you she's been doing her best to give us the shaft?"

"I already heard about the death threats."

"Oh?"

"A police detective was here earlier."

Lane's brows rose, but if there was panic in his heart, he carefully disguised it. As always, he was in control of his emotions. "What did he want?"

"The bottom line was he wanted to see if I was behind the death threats."

Lane studied him. "Because you're a spurned lover or because you're a partner at Cedrick & Betts?"

"Because I did something really stupid last night." Frank told him about the car chase.

"You'd be well-advised to have yourself surgically neutered, Frank," Lane said over his steepled fingers. "Your sex drive is going to do you in one of these days."

"Dana's going to be the death of me, I know."

"Let's hope not the death of C&B. If you want to take yourself down, that's your business, but I'd appreciate it if you didn't take me with you."

"Well, you can save worrying about that. I'm innocent, so there's nothing to fear from the police," Frank said. "But I still feel like shit."

"Where was it left?"

"I admitted what I'd done. It seemed the thing to do. After all, I wasn't guilty of anything but stupidity. Once I apologized, the conversation was pretty much over, so he left." Frank sighed. "What I've been worrying about is how this will affect Dana. How'm I going to negotiate with her now?"

Lane, his fingers still steepled, contemplated the situation. "As I think about it, this might work in your favor, Frank. As long as you can convince her you acted because of your feelings for her and you're not the guy behind the letters, she may take compassion on you. What could be more pathetic than a grown man who's lovesick and desperate?"

"Thanks, Lane. Thanks loads."

"What the hell. Take advantage of it, if you can. If I were you, I'd call her, apologize for what you did, express your sympathy for what she's going through, and ask to meet with her to discuss business."

"What if she refuses to see me?"

"Frank, there's nothing as powerful as the truth."

Lane smiled slightly as he said it, mocking him, but Frank could see he had a point. Coming to Dana in shame and seeming weakness might disarm her. He hadn't often had to eat crow in his lifetime, but given the desperation of the circumstances, he wasn't above trying.

"I hope it'll work," Frank said. "I want this shit behind me. I'll tell you this, when I saw that cop, my first thought was that he'd come to ask about Oak Meadow Partners. I had visions of being led away in handcuffs."

Lane shook his head. "I hate to say this, but you don't have the guts for the big time, Frank. You should have stuck with selling houses and fucking the salesladies."

"I thought that stock deal was supposed to be a sure thing. It wasn't my idea. I listened when I shouldn't have."

"You went into it with your eyes open, Frank, just like me. We rolled the dice and lost. Now we've got to manage our mess. Winning doesn't take balls. Bouncing back from a setback does."

"I hope you know what you're doing with Dana."

"You get her to sell out her interest in the bank and I'll take care of the rest," Lane said.

"I'll do my best, but I sure didn't like having that detective coming around asking questions this afternoon."

"Do what you have to, Frank, and he won't be back. Take comfort in the fact that we aren't the only ones unhappy with Dana. Who knows? With a little luck, she'll go down in flames before we do."

"I hate to think whoever is threatening her is serious."

"It'll be mighty interesting to see how her salespeople react to all this," Lane said with a sadistic smile. "My guess is that it won't go down very well. This could be the break we need, Frank. Just what the doctor ordered."

Somehow Frank Betts wasn't as happy as he knew he was supposed to be.

* * *

San Rafael

Mitchell Cross pulled up in front of David Kirk's place.
There was a black-and-white on the scene with an officer
behind the wheel, listening to the dispatches on the radio,
and an empty unmarked car. It was undoubtedly Corinne
Smith's vehicle. She'd put in a call for him at Dana Kirk's
request. Mitch got out of the car, waved at the patrolman,
and went past an older woman standing on the sidewalk,
staring up at the house. She had a dog on a leash and pulled
it back to make way for him, looking like she wanted to ask
what was going on. He ignored her and made his way up
the walk.

He rapped on the door, not bothering with the bell.
Corinne appeared, wearing one of her blue suits. Brown
and blue were all she ever wore. Mitch had seen her at a
party once in a frilly pink-and-white dress and hadn't recognized her.

"Well, if it isn't Detective Cross, San Rafael's real-estate
cop."

He chuckled. "How'd they end up sending you out here,
Corinne?"

"Beats me, honey." She glanced back, then stepped onto
the porch, pulling the door to. "I guess dolls gettin' their
arms ripped off sounded like domestic violence. Besides,
everybody knows I carry Krazy Glue in my purse."

Mitch smiled. "So, how's Mrs. Kirk taking it?"

"She's pretty shook-up. She's with the girl in her room,
talkin'."

"What happened, exactly?"

Corinne gave him a rundown.

"Sounds like the guy is turning the screw," Mitch said.
"He must figure the girl is her Achilles' heel."

"Judgin' by the way she's actin', I'd say the sonovabitch is right."

"I don't imagine there's any chance of prints or other physical evidence."

"The girl handled the doll a lot. She thought the whole thing was a prank."

"Was there a note?"

"Yeah, pinned to the doll's dress. One word—'Boo.'"

"Boo?"

"That's right. Seems like our bad guy has a quirky sense of humor."

"He's been less than witty until now."

Corinne nodded. "Mrs. Kirk gave me the whole story, including how nice and thorough you are. Must say, you have a way with lady victims, Mitch."

He gave her a sideward glance. "Where's the girl's father?"

"He's teachin' a seminar or somethin' like that. Mrs. Kirk said rather than disturb him, she'd just stay here with the girl until he came home."

"Well, I've got good news for her. We picked up O'Connell about forty-five minutes ago."

"The one who slapped around his wife in the real-estate office?"

"Yeah, the same guy you told me about this morning."

"Hooray for us!" Corinne chortled. "You talk to him yet?"

"No. I was going over to see Mrs. O'Connell first. She's a little skittish and I want to make sure she'll hang in there with us on charges."

"Sounds reasonable. By the way, we did find a footprint in the muddy flower bed outside the girl's window. We're waiting on the lab truck. Looks to me like we might be able to get a cast."

"That's great. Now if we can find the shoe that goes with the print, we might have something."

"Prince Charming found Cinderella that way, honey. I don't see why we can't. Of course, it's yet to be determined which of us is going to run around and check out all the size tens in Marin County."

"That could be a problem," Mitch said with a laugh.

"I take it you're here to speak with Ms. Kirk before you go see Mrs. O'Connell. She's been patiently waiting for you."

Mitch couldn't help a smile.

"Don't get too wrapped up in the knight-in-shinin'-armor bit," Corinne said. "This job has a way of humbling heroes."

"Detective Smith, I take my victims as I find them."

"Yeah, honey," Corinne said, turning to open the door, "tell me another."

Mitch followed her into the house, aware that for the second time that day he was in the den of a man from Dana Kirk's past. It was hardly an observation to share with her.

"Is she back there?" he asked, pointing.

"Let me get her," Corinne offered.

She went to the entrance to the back hall and called out to Dana. "Mrs. Kirk? Detective Cross is here."

A moment later Dana appeared at the other end of the hall. Mitch saw her coming. She looked beautiful. A little stressed-out, but that only added an air of vulnerability. He liked that—the combination of being strong and weak at the same time. A young girl appeared behind her and followed Dana into the front room.

"Detective Cross," she said, seeming happy to see him. She extended her hand, just as she had that morning.

"Seems like you're having a bad day."

Dana rolled her eyes. "Tell me about it." She turned, putting her arm around her daughter's shoulders. "I'd like you to meet Molly.'' Then to the girl she said, "Honey, this is Detective Cross.''

Mitch smiled. The daughter was pretty, though not the beauty her mother was. The consanguinity was evident, however. "Hi, Molly," he said.

"Hi," she said shyly.

"I understand you had an unwanted visitor last night."

"I guess so. I thought it was a joke—that somebody from school had done it."

"We hope to catch the guy soon so you won't have to worry about it."

"Mom's more worried than me. I'm not scared or anything."

"How's Mom holding up?" he asked, looking at Dana.

"Not quite as well. This is not the sort of development I appreciate." She squeezed the girl against her.

"I've got some news that might cheer you. Ted O'Connell was picked up a while ago. We've got him in custody."

Dana's brows rose with surprise. "That's wonderful! Has he said anything?"

"I'm going to question him shortly. But I've got to run over and see his wife first. We'll need her cooperation if we're going to hold him."

"I see."

"Actually, I wanted to talk to you about that a little and also brief you on some other developments. Maybe we can take a walk," he said, glancing at Molly.

"I can go to my room," the girl volunteered.

"That's all right, Mol," Dana said, "I could use some air. Why don't you do me a favor and call your dad's office and leave a message on his machine in case he goes back there after his seminar."

"What do you want me to tell him?"

"Just say I need to talk to him and I'll be waiting here with you."

"Okay."

Dana went to the hall closet and got her trench coat.

"Nice meeting you, Molly," Mitch said. "Next time I see you I hope it will be under better conditions."

"Yeah, I guess."

He winked and went to the door in time to help Dana with her coat. He casually saluted Corinne, who'd remained in the background, taking it all in. "See you back at the office, Detective," he said.

"I'll be here until we get our glass slipper."

"Just don't turn into a pumpkin," he said, opening the door.

"And you watch out for the ugly stepsisters."

Mitch laughed and followed Dana outside. He closed the door behind them and glanced up at the sky. It was overcast and getting dark due to the lateness of the hour. It hadn't rained for a while, but the ground and pavement were still wet. A breeze had come up and it seemed cooler. "Would you like to walk or sit in the car?"

"Do you mind walking?" Dana asked. "I really could use the air."

"No, just let me get my trench coat."

The patrolman was talking on the radio and Mitch gave him the high sign. The officer waved back. There were two boys on bicycles across the street, watching. Mitch glanced at them as he took his coat from the car. He rejoined Dana Kirk and they went up the sidewalk.

"I guess these are your old stomping grounds," he said.

"Don't remind me."

"Unhappy associations?"

"Are you married, Detective Cross?"

"Detective is fine for the first crime. By the second my first name becomes Mitch—unless you're a stickler for formality, Mrs. Kirk."

"I'm not. Call me Dana, if you like."

"Thanks," Mitch said. "But to answer your question, I'm not married."

"Divorced?"

"No, just a stodgy old bachelor."

"Then you don't know about former spouses."

"Enough to avoid being one."

"Good for you."

He looked over at her. "I think I know what you mean about the associations, though. I'm a child of divorce."

"Molly keeps David and me together, in a manner of speaking. But I suppose you understand that, too."

"No, as a matter of fact. My old man took off when my parents split. I've seen him twice since I was in grammar school."

"That has to be rough."

"Your daughter seems to have both her parents, though."

"Yes, David's been a good father."

They passed under some trees that were dripping. Mitch noticed Dana wipe a drop of water off her nose. The way she did it appealed to him. It was a small thing, but he noticed it.

"What do you think will happen now that Ted's been arrested?" she asked.

"It's too early to say. My hunch is he's not the boy who's been harassing you, but we'll see."

"Can you let me know somehow? I'd like to get a good night's sleep. It's been a month, I think, since I have."

"Sure, but don't get your hopes up."

"Don't worry. I've learned to be stoic, if not accepting."

He could see tiny lines at the corners of her eyes. He wasn't the only one who was bushed, it seemed.

"I also wanted to tell you about my conversation with your old . . . boss, Frank Betts."

Dana whipped her head in his direction. "You talked to Frank?"

"Yeah. Went by his office this afternoon. He confessed to being up at your place last night. Didn't even try to deny it."

"Did he say what he was doing there?"

"The guy seems to have a crush on you."

Dana looked down at her feet.

"He was apologetic about it," Mitch went on. "I think he was embarrassed, too."

"So you think it was innocent?"

"I don't know. What kind of actor is Betts?"

"Frank has a line of bullshit, but he's not a pathological liar. In a funny sort of way he's honest. You have to be able to see through all the song and dance, but the real Frank is there."

"Maybe I don't know him well enough."

They'd come to a cul-de-sac and followed it around. All the homes were about the same age as David Kirk's and in roughly the same condition. Mitch didn't know real estate but if he had to guess, he'd have said when the subdivision was new the houses sold for twenty-five or thirty thousand and now went for between three-hundred-fifty thousand and half-a-million dollars.

Dana hadn't said anything for a while. "So you aren't prepared to say Frank's somehow involved in my problem."

"The conversation was brief, but I didn't get any clear signals of guilt," he replied. "I'm not prepared to say he's innocent, though. The man seemed troubled to me."

"Neither Frank nor Lane is very happy these days."

"Lane's the partner."

"Yes, Lane Cedrick."

"What's he like?"

"Coldly efficient. A hard-driving businessman. Of the two, Lane is definitely the back-room guy. He handles the numbers and the money. He's not a gray accountant, by any means. He's a got style of his own. In fact, he's more sophisticated than Frank. But Frank has always been the front man, the one who's dealt with the sales force and the public."

"I had that impression talking to him. But it's too soon to say what's going on in the guy's head. I'm reserving judgment."

Dana carefully stepped over a large banana slug on the sidewalk. "Do I have reason to fear him, Mitch?"

"You have reason to be careful. But do you reach for your gun if you see him coming? I don't think so."

She grinned at that and her face seemed to light up, looking younger. "You cops are like politicians, aren't you?"

"I'm hedging. Is that what you mean?"

Dana nodded.

"Well, cops don't like to make mistakes when we're talking about matters of life and death. As soon as I say I think Betts isn't our man, it turns out he is—which is fine unless he hurts somebody in the meantime. So I hedge."

"I won't hold you to your gut instinct."

Mitch reflected. "Sending threatening notes and hanging dolls outside your daughter's window doesn't strike me as Betts's style."

"No, it doesn't strike me that way, either."

"People do some pretty strange things under stress, though," Mitch said.

"Don't worry. I'll be careful."

He checked his watch. "Maybe I'd better get back. I've got to get over to Mrs. Hansen's place to talk to Mrs. O'Connell. That's the other thing I want to discuss with you."

"Bev?"

"Yes."

They started heading back toward the house.

"Ted O'Connell is not somebody I want to see out on the streets," Mitch said. "But I'll need his wife's cooperation and maybe yours to hold him. Even then, he's going to get out on bail, though with luck we can put it off a few days. I think the DA will cooperate. But without Mrs. O'Connell's help he'll be out tonight."

He saw her shiver.

"Can you give me a little insight into Mrs. O'Connell's attitude, so I can manage this the best way possible?"

She stuffed her hands into her pockets. "Bev's not going to want to hurt Ted. I believe she realizes their relationship is destructive, and I think she wants to end it, but he does have a hold on her."

"You're saying she's not likely to cooperate."

"My guess is she doesn't want to see him in jail."

"Great."

"But if you think it will help, I'll call her," Dana said.

"Sure. It can't hurt."

They walked for a while in silence. Mitch felt a curious sort of closeness, a protectiveness toward Dana Kirk. He thought of Corinne's knight-in-shining-armor remark and knew there was a ring of truth in it. The bald fact was that he was attracted to the woman. That wasn't good. Not considering who she was.

Her affinity for him was easier to explain. He was a policeman, the law, a protector. She was vulnerable and in need. Once her problem was solved, she'd forget he ever existed.

"Mitch," she said, breaking the silence, "I was wondering if maybe I could ask a favor."

"Sure. What do you need?"

"Actually, I need advice more than a favor. I've been sort of muddling along through this thing, taking it a day at a time. I've tried to be careful, but frankly I'm not sure I'm doing the things I should be doing."

"What do you mean?"

"The death threats are virtually public. And now that Molly has been brought into things directly, I'm more worried about her than ever. Lots of other people are affected, too—her father, my agents, even my neighbors to some degree. What I'm getting at is the broader question of security."

"I think I understand."

"I tried to discuss this with Detective Brockmeyer, but he was pretty straitlaced and formal."

"You'd like some advice without all the B.S."

"Yes, I guess that's what it amounts to. I know this isn't the time, but if you could find half an hour sometime in the next few days to give me your professional appraisal of the situation, I'd appreciate it. I guess I need an objective analysis from somebody who knows what they're talking about."

"I hear you."

The wind gusted and Mitch pulled the lapel of his trench coat over his chest. The Kirk house was a few doors away. He saw that the lab truck had arrived. The technicians would be at work soon. And he had to get going.

"Look, Dana, I'm going to be tied up with the O'Connells for two or three hours, which puts me at the end of my shift," Mitch said. "I can stay in town for dinner. How about if afterward I swing by your place. I'll brief you on what happened with O'Connell and we can talk about security."

"Oh, that would be great. But I don't want to impose on your personal time."

"No problem. I'll take a few extra coffee breaks this week. Things have a way of evening up."

"Could I take you to dinner instead?"

Mitch turned to her. Her expression was earnest. There wasn't a trace of guile in her eyes. He realized Dana wasn't propositioning him; she was just looking for someone who could help her evaluate her situation. Funny, but a part of him was disappointed by that.

"I normally don't sell out so cheaply," he said, tongue in cheek, "but since the safety of an innocent girl is involved, I suppose I could make an exception."

"I'll take you to a very nice place."

He smiled. "Now I know how a woman feels being wooed with fancy meals and nights on the town."

She nodded, indicating she understood the message behind his teasing. "My intentions are completely honorable, Mitch."

"Yeah, that's what they all say." He winked.

Dana Kirk blushed. He liked that.

"To be honest, Mrs. Kirk, you're looking at a meat-and-potatoes guy. I ride a horse, not a Porsche. I eat a T-bone, not filet mignon."

"I'm sure we can find a place that you'll like."

He grinned. "You're a hard lady to say no to, aren't you?"

"How do you suppose I got rich? The first thing I learned in sales is you don't get the order without asking for it."

"There must be a lesson for me in that," he said.

"You aren't looking for property by any chance, are you?" she rejoined.

Mitch couldn't help laughing. "I was warned about you."

"Oh?"

"I have no further comment."

Dana gave him an elbow in the arm. He liked that, too.

* * *

San Rafael

David Kirk took his notes from the podium and sat down to stuff his materials into his briefcase. It felt good to be off his feet after standing for several hours. Seminars were tiring, but he enjoyed them. In therapy he listened. In a seminar he was free to pontificate. Every thinking person needed to do that once in a while. He also didn't mind the adulation. It was his one small opportunity in life for celebrity.

He hardly had a chance to catch his breath before people started coming up with their thanks and their questions. He patiently dealt with each person until the last one was through. Then, taking his briefcase and his raincoat, he looked up and saw that the redhead was still sitting at the other end of the room.

All afternoon he'd been aware of her, first because she was attractive and very unlike the rest of the participants, second because she didn't say a word the entire time, and third because she looked familiar and he couldn't place her. When they'd had their break, he'd subtly observed her. The tight leather pants and glamorous face made it hard not to. She looked more like she belonged on Rodeo Drive than in a self-image workshop at Dominican College. Who was she?

Making his way around the perimeter of the room toward the exit, he watched her as she watched him. She had an expectant expression on her face, but also a sort of wariness. And she'd made no move to gather her things. It was as though she was waiting for him.

David stopped and spoke directly to her. "I've been to movies where people stayed in their seats afterward, not wanting the experience to end. Would it be immodest of me to wonder if that's why you're still here?" he asked.

"I don't know about 'immodest,'" she said, a smile of triumph forming, "but your conclusion's right. I really liked the seminar. And it would have been fine with me if you'd kept going."

David smiled appreciatively. He couldn't help being aware of her voluptuous body. She was pretty in a showy, obvious way. Also a bit older than he'd first realized, possibly older than he. "That's high praise," he said.

"Take it as flattery if you want."

"Is that how you intend it?"

She chuckled. "You're sounding like a shrink."

"Sorry. Habit."

"I don't mind."

David moved closer and set his briefcase on a chair two down from her. She crossed her legs in a way that drew attention to them and looked up at him through her lashes. She was a sexual creature, without qualification or apology. He studied her face, knowing he knew her, though he still couldn't say from where or how or through whom.

"You don't remember me, do you?" she said.

He could see he was more transparent than he'd thought. "No. But I've been racking my brain."

She smiled. "That's not very flattering, but it does give me an advantage, doesn't it? Should I tell you, or would it spoil the fun?"

He studied her. "It wasn't in therapy, was it?"

She shook her head.

He struggled to remember. Could it have been at a social occasion? he wondered. Was she a neighbor? Maybe the PTA. He'd been doing PTA since Molly was in grammar school. "I'm drawing a complete blank, I'm sorry to say."

She turned her shoulders toward him, enabling him to see the name tag on her sweater. Hand-lettered with a marking pencil was the name Nola. That sent a pulse of recognition through him, but he couldn't quite make the connection.

"I'm embarrassed, Nola," he said, shaking his head.

She gave him a coy look. "I've a confession. Until you walked into the room, I couldn't have said for sure what you looked like, either. It was vague for me, too."

"It's apparently been a while."

"You'll laugh when you find out." She paused long enough to measure him. "Let me buy you a cup of coffee and I'll tell all."

David contemplated her, trying to discern her intent. One thing was sure, he was strongly attracted to her. That surprised him because he didn't normally react this way to women. He had to desensitize himself in therapy, and out of habit he often did so in life.

But the tug he felt from this woman, Nola, was palpably different. Sure, he'd been the seminar leader—the father figure, after a fashion—but this sensation he was experiencing was gut-grinding sexual attraction, something he wasn't accustomed to.

"Was that too brazen of me?" she asked.

He clicked back to the moment at hand, telling himself this was not a clinical situation where he needed to fight his feelings. "You've piqued my curiosity, I must confess."

"I don't mean to be cruel, David. Honest."

He checked his watch.

"If you don't have time for coffee, I won't torment you," she said.

"No, I'm just trying to calculate how much time I have. I'm supposed to take my daughter to dinner."

"If you'd rather another time—"

"I've got an hour. That should be enough to clear up the mystery of the lady in purple."

She gave him a coquettish smile and began gathering her things. He was very conscious of her voluptuousness, the way she filled out a sweater. But more than anything he was curious.

Nola slipped on her coat, looking into his eyes as she did so. He snatched up his briefcase and they headed for the door.

"Have any particular place in mind?" he asked.

"Why don't you follow me in your car? I'll pick a place."

"More machination," he said.

Nola giggled. "You'll die when you find out, David. You'll really die."

San Rafael

Ted O'Connell sat with his beefy arms folded, glaring across the table at Tony Lugretti as Mitch watched from the corner of the room. Tony, a San Francisco native who lived in North Beach, had been doing most of the questioning. And was getting nowhere.

Mitch could tell that O'Connell, who'd been mostly wearing a smirk, had been interrogated before. It usually showed. His rap sheet wasn't bad by most standards. The only thing in the past five years was a drunk and disorderly. He'd been arrested on a DUI but hadn't been convicted. The worst thing on the sheet were two assault raps dating back to his college days at San Jose State. "Barroom brawls" was the way he described them. He'd done two months in the county jail on the second conviction. "The worst was I lost my football scholarship." That was all he'd said about his past.

"Look, how many times do I have to tell you," he was saying to Lugretti, "I don't write letters to people who fuck with me. I break their goddamn heads."

"You threatened to break Mrs. Kirk's head, or words to that effect, didn't you, Ted?" Lugretti said, pushing his dark hair off his forehead.

"The bitch was pointing a gun at me."

"But you're pissed at her. Pissed enough to threaten her life."

"Damn right, I'm pissed. Pissed because of what she did today, this morning."

"Your wife says you and she have been arguing about Mrs. Kirk for weeks."

"Look, officer. I don't like the woman. I admit that, all right? Am I writing her letters? No. Do I tell my wife she's nuts to leave the biggest company in Marin to join some arrogant bitch on an ego trip? Yes."

"What do you have against Mrs. Kirk, Ted?" Lugretti asked. "What did she ever do to you?"

"Jesus," O'Connell complained, rolling his eyes, "what's with you guys? Haven't you ever had anybody you didn't like? She's an arrogant bitch. Period. What can I say?"

Mitch moved toward the table. "It doesn't compute, Ted. You're hiding something and we both know it."

O'Connell shook his head. "Look, I've been sitting here for an hour taking this shit. If you want to charge me for murder because I don't like Dana Kirk, then do it. All you're doing is flapping your lips and the reason is because you don't have anything. Nothing. Nada. I want to know right now, is my wife bringing charges against me or isn't she? Because if she isn't, I want out of here.

"You can't hold me and you know it. I haven't screamed for a lawyer because I've got nothing to hide. But if you don't give me my hat in about three minutes, I'm going to start screaming. Now put up or shut up."

"Listen, O'Connell," Mitch said, standing over him, "and listen good. I'm going to give you your hat even though I can keep you. I've got enough to hold you a couple of days, but that's not what I'm after. Two things matter and I'm going to explain them to you nice and slow, so you'll understand.

"First, I want you to stay away from your wife unless she wants to see you. If she does, she'll let you know. Second, I want you to stay away from Mrs. Kirk. I don't want you going near her office or her home. If you show up in either place I'm going to slam you in the can so fast it'll make your head spin. And if you hurt either of those ladies, I'll make it my personal mission in life to make you pay and pay dearly.

"Now I want you to get your ass out of here and I don't want to see it or hear any complaints regarding you again. Do we understand each other, Mr. O'Connell?"

"I take it that means my wife is not filing charges, officer."

Mitch rarely had the desire to club anybody he was interrogating, even some of the worst slimeballs, but Ted O'Connell was one jerk he really wanted to put on his ass. "Let me tell you this, O'Connell you don't deserve that woman's indulgence. You should count yourself fortunate she doesn't have you put away."

"Maybe she loves me."

"Let's just hope that doesn't mean she's a fool."

"Is that goodbye?"

Mitch indicated the door with his chin. "Get out of here."

Ted O'Connell smiled and got to his feet. "Thanks for the hospitality, fellas." He went to the door and looked back at Mitch. "I don't mean to tell you your business, officer, but it sounds to me like Dana Kirk's given you a hard-on. As one friend to another, don't be surprised if there isn't any payoff. She's a prick tease. Take it from one who knows."

Ted O'Connell left the room. Tony Lugretti glanced at Mitch and followed him out.

* * *

Terra Linda

Dusk was falling as the BMW convertible exited the freeway at the Manuel Freitas Parkway. It immediately turned right into the parking lot of the Holiday Inn. David followed it, his heart beating nicely at the illicitness of it all.

He'd counseled many people plagued by compulsive sexual behavior, usually tied to a deep psychological problem or need. He was also aware that perfectly normal, healthy people—people who were usually guided by reason and sound judgment—would occasionally find themselves in the grip of such a compulsion. That's what was happening now. This woman could lead him almost anywhere and he would follow. It made no sense, but it was true.

In a way he didn't want to understand it or analyze it. He just wanted to go with it. After all, Nola was not a patient. She was available and interested, and that was enough for him.

Of course, he had experienced desire in the clinical setting more than once, but he'd never come close to doing anything about it. That would be unprofessional. And since the divorce he'd had both romantic and sexual relationships. But this was something new. It was very sudden, very powerful, and it undoubtedly said a great deal about the way his life had been of late. He didn't want to think about that. He simply wanted to enjoy it.

Nola pulled into an empty parking space and David pulled into the one next to it. He glanced over at her, his heart tripping. The Holiday Inn. He secretly wanted to believe she was taking him to the hotel, but he knew there was a restaurant there where they could have a cup of coffee.

Nola got out of her car. David did, as well. The excitement he felt told him how extensive the neglect of his emotional life had been. When you did that, your subconscious found a way to get even. He'd preached that to others, and now he was preaching it to himself. Nola was smiling with girlish glee as she came around her car to meet him. He wondered if she, too, might be in the grip of some sort of compulsion. The joy in her seemed to mirror his own.

"I feel so guilty dragging you here," she said, taking his arm.

"No need to feel guilty. I could have said no."

She pressed her breasts against him as they walked toward the entrance. "It's your curiosity that made you come, isn't it?"

"Partly."

"I hope you won't be disappointed or angry."

There was a strong undercurrent of insecurity in the woman, which made him secretly glad. "I won't. I promise you."

Nola laughed as though it were a wonderful joke.

They went into the lobby. The entrance to the Café Pacific was beyond. It was a rather fancy coffee shop. David had eaten there with a colleague once years ago, but didn't remember it well.

They were shown to a booth adjacent to the window that overlooked the central garden and swimming pool. It looked strangely inviting, reminding him of the hotel pool in Hawaii where he and Dana had spent their honeymoon.

Nola was looking around at the teal-and-purple flowered decor. Then, she, too, gazed out at the pool. "Makes you want to go skinny-dipping?" she asked.

"In the moonlight?" he said, playing along.

"I skinny-dip in my spa all the time," she stated wistfully.

The comment evoked an erotic image. But before he could decide whether or not that was her intent the waitress arrived with menus. Nola told her they just wanted coffee.

"Or would you prefer something else, David?"

"Coffee's fine."

They looked out at the pool until their coffee was poured. Nola sipped hers and gazed at him intently.

"You and I have danced before," she said, her voice sultry.

He gazed at her with surprise.

"Surprised to hear that?"

He nodded. "Yes. When was that?"

"Eight or nine years ago."

He strained to remember. The corners of her mouth lifted with amusement.

"I'd forgotten all about it until it suddenly came to me during the seminar. You have a pleasant voice. I guess that was what reminded me."

"You're going to have to tell me."

"My former husband's name will mean more to you than mine. Frank Betts."

David's mouth dropped. "Nola Betts. Frank's wife. Of course."

"Former wife."

"Jeez, Nola. Yes. Of course. I remember now. How stupid of me. Your name isn't a common one. I should have made the association."

"We didn't really know each other that well," she said. "We only talked a few times. And danced that once. At a C&B party. I don't know about you, but I was probably loaded. I drank a lot at parties."

He shook his head, uncertain how he felt about the unexpected revelation. "So you're divorced now, too."

"Frank and I split a couple of years ago."

"How do you feel about that?"

"Doc, that's a shrink question."

"I'm sorry, it is. Forgive me."

She drank some more coffee and studied him. Her look wasn't seductive, but it was approaching that. "I want to know it's all right," she said.

"That what's all right?"

"That I am who I am."

"Of course. Why shouldn't it be?"

She sighed and looked off toward the pool. "I don't know. Certain associations bother some people."

"Dana and I have been divorced for seven years and were separated before that."

"So the name Betts is not a problem to you?"

He shook his head. "There's no reason why it should be."

David knew he was being overeager, overcompliant, but he didn't care. Ironically, the realization that this sexual creature also happened to be Frank Betts's ex-wife added to her allure. He couldn't say exactly why, unless it had something to do with illicitness and revenge.

Not that he'd had a particular problem with Frank. Dana had told him during their marriage that Betts wanted to seduce her. David knew it was because Frank wanted to seduce everyone. Sex was part of his management style and an important part of the way he defined himself. Frank's rapacious ways hadn't been an issue in their marriage, however. Dana had never gotten involved with him while they were married, David was sure of that.

Nola, whose mind was off somewhere else, smiled sadly. "A whole day of self-image training and I'm blowing it already."

It took a moment for him to realize she was talking about her insecure musings. "You aren't blowing it, Nola. You had a concern and you voiced it. We can put it behind us and move on."

"'Move on.' That's a nice term, isn't it? There's comfort in it." She chuckled. "I guess that says a lot about me, doesn't it?"

David took a drink from his cup. He did not answer her. His mind was focused on her sexuality. It was a liberty he didn't allow himself often, and it was almost scary how firmly in its grip he was.

"Let me make a confession right up front," she said. "I sort of developed a crush on you during the seminar. It's not a shrink-patient thing. This is more man to woman. You seem kind, David. I like that. I'm very attracted to it."

He felt a rush of pure joy. He'd already assumed that she felt some attraction, but what she was expressing sounded parallel to his own. How fortuitous and rare there should be such mutuality.

"You're very brave to speak your mind that way," he said, struggling to conceal his elation.

"I've never lacked guts. Judgment maybe, but not guts." She ran her tongue over her lips. "I'm capable of doing anything my desires tell me."

David felt himself harden. It sometimes happened in therapy when a client talked about sex in graphic terms, but that was always impersonal—like an erotic film. This was different. "What do your desires tell you?" he asked.

"I think it's too soon to say. We're only on our first cup of coffee." Her brow arched suggestively.

David wondered if it was no accident that they were at the Holiday Inn. She had to have been aware how easy it would be for him to go out to the desk and ask for a room. He hardened at the thought. What great, wonderful luck! But then he remembered Molly. His irresponsibility hit him with a jolt. He couldn't leave his daughter alone all night. He already should have been home.

Nola had a grin on her face. "You look to be in such torment," she said.

"I am."

"Why?"

"I have other obligations, but I'd rather spend the evening with you. If it were possible, I'd suggest dinner."

There was a look of momentary disappointment on her face. "There will be other evenings."

He thought, knowing in his gut he had to seize the moment. "Do you have plans for tomorrow night?"

"No."

"Dinner?"

"I'd like that," she said, nodding. "Very much."

"You'll let me go, then."

"I'll think about tomorrow night."

Another pulse went through him. He was more needy than he would have thought. The power of this had him completely off-balance.

Nola slid a hand across the table. He took it, rubbing his thumb over the back of it. She pursed her lips ever so slightly. He knew then that he was going to have an affair with her. An affair with the former wife of his former wife's former boss. The notion was irresistibly taboo.

"I'm going to have to go now," he said softly.

"Shall I give you my address?"

"By all means."

San Rafael

Mitch Cross sat at his desk, drumming a pencil on the blotter. He stared at the dark windowpane. He'd put in eleven hours, and he was beyond tired. He was running on adrenaline and thinking about Dana Kirk.

Funny thing was, he felt about equal parts annoyance, compassion, admiration and lust, though the order wasn't entirely clear. The annoyance part was the stickler. Why did she annoy him? Was it the germ of the same thing that had gotten to Ted O'Connell?

No, he dismissed that quickly. Nothing that scumbag said was worth a second thought. Dana did not strike him as a tease. She was a dynamo. Single-minded, in a way. Maybe it had something to do with that.

He also worried about her. She struck him as extremely vulnerable. And she'd reached out to him, almost as a friend. Maybe what he resented was her seeming indifference to the angst she'd caused. Or maybe she wasn't aware that he was attracted to her. Either way, he had to deal with her.

He consulted his watch and decided to give her another call. There'd been no answer earlier, which meant she'd gotten hung up—if not with her daughter, then with business. But he was still reluctant to flick it in and go home. She'd seemed very eager to talk to him, to get his advice, so he'd do his best to accommodate her. If she didn't answer this time, though, maybe he'd grab a bite, then phone her afterward. There was no reason they had to talk over dinner.

As he looked in his drawer for her number, his direct line rang. Mitch picked up the receiver.

"Cross."

"Hi, Mitch. It's Liz Rogers."

"Hello, counselor."

"Thought I'd get an update on what's happening with Dana. I tried calling her, but was only able to leave messages."

"I apologize for not getting back to you, Liz. I'd promised to keep you advised."

"I know you're busy, but I'm working late and Dana came to mind. I took a chance I'd catch you in."

"Are pregnant ladies supposed to put in long hours?"

"They run marathons, so I imagine they can put in a few extra hours at the office. But please, Mitch, 'pregnant women,' not 'pregnant ladies.'"

"Political correctness was never my long suit."

"Sorry if I'm being irritable," Liz said. "Pregnant *ladies* do that sort of thing. *I* have no excuse."

"I absolve you, if you absolve me."

"Agreed." She paused. "So what do you think of Dana?"

"She's a go-getter, like you said."

"But likable, too, don't you think?"

"Likable, attractive, nice."

After a moment Liz said, "I thought you'd like her."

"I do."

"Well, that's good."

Mitch wondered why she was sounding like a matchmaker. Or was he presuming?

"So, how's the case coming?" she asked.

"Not well. One step forward, two back." He gave her a brief account, including the most recent setback with Ted.

"Well, it's early," she said. "You've only just gotten started. But it's disgusting to think the guy is harassing Molly, too."

"Yeah, but I think that little trick was aimed at Dana. I admit to being concerned, though. I don't want anything happening to her on my watch."

She let his comment hang, as though she might be making something of it. "That's why I wanted you on the case," she finally said.

Mitch waited, sensing there was something else she had to say.

"I guess I'd better get out of here," she said. "This chair is starting to get to me."

"Go on home, Liz. Maybe Martin will have dinner waiting on the table."

Liz laughed derisively. The tone was unmistakable. Mitch knew his comment had been bitchy. Martin Rogers, from what he remembered of the guy, would be the last man on earth to cook his wife a meal, whether she was pregnant or not. The temptation to say it had simply been too great, though.

"Martin is in Phoenix," she said. "He'll be gone for several days. So I'm on my own."

Mitch wondered if the forlorn tone was a bid for sympathy, or if she was sending him some kind of message. If she hadn't been eight months pregnant, he might have thought the latter. Under the circumstances, it was hard to believe she would be suggesting anything.

Reading between the lines, Mitch decided something was wrong. Unless he was mistaken, he was talking to a very unhappy wife.

"Maybe we can have lunch," he said. He wasn't himself sure what he had in mind, unless it was simply his instinct to comfort her. Pregnant women were definitely beyond his range of experience, and he planned to keep it that way.

"That would be good," she said.

"I'll give you a ring, then."

"Do that, Mitch."

He hung up the phone and scratched his head. Why did it seem like every guy in the world was fucking up and the broken pieces were falling on him?

With Dana Kirk's home number on the slip of paper before him, Mitch dialed. The answering machine didn't pick up his call, but neither did she. That made him begin to worry. But finally on the sixth or seventh ring she was there.

"Hello," she said breathlessly.

"Mitch Cross," he said. "Did I make you run from the garage?"

"Oh, hi, Mitch. No, I was changing."

The visual image that came to him was very appealing. Dana Kirk undressed. "Sorry."

"No problem. I usually get out of my business suits the minute I hit the door. I assume you don't mind if I'm dressed casually for dinner," she said. "You're still letting me take you, aren't you?"

"Yeah, sure. I called to get a reading on how your schedule is."

"I'm running behind, but that's pretty normal for me. My damned former husband was late getting home, and by the time I explained what had happened and we discussed what to do about it, happy hour had come and gone."

"I've been busy myself," he said. "And I have bad news, I'm afraid."

"What?" Her tone was wary.

"We had to release O'Connell."

"Oh, shit."

Somehow the word on her lips was all right. In fact, he liked it. The incongruity appealed to him. And it was honest. Perhaps he liked that about it best.

"Bev wouldn't bring charges, is that it?"

"Yeah. Said she didn't want him in jail."

Dana sighed. "I'm not surprised. That's Bev."

"So keep your doors locked."

"You don't think Ted will pull anything else, do you?"

"I tried to put the fear of God in him, but I wasn't successful, to be honest. As to what he might do, I have no idea. It was clear that the man is not a fan of yours."

"Did he elaborate on what his problem is?"

"Nothing more than what you already know."

"Oh, my," she said, sounding resigned.

"Keep your dauber up," Mitch said.

"Don't worry, I will."

"How long do you need?"

"Doesn't matter. Come when you can."

He heard a tremor in her voice. "You feeling jumpy?"

"Yes, I guess I am."

"I'll be there shortly, Dana."

Mitch hung up the phone, with the mental image of her gliding across the floor, undressed, still on his mind. He didn't like thinking of her as nervous or upset, but that didn't erase this new picture of her. It afforded one of the nicer moments in what had otherwise been a very long and trying day.

Marinwood

Ted O'Connell drained the last of his beer and gazed down at the can before crushing it and hurling it across the family room and into the kitchen, where it rattled around on the tile floor before coming to a stop against the refrigerator. He pounded the cushion of the black leather couch with his fist, having half a mind to tear it to shreds. He had a terrible urge to beat on something.

It was ironic he'd think of the family-room furniture. They'd gotten the leather set at his insistence. Bev had wanted something cutesy, but if he was going to put his feet up and watch a game, he wanted to do it in comfort on stuff he liked. He told her she could put any goddamned thing she liked in the front room, but the family room was his.

He drew a deep, agonizing breath. *Family room*—that was a laugh. With Bev gone there wasn't any family. If it wasn't for that goddamned Dana Kirk, everything would be all right. Bev would have listened to him. She always did—eventually. But this time Dana had gotten to her. She'd reamed her husband and she figured every other woman should do the same. That was the trouble with the fucking real-estate business. A woman makes a few bucks and all of a sudden she thinks she's got balls.

"Frigging bitch," he muttered.

He went to the refrigerator, kicking aside the crumpled can. After staring at the half-depleted stock of beer, he decided against having another and slammed the door shut. Then he again went to the phone on the counter. He grabbed the receiver and dialed. He waited.

"Kirk & Company." It was a woman's voice, but not the one who'd been answering. This one didn't have an accent. Probably some agent working late.

"Let me speak with Bev O'Connell," he said, thinking he might have an opportunity to bluff his way through this time.

There was hesitation at the other end of the line. "I'm sorry, but Bev's not in. May I take a message?"

"I need to talk to her," he said. "It's urgent. Where can I reach her?"

"I can't say," the woman replied, "but if you'll leave your name and number I'll see that she gets the message."

"I don't want to leave any message. I want to know where she is!"

There was a silence, then the woman asked, "Is this Mr. O'Connell?"

"Shit," he said through his teeth and slammed down the receiver. "Fuck!"

Ted headed for their bedroom. He passed through Bev's hoity-toity Chippendale living room with all the claw-footed table legs and pictures of hunting scenes with English faggots sitting on their horses—noses in the air. The faggots and the horses both. He went up the stairs, taking them two at a time.

His pulse was racing as he burst into their bedroom. He looked around, hating the sight of the fancy velvet drapes and bedspread. The closet door was open and Bev's scent wafted out, making him feel all liquid in the gut. God, he missed her. And he was mad as hell she'd abandoned him. It was hard to know which feeling was stronger. Tears filled his eyes and he felt wretched. No broad should be able to do this to a man.

Feeling the need to fight back, he grabbed hold of one of her dresses and ripped it off the hanger. He wanted to tear everything she had to shreds. He wanted to hurt her for hurting him.

Then he saw her nightgown hanging on a hook. He grabbed it, crumpling it in his fists. He pressed it to his face, inhaling the scent of her body. He began weeping then, sobbing like a baby. Damn her. Damn her to hell!

After a few minutes Ted pulled himself together. He threw down the gown and stomped from the room, heading for the garage. He was going to get out of there. Go someplace. Do something. Pushing the button, he opened the garage door and climbed into his Porsche.

The engine roared to life and he backed out. He didn't bother to use the remote control to close the door. He didn't care. Once he was in the street, he rammed the gearshift into first and took off. The tires screeched. He gripped the wheel tightly. He was determined. He was going to find her and settle this, once and for all.

Ross

Dana stood before the mirror in the master bathroom, trying to decide if the black V-neck cashmere sweater, slim black suede skirt, black hose and shoes looked too funereal when the doorbell rang. She consulted the tiny Waterford clock she kept on the marble vanity. Mitch Cross was punctual if he was nothing else. That was a trait she valued.

Making her way through the brightly lit house, she realized she'd neglected to put on her pearl stud earrings. Well, she'd just have to take a minute to put them on after she let him in. She felt undressed without them.

She checked the peephole to make sure it was Mitch before she opened the door. He took her in, looking surprised and maybe pleased, as well. Although the wind was cold, he wasn't wearing a topcoat. She noticed his tie was loosened a bit at the neck. He had an air of insouciant casualness about him. In combination with his manliness, it was appealing.

"I neglected to bring a tux to work this morning," he said, checking her out a second time. "When you said casual I expected you to be in jeans."

"What I'm wearing dresses up or down, Mitch."

"You look lovely."

"You're the first police officer who's ever said that to me," she replied with a broad smile, gesturing for him to enter.

"You obviously spend all your time on the right side of the law."

She closed the door and turned the dead bolt. "I try."

Mitch peered around with obvious curiosity before turning back to her, rewarding her with another admiring glance. "You survived the day intact. That's an accomplishment."

"It's been a while since I've had a day like this."

"Hopefully it'll end on a higher note."

She wasn't sure what he meant, but assumed he was just making friendly talk. The eye contact they'd made persisted; nonverbal messages of uncertain intent passed back and forth between them.

"I'm only ninety-percent ready," she said, breaking the moment.

"Oh? I would have guessed ninety-nine and forty-four one-hundredths percent. What's left?"

"Earrings," she said, touching her lobe.

"I never would have noticed."

"What men see and don't see is not the standard women dress to, Mitch." She gestured toward the front room. "Make yourself comfortable while I finish. I'll only be a minute."

He stepped into the front room, peering around like he was entering a museum. Dana noticed, recalled the feeling. The first time she'd previewed a million-dollar home she'd only been in real estate a few weeks. God knows, she didn't have a client for anything that expensive, but she'd known she would someday and she wanted to learn. The house had seemed like Buckingham Palace, far removed from everything she'd ever experienced.

"Nice place you've got," he said, probably not intending to sound as glib as he did.

"Thank you."

Dana looked with him. The front room was her favorite. She and the decorator had worked hard on it. The decor was a kind of California modern with a splash of the Orient. The walls were the color of sand; the ceiling, trim and carpeting, off-white. The woods were dark. There were big nubby white sofas and chairs, and the decorator had found a huge Oriental lacquered cabinet that served as the centerpiece of the room. Large leafy palms softened the effect.

"How about a drink?" she asked, noting how uncomfortable he looked. "You are off duty, aren't you?"

"Yes, but I think I'll pass."

"Are you sure? I'll have one. I'm hungry, but I also feel the need to unwind."

"All right. I'll be sociable."

He was still standing, looking as though he didn't want to get the chairs or sofas dirty.

"Sit down," she said. "I'll finish getting ready, then I'll get the drinks." She headed off, leaving him to his own devices. "Be thinking about what you want," she called over her shoulder. "I've got everything you'd find in your average well-stocked bar."

There was a bounce in her step as she returned to her bedroom. Dana suddenly realized that except for the odd lunch or dinner date, and having gone to the opera once in December with the regional vice president of First Security Title, she hadn't socialized with a man in a year. True, Mitchell Cross wasn't exactly a date, but he already seemed like a friend. There was a warmth and a rapport between them, and that gave her a nice feeling.

After she'd put in her earrings and smoothed her hair, she returned to the front room. Mitch was standing at the window, his hands on his hips, looking out at the panorama of lights. He glanced over his shoulder and saw her.

"Quite a view you've got."

Dana joined him at the window. "It's still new enough that I occasionally stand here myself and take it in."

"How long you been here?"

"Since December."

"You have the place custom built?"

"Yes."

"Nice job."

"Thank you."

During their exchanges, both had been staring out at the view. Then Dana saw his reflection in the glass and realized that he was looking at her. She turned to him. "How about that drink?"

"Does your well-stocked bar include beer?"

"Heineken, Sapporo, Guinness, Tsingtao, Dos Equis, Corona, San Miguel, Samuel Adams, Coors, Miller. And probably a few I left out."

"All on ice?"

Dana frowned. "No, that's an important consideration, isn't it."

"Cold's better when it comes to beer."

"Then I guess it's Coors."

"You were just showing off, eh?"

"Yes, I guess I was."

"What do you have all those brands for, anyway?" he asked.

"Well, to show off, what else?"

He grinned. "Your candor is refreshing, Dana."

"Some friends of mine had a wine-and-beer-buying party where a wholesaler came and sold everybody cases of the stuff. I got a variety pack of beers in addition to some wines."

"How chic."

"Don't you mean pretentious?"

"You said it."

"You'll settle for Coors then, I take it."

"If that's the best you can do," he replied, winking.

Dana gave him a look of mock anger. "I think I'll make you drink it from the bottle." She headed for the kitchen.

"Need some help?"

"Sure."

"I'm experienced when it comes to beer," he said, following her.

"What does that mean—that you open bottles with your teeth?"

"Only if I'm desperate."

They entered the family room and he checked it out.

"Look at this, another living room," he quipped. "How many do you have, anyway?"

"Only two. It makes it easier to segregate your guests that way."

"Between beer drinkers and wine drinkers?"

"Something like that."

Mitch stopped at the counter, watching as she got him a bottle of beer from the refrigerator. She poured herself some wine and put the beer on the counter in front of him.

He twisted off the cap and touched the neck of the bottle to her glass, then looked into her eyes, smiling.

"Cheers." Dana took a small sip and watched as he took a long drink. They stood that way—he on the family-room side, she on the kitchen side—the counter between them.

"So tell me, Mitch, is your class bias political, economic or social?"

"Hmm," he said, "I was being blatant again."

"I'm not sure if that's a chip I see on your shoulder or something else."

He took a smaller sip of beer. "It's a chip, and I'm sorry. I apologize."

"Did I say something to offend you?"

"No, it's me. Don't think a thing of it. I'll try to behave."

Curious, Dana gazed at him. Until now, the only glimpse he'd given her of his inner self was when he'd commented on the pain of his parents' divorce. She wondered if he'd had some other traumatic experience—perhaps a related one—that had turned him against wealth.

"Let me guess," she said. "You were in love with a rich girl once, but her father wouldn't let you marry her."

"No, nothing that pat." He took another drink.

"Are you going to explain, or is it none of my business?"

"It's none of your business," he said, "but since I'm among friends I won't hide behind that. I have to warn you, though, it's not a very interesting story. Childhood stories usually aren't."

"Now you've really got me curious." She walked around the counter. "Come and sit down."

She went to one of the plaid chairs. Mitch sat on the sofa, facing her.

"Where did you live growing up?" she asked.

"Mostly in Nevada. Reno. That's where my mom was from originally."

"So what happened?" Dana asked.

"After my old man took off my mother and I scraped by. Then, when she died, things got even tighter. My grandmother put food on the table, but there was never a dime for anything extra. I went to college on a scholarship and never had anything until I went to work as a cop and started drawing regular paychecks. I felt rich, believe me. I was able to send my grandmother money and still have everything I felt I needed."

"You had a rough childhood, then."

"Yes, but I'm not complaining. I didn't tell you as a bid for sympathy. It was only because you asked."

He leaned back and watched as she recrossed her legs. Dana tasted her wine, wondering about Mitch Cross.

"I don't mean to incite a controversy or anything, but what drove you to build your empire and accumulate all this wealth?" he asked, indicating the room with a sweep of his hand.

"What do you think was behind it?"

"I asked you first."

"I know, but indulge me anyway," Dana said. "I'm curious what someone like you sees in me."

"That's a trap, if I've ever seen one." He chuckled good-naturedly. "You want me to hang myself with my own prejudices."

"All right. I plead guilty."

"I suppose I deserve it for opening my mouth."

"I won't argue with that," she said with a smile.

Mitch sighed. "Well, let's see.... Who was Dana Kirk? Your father was a doctor and you were the apple of his eye. He taught you the value of good hard work and instilled the belief that you could achieve anything you wished. You had ballet lessons, music-appreciation courses, but came to realize the real sizzle in life was out competing in the business world. I don't know if it was before or after college, but eventually you decided the mark of a person was in their ability to make money. What mattered most in life was what was in the bank and in the garage." He stopped and studied her. "Am I in the ballpark?"

Dana shook her head. "Not even close, Mitch."

"No?"

"Forgive me for saying this, but it wasn't even a very good guess. The people who have the most to prove usually start out with the farthest to go."

"Don't tell me you were a sharecropper's daughter."

"Just about. I grew up in the Napa Valley where my father worked in the wine business as a laborer. He was a warehouseman at the pinnacle of his career, but he was an alcoholic and couldn't keep a job. Toward the end, he'd get temporary work doing any manual labor he could find. I made as much money working after-school jobs in high school as he did.

"I never got my degree. I completed a number of classes at the community college, but I had to quit about the time my father died in the VA hospital." She stopped and took a sip of wine. "Want to hear more?"

"I feel duly chastened."

"That wasn't my intent, Mitch. If there's a point, it's that making assumptions is dangerous. When you think about it, our backgrounds are very similar. We both grew up in poverty in one-parent families."

"But that's where the similarity ends. We took two entirely different roads."

"And, you don't have much respect for the course I took," she said.

"Let me ask you, deep down, do you feel better about yourself because you've got money?"

"That's a loaded question if I ever heard one, Detective Cross."

Mitch chuckled, shaking his head. "I've gotten off on the wrong foot with you, haven't I? I withdraw my question— it's none of my business anyway. Maybe we should get on to the topic at hand. You wanted to discuss security."

Dana regarded him, appreciating the fact that he felt badly that they'd sparred. He was trying to be constructive. But in a way she wished he hadn't changed the subject. Mitch was starting to open up, let her see past the tiny crack in his shell. The man she saw interested her.

"How about another beer?" she said, hoping to delay just a bit the point where they'd get down to business.

"Being in law enforcement, I try to drink modestly while driving."

"I'll drive, if that's a concern," she said.

"I thought you wanted to unwind."

"A few sips of wine usually does the trick."

"You're a cheap drunk, Mrs. Kirk."

"I'll have you know this is the most expensive cheap jug wine money can buy!"

Giving him a challenging look, she got up to get him another beer. She was on her way to the kitchen when the telephone rang. Out of habit she checked the caller ID device. The number looked familiar, but she couldn't place it. She picked up the phone.

"Dana, a dozen roses will be delivered tomorrow, but I hope you'll give me your forgiveness tonight," Frank Betts said. "I was an ass, going up to your place like I did. And I want to apologize. I hope I didn't give you a scare."

"Frank," she said, "what were you doing?" She glanced over at Mitch.

"Being an idiot. You know what a sentimental slob I can be. I was out driving in the rain, I had *Willow Creek* on the CD player, and the next thing I knew I was going up your hill. Don't ask me what I expected to accomplish. I didn't even give serious consideration to ringing your bell. I was about to leave when you came out.''

She was stunned by the abjectness of his apology. "It wouldn't have been such a big deal if I hadn't been having problems with a stalker.''

"Yes, I heard about that today, Dana. Had I known last night, I wouldn't have done it. That's the truth.''

"Why did you drive away so fast? I thought for sure it was the guy who's been harassing me. People don't run unless they're guilty, Frank.'' She glanced again at Mitch, who looked somewhat bemused.

"I *was* guilty. Guilty of doing something stupid and childish. I was embarrassed at the thought of being there and even more embarrassed at the thought of being caught. So I just took off. I didn't expect you to follow, and when you did, it only made my embarrassment worse. I'm sorry.''

"It's over now, Frank, we can forget about it. I appreciate you calling, though. Under the circumstances, it was thoughtful. And it couldn't have been easy for you.''

"Will you indulge me a few minutes more?'' Frank asked.

"Sure.''

"I'd like to talk business, if that's all right with you.'' Dana looked at her watch, then at Mitch, who was taking it all in.

"Okay, I'll discuss business, if you wish, but I don't have time for a long discussion. I've got a dinner engagement.''

"I'll be brief.'' He cleared his throat. "I guess I'd be less than gracious if I didn't compliment you on your competitive skills, Dana. I thought you'd be successful, but I didn't think it would be at our expense. At least, not to this degree.'' He laughed nervously. "Our Kentfield office will be empty in a month at the rate you're going.''

"I know you too well, Frank," she said, "you're not calling to surrender. What's on your mind?"

"Let me take you to lunch."

"What for?"

"To talk," he said.

"About what?"

"Do we need a formal agenda? Isn't it enough that I'd like to discuss topics of mutual interest?"

"It may be what I've been going through lately," she said, "but I've gotten a little paranoid. Somehow this is sounding like a conversation from *The Godfather*. You aren't planning on sending a hit man in your place, are you?"

He laughed. "Are things really that bad between us?"

"Maybe I should ask you," she replied.

"They aren't. Trust me, Dana."

"Trust is something I've been very short of recently."

"Hey, Lane and I don't have hard feelings. Screwing the competition is the American way."

"So why lunch?"

"The official answer is to discuss bank business. The unofficial reason is I wouldn't mind seeing you someplace beside the Board of Realtors breakfast meeting."

"I think you've already demonstrated that, Frank. But listen, don't make me talk about my feelings," she said. "You know how I feel."

"Yes, I do." He drew a deep breath. "All right. It will be strictly business, if that's the way you want it. On my honor as a gentleman. Just lunch and a business discussion."

"Okay, fine," she said. "When and where do you want to meet?"

"Does Monday sound overeager?"

"No. What time?"

"Let's make it one-ish, if that's okay. You pick the place, I'll pay."

"Dominick's," she said.

"I'll meet you there."

Dana hung up the phone and turned to face Mitch. "Frank Betts," she said. "He wants to meet for lunch."

"So I gathered."

"He said he wanted to discuss business."

"Did he sound sincere?"

"I guess so," she said, returning to her chair. "Do you think I'm doing the right thing?"

"My theory is the more you talk to people, the more likely it is you'll find out what they're thinking. Unless you have some reason to fear him, I'd say go for it."

"I've never thought of Frank as dangerous. I'm inclined to believe him about last night."

"Then there's your answer."

"What do you recommend, Mitch? Anything in particular I should say?"

"I'd listen carefully and take your cue from him."

"That's what we do in sales. Listening is the key."

"Well, maybe we have more in common than I thought," he said.

Dana looked at him and he returned her gaze. There was a chemistry there and it seemed to be getting stronger. "Oh, I was getting you a beer," she said, rising. "I almost forgot."

"Let's skip it," he said.

"Are you getting hungry?"

"As a matter of fact, yes."

"Then let's go eat."

Mitch got to his feet and Dana led the way toward the front entry hall. She got her coat and he helped her on with it. She took her purse from the table.

"We can go down the inside stairs to the garage," she said. "Back this way."

She turned on the alarm, then led the way down the staircase to the garage. Because Mitch was with her, she opened the garage door before getting into her car, as she usually did. She unlocked the passenger door on the Mercedes, then went around. Mitch had already gotten in and pulled up the door-lock button for her.

"Thanks," she said, climbing in. She put her purse on the floor next to her feet and glanced over at him. "This is the most normal I've felt getting into my car in a month."

"Why's that?"

"I guess I feel safe with you. That's a gift, Mitch. A very nice gift. Thank you for indulging me."

"Hey, you'd be surprised what some guys will do for a free meal."

A smile touched her lips. "You know what? I think your bark is worse than your bite."

"Have I been barking?"

"What I mean is, that tough, sardonic exterior is all for effect. You go out of your way to hide a pretty decent guy."

"Thanks, but it's not what a cop wants to hear. The vicious-bite illusion is one we work hard to maintain. Theater is as important in police work as sales."

"We *do* have a lot in common, Mitch. You may be right about that." She started the car.

The admission was probably too candid, but that was all right with Dana. She was feeling a little reckless. It had been a long time since she'd felt secure enough to take a risk of any kind. And this one felt good.

Ted O'Connell backed deeper into the shadows when he heard the car's engine start. The garage door had been open a minute or two already and he was beginning to wonder what was up. There'd been the sound of two doors slamming. If Bev was here, she could be leaving, possibly with

Dana. He assumed she'd have put her car in the garage. It made sense.

But who belonged to the Bronco parked out front? It wasn't a real-estate car.

When the car's taillights appeared, O'Connell squatted down behind a rhododendron bush. It was Dana Kirk's Mercedes. If Bev was in the car, he wondered if he should risk dashing out to stop them. About then, he saw there was a man in the passenger seat. And Dana was driving. Shit.

O'Connell watched as the vehicle rolled down the drive past the spot where he'd hidden. He got a good look at the guy. It was that detective, Cross.

A surge of anger went through him. What was he doing at Dana's at this time of the night? Fucking her? The remark he'd made at the police station that afternoon about Cross having a hard-on over the bitch had been a joke. He'd taken a shot, but now it looked like he was a prophet. No wonder the bastard got on his case about hanging around Dana.

The Mercedes backed into the road, then proceeded down the hill, its taillights disappearing from sight. O'Connell got to his feet and stared up at the house, which was still lit up like a Christmas tree. Bev could be in there, but he sort of doubted it, now.

Then it occurred to him they might be going to pick Bev up. Maybe he'd hang around for a while longer. Thrusting his hands into the pockets of his windbreaker, O'Connell looked again at the Bronco. Maybe he'd take the opportunity to prepare a surprise for Mitchell Cross. Anybody who gave Ted O'Connell grief should be prepared to get a little in return. That was the way the fucking cookie crumbled.

* * *

Strawberry Manor

Chiara Fiolli descended from the bus at the Town &
Country Village shopping center. From there it was only a
few blocks to her apartment complex. A short walk, though
one she wasn't fond of making at night. As she trudged
along in the cold wind, she thought of winters at home in
Milan—the walk along the boulevards from her school to
the apartment block where she'd lived with her mother and
older sister, Rossella. Winter in northern Italy and northern California were not the same, but they were similar.

When she'd left Milan with Walter Brooks, she was sure
her climb to stardom as a big-time model had begun. Walter claimed to be a fashion photographer, but he'd turned
out to be a phony. He'd earned a living doing photogra-
phy, all right, but he was small-time and a creep to boot. All
he wanted was her body. She had given that in exchange for
his promises of stardom, but she'd ended up with a green
card and little else.

So she'd left New York and headed for California, the
land of opportunity. Everybody in L.A., she soon discovered, was on the make. The guys were worse than in Italy.

Eventually she made it to San Francisco, where she
signed on with a modeling agency. Jobs were scarce so she
supported herself working as a receptionist—first in a hair
salon, then in a law firm, and finally in a stock-brokerage
firm. When she got tired of the men hitting on her, and the
high San Francisco prices, she decided to look for work in
the suburbs, ending up with Dana Kirk.

Now that she was twenty-five, Chiara knew that her
chances of becoming a successful fashion model were
growing slimmer each day. The agency in San Francisco
occasionally got her jobs, but with expenses what they
were, she couldn't earn a living at it—not without a big
break. She'd be facing thirty before long, and there was no

way to turn back the clock. Her chance, she was beginning to realize, had nearly passed her by.

Chiara felt the weight of her failure. Her image of a glorious return to Milan had flickered dimmer with each passing month. The worst had been around the holidays. Her mother had asked her to come home to Milan, even saying she'd ask Rossella, who'd married well, to send her a ticket. Chiara had been too proud to accept. She'd insisted she was too busy modeling to consider a trip back.

In fact, she'd been hopeful of landing a job that would have taken her to Japan for two weeks. She'd gotten her hair styled, bought an expensive new dress at Nordstrom and gone in for the interview, determined to let her star quality show through. But they passed her over, deciding, they'd said, to hire nothing but blondes.

Word of this had come from her agent two days before Christmas—just before Dana had taken the entire office to lunch. Chiara had felt like killing herself right then. Instead she had too much wine and got drunk. Dana had Sylvia drive her directly home from the restaurant.

From the first, Dana had been good to her. Chiara could hardly claim she'd been mistreated. Dana paid her as much as she'd made at the brokerage firm, though salaries were lower outside the city. Dana had given her a clothing allowance, had arranged for her to get a deal on her apartment because she owned a part of the building, and even gave her time off when she had a modeling assignment. But in a way, it was like charity. Chiara didn't want to spend her life beholden to others. She wanted success in her own right.

The thing that impressed her most about Dana was that she was smart and strong and she'd made her own money, instead of marrying it. Still, Dana reminded her of her older sister. Dana was prettier and not so arrogant as Rossella, but she had the same way of making Chiara feel inferior. In a way, Dana's success made her own failure all the more apparent.

Chiara noticed a young man in a passing car check her out as he drove by. Men were all alike. If they had class or money they wanted a woman with a college education and a good-paying job—secretaries were for sex. And once they heard she did modeling, they were sure she would be easy.

She'd hardly dated since moving to Marin. There was no point. The last guy she'd gone out with who had been nice to her was one of the messengers at the San Francisco stockbrokerage firm. Ed wasn't handsome but he was kind. He had long stringy hair and he reminded her of Gérard Dépardieu. When she found out that he was in love with her she'd ended the relationship. She'd felt sorry for him, and that wasn't enough. She didn't want to hurt him.

Mostly she stayed home alone or went to the movies, as she had that evening. She'd seen every movie Harrison Ford ever made. At least three times. All day long, though, she'd been thinking about that police detective, Mitchell Cross. She liked his name. And she liked the way he joked with her. He was one man she'd go to bed with, even if all he wanted was to have sex. There were very few men she could say that about, but he really seemed different. He reminded her of Harrison Ford a little. Strong and sensitive.

But he wasn't interested in her. It was Dana he was attracted to. She saw the way he looked at her. And why wouldn't he be interested? Dana was beautiful and she was a millionaire. For a cop, that had to look pretty good. Dana didn't need him, of course. She could have any man she wanted. But that was why they all wanted her.

Chiara had come to her apartment complex. Her little studio was in the first building, ground floor. It wasn't fancy, but it was better than what she could get in the city for the same money.

She went into her apartment and turned on the lights. She took off her jacket and put on the heavy sweater her mother had knit. The utility bills were horrible in the winter, so she kept the heat at sixty-four. It wasn't unbearable. Growing up they'd worn heavy clothes indoors during the winter. Sometimes even mittens. Chiara remembered how hard it had been to use her crayons with them on.

She went to her tiny kitchen and put some water on the stove to make tea. Maybe she'd watch the news before she went to bed. There might be something on about Ted O'Connell. All day she'd thought about the commotion in the office and Dana getting death threats. It was a shock. Yet, oddly, the thought of someone being after Dana— someone mean like Ted O'Connell—pleased her. Chiara knew she ought to feel sorry for her boss, but secretly she was almost glad. It had been like that with Rossella when they were little. She used to amuse herself by imagining her sister dead, picturing what it would be like attending her funeral. The thought never made her sad. It didn't with Dana, either.

San Anselmo

They'd circled the downtown area twice, looking for a parking place. Mitch noted her annoyance and found it amusing. Actually, he found that observing her was an enjoyable pastime under any circumstances. Dana Kirk appealed to him. There was no point in denying the fact.

"What good does it do to have a cop for a friend, if he can't even fix parking tickets?" she muttered. "I've found two perfectly good spaces—or they would have been if it weren't for the fire hydrants."

"Cops have to park in legal spaces like everybody else," he said. "Unless we're in an official vehicle, of course."

"When was the last time you got a traffic ticket?" she asked.

"I guess when I was a kid."

"Have you ever been stopped since you became a policeman?"

"Yeah."

"I rest my case."

Mitch gestured as they approached the next intersection. "Why don't we drive up a side street and park in a residential neighborhood?"

"I guess I don't have to be in a well-lit, public place when you're riding shotgun, do I?"

The remark made him realize how vulnerable she truly was. The most routine act, like parking, required vigilance on her part.

The commercial district of San Anselmo was not large. It was just a village wedged in the hills with a creek running along the main drag. She found a parking place a block and a half from San Anselmo Avenue. They walked back toward the business district.

Dana, who seemed a little nervous, had been talking almost constantly since they had left her house. Now she was saying something about the restaurant she was taking him to, but he hardly listened. He was concentrating more on the unspoken communication, the physical person.

He observed her face change with the shadows from the streetlights. He saw her engaging smile...smelled a whiff of her perfume in the cool air...heard something about vegetarianism and her personal trainer...the pressure of making payroll and keeping the doors of a business open...the click of her heels on the sidewalk—and then he realized her monologue had stopped.

"You have a busy life," he said, filling the silence with the first remark to pop into his mind.

"I'm boring you," she said. "I'm sorry."

"You aren't boring me at all."

"Your mind was elsewhere, Mitch. Don't pretend otherwise. I can't blame you, though."

"I was thinking about you, actually."

She looked dubious. "Thinking about me instead of listening to me babbling on?"

They'd come to San Anselmo Avenue and she indicated the way. They crossed the street.

"I'm trying to decide how real you are," he said, explaining what he meant.

"You mean whether I'm a phony?"

"I knew a woman once when I was young, still in high school. She was very charming and I was completely taken by her, really fascinated. In the end it turned out that she was something very different than what I'd thought. The experience made me distrustful of beautiful, sophisticated women, and I tend to get sidetracked on the point."

"Is that a left-handed compliment?"

He laughed. "Yes, I suppose it is. But well intended."

They walked in a companionable silence. He felt like he was on a strange date, unsure what hat he was wearing or was supposed to wear. His instincts kept urging him in the wrong direction—toward greater familiarity. They were flirting with each other, but he didn't understand why, and he didn't think she did, either.

"I believe this is the place he called me from," she said, indicating a tavern they were passing.

"Who? What are you talking about?"

"Didn't I tell you about the calls?"

"I'm aware that somebody's been phoning and hanging up, but—"

"Oh, in all the excitement, I must have forgotten."

She recounted how a friend had given her a caller ID device and how she'd received one call from a service station and another from a bar. She told him about phoning back and talking to the kid and the barmaid.

"I hope I'm not going to get in trouble for having the thing," she said. "You won't arrest me, will you?"

"Arrested by a man who gets his tickets fixed?" he said with a laugh. "No need to worry, but I am very interested in these calls. Did you make a note of the numbers and the times when the calls were made?"

Dana told him that she had.

He asked if she'd give him the information when they got back to her place. "It might be useful to drop by and talk to the folks at those locations," he explained.

"Poor Mitch, you can't go out to dinner without having to think about work, can you?"

"It comes with the territory. But you must do the same in real estate."

"A good agent always has her ears open for somebody with a need."

"There you go," he said.

"Let's make a deal. During dinner I won't talk about real estate or my problems and you won't talk about police work or the case. And we'll try not to think about it, either."

"I thought the purpose of this was to discuss security," he reminded.

"It is, but let's wait and discuss it over coffee."

"What *do* we talk about, then?"

"That's the challenge."

Mitch thought. "I suppose I can tell you about my horse, my dream ranch. What do you have?"

"My daughter."

"What else?"

Dana pondered the question. "That may be something I have to work on. I don't particularly like the alternatives that come to mind."

"Life has a way of standing up and slapping you in the face every once in a while, doesn't it?"

"Have you been slapped in the face recently?" she asked.

Mitch reflected. That wistful, lonely night of sex with Carole came to mind, as had other empty nights with her warm body beside him, and the many women who'd preceded her—years of other women. He hadn't anguished over his life-style, rather he'd accepted it as a given. Now he saw it in a different light for the first time, and realized he might be more unhappy than he'd even known.

"Yeah. I've been slapped in the face," he said, as a gust of wind blew up the street, making him shiver. But he didn't elaborate on his response.

San Rafael

David watched Molly shuffle the cards. He glanced over at the scorepad by her elbow. He was so distracted he'd lost track of where they were in the game. She must have ginned three or four times in a row.

"Last chance, Dad," she said, starting to deal, "if you want to keep me from sweeping all three games."

"Can't have that, can we?" He began picking up the cards.

The queen of hearts. It made him think of Nola Betts's rubescent lips. Everything made him think of Nola.

He glanced up at his daughter. Thankfully she'd been cavalier about the doll being left outside her window. It had upset him and Dana much more. They'd talked about it and decided Molly shouldn't be left alone and that he'd have to be even more vigilant. Yet, short of hiring a bodyguard, there wasn't a lot more they could do.

David became aware of the kitchen window and got up from the table to close the blind. He returned to his place and picked up the last of his cards.

Molly had finished dealing and turned over the top card on the deck. "Your play, Dad."

David studied his hand. He quickly regrouped his cards. Molly drummed her fingers, waiting for him.

"Are you worried about Mom?" she asked.

"She's going through a rough time, so, naturally I'm concerned for her. I'm also concerned about you."

"Personally, I think it's all a game," she said.

"Oh?"

She studied her cards. "I think it's Frank Betts."

"Frank Betts? Why?"

"Because Mom dumped him."

"Your mother dated him for a while, Molly. That's hardly—"

"Dad, how can you be so naive? They were lovers!"

David felt the color rising in his face—not so much because of what Molly said, as the fact that she was saying it. They had talked a little about Dana and Frank back when they were seeing each other, but in more subtle, euphemistic terms. Now Molly's remark brought home the fact that the woman he'd had coffee with that afternoon was the former wife of the man they were discussing. Good old Sigmund would have had a field day with this one!

"Just because they were involved, doesn't mean Frank's the one who's been harassing your mother."

"I know it was him," she said. "Your turn."

David mindlessly drew a card, then discarded another with equally little thought. "What makes you so sure?"

"It smells like Frank." She took his discard and put down another.

"Oh? Why's that?" David studied his hand without seeing it.

"Don't you ever just know something, Dad?"

"The older I get, the more I doubt my infallibility," he said. In the context of Nola Betts, his remark struck him as ironic, even stupid. He knew why she fascinated him; he knew he could explain her away, but he was powerless to do so. No, that wasn't right. He had the power to do it; he lacked the desire.

"Your turn," Molly said.

He drew another card, making a triplet. He discarded a solitary ace, which Molly immediately picked up. She put down a king on the discard pile.

"Well, I bet it turns out to be Frank," she said.

"Why don't you like him?"

"He's a jerk." She shivered, as though a disgusting thought had gone through her mind.

"You're entitled to your opinions, but be careful who you say them to."

"Mom knows I hate Frank. To be honest, I think she does, too. I don't think she ever liked him. Play, Dad."

David picked up the king and discarded the queen of diamonds. Molly snatched it up, giving back the nine of clubs.

His daughter's insights, prejudiced though they might be, surprised him. "Maybe you wouldn't like *any* man your mother went out with," he said, drawing from the deck.

"No, that's not true. I don't care what she does. I just didn't like Frank. He's a phony."

He discarded. Molly drew, discarded onto the pile, facedown, and announced gin. "I think this wipes you out," she said. "What have you got?"

He put his cards down on the table. She calculated the hand.

"Yep. I swept you."

David looked at his watch. "I wasn't much competition. Sorry."

"That's okay. Winning is good for my ego." She laughed and gathered the cards.

"I think I'll read for a while."

"I've got to read a book for English," she said. "Ugh."

"Seems like you're all right, honey."

Molly shrugged and got up, taking the deck of cards. "If you mean the doll, I didn't take it personally."

"I'm glad you're handling it well. But I still want you to be careful, Molly. You could be wrong about it being Frank."

"Don't worry, Dad."

He patted her hand. Molly left the kitchen and headed for her bedroom. David remained at the table. He pictured Nola in his mind and wondered if it was the time of life he happened to be in that made him feel such a strong sexual desire. He couldn't really say he was lonely, but not much had been going on apart from work and helping Dana cope with Molly. Maybe his need was greater than he'd realized.

He got up, left the kitchen and went back to Molly's door. She was digging through her book bag.

"Honey, didn't you say you had a school project you were doing with Tiffany?"

"Yes, a biology project. Why?"

"Is there any chance you could work on it with her at her house tomorrow night?"

"Why?"

"I have to go out to a dinner. I was planning on leaving you alone, but I promised your mother I wouldn't."

"I guess I could. But I have to call her in the morning. Her mother won't let her talk on the phone this late."

"I'd appreciate it if you would."

"What kind of dinner do you have to go to on a Sunday night?"

"It's a business dinner. A colleague from the seminar."

"Oh."

David felt a sudden pang of guilt. He didn't like lying to Molly. He didn't like lying at all. The only time he did was with a client when there was a compelling clinical reason.

Turning from his daughter's door, he went to the front room where he sat in his chair, more certain than ever that he was going to have an affair with Nola. Maybe there was a good "clinical" reason for it, too; and if so, he was beginning to realize it had to do with him.

San Anselmo

Mitchell Cross had finished his steak and the waitress took his plate away. Dana had been watching him, trying to figure out what was going on in his mind. He was one of the more confounding men she'd ever known. One minute he was flirting with her, the next he seemed annoyed. At times he went out of his way to keep his distance, then he would cozy up like a longtime friend.

They'd come to Bill's, a steak and fish place that she and Molly often went to when Dana didn't feel up to cooking. The fact that Mitch was a meat-and-potatoes guy was reason enough to bring him here, not to mention the fact that an exotic or romantic place wouldn't have sent the right signal. The ambience that was called for was down-to-earth and wholesome.

Bill's was about as down-home a place as you could find in Marin. The walls were wood paneled and there were a number of ceiling fans. It had the usual array of booths and tables, yet the decor was eclectic and without a notable theme. If nothing else, that saved it from having the numbing sameness of a chain restaurant.

The highlight of the place for Molly was their make-your-own sundae dessert. But Dana liked Bill's because of its homey frenzy. Normally dishes would be clanking, waitresses would be calling out orders, children could be heard yammering for dessert, dads would sit back contentedly, overseeing their brood while mothers wiped runny noses. But since it was late, Bill's was relatively quiet. There were no children present and, by the time they'd finished eating, only a handful of couples and solitary diners remained.

"Can I ask you a personal question?" Dana said after a long silence.

"If it's not too personal."

"Well, it is, but I'll try anyway. Do you have a lady friend?"

"Do you have a gentleman friend?" he returned, not missing a beat.

"No."

"Hmm . . ."

She waited.

"Well," he said, "I've been seeing someone for a couple of months, but it's not a serious relationship. Why do you ask?"

"I don't know. I was just curious. Nosy, I guess." She fiddled with her water glass. "Does your lady friend regard it as equally unserious?"

"I'll bet you don't do this with your clients," he said, draining the last of his beer.

"No, of course not. I wouldn't be *that* rude," she added with a chuckle.

"So, why do I rate?"

"I don't know. I guess I was curious if you play games. Men do that to protect themselves. But I shouldn't have let my curiosity get to me. Especially considering your relationships are none of my business. If I offended you, just forget I said anything."

"I'm not offended, but I am curious about your curiosity. Talk to me some more."

Dana regretted she'd said anything. She'd been a little too honest and began searching for a way to back down. "Maybe we should change the subject."

"That only makes things worse," he said.

She sighed. "In trying to understand you, Mitch, I started thinking out loud. It was a mistake."

"Might as well finish. Give me your analysis."

She didn't want to, but she could see she couldn't very well turn back now. "Okay," she said, "I have a feeling you're the sort of guy who's made a career out of breaking hearts. Perhaps not intentionally, but you do it just the same."

"I think maybe you've been listening to too many country-and-western songs."

"I don't listen to any, actually."

"Maybe *I've* been listening to too many, then."

"That says an awful lot right there," she said.

Mitchell Cross grinned at her. There was a dash of guilt in his eyes. And maybe a touch of embarrassment, as well.

"So tell me about your lady friend."

He wiped his mouth with his napkin and leaned back on the leather banquet. He crossed his arms, contemplating her. "You really want to hear?"

"Yes. I wouldn't have asked otherwise."

Mitch rolled his tongue around in his cheek as he considered how to respond. "Her name is Carole and she says her feelings toward me are the same as mine are toward her," he said. "If we were married, it would be a marriage of convenience. It's not—what's the term?—a committed relationship. We have a—I'm not sure how to put it—a special kind of friendship."

Dana looked down at her hands.

"Does that satisfy your curiosity?" he asked.

"I shouldn't have pressed you."

"Don't worry about it. The truth is the truth. Somewhere along the line I learned there's not much to be gained by trying to avoid it. In the end it's always there, isn't it?"

She gave an embarrassed shrug. "Far be it from me to pass judgment, Mitch."

"Everybody passes judgment all the time. It's in the character of the human race."

"You're a philosopher on top of everything else."

"Am I pontificating?" he asked.

"No, I don't mind at all. In fact, it's rather refreshing." She wasn't going to tell him how much she liked it that he was different, not just a run-of-the-mill sort of guy.

"I guess that goes to show the passing of judgment isn't necessarily bad," he said.

There was whimsy in his eyes. She liked that, too. But the growing intimacy was beginning to feel a little uncomfortable. She'd ordered a glass of Chenin Blanc with her swordfish and had drunk less than half. She picked up the wineglass and took a long sip. Then she glanced around the dining room, avoiding his scrutiny. "Maybe we should discuss security."

"Whatever you wish."

"Did you want to fix yourself a sundae?" She'd already told him about the sundaes and how fond Molly was of the hot fudge.

"I think I'll pass."

The waitress came to clear the dishes. Dana asked for coffee and Mitch said he'd have a cup, as well. Once a couple of steaming coffees were before them, she felt better.

"Here's my concern," she said, fingering her cup. "After that business with Ted this morning, and the armless doll being hung on Molly's window, I began wondering if I should take any special steps. I thought you could help me review my options."

"Are we talking about at the office or at home?"

"Both."

"There's never a way to make yourself absolutely safe, not without locking yourself in a bunker. The more you're out and about, the more difficult it becomes."

"I don't want to change my life-style. I have to go about my business as usual. That's very important. My salespeople are nervous enough as it is. I've got to appear confident and unafraid."

"You're saying you want security, but won't change anything to get it."

"Can't it be done unobtrusively?"

Mitch gave her a sardonic grin. "You're worse than a politician, Dana."

"All right, you know my situation. What do you recommend? What would you do if you were in my shoes?"

"I'd get a security guard at the office. Fancy jewelry stores do it. True, it would be a visible precaution, but I'm not so sure that's bad. Seems to me you want to discourage the bastard or bastards. If O'Connell comes by, he might think twice about coming in with a guard on duty. And rather than scaring your people, it might make them feel more secure."

Dana sipped her coffee. "You make a convincing argument. What about home?"

"I'd have a security guard there, too, at night. They can put a car in your driveway. It won't make an unwelcome visit impossible but it will discourage it."

The waitress came with their bill and Dana picked it up immediately. She took her wallet from her purse, removed a credit card and put it down on the corner of the table.

"It's going to be an expensive proposition," Mitch said. "But with luck it won't be for long."

"Is that confidence speaking, or wishful thinking?"

"Plan for the worst, hope for the best, accept what happens. That's my motto."

"In life or in police work?" Dana asked.

"Both, I guess."

She wondered how his friend, Carole, fit into that philosophy, but she certainly wasn't going to ask. "Do you have a particular security company you'd recommend?'' she asked.

''I can give you a name. A former deputy sheriff in Marin County who opened his own security agency a few years ago. Bob Howard. I don't know him well, but people I respect speak highly of him. I believe his company is called North Bay Security and Investigation. He's in the book.''

The waitress came and took the bill and Dana's credit card.

''What's your feeling about Molly?'' she asked. ''How serious is the danger?''

''I wouldn't let her run around alone in public.''

''David and I have already agreed on that. Do you think I should hire somebody to guard David's place at night?''

''My gut instinct is that it would be overkill, but then there's always a chance that it could make a difference. If your secret admirer follows up with more threats aimed at Molly, then I'd beef up security for her. But right now I think the guy's aim is to unnerve you, and he's using whatever means he can find.''

Dana shivered, rubbing her arms. ''What a decision to have to make.''

''I could talk to the patrol commander about running a black-and-white up and down the street three or four times a night. It could discourage anybody watching the place.''

The waitress brought back the credit-card slip. Dana added a tip and signed the slip, tearing off a copy.

''I'd appreciate anything you can do along those lines,'' she said. ''But I think I'll talk to David in the morning about hiring a security guard. He'll expect me to pay for it, but that's all right.''

''You're starting to talk big bucks.''

''What can I spend my money on that's more important?''

"I guess it can come in handy. Money, I mean."

"Believe me, I'd rather not have any than have to spend it to protect my daughter's life."

"Funny how things get turned upside down, isn't it?"

"Seems like everybody's meant to be slapped in the face by fate every once in a while," she said.

"Maybe."

"Have you been slapped around by fate much?" she asked.

"Same as everybody else, I suppose. But I don't think we want to talk about it."

"Wash my mouth out," she said. "I promised myself I wouldn't do that again. Sorry." She slid out of the booth and so did Mitch.

He helped her on with her coat. She glanced at him.

"Thanks for being indulgent," she said.

"Thanks for the dinner."

They headed for the exit. When they came to the door, Mitch opened it for her, touching her waist as he ushered her through. It was the first time, other than shaking hands, that he'd touched her.

San Rafael

Ted O'Connell went east on Third Street, passing under the freeway. He turned right on Grand Avenue, then went to Francisco Boulevard, the frontage road running along the north side of the freeway. At Harbor he made a left and went to the entrance of the yacht harbor. He parked the Porsche under the streetlight as he'd been told. Then he waited.

After a minute he turned on the radio. The Warriors and Suns were in the last quarter, the score was close. Chris Mullin hit a three, putting the Warriors in the lead. Charles Barkley slammed at the other end, putting the Suns back on top. Ted's stomach clenched. Listening to basketball made him more nervous than any other sport. A case of the nerves was all he needed just then, so he spun the dial, looking for a soothing sound, but ended up shutting the damned thing off.

Ted kept his eye on his rearview mirror, hoping this wasn't going to turn into a wild-goose chase. Donnie promised him this guy could be trusted. He checked the clock on the dash. Five minutes late.

He tapped his fist nervously on the steering wheel and looked around. Reaching behind the seat, he found the six-pack and pried loose a can. Popping it open, he took one long swig, then another.

He'd just put the can on the floor between his feet when there was a tap on his window. It scared the shit out of him and he jumped. It was a guy. He was standing close to the window. Ted couldn't see much besides his pants and Levi's jacket. His head was above the window. Ted lowered it. The guy leaned over and peered in at him. He was younger than he'd expected. He had zits and stringy hair.

"You O'Connell?" the guy said.

"Yeah, I'm O'Connell."

"Open the passenger door."

Ted leaned over and pulled up the door-lock button. The guy went around the car, opened the door and climbed in. He smelled like onions and tobacco.

"You got the piece?" Ted asked.

"Let's see your money."

O'Connell took five one-hundred-dollar bills from his hip pocket, unfolded them carefully, but kept them clenched in his fist. The guy took a package wrapped in brown paper from under his jacket. Breaking the tape, he unwrapped it, holding the chrome-plated 9-mm automatic in his hand.

"That baby can't be traced?"

"How long do you think I'd be in business if I didn't deliver what I promised?"

"Yeah, but if you didn't I might not be around to complain about it."

"Look, O'Connell, you going to give me shit, or what?"

Ted held out the five bills. The guy took them, checked each one, and handed the gun over.

"What about the ammo?"

The guy took a box of shells from inside his jacket and put it in Ted's hand. "Pleasure doing business with you," he said.

"Thanks for coming up."

"I like the view from the Golden Gate at night. Look, do me a favor and wait here for a couple of minutes before you leave, okay?"

"Sure."

The guy opened the car door. "If you need anything else down the line, Donnie knows how to get ahold of me."

"Thanks."

The skinny pimply-faced guy got out, shut the door and walked toward the rear of the Porsche. Ted watched him in the mirror until he disappeared up the dark street. Then he picked up the can of beer and put the pistol and the shells under the seat. He took a long drink and turned the Warriors game back on. The Suns were up by four.

"Shit," he said, and turned the radio off. Draining the rest of his beer, Ted tossed the can into the street and started the engine.

He turned the Porsche around and went back the way he'd come. There was no sign of the guy anywhere. Ted heaved a sigh of relief. He had his gun and was ready to play this game his way.

*   *   *

Ross

They were headed south along Sir Francis Drake Boulevard when Dana's car phone rang.

"The life of a broker," she said to Mitch, as she picked up the receiver. "It's worse than being a drug dealer."

He chuckled.

"Hello."

"Dana, it's Bev."

"Hi, Bev, how are you?"

"I'm okay. Sorry to bother you when you're out, but I wanted to make sure I talked to you tonight."

"Is something wrong?"

"I'm going to pick up my things at the house tomorrow and I was wondering if you'd go with me. Sylvia has out-of-town clients she'll be with all day."

"Of course I will, Bev."

"Sylvia thinks the police would probably be willing to be there just in case Ted causes trouble. Do you know anything about that?"

"I'm sure it can be arranged. In fact, let me handle it. What time do you want to go?"

"Eleven okay?"

"Fine. Shall I pick you up at Sylvia's?"

"If you don't mind."

"I'll be there at ten-thirty."

"Oh, Dana, did you hear?" Bev asked.

"What?"

"Ted was on a rampage tonight, looking for me. He called the office at least ten times, trying to coerce people into telling him where I was. He upset everybody."

"Well, don't worry about it. He'll calm down once he knows you're serious."

"I don't know. Ted's weird about things like that."

"You get a good night's sleep, honey. We'll deal with Ted in the morning."

Dana hung up and glanced over at Mitch.

"Mrs. O'Connell?" he said.

"Yes. She was pretty upset." Dana recounted the conversation and asked him whether the police would accompany them to Bev's house.

"Sure. I can arrange it. In fact, if I can borrow your phone, I'll do it now."

Dana handed him the phone and listened as he spoke with the watch commander. She guided the Mercedes up her hill. Mitch hung up the phone.

"Done," he said.

"I appreciate all your help, Mitch. You've really gone the extra mile for me and I'm deeply grateful."

"Hey, anything for a taxpayer."

Dana chuckled. "This has been a long day."

Mitch checked his watch. "Just over eighteen hours."

"Oh, Lord. How long is your drive home?"

"This time of night, under an hour. But that's okay. I've got tomorrow off."

"Lucky man."

They were nearing the top of the hill. Dana slowed. She was happy that Mitch was with her—for once she didn't feel the usual trepidation of arriving home alone. In fact, if she wasn't sure he'd decline, she'd invite him in. He had to be dead tired. God knows, she was.

They came to the driveway and Dana drove up it, stopping as she always did to wait for the garage door to lift. She glanced over at Mitch's Bronco and blanched. The windshield had been smashed in and the tires were slashed.

"Christ," Mitch said, seeing it at the same time. He got out of the car and went over to his vehicle.

Dana drove the Mercedes into the garage, then walked back out to where Mitch was inspecting the Bronco.

"Looks like your secret admirer isn't any more fond of your friends than he is of you," he said.

"Oh, Mitch, I'm so sorry. You don't deserve this."

He glanced up at the house. "Doesn't look like anything else has been vandalized."

"So, what was the point?"

Mitch shook his head. "Who knows? I suppose it's possible this wasn't even meant for you. It could have been somebody who was unhappy with me."

"But that means it would have to be somebody who knew you were here and who would recognize your car."

"There's no way to know for sure. I'll get a technician up. It could be that our friend got careless and left some prints or other physical evidence."

They looked at each other. Dana felt as badly as she knew Mitch felt. "I'm turning into the kiss of death for everybody I come into contact with," she said.

He managed a weary smile. "I'm not giving up on you yet," he said.

Dana couldn't help herself. She stepped over and gave him a big hug. Mitch held her for a minute as the cool wind blew against them. Despite everything, the affection felt good.

They parted then. "I guess we'd better go inside so you can call," she said. "I'll make a pot of coffee."

"And I'd better see if I can get a rental car delivered. I won't be driving that baby tonight."

They went in through the garage and up the inside stairs. It occurred to her that she could invite him to stay the night. She would have liked knowing he was in the house, but it seemed like an awfully big step, despite the sacrifices he'd made for her.

"This has been a day I won't want to relive anytime soon," she said, unlocking the upstairs door and turning off the alarm.

"It had its ups and downs," Mitch said. "At least I got a free dinner."

"And I'm paying the deductible on your auto insurance."

"It's only fifty dollars."

"Fifty bucks is fifty bucks," she said, leading the way to the family room."

"To tell you the truth, I'd rather have another steak dinner."

Dana tossed her purse on a chair and proceeded to remove her coat. "I think you're entitled to both, Detective Cross. Fifty bucks *and* a steak dinner."

"Hey, this may not be such a bad day, after all."

She pointed to the phone. "Make your call."

Four

Ross
Sunday, March 1

Robin Cohen went from the empty guest room to the master suite. It, too, was empty, though the impressions were in the carpet where the furniture had stood. The cleaning women hadn't quite gotten out all the traces of the previous occupants. The closet still had a faint smell of body odor, though it was mostly masked by disinfectant. What was it about a vacant house that was so sad? Did the emptiness suggest an absence of life?

Robin shook her head. She was being too philosophical for eight-thirty on a Sunday morning. She retreated to the hallway, popping her head into the guest bath long enough to check colors and the condition of the tile.

As she made her way back downstairs, she wondered how long she'd been in the place. Three minutes? She couldn't preview a property without thinking of the first time Dana had taken her on tour. They'd seen eight houses spread from Mill Valley to Terra Linda in an hour and twenty minutes, including driving time. It was incredible how quickly Dana moved. Robin practically had to run just to keep up with her. "Why bother touring?" Robin had asked. "It's all a blur. I don't remember a thing."

"Every woman is born observant," Dana had replied, "but you have to train yourself to take it in quickly. The only time you slow down is when you're with clients. Nobody wants to be rushed when they're buying a house. Just remember when you're scouting, you're not a buyer."

And to prove how observant she could be in fast motion, Dana had given Robin a rundown of the color schemes, basic layout and prominent features of all eight houses. Not surprisingly, she'd proceeded to sell one of them within three days of their whirlwind tour.

Robin left the house, putting the door key back into the lockbox before returning to her car. After the daylong respite in the weather, another storm had moved in and it was starting to drizzle. She consulted her notepad. The next place on her list was on Alta Terrace in Corte Madera. She checked her watch. She was in lower Ross, only a couple of blocks from Dana's street. She decided to give her a call.

Robin took her cellular phone from her briefcase and dialed. While it was ringing, she started her car and pulled into the street. Dana picked up the phone in the middle of her recorded message.

"Hey, hotshot," Robin said, "what are you doing home? I've already previewed two houses for my buyers from Dallas. You getting lazy in your old age?"

"Hi, Robin. No, I'm hand-holding this morning. I'm going with Bev to pick up her things in an hour or so."

"The rigors of managing an office."

"You got that right, sweetie."

"Have you got the coffeepot on?" Robin asked. "I'm at the bottom of your hill, haven't had breakfast, and could use a shot of caffeine."

"If you can take my coffee, and me without makeup, on an empty stomach, you're welcome to come on up."

"You're just getting up? My God, what happened? Did you get laid last night?"

"No, but I didn't get to bed until nearly two in the morning. I was entertaining the police."

"What happened?"

"Come on up and I'll tell you about it."

Robin proceeded up Dana's street, wondering what could have happened now. The entire Marin real-estate community was talking about the problems over at Kirk & Company. She'd have expected Dana to sound depressed, in need of a lift. But she seemed her old self. It had to be that Kirk resilience.

Robin pulled into Dana's drive. Getting out of her car, she noticed what looked like broken glass on the pavement. Dana was waiting for her at the open front door. Robin took in the smell of coffee wafting out from the kitchen. It was especially nice, considering the dank weather.

"Is that glass down on the driveway?" she asked, stepping inside.

"Yes," Dana said, closing the door and turning the dead bolt. "Somebody vandalized Mitch's car—he's the detective on the case—while we were out to dinner."

"Lord," Robin said, "I feel like I walked into the middle of a movie. You went to dinner with the cop?"

"It's a two-cups-of-coffee story. Come on in."

They went back to the kitchen. Robin sat on a stool at the counter while Dana poured her some coffee. Dana also got a sweet roll from the refrigerator, but Robin pushed it away.

"You skinny broads love to wave around pastries. Why is that? Give you some kind of sugar rush?"

"Molly eats them, not me." Dana sipped her coffee. "Did you hear about Ted O'Connell coming to my office and trying to drag Bev off by the hair?"

"Honey, that's old news. I called when I heard, but I never was able to reach you, either at the office or at home. And last night I was out. I went to a party in the city."

"Oh?"

"Nothing worth talking about," Robin said, with a wave of her hand. "But tell me about this Mitch."

"There's a lot more." Dana filled her in on the details about the confrontation with Ted, and how Mitch Cross had arrived shortly after Ted left. Then she told her about the armless doll outside Molly's window at David's, Ted's arrest and subsequent release. She skipped quickly over her dinner with Mitch, but described their discovery of the vandalism when they got back from the restaurant.

"Hell of a way to meet a man," Robin said.

"You know the funny thing is, he's an awfully nice guy."

Robin gave Dana an inquiring look. "You aren't depressed. I see a hint of a smile when you should be in tears. Something tells me this cop is more than just a nice guy."

"Oh, don't be silly. He *is* nice, yes. He's also compassionate and kind."

"Kind? *David* was kind."

Dana shook her head. "Not that kind of kind."

"Oh, you mean the kind of kind with great buns."

"In my condition you're a lot more aware of compassion than broad shoulders, believe me," Dana said.

"Yeah, sure. Tell me another."

"No, it wasn't that sort of thing. We talked a lot, which is not surprising, considering we were together for hours. I'd say we got to know each other pretty well. We're friends."

Robin knew telltale signs when she heard them and these were telltale signs. "So, what does Mitch look like?"

"He's good-looking. Quite attractive, actually."

"Uh-huh." Her interest was really piqued now. She scooted to the edge of the stool. "How old?"

"Late thirties."

"Not married?"

"No."

"But he's a cop. Not the job profile you find at the top of most women's list."

"Oh, Robin, it's not that sort of thing. Really. We're from different planets, but it's not because of his job. The guy's got a chip on his shoulder about money. But we sort of laugh about it."

"You talked about stuff like that?"

"We talked about a lot of things."

"Listen, Kirk, I know you. If you spent that much time talking to the guy, you weren't just being sociable. And if he's a cop, he's probably not in the market for property. At least not around here. That only leaves one thing."

"It's not like that, Robin."

She gave Dana a long, hard look. "You like the guy. You like the guy a lot. It's all over your face."

"Of course I *like* him. But it's not what you think."

"Why?"   .

"Because . . . like I said, we're . . . very different. I annoy him. And frankly, he annoys me at times, too. He lives up in Sonoma and has a horse. He thinks I'm a spoiled rich bitch from Marin."

"He said that?"

"No, but I can tell he thinks it. Underneath the politeness and compassion, there's . . . resentment. Disdain, maybe."

"Well," Robin said, "you *are* a spoiled rich bitch, but that doesn't keep *me* from liking you. He might feel the same as I do."

"Thanks. Maybe I ought to introduce *you* to the guy, since you have so much in common. Who knows? Your elusive Mr. Wonderful might be a cowboy with a star on his chest, Robin."

"Somehow he doesn't sound quite right for me," she said. "Sheep don't get along too well in cattle country, especially if the lamb in question is a Jewish princess. Thanks for thinking of me, though.'' Robin noted the bemused expression on Dana's face. She could tell there was another mischievous thought rolling around in her head. ''What, Kirk?''

''My head isn't the only one Mitch has turned.''

''Yeah?''

''I had a call from Liz Rogers this morning. She was following up, making sure everything was going all right and so forth.''

''And?''

''Well, we talked about Mitch.'' A little smile touched the corners of Dana's mouth. ''If it wasn't so ridiculous, I'd say she has a crush on him.''

''Liz Rogers? She's pregnant!''

''A woman's body doesn't go comatose just because she's pregnant, Robin.''

''Do you think they were an item?'' Robin asked, her mouth sagging open.

Dana considered that. ''I don't think so. They spent a lot of time together working on a case sometime back. I imagine Liz did some fantasizing at the time. And, well, being married to Martin...''

''Yeah, he's definitely a schmuck. I know that much about him.'' She grinned. ''So Liz has a crush on your cowboy, too.''

''I suppose it shows the man has wide appeal.''

''It also sounds like he has champagne taste in women.''

''I admit it's reassuring to know that other women see the same virtues in a man.''

''So, tell me, is there a future in all this?'' Robin asked.

''Mitch is a nice diversion,'' Dana replied, ''but I've got a lot more important things to worry about. Today is going to be another bitch, I can tell.''

''I don't want to add to your misery,'' Robin said, taking a sip of coffee, ''but you might want to put a little time in at the office patting butts. Rumors are flying fast and furious. I had calls from a couple of different people asking me if your ship is sinking.''

"Really?" Dana looked surprised.

"And just before I left for the city last night, I got a very surprising call. Lane Cedrick.''

"Lane?"

"Yeah. You know how many times Lane has called me since I've been at C&B?" Robin held up her hand, making a circle of her fingers and thumb.

"What did he want?"

"Nothing. Just wanted to see how I was getting along."

Dana adjusted the belt on her robe. "They're afraid you're going to jump ship. They don't want the cancer to spread to the Corte Madera office. That's all.''

"No, I don't think that's it.''

Dana seemed to read the insightful expression on her face. "What do *you* think his motive was, then?''

"I think Lane was probing to see where my loyalties lie. It's just a hunch, but I think ol' Lane was wondering if he could find a way to use me against you.''

"Robin, that's ridiculous. What could you do to help Lane and Frank against me?''

"I don't know, but that man's got a woman's mind—no offense intended. He's up to something.''

"You're imagining things."

Robin shrugged. "I've told my story. Do with it as you like." She got up from the stool. "There are houses out there awaiting my inspection. Got to go.''

They walked together to the front door. As Dana opened it, they heard a car roar by and the screech of tires on wet pavement. Dana peered out, craning her neck. When she turned to Robin, she had an ashen look on her face.

"What's the matter?"

"It was a red Porsche."

"So?"

"Ted."

San Anselmo

Two hours later Ted O'Connell sat in the back seat of the police cruiser, looking at the front of his house. His fists were clenched, his teeth grinding. The middle-aged cop in front was trying to get his mind off what was happening.

"So, did you play ball in college or what?" the officer asked.

"Yeah, in college."

"Where?"

"San Jose State."

"I played a little high school ball myself. Offensive line." He laughed. "Hundred-sixty-pound guard. And I was slow as molasses."

"That's great," Ted said sarcastically. He glared in the direction of Dana Kirk's Mercedes, sitting in his drive. The other cop, in a rain slicker, stood next to it, his hands in his pockets, looking bored. Dana had to be the one responsible for the armed escort. Bev wouldn't have brought police to their home on her own.

At that moment he hated Dana Kirk with his very soul. Their lives weren't any of her goddamned business. If it wasn't for her, he and Bev might have already settled things. They might have made up and got laid. It wouldn't have been the first time.

It was misting lightly as Bev came out the front door with two suitcases. Dana was right behind her with two more. They came down the twisting flight of stairs to the drive. Bev seemed shaken, her eyes still red. She looked toward the cruiser, then went to the rear of the Mercedes. Dana opened the trunk.

Ted had a desperate, sinking feeling. How could this be happening? His wife was leaving. Next thing, she'd be serving him with divorce papers. He didn't want that. Bev didn't want that, either. Not in her heart. And she wouldn't go through with it unless somebody talked her into it. Only Dana Kirk had that kind of influence over her.

Ted reached for the door handle. "I've got to talk to my wife."

"Just stay in the car, Mr. O'Connell," the officer said. "This isn't the best time."

"She's *my* wife! I can talk to her any goddamned time I want to!" He got out, and the cop opened his door, as well. The other officer up by the Mercedes reached under his slicker and grabbed hold of the handle of his billy club. He came a step or two down the wet, slippery drive. Ted groaned, knowing he was outgunned. "Bev!" he called out. "Talk to me before you go. Don't just walk out."

Her back was to him. She didn't turn around. She and Dana were putting the last suitcase in the trunk.

The middle-aged cop was standing next to him now. Ted knew not to move. "Bev!" he called out again. "Don't do this, honey. Swear to God, I won't fly off the handle anymore. Stay and talk to me. Please."

She looked over her shoulder at him, appearing terribly distraught. Dana slammed the trunk closed. Bev went to the passenger side of the Mercedes, looking down the drive at him, obviously on the verge of tears.

"Beverly," he pleaded, "don't let them do this to us. Don't let them!"

He saw her wipe her eyes as she waited for Dana to release the automatic door locks. When the button popped up, Bev got in.

Ted couldn't stand it. He started up the drive, but the cop took hold of his arm.

"Hold on, Mr. O'Connell. If your wife wants to leave, that's her right."

The engine of the Mercedes started. Dana Kirk looked over her shoulder and began backing down the drive. The other cop walked alongside the car. The mist turned into a slow drizzle.

Ted felt helpless, yet enraged. As the Mercedes rolled past them, Bev stared straight ahead, tears streaming down her cheeks. The sight was just too much. Ted jerked his arm free and lunged for the car, grabbing the door handle on the passenger side. It was locked.

The Mercedes lurched backward to escape, and Ted brought his fist down on the hood as both cops landed on his back. The next thing Ted knew, he was on the wet cement and the Mercedes was in the middle of the street. The cops had him pinned. Instead of struggling, he looked at Bev, beseeching her. Dana got out of the car and looked toward Ted and the two cops. "Is anyone hurt?"

"Go on, lady," one of them called to her. "Just get out of here."

Ross

Bob Howard, a large gray-haired man of sixty, was waiting at Dana's home when she and Bev O'Connell arrived. He was sitting in his car in the drive and got out to greet them.

Dana shook his hand. "I appreciate you coming on such short notice, Mr. Howard."

"Whenever there's an emergency I try to accommodate people. Besides, who can play golf on a day like this?"

He helped carry the suitcases up to the door. Dana had him wait in the front room while she showed Bev, who was still teary-eyed and had hardly said a thing, to the guest room.

When she returned to the front room, Bob Howard was standing at the window, looking out at the view just as Mitch had the previous evening. That already seemed like a week ago. Howard turned.

"You've got yourself a million-dollar view here, Mrs. Kirk," he said affably. "That probably doesn't begin to cover it though, does it?"

"Ross is expensive, all right."

"Don't need to tell me. I've been around for thirty years. Sheriff's Department before I started doing this."

Dana gestured for him to sit down. She took an adjoining chair. When she'd called she'd briefly explained her situation. He had a few specific questions. Dana answered them as best she could.

"So, the danger seems to be from O'Connell and the person who's been threatening you, which may or may not be one and the same."

"Yes."

"And we're talking ten hours of security presence at your office, daily, and round-the-clock security here at your house."

"Round-the-clock here only as long as Bev's here. Once she's made other living arrangements, it would only be nights here at the house."

"I think the proposal should be based on the maximum schedule and we can amend it as conditions change."

"Mr. Howard, just give me your best price and I'll sign the contract. I'm not getting competing bids. You've come highly recommended and the most important consideration is getting a security guard in place both here and at my office immediately. And as soon as I've talked to my former husband, we may want to add security there to protect my daughter."

"I understand, Mrs. Kirk. I'll just need a few minutes to prepare a contract. I have a form right here in my pocket."

"Fine, I've got some telephone calls to make. Take your time."

Dana went into the family room. She phoned the office and talked to Helene Whitford, who was on floor duty. Dana told her she'd be there in forty-five minutes, so if any of the agents wanted to speak with her she'd be available. Then, she phoned David's again, but still got the machine. Her former husband liked going out for breakfast on Sundays, and though it was already almost noon, she assumed that's where he and Molly had gone. They might also have gone for a drive. Sunday drives had been a tradition in his family and he'd carried it on with Molly.

"It's me again," she said, after the beep. "Please give me a call, David. I'll be at home for another twenty minutes, then at the office. It's a few minutes before noon."

Next she dialed Mitch's number at his home up in Sonoma. He'd written it on the back of his card before leaving last night. It rang and rang. She waited an extra-long time because he'd told her if he was outside it took him a while to get to the phone. Finally he picked it up, giving a breathless hello.

"Didn't wake you, did I?" she said without identifying herself.

"Oh, hi," he said, still catching his breath. Only then did she realize she might have been presumptuous in not identifying herself. "No, I was cleaning out the barn. Up to my ankles in you know what."

"Sounds delightful."

"Were you able to get one of O'Connell's shoes?"

"I asked Bev, but she wouldn't cooperate. Said she didn't want to cause Ted any problems."

"That's rather shortsighted, considering the way he's treated her."

"I know, but when you've been traumatized you don't always think clearly. I tried to explain that my concern was for Molly, but it was hard telling her I was afraid Ted might be involved in terrorizing my daughter. She insisted that Ted is definitely not the one who's been writing the letters.''

"So we came up empty."

"No, not exactly," Dana said, glancing over her shoulder. She lowered her voice. "While Bev was busy packing, I grabbed one of Ted's slippers from the closet and stuffed it in my purse. I don't know if that's as good as a shoe, but it was the best I could do."

"Resourceful little thing, aren't you?"

Dana pictured the expression on his face that went with the tone. The image pleased her. "Well, when your daughter's safety is at stake, you cut corners. Will you be able to use it?"

"Probably not in court, considering it was an illegal seizure. But if there's a significant difference in shoe size, we may be able to eliminate O'Connell as a suspect in the doll charade."

"What if Ted's size is the same as the footprint outside Molly's window?"

"Then we take more direct steps."

"What do I do with the slipper?"

"I'll have a car swing by and pick it up."

"Could you have them go to my office? Bev's here at the house. Anyway, I'm going to be leaving shortly. As soon as I sign Mr. Howard's contract."

"You decided to go ahead with the security-guard arrangement."

"Yes. I'm going to fight this with everything I've got."

"Good for you, Dana."

There was a long silence and she realized that there were mutual feelings passing between them, even over the phone wires. "Well, I'll let you go," she said. "Sorry to have bothered you on your day off."

''Hey, anything for a friend. Besides, every now and then a fella needs a break from shoveling manure.''

''You really are a cowboy, aren't you, Mitch?''

''Yep, little lady, sure am.''

''Well, adios, partner,'' she said. ''I'll let you get back to your shoveling.''

''I'll talk to you tomorrow after I get in the office and have an update from the lab.''

''Okay. And thanks again.''

''Adios, sugar.''

Dana hung up the phone. She stood there for a minute with a smile on her face, thinking how crazy it was that she actually liked the guy.

Larkspur

Helene Whitford had the most professional image of any of the Kirk & Company salespeople. She favored suits over dresses and probably had twenty-five or thirty of various weights and styles. When Dana arrived at the office she found her sitting at the receptionist's desk in a bright red gabardine number with black trim.

Helene was forty-four, had dark brown hair, which she kept short, and normally wore a minimum of jewelry. She was average height and more handsome than pretty. After Sylvia, she was the closest to Dana and the most loyal among the agents in the company.

''Guess who's talked to everybody in the office already this morning?'' she said, as Dana checked her messages.

''Either Adrianne Stevens or Frank.''

''Adrianne. She called me at home and I know she tried to reach Sylvia this morning. She called Judy here half an hour ago, and I imagine Lucille, too.''

"She thinks she sees an opportunity and is desperate to get everybody who jumped ship back again," Dana said casually. She took off her coat.

"Everybody's jumpy, Dana. I wouldn't take it lightly."

"I'm not, believe me. I hired a security company this morning. There'll be a guard here shortly."

"Really?"

"I want everybody to feel comfortable when they're in the office. And I intend to discuss the whole business at the sales meeting tomorrow. But if anybody needs to talk before then, I'm available."

Helene nodded. "That's good."

"How are you doing?"

"I didn't like that business with Ted yesterday."

"I didn't, either."

Helene smiled. "No, I guess you didn't." She glanced toward the bull pen where a single agent, Lucille Fernandez, was talking on the phone. "Well, you don't have to worry about me. Sylvia and I aren't going anywhere unless they burn the place down."

"God forbid."

"Frankly, I'm a little worried about Nancy," Helene said. "She took off after the big to-do yesterday and nobody's seen her since."

"I'll call her. Thanks for the insights, Helene."

Dana went into her office and hung her coat on the hook behind the door. She dumped her briefcase on her desk and dropped heavily into her chair.

She'd maintained a cool demeanor talking to Helene but her stomach was in knots. Helene didn't want to sound alarmist, but Dana recognized the smell of trouble in an office, and this was big trouble. If one salesperson bolted, it wouldn't be disaster as long as everybody else stayed. But if a second toppled, it could start a domino effect.

The only two Dana knew she could count on were Sylvia and Helene. Bev would be a basket case for a few days at least, so she hardly counted. If Nancy, Lucille and Judy jumped ship, Kirk & Company would be reeling. It was essential that she get a grip on this thing now.

She left a message on Nancy Tong's machine and on Judy Povich's, as well. Since Lucille was in the office, she could walk on back and schmooze her a little, but first she'd call David. She dialed his number, but there was still no answer. She didn't leave a message this time, but she was beginning to worry. Gory images came to mind, but she dismissed them. She didn't need that eating at her.

Dana was on her way back to the bull pen when a San Rafael police car pulled up out front. An officer in a yellow rain slicker got out. She grabbed her purse and met him just outside the door. Taking Ted's slipper out of her bag, she handed it to the officer.

"Bet this is the first time you've driven out in a rainstorm to pick up a slipper," she said.

The cop, who was blond and youngish, grinned. "You'd be surprised at some of the things we have to do, ma'am." He put the slipper in his pocket.

"I'd invite you in for a cup of coffee, but we've had so many policemen around here the last couple of days, my people are getting gun-shy."

"I've got to get this back to the lab anyway, ma'am," he said, patting his pocket. "Detective Cross is eager for an analysis."

"Well, thanks for picking it up."

The cop saluted casually and returned to his car. No sooner had he pulled away than a North Bay Security patrol car pulled up, parking conspicuously right at the door. A black man in a light blue uniform got out of the car, putting his hat on. Only then did Dana realize how big he was. He must have been six-four, with a large meaty body.

There was gray at his temples, so he had to be forty or so. He appeared powerful and in excellent condition.

"Kirk & Company," he said, looking at the gold lettering. "This must be the place."

"And you must be my guardian angel."

"I don't know about the angel part, but the rest of it you got right," he said with a laugh.

Dana had been standing outside long enough that she'd gotten cold. The dampness had soaked right through to her bones. She stepped inside and the man followed her. She offered her hand. "I'm Dana Kirk."

"Just the lady I'm suppose to see. I'm James, but the boys call me Big Jim," he said, pumping her hand.

"What do you prefer?"

"James, if you don't mind."

"Then James it is. Let me show you around and introduce you to everyone. What do you need," she asked, heading for the receptionist's desk, "a chair or a desk?"

"I move and sit, move and sit," he replied. "Don't like to stay in one place too long."

"We'll put a chair for you here in the entry, then, and you can wander around as you see fit."

"That'll be fine."

Dana introduced James to Helene. Then she showed him the coffee room and told him to feel free to get a cup whenever he wished. While they were in back, he checked the supply room and the rear door, explaining he liked knowing where all the entrances and exits were.

Lucille Fernandez was just getting off the phone when they got to the sales floor. Dana introduced James, explaining that security would be a top priority in the office. Lucille seemed pleased. James excused himself and headed back toward the entry. Lucille, a chubby woman with perfect clear skin and bright red lipstick and nail polish, admitted to Dana she was relieved. "I hope I never see Ted O'Connell again," she said.

"That's why James is here."

"I've got a listing appointment in a while and I feel a whole lot better going on it," Lucille admitted.

She didn't say it, but Dana understood that to mean Lucille had considered waiting until she moved her license to another broker. The admission was a good sign, but it also showed how fragile things were.

"Where's the property?" Dana asked, deciding talking shop was the best palliative.

"Fairfax," Lucille replied. "Four-bedroom ranch-style in the hills on an acre."

"What price range?"

"Probably upper fours to low fives."

"Let me know how it turns out. I could have somebody for that."

Lucille beamed. "I will. Keep your fingers crossed."

She began packing her briefcase and Dana wandered toward her office. James had installed himself in one of the extra desk chairs at the entrance to the bull pen, but in sight of the front door. He had a cup of coffee in his hand.

"Like your coffee, Mrs. Kirk."

"We aim to please," she said. She glanced at Helene, who smiled.

"So far so good," James said. "By the way, what kind of car does this O'Donald fellow drive?"

"O'Connell," Dana said. "A red Porsche."

"Shouldn't be hard to spot."

"No. Ted's not, either. He's big. Used to play football."

The guard grinned. "That makes two of us. Maybe he's used to being hit."

"He's certainly used to hitting."

The telephone rang and Helene answered it. "Kirk & Company," she said, and after a pause, "Just a moment, please.'' She put her hand over the mouthpiece. "Dana, it's your ex.''

"I'll take it in my office.'' She went into her private sanctuary and closed the door. As she settled in her chair she saw Lucille heading out the door on her way to her appointment, a plastic rain scarf covering her glossy hairdo. Dana picked up the phone.

"Hi, David, how's Molly?''

"Fine. I'm sorry, we probably should have phoned you this morning. We went out to breakfast and drove over to Bodega Bay.''

"I figured it was something like that. No trouble last night?''

"No more dolls or prowlers.''

Dana sighed. "That's a relief.''

"Is that what you were calling about?''

"That and to see if you think we should have some security there at the house.'' She explained the arrangements she'd made with the security company.

"I understand your concern,'' David said, "but I wonder if it might not cause more harm than good. Unless of course, something else happens to indicate the guy's serious.''

"I thought the same thing myself, but I'd hate for something to happen to her in the process of us finding out how serious the situation really is.''

"I'm keeping a close eye on her, Dana. And we had a long talk about the things crazy people can do.''

That made her feel better. "You feel okay about it, then?''

"Yes, I do. Tonight, Molly's studying over at Tiffany's and she's going to spend the night. Mrs. Marks will drive them to school in the morning and I'll be picking Molly up after school.''

"I suppose she'll be safe at the Markses'.''

"You can't let yourself get completely paranoid," David said. "You've got plenty on your plate as it is."

"Easier said than done." But she appreciated his understanding. "Keep me posted, please."

"I will."

Dana hung up. Then she looked around her office realizing that, for the first time in days, nothing immediate was hanging over her head. She could turn her attention to business and try to make some money for a change. It seemed like weeks since she'd done anything constructive. Taking her appointment book out of her briefcase, she made a list of the follow-up calls she needed to make. As she worked, she noticed a flash of motion out front and looked up to see a red Porsche. Her eyes moved to James, who noticed at the same time. He got to his feet and began moving toward the door.

Ted parked and got out of his car. He didn't move; he just stood there, staring at the guard. James stepped outside. The men exchanged words. Dana could see Ted's face and he didn't look too happy. He got back in his car and drove away in a rush.

Dana's heart was pounding. After a few seconds she realized the crisis was over. Getting up, she went to her door. James was returning to his place in the reception area.

"What did he want?" Dana asked.

"The gentleman was looking for his wife. I told him she wasn't here and even if she was, he wouldn't be welcome. I told him if she wanted to see him, she'd call."

"He didn't look very happy."

"No, Mrs. Kirk, he sure wasn't. But worryin' about that's not my job now, is it? You aren't payin' me to make people happy, as I understand it."

Dana shook her head. "You got that right, James."

The guard grinned a big toothy grin and leaned back in his chair. Dana returned to her desk, silently blessing Mitch Cross for his wisdom and foresight.

Sausalito

It was raining lightly as David Kirk pulled up in front of Nola's place. He was ten minutes late. Fashionably late.

He'd been thinking about Nola all day. Even amid all the problems with Molly and Dana, she'd been on his mind. In the middle of the afternoon he'd taken Molly to her friend's house, only too happy to unburden himself of the responsibility of her safety for a few hours. It was the first time he'd regretted her coming to live with him.

He'd often heard the complaints from his single clients that kids could play havoc with their love life, but he hadn't fully appreciated the breadth of the inconvenience until now. The simple truth was he was tired of denying himself. He was eager for a romp—and Nola Betts appealed to him at a gut level. She'd given his libido a wake-up call.

Taking the bouquet of pink and yellow tea roses from the passenger seat, he got out of the car and carefully locked the door. Nola's tiny house was probably thirty years old, but it was modern in style. It had a flat roof and was built on a steep hillside that dropped sharply away from the road. The branches of two oak trees sheltered the house, making it seem almost nestled into the hill. The view out the back had to be fabulous. Views of the bay and the San Francisco skyline were what made Sausalito desirable and exclusive and expensive. Nola's garage was right on the street. To get to her front door, he had to traverse a narrow wooden deck that ran alongside the garage.

David was nervous with anticipation. Nola had been friendly when they spoke on the phone that afternoon. Rather than going out, she'd suggested fixing him dinner at her place, saying it had been a while since she'd cooked for a man. He'd taken it as a signal that she wanted an intimate evening, and he couldn't have been more pleased.

He hadn't given a lot of thought as to her motives. Women approached seductions differently than men, but there were often parallels. What excited him most was that Nola seemed to be thinking in sexual terms right along with him. He could only hope that he was reading the situation right. He pressed the doorbell and waited, the thrill of sexual adventure pulsing in his veins.

The door swung open and Nola stood there, rubescent and voluptuous in a pair of tight black silk pants and a black Chinese jacket that hung open, revealing a low-cut white silk tank top. He stared at her for a long moment.

"Good evening, Nola," he said, recovering. He extended the flowers.

"How sweet," she said, taking them and sniffing the buds. "Come in, come in," she said, grasping his hand and drawing him into her den. The cozy living room was a festival of chintz. It had the feel of a boudoir. He went to the sliding-glass door that opened onto a redwood deck and a view of the lights of the city at dusk. Nola drifted up beside him.

"I'd offer you a drink, but I don't have a drop of liquor in the house," she said. "I've recently given up alcohol."

"Good for you," he said.

"I hope you won't feel deprived."

He shook his head. "I don't drink much myself. When I do, it's just to be sociable."

Nola pressed her breast against his arm as she sidled closer. "Maybe we can find other ways to be sociable, David."

He was looking at her full red lips. Though he'd scarcely been there a minute, he wanted to kiss her. His loins already tingled.

Nola interlaced her fingers with his and squeezed his hand. "The only thing I've thought of the last twenty-four hours is seeing you again," she said in a sultry voice. She touched his lower lip with her finger and he got an instant erection.

"I've made you a nice dinner, David. I hope you like filet mignon."

"Love it."

She smiled coquettishly, took his hand and pressed the back of it to her cheek. "Why don't you sit on the sofa and I'll go get the nibbles?"

With that, she turned and walked away, swaying her hips as though she knew they were being watched. David swallowed hard. He was being seduced and he loved it.

Ross

Bev O'Connell had hardly eaten and Dana could tell she was in misery. She'd been pushing her food around with her fork and had finally set it down.

"You know," she said, "I'm not doing anybody any good. Ted's miserable. I'm miserable. I've messed up your office and upset your home. I should have stayed with C&B and none of this would have happened."

"You can't worry about that. What's done is done. All you can do, Bev, is go on with your life."

"It's not fair that you should suffer just because I'm having problems."

"Bev, you're a fine agent and I'm proud that you wanted to join my company. My loyalty and support do not depend on you making a ton of money for me. After all, you're a friend first. And if you were still at C&B and I could have helped you, I would have."

"I can't tell you how much I appreciate it."

Dana had finished her share of the lasagna and carried her plate to the sink. Bev got up, too.

"Let me clean up," she said.

"All that's necessary is to rinse off the dishes. Anita will be here in the morning."

"I don't mind. Actually, I prefer to stay busy."

She dumped the rest of her food down the garbage disposal and Dana went to the breakfast nook to get the serving dishes. As she returned to the kitchen the telephone rang again.

"Oh, Lord," Bev said, "why can't he leave us alone?"

Ted had called three times since Dana had been home. They'd let the answering machine take the calls. Bev said he'd phoned all afternoon once he'd discovered the security guard out front wasn't going to let him onto the property. She hadn't talked to him, but hearing his imploring messages had been almost as bad.

"Bev, honey—" Ted's voice came over the speaker "—for God's sake, please talk to me. Just pick up the phone. What harm's it going to do?"

Dana looked over at Bev, whose head had dropped. She stood at the sink, crying. Dana had tried so hard to stay out of it—especially considering what had happened the last time—but her anger flared. She marched over and picked up the phone.

"Ted," she said, "don't you understand Bev doesn't want to talk to you? Why do you do this? You're only making everything worse."

"I don't need you telling me how to run my life!" he roared. "Put my wife on the phone."

"I can't make her talk to you even if I wanted to. But this is my phone and you're not accomplishing a damn thing by tying it up and filling my machine with the same old lament. If Bev wants to speak with you, she'll call. Now please, for your own sake, let it go."

"Put her on the phone!" he bellowed.

She started to hang up but Bev called for her to stop. "There's only one way to end this," she said, walking around the counter. "Let me talk to him."

"Are you sure?"

Bev nodded, biting her lip. Dana held up her finger, indicating to Bev that she should wait.

"Okay, Ted," Dana said into the phone, "I'm going to put Bev on and she'll speak with you under one condition. This is the last call. She's going to let you have your say, but you've got to accept what she tells you."

"Just put her on," he said, sounding halfway human.

Bev took the receiver from Dana, looking as frightened and childlike as she had at the office when he was threatening to drag her away. Dana went into the living room. She found a copy of *W* on the chair by the fireplace, probably something Bev had been looking at that afternoon. Dana picked it up and began paging through it absently, trying not to think about what was going on in the next room.

Turning the page she came to "Suzy," the gossip column. There were the usual pictures of celebrities and socialites, which Dana skimmed as she always did, reading the squib on someone who particularly interested her. On the second page a picture of a man jumped right out at her. He was an attractive white-haired gentleman in perhaps his early sixties. But what struck her was how familiar he looked. It could have been Mitchell Cross in twenty-five years.

Checking the caption, she was shocked to see that the man's name was Bill Cross. He was identified as an airline executive from Dallas. She wondered if he was a relative. The resemblance was uncanny. She read the accompanying text. It indicated that Cross was stepping down from his business to devote more time to charitable endeavors, one of which was a home for boys that he'd founded in Nevada. He enlisted the support of a number of prominent politicians and celebrities, several of whom were named in the article.

It could all be a coincidence, but Dana suspected that it wasn't. She tore out the page and decided to show it to Mitch.

Her attention drawn for a few moments from Bev, Dana paused to listen for her voice. Instead she heard what sounded like crying.

Getting up, she went into the family room. Bev was sitting on the sofa, her face in her hands. Dana sat next to her and put her arm around Bev's shoulders.

"Sorry you have to go through this," she said. Bev stopped crying and drew a ragged breath. "I told Ted I'd talk to him," she announced, trying to sound resolute.

"You did?"

"Yes, I figured I owe him one last meeting. He promised he'd accept whatever I said, once we had a chance to talk."

"Bev, do you think that's wise? I don't know how reasonable Ted is. He's been emotional and volatile."

"I know. I told him I'd only see him in public, and he agreed. We're meeting for breakfast at the Holiday Inn across from North Gate Mall." Bev wiped her cheeks and attempted a smile. "I may be a fool, but it's what I want to do."

"It's your life, Bev. I just hope you'll be safe."

She drew a deep breath. "Ted knows this is his last chance. I think he'll be on good behavior."

"What if he doesn't like what he hears?"

"I told him not to expect me to change my mind."

Dana sensed that was a mistake, but what could she do? She patted Bev's hand and tried to be understanding.

"At least he won't bother us anymore tonight," Bev said.

Dana nodded. She was glad of that, of course, but somehow she didn't think it would be enough.

Santa Rosa

Carole looked the prettiest Mitch could ever recall. She wore a red dress and her hair looked extra good. She'd twisted it up somehow and had done something with her makeup that was more sophisticated than usual. Her eyes shone in the candlelight.

She'd seemed happy through dinner. They hadn't talked about anything special, just the things they normally discussed. He'd spoken less than usual, letting her carry the conversation, which she could do without much trouble. But underneath her outgoing cheerfulness there was a wariness, and he figured she knew.

The band had arrived about ten minutes earlier and they were setting up. Hogg's wasn't as lively on Sunday nights as it was on Fridays and Saturdays. The crowd was older, the music older, running more to Patsy Cline than Loretta Lynn. But that was all right. Mitch felt older himself.

The leader of the band, wearing his Gene Autry hat, finished his little spiel and they began playing a quick-tempo piece with lots of country fiddle. The older cowboys—fifty-five- and sixty-year-olds with guts spilling over their wide leather belts—got their ladies up for a spin around the floor. The women with their dyed hair and petticoats or wide-hipped jeans kicked up their heels and the guys hooted. The girl singer stood off to the side, clapping and tapping her booted foot to the music, a grin running from ear to ear.

He sipped his beer, half listening to the music and half watching Carole, nostalgically remembering having made love with her. He'd moved on to other things, though. He was thinking about the change in his life—especially his frustrating preoccupation with Dana Kirk. He hadn't yet decided if she was a cause or a symptom. All he knew for sure was that she was in the middle of it.

The band finished its opening number to hoots and hollers and immediately went into a slower ballad. The girl singer went to the mike.

"Want to dance, Mitch?" Carole asked.

They went onto the dance floor and she melted right into his arms, her big soft breasts pressing against his chest. Mitch was aware of the smell of her hair spray and perfume as well as her own natural musk. He felt terribly sad.

"This is our last date, isn't it, Mitch?" Carole said.

"Huh?"

She pulled her face back to look at him in the low light of the dance floor. "This is thanks and farewell, isn't it?"

Mitch looked into her eyes but didn't say anything. She managed to smile even though her eyes were shimmering.

"Relationships have a natural life span like anything else," she said. "Ours is like a fifteen-year-old dog, loved for his loyalty and the good times, but fading fast."

"It's not like that," he said, unconvincingly.

"Yes, it is. I can tell." She put her face against his again. "The last time we made love there was something different," she said. "I sensed it."

"The best things end well, Carole."

She was silent for half a minute. "We've had a good ride, good times. I learned some things."

"Yeah, me too."

A minute passed without conversation, and the song ended. They returned to their table. Carole wore a brave smile. Mitch felt like hell.

"Is your new woman someone special, or is it just the old thing of needing a change of scene?"

He wasn't sure which answer was kinder. Both were true, yet, at the same time neither was. "Someone special, I guess."

Carole smiled. "That's good."

"It's more in my head than an actual relationship," he said, thinking an explanation was called for.

"That's what counts—how you feel."

The slightly chubby cocktail waitress, wearing a toned-down version of the Dallas Cowboys Cheerleaders' outfit, came by and asked if they wanted another drink.

"Not me," Carole said. "I gotta work in the morning."

Mitch shook his head and the girl went off.

"Want to dance again?" he asked.

"No, I think I want the last one to be the last. It's a nice way to remember you."

Her smile had turned somewhat brittle and Mitch knew she was protecting herself. He couldn't blame her. He wouldn't have blamed her even if she'd gotten bitchy and angry. People had to protect themselves any way they could.

The last date was the worst thing about relationships. He always ended them face-to-face, though. It was cowardly to run off without saying anything.

"I don't want to sound like a spoilsport," Carole said, bucking up, "but I'd like to go home. I've got an early morning and I know you do, too."

"Sure. Whatever you want."

They got their coats from the coat check and went out into the misty night. The rain had stopped but the air smelled of wet grass and wet fields. A semi went by on the highway. They made their way through Hogg's gravel parking lot. The vehicles were mostly pickups, four-wheel drives and old gas-guzzlers from the seventies. He finally spotted his rental car.

"You going to be all right?" he asked.

"Hell, yes," she said, almost sounding like she meant it. "I would have broken it off in another month or so if you hadn't."

"I'm glad." Somehow he didn't believe her, though.

"I've been in it for the sex," she said. "But you know that." The sadness in her voice was not terribly well disguised.

"It's meant more to me than that, Carole. I hope you believe that." He wasn't just blowing smoke. He was being sincere, though in truth he would have been hard-pressed to explain what he meant.

"Yeah," she said, taking his arm, "men are such romantics."

Sausalito

The only light in Nola's bedroom came from three candles on her white French Provincial dresser. She'd gone into the bath, leaving him alone with the rich aroma of her perfume and the lush scent of the roses. She'd put his flowers on the nightstand, almost as though they were a calling card.

David had already removed his jacket and loosened his tie. Now he took off the tie and shirt. He kicked off his shoes and finished undressing. Once he was naked he carefully hung his trousers over a chair. He could not help shivering. There was a slight chill in the room. He went to the sliding-glass door and looked out at the roiling water of the spa. Nola had turned on the pump before repairing to the bath, promising that the water was well heated. It was frothing with steamy bubbles.

David pushed open the glass door. Chilly air rushed in the crack. He quickly stepped out onto the deck, closing the door behind him. The wood was slippery and wet, the icy mist in the air stinging his bare skin. He shivered again as he tiptoed to the spa, tentatively testing the water with his foot. It felt hot, but inviting.

He carefully got into the tub. The heat of the water was as shocking as the cold air had been, but it was a welcome jolt. He squatted down, sinking to his chin. He sighed with contentment and edged over to the seat that ran around the circumference of the spa.

It was not a large pool as they went—probably designed to accommodate four, capable of holding six, yet intimate enough for two. David wondered if Nola used it often when she entertained. He suspected he wasn't the first man to be invited into it, but he didn't know if there had been many. Instant success with a woman always raised that question.

Light spilled out of the bedroom behind him and David turned to see Nola exiting the bath. The light was quickly extinguished but not until he'd seen that she was wrapped in a sarong. She came to the sliding-glass door and stepped out onto the deck.

"How's the water?" she purred.

"Perfect."

Nola's gown was white and tucked under her armpits, running in a slender tube all the way to her ankles. She had on gold sandals, a chunky gold necklace, and nothing else. She'd pinned her curls up on top of her head, but he could see a few tendrils hanging loose at her neck. She had a couple of fluffy bath towels under her arm. She set them on a lounge chair, then, looking up at the night sky, she rubbed her bare arms.

"Burr, it's chilly."

"Not in here, it isn't."

"Then, I'll join you."

"Please do."

Turning her back to him, she untucked her sarong, unwinding the loose fabric and holding it in her outstretched hands like a screen. Glancing over her shoulder at him, she giggled and let the cloth slide down her back until she was standing naked.

For a moment she didn't move, giving him a chance to look her over. He scanned her body, his eyes drawn to her buttocks. It was fleshy, but nicely rounded. And her legs were good. All in all she had kept her figure and wonderful smooth skin. It had the look of marble in the moonlight.

Keeping her back to him, Nola stepped out of her sandals and then turned. His gaze moved to her pendulous breasts and her pubis. Showing only a minimum of modesty, she approached the edge of the spa. He stood, offering his hand to assist her into the water.

Once she was in the tub, she lowered herself to her chin as he had, moaning with pleasure at the warmth. He returned to his place on the seat and Nola scooted back, sitting opposite him.

She smiled a broad, pretty smile that was unmistakably coquettish. "The colder the night, the better it feels," she said.

Her voice was low and sensuous. If this was theater, Nola had the act down pat. But he was reveling in it, liking—loving—every moment, every trick.

"Do you use the spa often?"

"Yes, I love it," she replied. "Sometimes, if I wake up in the middle of the night and can't get to sleep, I come out here and in ten minutes I'm ready to drop off. It's like a ... soporific—isn't that the word?"

"Yes."

"I was hooked on pills until I got my spa. Funny, a thing like this could save a person, don't you think? Of course, I got treatment, too. It's crazy what people put in their bodies just to function."

"Yes, it is."

Nola was keeping a tantalizing distance from him, teasing him. "Do you have a spa?" she asked.

"No."

"Oh, you should get one, David."

"Probably."

Nola smiled the smile of a seductress. "I hope I haven't scandalized you," she said, her foot finding his under the roiling water. "I invite you over for dinner and the next thing you know we're naked in the hot tub."

"How could I possibly object to that?"

"You're very proper, David. I already know that about you."

"What makes you say so?"

She looked off toward San Francisco and, as she did, she ran her foot up and down his shin. "Men are either users and abusers or they're protective and moralistic. It took me forty years to figure that one out, but I know I'm right. You're definitely in the second group, David."

"I'm not sure that's good," he said.

"You don't want to be a user and abuser, do you?"

She'd run her foot farther up his leg and was now rubbing the inside of his thigh with her sole.

"No, but I don't know if I like the moralistic part."

"It can get tedious, I grant you. But on balance it's better than the alternative."

"So what are you saying, Nola, that a woman has to choose between an animal and an uptight saint?"

"Basically. Ironically, though, women want both. I used to think the solution was to turn the animal halfway into a saint. Recently I decided the better solution is to do it the other way around." Again she smiled at him. This time there was challenge in it.

David was surprised by her insightfulness. In combination with her sexuality it was very, very arousing. "Do you think I'm a candidate for conversion?"

"Well, I didn't invite you into my spa to debate welfare reform."

He laughed.

Nola moved toward him, keeping herself low in the water, as though she were swimming. Stopping just before him, she put her hands on his knees. He felt his scrotum tighten.

She learned forward, pressing her breasts against his knees as she ran her hands up the outside of his thighs and over his hips. He made himself hold still, even as he swallowed hard, wanting badly to grab her and kiss her.

Nola caressed the inside of his thighs, running her hands up and down without venturing too close to his genitals. Without any resistance, or even gravity, it was hard for him to tell just how erect he was.

"You're a terrible tease," he said.

"Why, because I like to touch your body?"

"Because you tantalize."

"Would you rather I stop? Or would you prefer more?"

David studied her. "You're bringing out the animal in me."

Nola's look was self-congratulatory. "Oh, really? Well, let's see about that."

She moved her hands slowly up his thighs until she reached his crotch. She gently cupped his balls, then drew both hands lightly along the shaft of his distended penis.

"Hmm," she moaned softly, "I think you're right. This could be a real animal."

Nola floated forward then, bringing her face against his. She gave him a long, sensual kiss, parting her lips to give him access to her mouth.

"I put on lots of Vaseline," she whispered when their kiss ended. "It keeps me lubricated in the water."

He realized she meant for him to have intercourse with her in the spa. He had brought condoms with him, but they were still in his jacket pocket. But before he could mention them, Nola took his wrist and guided his hand between her legs. His finger found the slit in her plump center. It was slippery, smooth to the touch. He rubbed his finger over her nub and she moaned, closing her eyes. She seemed to sink farther into the water. After he'd caressed her for a couple of minutes, she began stroking his cock and asked if he was going to fuck her.

"Yes. I want to make love with you," he said.

She floated toward him, kissing him lightly on the lips. They tantalized each other with their tongues.

"You know why this is different for me, especially exciting?"

He shook his head. "No, why?"

"Because I'm sober. I haven't made love sober in a hundred years."

"Then, in a way, this is like a first time."

She slowly nodded, taking his penis in her hands. "And I'm liking it a whole lot."

His cock began throbbing harder than ever.

"Let me sit on your lap," she purred.

David scooted to the edge of the seat and Nola sat astride him. Then she guided his cock into her. They sank deeper into the water and she spread her legs wide. It was an incredible sensation—their bodies were weightless, but their genitals were fully engaged.

Nola was moaning, her eyes now closed. He began undulating against her. Her head fell back and her body floated, suspended only by the least support from his thighs.

There was perspiration on David's brow, but he hadn't really noticed until the icy rain began falling in heavy drops. He saw water collecting on Nola's face. Strands of hair were plastered to her forehead.

Her hips started rocking in concert with his thrusts. He had an urge to grab the heavy gold necklace around her neck, to wrench it and take control of her body. Instead he grabbed her buttocks, taking a cheek in each hand. He pulled her against him, driving into her. She whimpered with pleasure. He could tell she was about to come and his heart started lugging.

"Almost," she said, "almost, David. Don't stop."

He couldn't wait. He thrust against her, lifting her from the water as he ejaculated. Once he'd come, he sank back down. But when he looked into her face, he realized she hadn't climaxed.

As he waited, helpless and spent, Nola reached down and began caressing herself, her pelvis rocking forcefully enough to separate her from his limp penis. She drifted away then, floating back until her head rested on the far edge of the spa. Then, with her eyes closed, and completely oblivious to him, she caressed herself until she came.

Five

Chiara did her best to ignore Shawn, the young security guard who'd spent more time watching her than looking out for Ted O'Connell. The first twenty minutes after she'd arrived at work no one was in the office except the two of them. He'd spent most of the time asking her questions. Had she ever seen the pope? Was the pizza in Italy better than at Round Table? Did Italian men really pinch all the women on the ass? What a jerk.

For once she was glad when the agents started arriving. Shawn had to pretend he was guarding, then.

Everybody was talking about Bev and Ted. Chiara had heard Judy Povich say she thought Nancy Tong would be leaving. Then she heard her tell Lucille that she was considering having lunch with Adrianne Stevens over at Cedrick & Betts.

Chiara glanced into the bull pen where Dana was leading the sales meeting. She could only pick up bits and pieces of what was being said. People were asking lots of questions and even at a distance she could tell that Dana was on the defensive. She was struggling.

Chiara wasn't sure how she felt about that. In a way, she was glad she wasn't the only one with troubles—Dana deserved to lose occasionally. But at the same time, if Dana was to go under, Chiara would be out of a job.

She'd felt torn like this when Rossella married Renato. Her sister had gained instant wealth and security. She had ensured their mother a decent life and she'd even given Chiara money a time or two. Yet sometimes she had secretly wished her sister would lose Renato and all his money, just so she'd know what it was like to do without.

Seeing the salespeople doubt Dana's infallibility sparked a secret joy in her. If Dana lost her company, she'd probably have to sell that big house of hers and come down to earth like the rest of the human race. It would almost be worth seeing it happen—*if* she was able to find another job, of course.

The telephone rang and Chiara picked up the receiver. It was Nancy Tong.

"Chiara," she said in that singsong accent, "is the sales meeting over?"

"No, not yet."

"Could you interrupt, please? Ask Dana if I can come talk to her at one o'clock."

Chiara, swelling with secret knowledge, put Nancy on hold and headed toward the bull pen. The security guard watched her. He grinned. Chiara did not acknowledge his existence.

"Yes, Chiara," Dana said, seeing her waiting expectantly at the back of the room. She relayed the message, watching the other women exchange looks. Dana remained serene despite the buzz that went around the room.

"Tell her one is fine."

Chiara nodded and returned to her console. She gave Nancy Dana's response. Just as she hung up, the front door opened and Mitch Cross came in. Her heart made a little leap at the sight of him. Out of the corner of her eye she saw Shawn lumber to his feet. Mitch looked first into

Dana's office, then in the direction of the sales floor, but proceeded to her desk, stopping in front of it.

Chiara gazed up at him, feeling elation without any real justification. Mitchell Cross hardly knew she existed, yet she had a crush on him. She'd awakened that morning thinking of him. She'd probably dreamed about him, as well.

"Hi," he said with that friendly grin. "Looks like they're having a meeting."

"Yes, sir, it's the sales meeting."

"Will it last long?"

"I don't think so. Usually it's over by now."

"I'll hang around then, if it's all right."

"Sure. Would you like to wait in Dana's office? I'll bring you a cup of coffee, if you like."

"You're certainly accommodating," he said with a wry smile. "Did you bring your charm with you from Italy, or is it something you picked up here?"

She blushed violently. Somehow she managed to look into his eyes. If she was a rich businesswoman like Dana, men like this would worship her, want her. "I don't know," she said ineffectually.

"I'll bet your mama taught you," he said with a wink.

Chiara nervously got to her feet. "Make yourself comfortable in Dana's office. I'll get the coffee."

"Hey, could I have a cup, too?" Shawn called to her.

She ignored him and went to the coffee room. When she came back out, Mitchell Cross had already installed himself in Dana's office. She gave the security guard a sideward glance as she walked past. "I only serve customers," she said out of the corner of her mouth. "You'll have to get your own."

She approached Mitch, feeling all shaky. He took the mug from her. Their hands briefly touched, sending a charge through her. He'd looked at her body when she entered the office. She wished that meant he was attracted to her—that he'd been thinking about her in romantic terms— but she had no illusions. Men simply looked at women's bodies. That was the way things were.

"Thank you, Chiara," he said. *"Molte grazie."*

Her brows rose at the sound of Italian on his lips. *"Prego signore. Parla italiano?"*

"Può raccomandare un ristorante?"

She began giggling.

"Is it my accent, or don't you know any good restaurants?"

She'd flushed again. "You're very funny, Mr. Cross."

"But it wasn't a joke," he said.

"Yes, it was."

Mitch winked. "Nobody's going to slip one by you, are they, Chiara?"

She backed toward the door, though she would have preferred to throw her arms around his neck. "I have to be at my desk in case the telephone rings."

"Dove posso far cambiare del denaro?"

She began giggling uncontrollably.

"Arrivederci, signorina," he called to her as she disappeared out the door.

Shawn looked at her strangely as she took her place behind the desk. Chiara pushed her hair back over her ear and glanced in at Mitch, who was smiling to himself. What a beautiful man, she thought.

Then she glanced toward the bull pen at elegant, confident Dana. *She* was the one Mitchell Cross had come to see. Chiara felt a terrible jealousy, the kind that made one woman want to plunge a dagger into another woman's heart. Life was unfair. Terribly unfair.

Through the blinds Mitch was able to watch Dana Kirk at the other end of the office. He'd seen her under stress.

He'd seen her vulnerable and threatened, but he hadn't seen her in her role as commander of her business enterprise. Women in positions of power were hardly novel in this day and age, even in police work. But in spite of that he'd never had a personal relationship with one.

Corinne Smith had seniority over him, and he considered her a friend, but they weren't lovers. Liz Rogers, as an assistant DA, was certainly higher in the food chain than he, and they'd had a flirtation of sorts, but you couldn't call it a relationship, either.

Mitch didn't know how he'd feel about being seriously involved with that kind of woman. He wondered if Dana had ever had a fling with the plumber or the club tennis pro. Did a self-made woman like her get off cavorting with a guy who couldn't afford to buy her car used, even if he plunked down a whole year's salary?

He wasn't sure why he kept asking himself these questions. The notion that they could have a relationship—a meaningful relationship—was pretty far-fetched. Dana probably thought of him as nothing more than her friendly protector. Admittedly she wasn't snooty or pretentious, but that hardly put them on the same plane.

He had developed a thing for her, though. He couldn't deny it. And the truth was it bothered him. He didn't see any future in it. Or any point. It actually scared him a little. Not so much Dana, of course, as his feelings about her. He'd ended a perfectly good relationship with Carole because he didn't want to screw one woman while he was thinking of another. What nobility. He had to smile at the thought.

Out on the sales floor the meeting seemed to be breaking up. Dana came directly to her office. She was in a suit that fit her like a glove. It was the color of the lupine on the hills out near his place. She seemed pleased to see him.

"Hi," she said, closing the door.

"Good morning."

She sat in the chair next to him. Her hair seemed especially shiny. "I saw you come in. Sorry to keep you waiting, but holding together hearth and home has been a struggle."

"You looked like you were in charge out there."

Dana laughed. "I was sticking my finger in the dike, believe me. Well, what's the word from the lab? Did Ted's slipper match the size of the footprint outside Molly's window?"

"I don't have a report yet. But I have other news, and it's not good, I'm afraid."

"What now?" she asked, a distressed look crossing her face.

"Ted O'Connell beat the hell out of his wife this morning. They were in the parking lot outside the Holiday Inn. Pistol-whipped her, apparently."

"Oh, no."

"She's at Marin General."

"How serious is it?"

"Nothing life-threatening from what I understand, but he banged her up pretty badly."

"Oh, Lord," she said, shaking her head. "Poor Bev is too damned softhearted for her own good. I knew it was a mistake for her to see him."

"How'd O'Connell lure her up there?"

"He pleaded with her to see him, and she finally gave in. They were going to meet for breakfast. Has he been arrested?"

"Not yet. But this time, when we get him, he won't be getting out. I wanted you to know he's on the loose, and desperate. God knows what he might do. You aren't one of his favorite people."

Dana glanced out toward the reception area where the salespeople were gathering. "I'm supposed to lead everybody on tour, but maybe I should go to the hospital instead." She shivered. "I dread having to tell them what Ted's done now. They're skittish as it is."

"Why not go on your tour and take the whole gang to see Mrs. O'Connell afterward? They say it's best to involve children in family tragedies rather than trying to hide them from them."

"That's not a bad idea, Mitch. Maybe you ought to consider going into management."

"The only critters I care to manage are steers."

She gave him her pretty smile. "You're serious about that cowboy business, aren't you?"

"What is it they say? You can take the boy out of the country, but you can't take the country out of the boy."

Dana contemplated him for a long moment. "Ever heard the expression, 'The lady doth protest too much'?"

"Yeah, what are you saying?"

She gave him a look. "I'm saying... Oh, never mind, it's none of my business."

"What were you going to say?"

"Forget it. I was speaking out of turn."

"No, really. I want to hear," he said.

Dana gave him her smile again, the one he pictured when he thought about her. "It's a shame the only compliment you seem interested in is commendation on your ability to rope and ride. But then, maybe I see more virtue in you than you do, Mitch."

He gave her a long, inquiring look. "I think I should be flattered, but I'm not sure."

"It was a compliment, but there was a little criticism thrown in, too."

She got to her feet. He rose, as well.

"You'll have to excuse me," she said. "Duty calls."

"Yeah, I should probably go out and look for Ted."

"By all means," she said with a laugh.

They went to the door. Mitch paused, his hand on the knob.

"I'm going to talk to Mrs. O'Connell. She might be able to give us an idea where Ted's likely to head. Hopefully she'll be more cooperative this time. Afterward I'll be going back to my office. Why don't you swing by after your tour? I'll probably have the lab report by then. I can update you."

"Okay."

Mitch opened the door and followed Dana into the reception. The women looked at them inquiringly.

"Let's take two cars," Dana said to her staff in a take-charge voice. "I've got a couple of errands after the tour. Who else wants to drive?"

"I will," a tall brown-haired woman with pearls said.

They put on their coats and went out the door looking like a mother hen with her brood. After the last one had left, Mitch turned to Chiara.

"Dove la farmacia più vicina?" he said with a straight face.

Chiara began giggling again. She covered her mouth and turned bright red.

It was a random question from a phrase book. He had gone through a period of fascination with languages in college and odd little bits had stuck in his mind.

"Why do you need a drugstore, Signore Cross?" she asked. "Does this place give you a headache?"

"No," he said, "the decor is much too lovely." He glanced over at the security guard. "Right, son?"

The young man blinked. "Huh?"

Mitch gave Chiara a smile and left the office.

* * *

Kentfield

Frank Betts stared out at the garden that was outside the glass wall of his office. In a few hours he'd be seeing Dana, but he wasn't as happy at the prospect as he should have been. It was going to be a humiliating experience. He knew that in advance. Plus, his task seemed impossible. And so much was depending on it.

There was a knock on his open door. Lane Cedrick glided in.

"Well, good news for the home team," he said. "I talked to Adrianne. The Chinese girl in Dana's office with all the foreign buyers is moving her license this afternoon. Adrianne talked to her yesterday."

"She wasn't even from C&B," Frank said.

"No," Lane said, sitting in a visitor's chair, "that's the beauty of it. She was with a franchise shop before joining Kirk & Company." He looked positively delighted.

"I wonder if any of the others are getting thoughts of coming home."

"Adrianne said Judy Povich was considering having lunch with her later this week. If Judy comes back, Lucille Fernandez won't be far behind."

"That'll leave Dana with Sylvia, Helene and Bev."

"Not enough to keep the doors open over the long haul. We might have her on the ropes, Frank. I wanted you to know going into your lunch with her. It's today, right?"

"Yes, I was just thinking about that. There isn't enough cash to buy her stock."

"Offer her paper, if you have to."

"Yes, but if she's got cash-flow problems of her own she's going to want cash on the barrelhead. This knocking her feet out from under her might come back to bite us in the ass."

"The only way to get to a woman like Dana is to shake her confidence."

"You don't know her, Lane, she's a fighter."

"She's also got common sense. At a certain point she's better off to cut her losses. Once the dam breaks it'll be too late and she knows it."

The intercom line buzzed. Frank picked up the phone.

"Dana Kirk on line three, Frank," Joan said.

"Thanks." He looked up at Lane. "It's Dana."

"Well, speak of the devil. It's too early for a surrender, but it might be interesting to see what she has to say. Put her on the speaker phone."

Frank pushed the speaker-phone button. "Hi, doll, what's up?"

"Frank, I'm going to have to reschedule. Can we meet next week? I've got a couple of salespeople who need attention. First things first, you know."

"You can't squeeze in lunch?"

"No, I've got one in the hospital and another who needs desperately to talk to me."

Frank gave Lane an I-told-you-so look. Lane signaled for him to put her on hold. "Can you hold a second, Dana? I'll be right back."

"Next week is too late," Lane said glumly. "Tomorrow maybe. Find a way to talk to her today, if you can."

Frank pushed the button. "A week of suffering is going to be sheer hell, Dana. I know I don't deserve it, but give me a few minutes. How about this evening? Do you have plans for dinner?"

"Dinner, Frank? Isn't that a bit much?"

"I intended a business lunch. Make it a business dinner. You get a better meal."

She didn't say anything for several moments. "This is really a rotten day."

"A martini and a nice lobster dinner will be something to look forward to."

"You have the martini," she said, "I'll have the lobster."

Frank glanced over at Lane, who was grinning. "All right, doll, you got a deal. Shall we say seven at Dominick's?"

"Yes, I think that will work. I'm on tour at the moment and can't check my office calendar. If there's a problem, I'll let you know."

"You're calling from your car phone, then."

"Yes. We're headed up to Fairfax. Lucille Fernandez picked up a new listing yesterday afternoon. Your San Anselmo office might want to have a look at it before it goes on the board tour next week."

"They probably would."

"I'll tell Lucille to fax you a fact sheet."

"Interoffice cooperation is the name of the game," Frank said.

Lane had that sardonic grin of his on his face.

"Got to go, Frank," Dana said.

"See you tonight." He disconnected the call.

"Pretty smooth," Lane observed. "Maybe she still worships your cock, after all."

"I wouldn't bet on it," Frank said somberly.

"Whether it's your cock or your silver tongue, it doesn't matter. Your ass is riding on tonight."

"Thanks, Lane. I function best under pressure."

Lane Cedrick got up from the chair and went to the door. "Let's hope so," he said. "Let's hope so."

San Anselmo

Ted O'Connell pulled into the parking lot in front of the Safeway and turned off the engine of the rental car. He'd have to abandon it. Every cop in Marin would be looking for a white Taurus before long, if they weren't already.

Wiping the perspiration from his brow, he reached over and took his 9-mm automatic from the glove compartment, shoved it in his belt, and covered it with his sweater. Christ, he was like a bank robber on the run. No fucking job, his wife leaving him, the cops after him. And it was all Dana Kirk's fault. If she hadn't butted in, everything would be all right by now.

Bev wasn't herself that morning, that was for goddamn sure. She was brainwashed. That wasn't her talking, saying she wanted a divorce. It was *fucking* Dana Kirk.

When a figure suddenly loomed up beside him, Ted jumped. Then he saw it was only an old lady loading her groceries into the car next to him. Shit, he had to get out of there, go someplace where he could think.

There was a deli at the far end of the shopping center. Ted got out of the car and walked toward it, trying not to act suspicious. It was hard not to look around. All he needed to see was a cop car come cruising along and he'd start running, he knew it.

He went into the deli, got a beer out of the cooler, ordered a ham-and-cheese on rye and sat in the back corner where he could see the door. He guzzled down half the beer before he made himself stop. He had to be careful not to drink too much.

He had drawn all the money he had out of the bank, a little over two grand. At least he wouldn't have to rob a convenience store to eat. One thing for sure, though, he wasn't going to South America on two grand. L.A. maybe, but not much farther.

The trouble was he didn't know what he'd do even if he got to L.A. Eventually they'd pick him up. Damn. He slammed his fist into the palm of his hand, making the mailman two tables over look at him funny.

Ted groaned silently. He shouldn't have hit Bev. That was a stupid mistake. But he was so goddamn mad. Why couldn't she see how Dana had ruined their lives?

He wasn't going to let the bitch get away with it. If she was going to fuck him over, then he'd sure as hell make her pay for it. But good.

The counter girl brought Ted his sandwich. He chomped it down, then finished the beer. He felt better. He sat there, trying to figure out what to do. He needed a place to sleep. He couldn't spend the night in a goddamned deli. They'd pick him up if he went to a motel. And he needed wheels, bad.

Ted started running through the friends he could turn to. The list wasn't long. Wayne Timmons was probably his best bet, if he was home. Wayne traveled a lot.

Ted checked his pockets, but he didn't have any change. He gave the girl behind the counter a dollar and asked for quarters. Then he went to the pay phone on the wall and dialed Wayne's number. He answered on the third ring.

"Hey, Ted, how's it going? You caught me on my way out the door, buddy. I'm headed to the airport."

"You drivin' your car?"

"Yeah. It costs a frigging fortune to park, even in the long-term lot. More than the frigging airline ticket if I stay long enough, but what else do I do? Why? What's up?"

"Wayne, old buddy, I need a favor. Me and the old lady are on the outs. Bev's pitched me out and had the dealer pick up the Porsche."

"Hey, that's the shits."

"I got drunk and I was out of it. By the time I sobered up it was too late. I seen a lawyer and he said he can fix me up but it's going to take a few days."

"So you need a pad."

"Sure do, Wayne. Any chance I could bunk at your place?"

"Why not? Shit, man," Wayne told him, "*Mia casa es su casa*. As long as you don't trash the place, of course."

"If you want I could drive you to the airport and pick you up when you come back. It would save you parking and I'd have wheels while you're gone. When my lawyer gets some dough out of Bev, I'll lay a couple hundred on you."

"Sounds good to me."

"Since you won't have to park at the airport, you'd have time to pick me up, wouldn't you, Wayne?"

"Sure, where are you?"

"At a deli in San Anselmo."

"Shit, Ted, your old lady's really pushing you around, isn't she?"

"Not anymore. I put a stop to that, but good."

"Well, give me an address."

"Wayne, you're a lifesaver. I won't forget this. I really won't."

San Rafael

Dana parked the Mercedes on Fifth Street across from the library and walked back to city hall. She realized then that in all her years in Marin she'd never been in the building before.

It was brick, contemporary in style—nearly as old as she. From the street it appeared to be two stories, but it had a full basement where the police department was housed. Dana followed the Police arrow pointing down the stairway near the main entrance.

After presenting herself to the clerk at the window, she waited in the reception area, feeling a little strange to be on Mitch's turf. He came out to greet her. He was in shirtsleeves and wore a shoulder holster. Seeing the gun strapped to him that way took her aback. Mitch noticed.

"I should have put on my jacket," he said, half apologizing.

"Oh, no," she said, "I just haven't—"

"Seen me undressed before?" he said, chuckling.

Dana colored.

"Do you want to run out someplace for coffee?" he asked. "I can grab my jacket. Or better yet, how about lunch? My treat."

"I've got to meet Nancy at the office at one, so I can't," she said. "But I'll take a rain check."

"I won't let you forget. Come on back to my office. It's not elegant, but it's private."

He led the way back through the corridor, stopping at his small office. It was cramped with government-issue furniture. The surfaces were stacked with files and documents. Mitch set the wooden armchair square in front of his desk for her and went around to his chair.

"I should have straightened up a little, knowing you were coming, but if I had, I wouldn't be able to find anything for a week, so please bear with me."

She sat down, glancing around. "You need a plant or something, Mitch. The room is dead."

"Had a plant once," he said affably. "Watered it to death."

"I have a tendency to do the same thing. I finally ended up hiring a plant service. They take care of all the plants at the office and my house."

"I don't think there's room for that sort of expenditure in the departmental budget."

She smiled. "Maybe the solution is an artificial plant."

"I'll put it on my list of things to do." Mitch folded his hands over his stomach. "So, how was your tour?"

"Nothing special. One of my people had a nice new listing up in Fairfax. Getting excited about that sort of thing is one of the age-old rituals of real estate."

"That and singing the company song?"

She gave him a look. "No, Mitch, that's door-to-door sales. We like to think we're a little more sophisticated than that. By the way, I wanted to thank you again for suggesting a group visit to the hospital. Bev appreciated it and I think it drew the rest of us together."

"The dike is holding, then?"

"It's too soon to say. I'm fairly sure I'm losing an agent this afternoon, and another one is shaky."

"What happens if they do go?"

"I scramble around like hell trying to replace them, do a little extra selling myself to make up the production, and pray."

"Sounds like a tough business."

"Yes, and it's starting to seem like it's just as dangerous as yours. I take it Ted hasn't been arrested."

"No, not yet."

Dana felt her shoulders slump. She'd been hoping to get that monkey off her back. "Well, I guess I'd better tell Bob Howard to move the security guard to David's."

"Why? What do you mean?"

"I called him a while ago and said I'd like to put on a full-time guard at David's, but Howard doesn't have the manpower. Rather than getting another company I told him to take the guard off my house and move him to David's."

"O'Connell's more desperate than ever, Dana. If anything, the guard for you is more critical."

"Yes, but with Bev in the hospital I don't need to stay at my place. I checked with my friend, Robin, and I can hang my hat there for a few days."

"I'm afraid there's another complication," he said.

Dana's heart sank. "You know, Mitch, I'm beginning to know when bad news is coming just by the tone of your voice."

"Yeah, it's not one of my more pleasant duties."

"So what now?"

"The lab report came back. The mud print outside Molly's window was either a size ten or a ten and a half. O'Connell's slipper was a size twelve."

"So Ted definitely wasn't the one behind the dolls."

"It appears not. It's almost certain we're dealing with two different people."

Dana groaned. "I knew that all along. I don't know why I'm disappointed."

"Because you want this over with. It's understandable."

There was compassion in his voice. It was a side of him she liked. But she also liked his quirky sense of humor, his warmth. Yet she knew he was holding back; that something—probably her money—bothered him. What she didn't know was whether that was all there was to it, or if there was more.

"Ted is definitely a bad guy," she said, "but the other guy, the one creeping around outside Molly's window in the size tens, has me confounded."

"Do you have any idea what size shoe Betts wears?"

The question came out of the blue and it was not until she thought about it for a moment that she realized she didn't like it. "No, I don't," she said pointedly.

"I thought along the way it might have come up," he said lamely, as if he'd only then become aware of his transgression.

"I don't make a habit of checking men's shoes, even if they happen to be on the floor next to my bed." Her cheeks burned as she said it.

"Sorry, Dana, I was doing my police thing."

She drew a deep breath. "No, don't apologize. I shouldn't be so sensitive. Frank's not a topic I want to think about just now."

"That's right, you were supposed to have lunch with him."

"I had to cancel because of Nancy. But he insisted on taking me to dinner tonight."

"He seems eager to see you. Or are you the one who's eager?"

"You said it would be interesting to find out what he wanted, right? So I figured I should see him."

Mitch nodded. "Yes, I still haven't quite figured Betts out."

She wondered if that was jealousy she heard in his voice. It sounded like it, though there was no reason why he should be jealous. They had no relationship and Frank Betts was old news anyway. "Maybe I should ask him what his shoe size is while I'm at it."

He chuckled. "That might be a little too unsubtle, Dana."

"I suppose I could seduce him to get his shoes off. I could toss them out the window. You could be waiting with a flashlight to check the size." She arched a brow. "Sound like a good plan, Detective Cross?"

"That might be a bit extreme. But we can always keep it in mind in case we get desperate." Mitch picked up a pencil and began thumping the eraser on his desk blotter. "It wasn't an entirely facetious question, though. His shoe size, I mean."

"Unfortunately, I don't know the answer."

"How about your ex?" Mitch said, "What's his?"

"Lord, you would ask." She closed her eyes to think. "I knew once." She opened her eyes and looked at Mitch, ignoring his bemused grin. "I think it might have been ten. You aren't suggesting that David hung a doll outside his own daughter's window."

"I don't suggest anything. I just ask lots of questions. Occasionally one turns out to be the right one."

"I don't know what to say, except that it doesn't make sense to me that David would do that."

Mitch shrugged. "Chances are he didn't. Ten is a fairly common shoe size. But in this business you take a look at the long shots as well as the more obvious candidates."

"Well, that's your area of expertise, not mine." She looked at her watch. "I have to get back to the office. It may be too late, but I'll try to talk Nancy out of leaving." She got to her feet and Mitch came around the desk.

"I'll walk you out."

"It's not necessary."

"Office policy," he said, tongue in cheek.

"Strange policy."

He took her elbow and ushered her through the door. "It's only obligatory if the visitor is good-looking."

It hadn't been necessary for him to touch her, but he seemed to want to.

"I see."

They walked down the hall.

"We keep score," he said, giving her a sly grin. "The guy with the most points at the end of the year gets a bottle of Scotch."

"What about the women officers?"

"They're too mature for this sort of thing."

"You're kidding about all this, of course."

"Yeah, but I got to walk you to the door."

They'd come to the entrance. He gave her a big smile. Dana felt a bit self-conscious. She didn't know why she should be so attracted to Mitchell Cross yet feel so prickly toward him at the same time.

"By the way, I've got a man out now, talking to people at the service station and the bar where our boy called you from," he said.

"Oh?"

"Yeah. He took a picture of O'Connell and also one of Betts that we got from the files at the I-J. It's a long shot, but worth a try."

"You don't like Frank, do you, Mitch?" Dana said what was on her mind without thinking it through.

"Liking and not liking isn't in the job description," he replied. "Being suspicious is."

"I see."

They stood looking at each other. He gave her an odd feeling. One that was comfortable and uncomfortable at the same time.

"So, you're going to be at your friend's tonight?" he asked.

"Yes. Robin has a condo in Corte Madera."

"Could I have the number in case I need to reach you?"

"Certainly."

Dana took a business card from her purse. She wrote down both Robin's phone number and her address. She handed him the card.

Mitch slipped it into his pocket. "If there are any developments, I'll get ahold of you."

"Thank you," she said.

He looked down at his shoes. "I hope I didn't offend you with my remark about Betts. I really wasn't trying to give you a bad time. It was just thoughtless of me."

"Don't apologize. I was being overly sensitive. If you want to know the truth, my relationship with Frank was not one of my prouder moments."

Mitch shrugged.

There were other things that needed to be said, or at least she felt as if there were, but Dana didn't know what they might be. "Bye," she said. "I'll talk to you later."

"I'll probably work late. And I have to pick up my vehicle at the repair shop this afternoon, so maybe I'll give you a call tonight, if that's all right."

"Sure. And if I'm not in, Robin can take a message."
Mitch nodded.

"Bye," she said again. This time she left.

San Rafael

Ted O'Connell slipped the key into the lock and opened
the door to Wayne Timmons's apartment, neat as you
please. He went inside, put on the safety chain, and leaned
heavily against the door. For the first time in two days he
could relax.

Wayne's place was nothing to write home about. It had
the basic furniture a guy needed and that was it. Wayne had
lived there three years. He still hadn't put any pictures on
the walls. The most outstanding feature was the big-screen
TV in the corner. A really big mother.

Ted headed for the kitchen and looked in the refrigerator. It was stocked with Budweiser, just like Wayne said.
Ted took one and guzzled half the bottle down before sitting at the table and kicking off his shoes.

Out the dark window he could see the traffic zipping by
on the freeway, half a block away. Wayne was a lifesaver.
Ted felt safe. He had a pad and wheels and the time to plan
his revenge carefully. During the drive back from the airport, he'd decided that's all he had left—revenge. Taking
care of Dana would cost him, but he didn't have anything
to lose anymore. And it would feel damned good to knock
her off her high horse. Damned good.

One thing for sure—he'd have to be careful stalking her.
Between the security guards and the police, it wouldn't be
easy getting to her. His best bet would be to catch her alone
someplace—in the parking lot of the grocery store, out
touring houses, on her way to her fitness club, or headed
home from work.

Dana worked pretty long hours. Bev always talked about how hard Dana worked. He might even be able to catch her alone late at the office. She'd be a sitting duck at night.

On an impulse he went to the phone in the front room, taking his bottle of beer with him. He tried calling her office just to see if she was there. One of the saleswomen answered. Ted didn't recognize the voice.

"Dana Kirk, please."

"I'm sorry, they left a few minutes ago. You just missed her. May I take a message?"

"Uh…no, I don't think so. I needed to talk to her about a house I'm interested in. She showed me property a couple of months ago."

"I'm sure Dana would be happy to help you with that. Why don't I get your name and number and I'll have her call you?"

"That's all right," he said. "I'll just try her at home. I have her home number."

"Dana's not going to be there for a few days," the woman hastily said, "so if you need to talk to her this evening, you'd better give me your number."

Ted quickly hung up. So, Dana wasn't going to be at home for a few days. And the woman had said *they* just left. Who did she mean? Dana and the security guard? Ted doubted it. More likely the woman meant Dana had left with whoever she was staying with. That made sense. Probably one of her salespeople. Bev had stayed at Sylvia Hansen's place. That might be where Dana went.

Ted stroked his chin and grinned. Wouldn't that be a hoot if he nailed her while she was hiding out, thinking she was being so smart. Poetic justice. That's what it would be.

But then it occurred to him Dana might have more sense than to hide out where Bev did. She could be staying with another agent, though. What was the name of the other one she was tight with? Helene Whitford. That was it.

Trouble was he didn't know where Helene lived. He didn't know her all that well himself. He could follow either her or Dana home. That'd be one way to find out.

Then it hit him. Dana's best friend was still working at C&B. Bev had talked about it. Dana and—what the hell was her name? The Jewish broad that worked out of the Corte Madera office. He'd heard the name, but he couldn't remember it. There was an easy enough way to find out. He could call the Corte Madera office and get the name by describing her. Real-estate agents made sure people could get hold of them, though it might take some talking to get an address. He'd find a way, whatever it took.

Ted took a long drink of beer, feeling good for the first time in days. Jesus, nailing Dana would be sweet revenge. He really wanted to put it to her. Make her suffer. He'd have to do it good, though, because the pleasure of it was going to have to last for a real long time.

Corte Madera

Dana kept her eyes on the taillights of Robin Cohen's Lexus as it exited the freeway at Tamalpais Drive. She stayed right behind it, not wanting to get separated in the darkness, although of course she could have made it to Robin's place with her eyes closed. It felt good for once to be the follower rather than the leader, though. Robin had swooped into the office and all but gathered her into her arms to take her home.

Robin had heard about Nancy Tong defecting—Adrianne had spared no time in spreading the word. Robin told her they had to be awfully desperate to have gotten the news out so fast. Dana lamented her bad luck, thinking about the pall that had settled over the office while Nancy had cleared her desk. Even Helene Whitford had looked glum. All in all, it'd been a pretty shitty day.

"Only one step back," Robin had said about Nancy's defection. "Tomorrow it will be two steps forward." Funny, that was the sort of thing she used to say to Robin her first year in the business, when the going had been tough. Now it was Robin in the mommy role.

The Lexus went west on Tamalpais Drive. Dana had been watching the rearview mirror and had seen nothing suspicious. When they made a turn, none of the headlights behind her followed. Another quick turn and they came to Robin's neat little condominium project tucked into a pleasant residential neighborhood. Robin's unit faced the street, but the parking was in back. The Lexus entered the drive, but Dana pulled up at the curb. She got out, locking her door.

She had her briefcase in one hand and her purse in the other. The purse was a lot heavier with the gun inside, but she'd decided to carry it with her, legal or not. The point was, she didn't want it to be in her desk drawer at the office if she needed it at home, or vice versa.

She waited on the sidewalk for Robin to arrive, glancing up and down the quiet street to make sure nobody suspicious was lurking about. Robin came around the corner of the building, moving briskly, probably aware Dana would be anxiously waiting in the street alone.

"What about your suitcase?" Robin asked.

"Oh, yes, I forgot about that."

"Let's open up the house," Robin said, "then I'll help you with the luggage."

Robin unlocked the door, took both of their briefcases and purses and put them on the straight chair inside the door. Then they went back out to the Mercedes. Dana opened the trunk. Robin took the larger suitcase. Dana took the overnight case and the clothes bag.

They went inside and carried everything directly to the guest room. It was the only room in the apartment that wasn't really decorated. Robin called it her memorial to dorm life in college. Dana hung the clothes bag in the closet and they returned to the elegant front room.

Robin's "nest" as she referred to it, was cheerful and homey. She'd put a lot of money into the decor even though she considered it an interim home. The real one—the dream house she planned—would be the one she bought with Mr. Wonderful. Until Sir Galahad came along, she'd have a bachelor pad.

Robin loved Queen Anne. She had a beautiful dining room set that was far too large for the room—an unimportant detail, considering its ultimate destination was elsewhere. She also had a beautiful writing desk in the front room. It was an antique she'd inherited from her grandmother. Other pieces were reproductions, but all of them were excellent quality.

Robin, who'd pronounced herself too far removed from her Stone Age ancestors to build a fire, turned on the gas jet in the fireplace, creating an instant cozy ambience.

"Oh, Robin," Dana said, plopping into a big wing chair, "I wish I could get in my bathrobe and sit by the fire with you this evening and forget my troubles."

"Call Frank and tell him you're not feeling well. Going out with him is not for your benefit, anyway."

"No," Dana said, "I already canceled lunch on him. Besides, he'll think I'm hiding because of Nancy. Better I look him in the eye."

"It's a little early for him to gloat," Robin said, warming her legs by the fire.

"Yes, but I'm not sure what he has in mind. He says he wants to talk business, but I'm suspicious."

"Everybody knows he's still carrying a torch for you."

"I hope after the other night, he's got that out of his system."

"Don't count on it."

Robin didn't sit. She went into the kitchen. Dana could hear her open the refrigerator and rummage around. It sounded like a before-dinner snack was in progress.

"Want something to eat or drink?" Robin called from the kitchen. "Glass of wine?"

"No, thanks. I want to be stone sober when I see Frank. Anyway, I should probably get ready."

Dana checked her watch. She had to leave in forty-five minutes at the latest. If she hurried she could get in a quick shower, but she was tired and didn't want to expend the effort. Besides, Frank didn't deserve it. Now, if it were Mitch she was having dinner with, it might be a different story.

Funny how the guy kept insinuating himself into her thoughts. During the afternoon, despite all the upset over Nancy, she'd kept thinking of him, her champion.

Robin returned with a glass of wine in one hand and a cracker with cheese on it in the other. "Sure you don't want something?"

"No, I'm just going to sit here until I have to go in and brush my teeth and put on some lipstick."

"Guess that says as eloquently as anything how far ol' Frank's stock has fallen."

Dana laughed. "It's definitely bottomed out."

"You haven't mentioned your detective friend. Did you see him today?" Robin asked.

Dana smiled.

"I thought there was a glow in those cheeks, the long face notwithstanding."

"Robin, I don't know what it is I see in the guy, but it's definitely something."

"Does the name Oliver Mellors give you any insight?"

She ruminated on that. "Even if that described him, I am definitely not the Lady Chatterly type. This is not a class thing. Lord, the guy has a college degree, which is more than I can say."

"It may not be that sort of thing as far as *you're* concerned, but it could be to him. Didn't you say he has a chip on his shoulder?"

"About the size of Mount Tam."

"Lady Chatterly's guy had a lot of pride, too."

"You want to hear something funny? I think Mitch's father or uncle or some other close family member is a millionaire."

"What?"

Dana went to her purse and got the page she'd torn out of *W*. Robin looked at the picture.

"Nice-looking man. Is it just the name, or is there a resemblance?"

"That could be Mitch in twenty-five years, easy."

"Not bad. The guy's a cop, but still an heir."

"From what he said, he and his father are completely alienated. He's probably disinherited."

"Bummer."

"I don't think he cares, to tell you the truth."

The telephone rang. Robin groaned and went into the kitchen to answer it. Dana could hear her talking, but she couldn't make out more than the odd word. Judging by the lilt in her voice, it was either a man or a hot client, possibly both. When Robin returned her cheeks were all aglow. "I'll be damned."

Dana looked at her. "Care to elaborate?"

"That was Morton Feldman."

"The mensch from Laurel's party?"

Robin smiled at Dana's use of the Yiddish term. "One and the same. He wants to meet me for a drink later. Said he's attending a business dinner here in Marin and thought I might be free for a drink afterward."

"Are you?"

"I told him I was, so I guess I am." Robin looked over at the clock on the mantel. She sat for a moment, evidently thinking over her conversation with Morton. She chuckled to herself.

"So, what haven't you told me?" Dana asked.

"You know me, I got a little cheeky with him. I asked him if he'd heard from Nola."

"And?"

"He said that as a matter of fact he'd called her to see if she might be interested in meeting a friend of his. Apparently there's a guy in his office who goes wild over redheads and Morton figured Nola was hot to trot."

"But she wasn't?"

"No. She told him that she'd started seeing someone. A shrink here in Marin."

"That sounds like Nola," Dana said.

"Doesn't it, though? Probably seduced him on his own couch." Robin got up. "Well, off I go to get gussied up."

"Where are you meeting him?"

"Sausalito. At the Casa Madrona."

"My, my. Morton's a real romantic. Suppose he's reserved a room, too?"

"Don't knock it, Kirk. Beats the hell out of spending the evening at home with Dan Rather."

"Or going to dinner with Frank Betts," Dana added.

"At least you're getting a free meal."

"I'd rather a bowl of soup in your kitchen, but a girl can't always have what she wants."

"My friendship has spoiled you." Robin went off, a definite bounce in her step.

Dana was happy for her. She curled up in the chair and watched the fire.

The phone rang again. Assuming Robin was indisposed, Dana went to answer it.

"Cohen residence," she said.

There was no response.

"Hello," she said again. "This is the Cohen residence."

Still no response. In the background she could hear noise. It sounded like a TV or a radio. She could hear breathing, then the phone went dead. Dana put down the receiver. That same old creepy feeling went down her spine. It couldn't be *him*. He had no idea she was at Robin's. It had to be someone else. A coincidence. Maybe Robin had been getting calls. The breathing was new. She hadn't noticed that in the past.

Dana returned to the fire. When Robin got out of her bath she'd ask if she had a secret admirer, a kid in the neighborhood, maybe. The very last thing she wanted to believe was that her tormentor had tracked her down. She shivered at the thought. Damn.

Corte Madera

Mitch sat at a window table in Denny's watching the nighttime traffic zipping up and down the freeway. He'd ordered chicken-fried steak for no particular reason other than the fact that it had been one of his grandmother's specialties. A little nostalgia trip in the vinyl-decked halls of Denny's.

He'd decided to hang around Marin because he wanted to see how Dana's meeting with Frank Betts went. He'd told her he'd call. He could have done that just as easily from home, of course, but for some reason he wanted to stick close by, maybe even go to her friend's place afterward—if he got invited. The simple fact was, he wanted to see her— a lot. He was also worried about her. The patrolman who'd taken O'Connell's and Betts's pictures to the service station and the bar had reported to him that a kid who worked at the station said Betts looked familiar. He couldn't say whether he'd seen him using the pay phone or not, but he definitely looked familiar.

Mitch knew he couldn't draw any firm conclusions from that. It could be that Betts bought gas at the station. Or that the kid had seen Betts somewhere else. Marin was not all that well populated when you got right down to it—a group of bedroom communities that anywhere else would just be small towns.

But being a cop, he was naturally suspicious. He couldn't dismiss the possibility that Frank Betts was his man. The guy had an emotional thing for Dana, and he'd been dumped. He'd seen thinner motives for hatred than that over the years.

And so he had drifted down the freeway to Corte Madera, wondering if he should let Dana go off to dinner without at least having a word with her first. He couldn't exactly drop in, but he could call. That wouldn't hurt, even if it might seem a tad overprotective. He pushed aside his dinner plate and went back to the pay phone in the hall outside the rest rooms. Consulting the business card Dana had given him, he dialed Robin Cohen's number. Robin answered.

"Ms. Cohen, this is Detective Mitchell Cross of the San Rafael P.D. Is Mrs. Kirk there, that I might speak to her?"

"No, you just missed her. She left maybe five minutes ago."

"She's meeting Frank Betts for dinner," he said.

"That's right."

Mitch considered letting it drop there, but instead followed his impulse. "You don't know where they were going to meet, do you?" he asked.

"Yes. At Dominick's in San Rafael. Why? Is there a problem?"

"No, I promised her I'd check in with her this evening. I just wanted to touch base."

"Can I give her a message?" Robin Cohen asked.

"You can tell her I called. I might give her a buzz later."

"All right. I'll be glad to pass that along."

Mitch hung up and returned to his booth with a view of the freeway. The waitress had cleared the table and brought his check. He didn't bother to sit. He put a dollar down, grabbed his coat, and went to the cashier.

It was crisp and cool outside, but at least the weather seemed to be clearing. Mitch got in his Bronco and headed for the entrance to the freeway. Going home meant driving north, through San Rafael, practically right by Dominick's. He hadn't decided yet whether he'd stop, but he was thinking about it.

Mitch wasn't sure where in Corte Madera Robin Cohen lived, but if Dana had only left ten minutes ago, she couldn't be very far ahead of him. He might even be able to catch her before she went inside.

When the moment of decision came, he exited the freeway at Second in San Rafael and doubled back on Francisco Boulevard. Dominick's was set off the frontage road, and backed up against the San Rafael Canal. Mitch knew the place well. The police department often had occasion lunches there. It was a middle-American sort of place that drew a diverse crowd.

The lot was half full. Mitch parked and headed for the restaurant. As he did, he noticed a woman approaching the well-lighted entry. Even at a distance, he recognized her. It was Dana.

He continued walking, thinking that if he should catch her before Betts showed up, he might get in a few words with her. Arriving at the door, he looked inside. Dana was there, talking to someone partially hidden. When the guy turned, Mitch saw it was Betts. They were waiting for the hostess to take them to a table.

He had another choice to make. Did he flick it in, head for home, or should he stick around? When Dana and Betts entered the dining room, Mitch stepped inside the door. What the hell. He wanted to observe the woman in action. He was curious how she'd act with Betts.

San Anselmo

Ted O'Connell drove up the street until he came to the condominium complex. He parked across from it and considered his next move. It appeared that the first unit was Robin Cohen's. The question was if they were both there.

He decided the only way to find out was to snoop around. But rather than leave the car in plain sight, he figured it would be smarter to park around the corner, just in case something went wrong and he had to make a fast getaway. He started the engine and proceeded half a block to the corner, where he turned and parked. He got out of Wayne's Plymouth, adjusted the 9-mm automatic under his belt, and walked back to the complex. He was a few doors away, on the opposite side of the street, when he saw the front door open.

Stepping behind a tree, he saw a dark-haired woman come out the door of the unit. For a second he thought it was Dana, then he realized that it wasn't. It was Robin Cohen. She looked dressed up, like she might be going out on the town or maybe to present an offer or something. She went around the building, probably headed for her garage.

Ted waited. Sure enough, a Lexus came out the drive a couple of minutes later. Robin was behind the wheel and she was alone. She went down the street and disappeared from sight. He glanced at the unit. Lights glowed from inside. Perhaps his sitting duck was in there, waiting. Moving from behind the tree, Ted crossed the street, knowing he'd soon find out.

* * *

San Rafael

Dana noticed the sparkle in Frank's eyes when the waitress put the martini in front of him. Her glass of Chardonnay would go largely undrunk but she'd ordered it to be sociable.

"Well," Frank said, picking up his glass, "to forgiveness." He clinked his glass to hers.

Dana took a sip along with him, but it was a small one. "You're making more of the other night than it's worth," she said. "If you don't mind, I'd rather move on to the business at hand."

Frank gave her a hurt smile. Dana could see he was as manipulative as ever.

"You don't want to eat first?" he said. "A little rapport building might make things go smoother."

"Frank, I think you and I have all the rapport we're ever going to have."

"Is it my imagination, or do women carry the bitterness of past relationships longer than men?"

Dana started to respond but he interrupted her. "No," he said, "the question doesn't deserve a response. It was bitchy, I'm sorry. Forget I said it."

"Let me be direct," she said. "The only reason I came tonight was as a courtesy to you. I owe you a great deal, Frank. I've told you that before. But this isn't a particularly good time for me to reminisce about the good old days. There's a wife-beating maniac roaming around, determined to get me because he thinks I messed up his marriage. Somebody else has been threatening my life for the better part of a month, and I'm trying to compete in the real-estate business with you and Lane. So I don't have a lot of extra energy right now. Please, let's get on with what you have to say."

Dana took a bigger slug of wine than she intended and sat back, giving him a level look. Frank fidgeted uncomfortably.

"I know you're having a rough time, and I'm sorry. I really am. Naturally, I don't want you to win the recruiting skirmish—at least, not at our expense—but I get no pleasure from your other hardships, believe me."

"Good. We've established our bona fides, Frank. Underneath our competitive natures, we're both decent people. Now what is it you want to talk about?"

Frank quaffed half his drink. His hand trembled slightly as he set down his glass. They were seated by the window, looking out over the black canal. It would have been invisible but for the lights across the way, reflecting off the shimmering surface of the water. Dana looked at him steadily.

"Lane and I want to buy out your interest in Marin Pacific Savings," he announced.

"I see."

"You're no longer a part of the C&B team," he went on to explain, "so it doesn't make a lot of sense that you play a central role in our bank."

"Friendly competitors," she replied with a smile. "But not *that* friendly."

Frank Betts fingered his glass. "You don't blame us, do you?"

"No, not really. And I don't have any intention of making an issue of it. I don't want to hold you up or anything."

He brightened. "Then you'll sell?"

"Sure, if the price is right. Do you have an offer in mind?"

His face fell.

Dana waited. "You don't expect me to give it to you gratis, do you?" she said, after several moments of silence.

"What do you want for your stock?" His tone had become no-nonsense.

She shrugged. "Market value. What it's worth. We're probably talking in the six figures somewhere, aren't we?"

He gave her a dark look. A very dark look.

"You don't seem to like that suggestion," she observed.

He stared down at his drink and she could see he was trying to control his temper. He started turning red, as he tended to do when he was angry. In a way, Dana knew him better than her former husband.

"Why don't you just tell me what you've got in mind," she finally said.

"I went out on a limb to give you that stock," he protested. "It was a gift. I had to twist Lane's arm to do it. I convinced him with the argument that you were an important cog in the C&B machine, that buying your loyalty was a worthwhile investment."

"So you're saying since I didn't pay hard cash for the stock, I ought to give it up for nothing."

"Not nothing, no. You're entitled to something, some cash."

"Spit it out, Frank," she said, growing irritated. "What's your figure?"

"We'll give you twenty-five thousand cash."

"Twenty-five thousand?" Dana was truly surprised. "That's not even par value. And probably not twenty-five percent of market."

"It was a *gift!*" he retorted.

"It was delayed compensation. You'd talked about bringing me into the bank for a couple of years before you did it. You admitted I helped you make C&B what it is today. I recruited for you, I promoted the company, did things I wasn't paid for because you were going to give me a piece of the action down the line. Had it not been for that, I'd have left the company long before I did. When I got the stock, it was for services rendered. There were no strings attached, no conditions. And I have participated actively on the board. I may not be a banking genius, but I *have* made a contribution!"

Dana was angry and she felt her own hands tremble. She folded them in her lap.

"Cash flow is a problem right now," Frank said, still looking down at the olive in his martini. "Lane and I have our personal funds tied up in several different investment ventures."

"Well, I'm not pressing you," Dana said. "You're the one who wants to deal. I can wait until you're more liquid."

"No, we want this settled now. Lane feels you're a fox in our chicken coop and we'd like to make the parting complete."

"Then come up with the money for the stock and it's yours."

Frank glared at her. She could see the hatred in his eyes, and it shocked her. Anger was understandable. Hatred was unexpected.

"Look, Dana, despite what you say, that stock was a gift. You're taking my generosity and you're cramming it down my throat. The least you can do is show a little flexibility."

"Be honest, Frank. In my shoes, would you take twenty cents on the dollar?"

"All right," he said, ignoring the question, "twenty-five in cash and twenty-five in paper. A straight note, simple interest, due in five years."

"Secured by what?"

"The stock."

"You're asking me to give up control for five years for a lick and a promise. What sort of rate did you have in mind? Prime plus one?"

"Let's don't let this disintegrate into a pissing match," he groused. "Whether you believe it or not, I'm trying to be constructive."

"Frank, you must take me for a fool. No business person in their right mind would accept your offer. Besides, I've pledged the stock against an operating line of credit at my bank. Your offer wouldn't liquidate it, even if the fifty was all cash."

"What collateral value did your bank put on the stock?"

She smiled. "I wouldn't see my stock based on appraised value any more than you'd sell your condo on appraised value. The figure is seventy-five thousand."

"So you'd need seventy-five in cash just to get the stock out of hock?"

"No," she said, "I haven't tapped out my credit."

"How much cash do you absolutely have to have?"

Dana chuckled. "Want to show me *your* checkbook, Frank?"

"I'll give you thirty cash and forty-five in a note," he said, his teeth clenched. "And I want you to know most of that is coming from me. Lane doesn't feel he owes you a thing. You were *my* mistake as far as he's concerned."

"Evidently in more ways than one," she said mildly.

Frank drained what was left of his drink. He put his glass down with a certain finality. Dana could tell he was on the edge and she wasn't sure why. There was more going on here than just a negotiation. She could feel his desperation. And it didn't make sense.

"So," he said, "what's your answer?"

"Let me think about it," she replied.

"I've got to know tonight, Dana," he told her in a low voice, brimming with emotion.

"I'm surprised to hear you say that, Frank," she said. "You were the one who taught me never to level ultimatums when it's the other guy who's got the leverage. I can say no as easily as yes."

"*Are* you saying no?"

"I'm saying, 'Let me think about it.'"

The waitress came by to see if they were ready to order. Frank didn't fool with her. He told her to bring him another martini. A double.

Mitch had been watching them from the bar all through their dinner, trying to stay objective about what he was seeing. Dana seemed to be handling herself well. She was cool, professional and damned sexy. He didn't know whether Betts was seeing her that way, but he sure as hell was.

Dana had class and brains and money, yet she was a poor girl from Napa. He'd thought a lot about that since she'd told him. He couldn't exactly say that had changed things for him, but it had made him reassess his initial feelings.

At the moment, though, he was more interested in what was going on at the far side of the dining room. The conversation didn't look as unfriendly as it had at first. Betts actually smiled occasionally. Mitch had heard his line of bullshit. The guy knew how to sling it. He wondered how Dana was taking it.

She must have bought it at one time, considering they'd been lovers. That wasn't a notion that he found either agreeable or understandable. Flashy and successful or not, Frank Betts just didn't seem worthy of her. But Mitch knew that was probably his jealousy speaking.

When it appeared that Betts was asking the waitress for his bill, Mitch grew alert again. Dana looked serious, but she did not appear threatened or frightened. If anybody looked upset, it was Betts. The question was, why? Was his disappointment of a business nature, or was it personal?

A few minutes later Dana and Betts got up from their table. Mitch turned his back so that if they happened to glance into the bar they wouldn't notice him. He wasn't particularly eager for either of them to know he was there.

And though his initial concerns about Betts had abated, he wasn't yet prepared to pronounce the guy harmless. Mitch had already decided that he'd follow Dana to make sure she got to her car safely.

Paying for his second glass of soda water, Mitch left the bar, checking the entry to make sure they'd gone outside. By the time he was out the door, they had walked halfway across the lot, still talking. They stopped, and Mitch moved into the shadows.

After another few seconds of conversation, Dana went one way and Betts another. There'd been no kiss, no hand-shake, no hug. They'd simply parted. Mitch liked that, but just the same he was curious as hell as to what had tran-spired.

When he saw that Dana was safely in her car and headed out the drive toward the street, he turned and went back inside. He'd already decided what he was going to do. He'd have a cup of coffee and a piece of pie. Then he'd give Dana a call and see how her dinner had gone. Of course, he wouldn't tell her he'd been watching practically every min-ute of the time.

San Anselmo

On her way back to Robin's, Dana called to see how Molly and David were getting along. Molly was asleep, so she talked to David.

"Having that guard out front has certainly changed the atmosphere around here," he said. "But I have to admit, in a way I feel better. The neighbors are wondering what the heck's going on, but that's all right. Can't worry about them."

"How's Molly? That's what matters."

"She's taking it fine. For the time being, anyway. I think she likes the extra attention."

"Hopefully it won't last long."

"Well, they haven't picked Ted O'Connell up yet," David said. "I called the police a while ago, hoping to go to bed tonight knowing he was behind bars."

"David, they don't think Ted's the one who put the doll outside Molly's window. His shoe size doesn't match the prints they found in the mud."

"Oh."

"So even if Ted's arrested, we've got to keep up our guard."

"You've made my day, Dana," he said gloomily.

"Sorry. But imagine how I feel."

"It's rough for us all, I guess."

David didn't seem eager to talk and Dana wasn't, either. She was exhausted, and looking forward to getting to bed, even though it wouldn't be her own.

"I've got to go. I'll be at Robin's soon. Tell Molly I called and give her my love."

"I will," David said.

Dana hung up. She was on Tamalpais Drive and approaching the cross street where she had to turn. As before, she checked the rearview mirror. Her purse with her gun inside was on the seat beside her. She was ready, but it didn't make her like living this way.

A minute later she was on Robin's street. There wasn't a parking place directly in front, but there was one across the street and up a couple of doors. She made a U-turn at the corner and parked.

Before getting out of the car, she looked around to make sure no one was lurking about. Everything seemed quiet. Exiting the car, she locked it and quickly crossed the street, not wanting to spend any more time out in the open than was absolutely necessary. She unlocked the front door with the key Robin had given her, stepped inside, turned the dead bolt, and heaved a sigh of relief.

She put her purse on the chair and took off her coat. Then she saw a note taped to the door handle of the coat closet. It was from Robin.

Dana,
I had a very strange call from one of the girls in the office. Some guy posing as a client of mine called, saying he needed my home address to drop off some papers. The name he gave was nobody I know. She thought I might have a secret admirer with questionable intentions. I'm wondering if the secret admirer isn't yours. Could be a false alarm, but maybe not. She didn't give him my address, but be careful anyway. There are all kinds of ways to track down a person's home address. Keep the door locked. See you later.
                                                    Robin

Dana swallowed hard as she hung her coat in the closet. She looked around the front room. Two lamps burned cheerfully. The place seemed the same as it had earlier, except for a slight chill, almost as if there was an open window or door.

The furnace kicked on and Dana decided she'd come back just when the temperature had dropped to its low point. She headed for the kitchen, turning on the light before entering the room. The dishes from Robin's dinner were in the sink, but everything else seemed in order. The phone rang and she picked it up.

"Dana, it's Mitch."

A wave of relief went through her. "Oh, hi," she said breathlessly, "I'm glad it's you."

"You all right?"

"Yes. I'm jumpy, though."

"What's the matter?"

She told him about Robin's note.

Mitch was silent for a second. "I don't like the sound of that. Maybe I should drop by. I wanted to hear about your meeting with Betts anyway."

"That would be great," she said, relieved.

"It'll probably take me fifteen minutes to get there. I'm in San Rafael."

"Perfect." That gave her time to freshen up a little. "See you then."

Dana hung up and returned to the front room. A distinctive cool draft blew across her legs and it seemed to be coming from the bedrooms in back. Before investigating she decided to light the fire. She went to the fireplace, struck a match and turned on the jet. A yellow-green flame popped up, its warmth bringing a smile to her face.

She'd just stood when a voice behind her and across the room said, "Well, isn't that romantic."

Dana spun around and let out an involuntary scream at the same time. Ted O'Connell was standing at the entrance to the back hall. He had a grin on his face and a gun in his hand.

"Oh, my God," she said under her breath. Her entire body began to shake.

Ted slowly walked toward her. Dana backed to the mantel. She could feel the heat of the flame on the backs of her legs.

"Ted," she croaked, "what do you want?"

"A little romance," he said ironically, "what else?" He stopped a few feet from her, chuckling. "It's time you and I settled accounts, dollface."

Dana struggled to summon her courage. "There's nothing we have to settle, Ted. Any problem that exists between us is all in your imagination."

"Don't tell me what's in my head and what's not!" he shouted. "I'm the one in charge here. *I* tell you what's what, *not* the other way around!"

She cringed at the depth of his rage. She could smell alcohol on his breath, but he didn't seem to be in a drunken craze. It was anger with rational undertones, and that bothered her even more.

"What do you want, Ted?"

"I want you to shut up, for starters," he growled. "If I ask you a question, then you answer it. Otherwise, keep your fucking mouth shut."

Her fear was so great she thought for a second she might faint. Dana told herself she had to keep Ted at bay until Mitch arrived. Fifteen minutes—it seemed like an eternity.

Ted inched closer. A funny grin touched his lips. He reached toward her face with his free hand. Dana's body grew rigid. His rough fingers touched her cheek.

"Where were you tonight, honey? On a date?" He drew his thumb across her cheekbone to the corner of her mouth.

Dana's body shook violently.

"Where were you, goddamn it!" he roared. "I asked you a question!"

"I went out to dinner."

"With who?"

"Frank. Frank Betts."

"Oh, really? Fraternizing with the enemy, huh? What did you do, offer to blow him? That's what you did when you worked for him, didn't you?"

She shook her head.

Ted laughed sadistically. Seeing she wasn't amused, he said, "I can see we have to lighten you up a little. Take off your clothes, Dana."

She recoiled.

"I said, take off your clothes!" he screamed. "Now!"

"Ted, this is insane. Please, listen to me. I—"

His hand lashed out and caught her on the side of the face. The force of the blow knocked her against the fireplace. Then he reached out and grabbed her by the scruff of the neck, jerking her close to him. His rancid breath spewed over her.

"When I say strip, I expect you to do it, understand?"

She nodded, trying to fight back the panic welling in her. Tears were forming in her eyes. She trembled under the force of his grip.

He glared straight at her. As he did he brought the muzzle of his gun up and pressed it against the pulsing artery in her neck.

"You're about to get a lesson in humility," he said. "The other day you humiliated me. Now you're going to see what it's like. It's payback time, baby. Payback time."

Ted slowly drew the muzzle of the gun down to her chest. He kept it moving between her breasts and over her stomach until it reached her pubis. He pressed it hard against her, making her flinch.

"Payback time." He took a step back. "Undress."

Dana slowly removed her suit jacket. How much time had passed? she wondered. Five minutes? How long could she drag this out? She dropped the jacket to the floor. Next she stepped out of her shoes. Then she began to unbutton her blouse. She did it as slowly and deliberately as she could.

Ted actually grinned. "You act like you've done this before, dollface. You do this for all your clients at the close of escrow? Is this the secret of your success?"

"This is going to make it much worse for you, Ted. If you hurt me, the sentence will be a lot stiffer when they catch up with you."

"Shut up," he snapped. "Just get your fucking clothes off. And hurry it up."

Dana loosened her skirt and stepped out of it. She was in her panty hose and her blouse hung open. Ted scanned her body and smiled. For a second or two she felt as though she might be sick.

"Come on, you goddamn whore. Get a move on!"

Dana took off the blouse, letting it slip slowly off her shoulders. Then she began to peel down her panty hose. Ted watched. She could feel the heat of the fire on her backside.

"Keep going," he said, "we're just getting to the good part."

She wasn't sure how much longer she could stall. Her bra and panties were all that was left. "Ted," she said, "I know you don't give a damn about me, but for your own sake, you'd better go."

Rage filled his face and he moved toward her, to hit her again. She lifted her hands to deflect the blow.

"The police are on the way," she cried.

Ted grabbed hold of her hair and, taking a fistful, jerked her head back. "What are you talking about?"

"Robin left a note for me," she stammered, "saying you'd called her office. That phone call a few minutes ago was the detective. I told him about the note. He's coming right over. He should be here any minute."

"Bullshit! You're a fucking liar."

"I swear it. Didn't you hear me talking on the phone?"

"Yes, I heard, but you didn't say anything about anybody coming over."

"Yes, I did. He's coming."

"Well, let's get ready for him, then. Take off your bra. Now, goddamn it!"

Dana reached back and unhooked her bra. The cups dropped away from her breasts and she let it fall on the pile at her feet. She knew Ted was ogling her. She didn't look into his eyes, though. Her body ached with dread. Oh, God, how much longer till Mitch arrived? Five minutes?

Ted reached out and pressed the barrel of the gun between her legs. He rubbed it back and forth.

"How does that feel, honey? Like it?"

Dana looked at him for the first time. Her heart ached with hatred and contempt, but her body felt numb, lifeless, especially where he was touching her. She slowly shook her head.

"Well, let's see what you can do for me," he said. "No reason you should have all the fun." He slid the barrel under the elastic of her panties. "Take these off."

She did as he commanded, her body trembling with a dread of what was coming. Ted looked her over.

"You know, you're not a bad piece of ass with your clothes off. Some broads don't look so good naked, you know. Turn around."

Dana did as she was told.

"Maybe if you'd been nicer to me at that party, we wouldn't be here now. We might even like each other."

She almost felt like she could throw up on him, if she let herself. Her shoulders slumped. She closed her eyes. Oh, God, she thought to herself, how much time?

"All right," Ted said, unbuckling his belt. "On your knees."

She froze.

"On your knees, damn it!" he screamed. "You're going to suck my cock."

Dana got on her knees, her stomach lurching. She could feel the heat of the fire on her back. Tears filled her eyes. "Please, Ted," she sobbed. "Don't do this."

He'd lowered his pants to his knees. She could see the bulge in his shorts. He pulled down his underpants and his erect penis sprang toward her.

Ted took a couple of steps backward. "Now crawl over here, you fucking bitch," he seethed. "Crawl over here and suck me."

She crawled toward him, going as slowly as she could. She was only a couple of feet from him when there was the sound of a car in the street.

Dana turned her head and so did Ted. A car door slammed. She listened for the sound of footsteps and prayed.

The doorbell rang a moment later, and her heart leapt for joy. But before she could breathe, Ted clamped his hand over her mouth. He bent down close.

"If you so much as whimper," he whispered, "I'll blow your fucking head off." He pulled up his pants.

Dana stayed on her knees, motionless. The doorbell rang again and there was pounding.

"Dana, open up," came Mitch's voice. "It's me."

She looked up at Ted, who was trying to hold the gun and fasten his pants at the same time. He looked panicked. Mitch pounded on the door again and shouted for her to open up. He had to know she was in trouble.

Ted jerked her to her feet and dragged her back toward the bedrooms. She wasn't sure what he planned to do, but with Mitch outside he couldn't chance raping her. Mitch would be forcing his way inside at any minute.

They entered the master bedroom. The sliding-glass door to the patio was open. Ted, still gripping her arm, dragged her to it. He stuck his head out to make sure the coast was clear. Then he jerked her up against him, his sour breath washing over her.

"You lucked out this time," he growled, "but I'll be back. And I'm going to get you good. In the meantime, here's something to remember me by."

He raised the gun hand. Dana lifted her arm to deflect the blow, at the same time falling to the floor. Ted swung, but he only managed to hit her upper arm.

There was a jolt of pain and she screamed. Ted started to hit her again, but they heard a loud crash in the front room. It sounded like Mitch was trying to kick down the door. Ted froze indecisively, then darted through the open glass door and into the night.

Pulling herself to her feet, Dana rushed frantically through the house. She got to the front room, opened the door, and threw herself into Mitch's arms.

"It's Ted," she managed between sobs. "He just ran out the back."

"Are you all right?" he asked, taking her by the shoulders.

She nodded, unable to stop weeping. The tears flowed down her cheeks. "He was going to rape me."

Mitch led her to the sofa. She fell onto it, pulling a pillow over her naked body and hugging it as though it were a teddy bear. She looked up at him through bleary eyes.

"I'm going to try and catch him, Dana," he said. "Wait here. I'll be right back. You're safe now."

She clutched the pillow and nodded. Mitch ran out the front door, pulling it closed behind him.

For a minute or so Dana sat shaking, unwilling to let go of the pillow. She knew she had to get dressed, though. Finally she staggered over to the fireplace where her clothes lay heaped in a pile. She slipped on her panties, then put on the blouse. There was a big red welt on her arm where Ted had hit her. She'd have one hell of a bruise. Next she stepped into her skirt. She'd just got it fastened when Mitch came flying in the front door.

"The sonovabitch got away," he said angrily. "Where's the phone?"

"In the kitchen."

Mitch started back, but diverted to where she stood in front of the fireplace. He reached out and touched her face tenderly. "You really okay?"

"Yes," she said, sniffling. "He hit me a couple of times, but if you hadn't come when you did, it would have been much worse."

Mitch pressed his cheek to hers, kissed her forehead, then went to the kitchen. Dana dropped into a chair, hugging herself to try to stop the trembling. She heard Mitch talking to the police dispatcher, saying something about a white car. A minute later he came back into the front room.

He approached her chair. Dana stood. "You saved my life," she said, her voice cracking. Tears streamed down her cheeks.

He took her into his arms and held her. In the safety of his embrace the dam broke and she began to weep uncontrollably. He stroked her head lovingly. Being held by him was the most wonderful feeling in the world.

"I'm sorry I didn't make it a few minutes sooner," he whispered. "You didn't deserve this."

She pressed her face against his jacket and continued to cry. All she could think of was that she never wanted him to let her go. Ever.

Sonoma County

Mitch had tilted the seat back for her and Dana reclined, hugging herself as she stared at the ribbon of red taillights stretching up the long incline ahead of them. She had changed into a bulky sweater and jeans. Her emotions had bounced around from helplessness to gratitude, to shame and then rage. It had been a close call. She had a deep contusion on her arm, a welt on the side of her face, and a battered ego.

Mitch had been doing a lot of talking during the drive up from Marin, probably sensing she wanted the comfort of his voice. The hysteria and the immediate fear were behind her, but she was still sorting out what had happened.

"If you hadn't arrived when you did, Mitch, Ted would have raped me. I know he would have."

"Well, he didn't. That's what matters."

"I feel violated, though. And angry."

"That's a normal reaction."

"I want you to know how grateful I am for what you did," she said. "You've been kind and compassionate, above and beyond the call of duty."

"I haven't done anything special."

"You mean you take all your crime victims home to nurse their wounded psyches?"

"Only if I consider them a special friend," he said, smiling.

Dana looked over at him. He seemed so strong and calm and confident and decent. Yes, and kind. That word came back to her again. She smiled at the recollection of the last time. "Kind?" Robin had said. "*David* was kind." She'd meant to chide her—it was a sort of put-down. But Dana saw significance in the parallel. It was no accident she'd married David Kirk, even if for reasons unrelated to his kindness it had been a mistake.

"Did you save wounded animals when you were a boy?" she asked.

"No, I was a feisty little kid. I didn't pull the legs off grasshoppers, torture mice or anything like that, but I acted out a lot of anger."

"Because of your parents' divorce?"

"I suppose that was part of it, though I didn't see my life in those terms. I was battling the world, even at an early age." He glanced over at her. "What were you like as a kid?"

"Conscientious. Ambitious. Determined to make something of myself from about the first time I discovered a part of the world lived a lot better than we did."

"You wanted your piece of the pie."

"Yes, I guess I did."

"Where'd you get your courage?" Mitch asked.

She thought about the question. "I'm not sure, unless it was discovering that my father wasn't up to carrying the load. Necessity gave me backbone, I guess."

Dana rubbed her arms and shivered, though the temperature in the Bronco was quite pleasant. It was odd to be talking about her courage when she felt anything but courageous. She'd just lived through one of the uglier experiences of her life. And yet, her decision to come with him had been easy; Mitch had made it for her. "I'm getting you out of here," he said as the Corte Madera police did their thing. "You don't need this."

At that point Robin was Dana's only concern. Ted had knocked the sliding-glass door in her bedroom off track breaking in, and Mitch had done a number on the front door. It was serviceable, but would have to be replaced. Dana had already decided to see to that.

But poor Robin hadn't arrived home by the time the police had finished up and Dana had given her statement. She figured the drink with Morton had turned into a night with Morton, but didn't know how to reach her. Robin had resolved the problem by calling from Morton's place in San Francisco at around eleven to say she wouldn't be coming home that night.

Dana had filled her in, told her they would make sure the place was secured, but that she was going with Mitch to

Sonoma. Robin was upset for her and concerned, but she was relieved that Mitch had taken responsibility. "Joy can follow the darkest evil," Robin had said.

Dana had thought of him more in terms of refuge than joy. Mitch was her protector, pure and simple. She'd grabbed her overnight case from Robin's guest room and once the condo was locked they'd jumped in the Bronco and headed up the Redwood Highway for Sonoma.

Whenever Mitch fell into silence, as he had now, Dana's thoughts would wander back to Ted. The worst had been when he'd caressed her with the gun. He wanted to hurt and humiliate her, and a sexual assault was the best way he knew to reclaim the manhood he thought she'd stolen from him. Dana shivered more violently than before.

Mitch took her hand without saying anything. He evidently had read her thoughts. She closed her eyes, savoring his firm-yet-gentle grip. He rubbed the back of her hand with his thumb. They stayed that way for a long time, most of the rest of the way to his place.

By the time they turned off the road into his drive, Dana was almost asleep. She was exhausted. But she sat up to see what she could in the headlights of the car. Mitch had described his home earlier, but she was curious about seeing it.

When the house itself came into view, she saw that it was modest, as he'd said, but not to the extent he'd let on. He pulled directly into the carport. Dana opened the door and got out. Her arm was throbbing. Mitch grabbed her bags and carried them to the door. It was quite cold and her teeth chattered as she stood waiting for him to unlock it.

She stepped inside and Mitch switched on the light. She glanced around at the sparse furnishings. Her eye was drawn to the map of Nevada.

"I told you it wasn't much to look at," he said. He put down her case and went over to turn up the thermostat. The furnace kicked on.

"It's a definite improvement over your office, but you could use some plants here, too, Mitch."

"Think that would do it?"

"No, but it would be a start."

"What's with women, anyway?" he chided. "I understand the importance of 'clean.' I understand the importance of 'comfortable.' Why aren't the aesthetics of functionality enough?"

"You don't eat your food raw, do you? Women like to please their eye as much as men want to please their stomach."

"It's remarks like that that keep old bachelors like me on the run," he said, wagging his finger.

"Don't be alarmed, Mitch, I'm not planning on marrying you."

He laughed. "I've been worrying about that."

She gave him a look. "I bet." She picked up her overnight case. "Where's the guest room?"

"Right this way." He led her into the bedroom. "You'll have to forgive the shoddy housekeeping," he said, picking up some socks and a shirt from the floor. "The maid's been sick."

He tossed the things in the closet, then hung up his coat. She watched as he removed his shoulder holster and put the gun in the top drawer of the dresser.

"This is your room," she said, looking over at the unmade bed.

"Only when it isn't the guest room. I sleep on the couch when I've got company—polite company, anyway."

Dana did her best not to laugh. "If I'd known I'd be putting you out of your bed, I wouldn't have come."

"I know. That's why I didn't tell you."

"Mitch . . ."

"It's no big deal. I'll have to change the sheets, that's all."

She put the case down on a chair. "I feel terrible."

"Don't." He went back to the closet and, after rummaging around for a minute, returned with an ice bag. "Here, take this to the kitchen and fill it with ice. We've got to take care of that arm."

"How do you know it was bothering me?"

"Body language."

She hated to think what else he might have read into her body language. Of course, considering that she was standing in his bedroom, and it was after midnight, she should figure that they were well beyond the point of coyness.

She turned and went to the kitchen. The sink was full of dirty dishes, but she could hardly fault him for that since he'd had no idea he'd be bringing her home. She had a peek in his refrigerator. A quart of milk, a stick of butter on a saucer, half a loaf of bread, a carton of eggs. Assorted condiments, an enormous jar of mayonnaise, carrots, jam, two bricks of cheese, a pound of hamburger, four bottles of beer. The man was not a gourmet cook.

The discovery was oddly reassuring. Dana filled the ice bag and returned to the bedroom.

Mitch had stripped the queen-size bed and was putting on a new fitted bottom sheet. "I don't iron them," he said, glancing up at her. "I hope you don't mind."

"I feel very badly about this," she said.

"Do you feel safe—as in, safe from O'Connell?"

"Yes."

"End of argument."

Dana put down the ice pack and helped him finish making the bed. There was a down comforter, but no bedspread. He folded it across the foot of the bed. Then he handed her the ice pack.

"Put this on your arm."

"Yes, sir."

"We really should have done it right away to keep the swelling down."

"You're a cop, a social worker, an innkeeper *and* a doctor," she observed. "Any other hidden talents?"

"Yes, but they're not the kind you'd be interested in right now." He gave her a wink, gathered up the dirty sheets and left the bedroom.

Dana looked after him. It was the most directly flirtatious thing he'd said. She was flattered.

Sighing, she sat on the bed and held the ice bag to her arm. The contact hurt, but after a moment or two the coldness started feeling good. Mitch returned with some towels.

"That help?"

"Yes, thanks."

He went into the bathroom. He rummaged around, running water, opening and closing cabinets. He reappeared. "It's not too bad in there," he said. "I cleaned up some. In the morning I'll do the tub before you have your shower."

"It's not necessary, Mitch."

"Yes, it is. I've learned from this experience that I have to reform my ways."

"I feel terrible for having intruded into your life this way."

"Don't, Dana. Really. I'm glad you're here. I'll sleep better, knowing you're safe."

It was a sweet thing to say. And she could tell he meant it.

He got a sleeping bag out of the closet and tossed it over by the door. She hated the thought of him having to spend the night on the sofa just because of her. She put down the ice bag and went over to him.

Mitch looked down at her, a surprised, uncertain expression on his face. She took his hands.

"Can I tell you something?"

He shrugged. "Sure. Tell me anything you want."

"The best thing that's happened to me the past week is meeting you."

The corners of his mouth lifted slightly. "We met three days ago."

"That's all?" She stopped to think. "God, you're right."

"Time flies when you're having fun," he said.

"It's a horrible cliché, but I feel like I've known you a long time, Mitch. Much more than three days."

"Yeah, I feel the same way."

She wanted him to kiss her. He appeared to realize it. Taking her chin in his hand, he leaned over and lightly kissed her on the lips. It was a tender kiss and it did not end right away. His mouth lingered near hers. He slid his fingers along her jaw, then under her hair at the back of her neck. He kissed her forehead and she turned her face, pressing her head against his chest.

Mitch held her to him. She closed her eyes and inhaled his scent. An odd, tentative sort of desire went through her. It wasn't exactly sexual, because that was the last thing she wanted, and yet it was.

"You need a good night's sleep."

"I know." She took another deep breath, drawing in his scent. "How early do you have to get up in the morning?"

"Tomorrow's my day off," he said. "I worked Saturday, so tomorrow I get to pitch manure instead of chase criminals."

She pulled back so that she could see him. "Nice change of pace."

"Believe it or not, it is." He looked into her eyes. After a second he seemed to notice her cheek where Ted had

slapped her. He turned her face for a better look at it.
"You're going to get some color here, too, it looks like."

She nodded.

"Might be a good idea to stick the ice bag on it, too."

"Yes, Dr. Cross."

"Fresh towels are in the bath. Anything else you need?"

"No, I feel duly pampered, Mitch. Thanks."

He kissed the end of her nose. "We mean to please.
Country hospitality." He went to the window and drew the
curtains shut. Then he went to the door. Grasping the knob,
he looked back at her, a wistful expression on his face.
"Good night, Dana."

"Good night."

He closed the door.

Suddenly alone, she deeply felt his absence. The solitude made her shiver. She got her case and went to the bath
to ready herself for bed.

After she'd gone to the bathroom, brushed her teeth and
put on her flannel nightgown, she returned to the bedroom. Pulling back the covers she slipped between the cool
sheets. That reminded her of the ice pack, which she took
from the nightstand to hold against her arm. She turned off
the lights and lay shivering in a strange bed with a bag of ice
pressed against her battered flesh. Outside she could hear
the gentle purr of the wind and the faint sound of a barking dog off in the distance. She felt the pain of the night's
events—in both her body and her heart. In the darkness
Ted—bitter, vengeful, cruel Ted O'Connell—came to her.
She chased the thought of him away by conjuring up an
image of Mitch holding her, and the feel of his protective
arms.

She realized the darkness and solitude of the strange
room made her feel alienated. She wasn't afraid, but she
was lonely. As her eyes grew accustomed to the dark, she
became aware of light coming from under the bedroom

door. Knowing Mitch was just out there, on the other side of the door, she realized she didn't want to be alone in his bed. She wanted to be near him, with him.

Dana threw back the covers and padded barefoot across the cold floor. Opening the door, she squinted into the bright light.

Mitch was seated on the sofa in his shorts, the sleeping bag spread open beneath him. He was reading the newspaper. Seeing her, he dropped the paper onto his lap.

"What do you need, sugar?"

Dana didn't answer. She went to the sofa and sat down next to him, taking his bare arm in both her hands.

"Mitch," she said, "do you have enough willpower to sleep with me, without wanting to make love?"

He grinned in a friendly, unthreatening way. "I wanted to suggest it, but I didn't know how without sounding insensitive."

"I'd love more than anything for you to hold me. I'd like to go to sleep in your arms."

Mitch put his paper aside. He took her hand, turned off the light, and led her to the bedroom. They climbed into the bed and he pulled the comforter up over them. She instantly glommed on to him, her arm around his chest, her head on his shoulder.

The surface of his skin was cool, but in a minute the deeper warmth of his flesh began radiating through her. She could smell the tang of his body and she felt an abiding sense of peace. Mitch began stroking her temple with his fingertips. Fatigue settled on her and in thirty seconds she was sound asleep.

Six

Forestville, Sonoma County
Tuesday, March 3

When Dana awoke the next morning it took a few seconds for her to figure out where she was. The clock on the nightstand said nine-thirty. Mitch was gone. She listened, but could detect no sign of him. She got out of bed and went to the window. It was a bright, sunny day. She saw blossoming trees and a green field. The air coming through the crack in the window smelled of spring. Were it not for the soreness of her arm, she might have concluded that Ted O'Connell had been no more than part of a vivid and awful dream.

She went to the bedroom door and opened it. "Mitch?" she called.

There was no response. She went to the bathroom. After brushing her teeth, she washed her face, ran a comb through her hair, and went to see if she could find him. She crept across the bare living room floor to the entrance to the kitchen. She was greeted by the aroma of coffee. A positive sign of life, but no sign of Mitch.

Then, through the window, she saw him walking toward the house. He was in jeans, boots and a jean jacket. He appeared at the back door, seeing her through the glass just as he opened it. "Well, Sleeping Beauty!" he said with a grin. "How do you feel?"

"Slept like a log."

He closed the door behind him. "No bad dreams?"

"Not that I recall."

Mitch came over to her and gave her a big hug. He smelled of the cool outdoors—hay, after-shave and earth.

"You're cold," she said.

"You're warm."

"Not my feet."

They both looked down at her curled-up toes.

"There's a remedy for that," he said. "Sit down. I'll be right back."

Mitch left and Dana sat at the table. She rubbed her flannel-covered arms and savored the aroma of the coffee. He returned with a pair of sweatsocks and a tattered white terry-cloth robe.

"Here," he said, holding the robe for her to slip into.

She stood and let him help her into it. The shoulders came to the middle of her arms and the hem to her ankles, but it would keep her warm. She tied the belt.

"These ought to keep your feet warm," he said, handing her the socks.

Dana sat to put them on. Mitch went to the cupboard.

"How about a cup of coffee?"

"I'd love one." She pulled the socks onto her feet. The tops of them came to her knees.

Mitch poured coffee into a mug and carried it over, putting it on the table. "What would you like for breakfast?"

"What do you have?"

"Eggs, toast, cereal. The sweet rolls I had got thrown out yesterday."

"Toast and coffee would be fine. But I can make it, Mitch. You don't have to wait on me."

He got the bread and butter out of the refrigerator and pointed to the toaster on the counter. "If you'd like to do the honors, I'll take the opportunity to clean the tub."

"You really don't have to."

"My reputation is at stake." He started to leave, then stopped at the door. "Not much to report from Marin, by the way. O'Connell hasn't been arrested, but they found the rental car he'd leased in a shopping-center parking lot in San Anselmo. I don't think it was the vehicle he was in last night, judging by the description. He may have stolen a car, or borrowed one from somebody."

"What does that mean?"

"That he'll be a little harder to pick up."

"Great."

"There are no reports of him headed this way. I think you can eat your breakfast in peace. In fact, my advice is to relax and kick back a little. You're welcome to spend the day, forget your troubles."

"My world is back there, Mitch. And it's falling apart. I've got to do what I can to shore things up."

"You're the boss."

"I'd at least like to make some phone calls. As a minimum I've got to tell people where I am and that I'm all right."

"Don't be too specific about your location—just to be safe."

"I won't. And I'll be using my calling card."

"Don't worry about it," he said.

"I don't want to be a total leech."

He gave her a smile and left. Dana fixed some toast. She ate it dry and drank the coffee. It was good and strong. There wasn't a phone in the kitchen, but there was one on the table by the recliner in the living room. Carrying her coffee mug with her, she ensconced herself in the chair.

First she phoned the office. Chiara told her that Sylvia was the only one in. Dana was glad—that was just the person she wanted to speak with. Dana told her she was going to be out of town for the day and asked if Sylvia would keep her eye on things.

"Dinner for you and Chuck anywhere you want, on me, for minding the shop," Dana said.

"That could really cost you," Sylvia said.

"If you hold things together until I return, you'll have earned it."

"Chuck loves Stars."

"You've got it." She gave Sylvia Mitch's number in case an emergency arose, but she didn't explain further.

Next she tried calling David's office. Molly would be in school, so there was no point in trying his home. She got his answering machine, which probably meant he was with a client. She left Mitch's number and asked him to call when it was convenient.

Mitch came out of the bedroom. "Milady's bath is pristine," he said, seeing she was between calls. "Shall I draw it for you, or do you prefer a shower?"

"A shower is fine, thank you."

"At your service, madam." He gave her a wink. "Would there be anything else, then?"

"No, thank you, Jeeves."

"If madam will excuse me, then, I'll finish grooming the horse."

"From one nag to another, huh?"

He strode over to her chair and brushed her cheek with the back of his fingers. "You aren't as desperately in need of grooming as my sorrel. And anyway, I thought to offer assisting you with your bath might be a bit forward."

She gave him an admonishing look. "Go tend to your horse, Mitch."

"I thought you'd agree."

He left and she leaned back in the recliner, savoring the moment. She liked the way they bantered with each other. In fact, she liked most everything about Mitchell Cross. His house was quiet, a perfect refuge. It looked no less benign by light of day, but it badly needed sprucing up. She wondered if he'd be offended if she offered to add some decorative touches. No, she decided, that would be pushy. Sleeping in a man's bed was one thing. Giving his digs a makeover was quite another.

For several more minutes Dana enjoyed the tranquillity. Though she had every reason to be anxious, she felt at peace here. She could go in and take a shower without wondering who might be lurking around outside the bathroom door.

The telephone rang. She figured it was probably David and she picked up the receiver. "Hello."

"Uh...is Mitch there?" It was a woman's voice, and she sounded rather surprised. Dana knew the tone well.

"He just stepped outside. Let me call him for you."

"No...don't bother. No need to disturb him. It's not important."

"Is there a message?" Dana asked.

"No. No message. Thanks." She hung up.

Dana put down the receiver. A lady friend, evidently—one who didn't like hearing her answer the phone. Ten in the morning was a suspicious hour for a woman to be there, so the reaction wasn't surprising. She'd have to tell Mitch, just in case there was a need for damage control.

She went off to get cleaned up, knowing she could do it at a leisurely pace without worrying about having to rush off someplace. It was almost like being on vacation, and she found herself wanting to make it last.

After she'd done her hair and dressed, she made the bed. As she did, she wondered how long it had been since he'd shared it—with a woman like the lady caller, for example.

She remembered Mitch saying he'd been involved with someone, but that it wasn't an exclusive relationship. At the time it had hardly seemed of consequence. Now she saw it in a different light.

Feeling a twinge of jealousy, she went into the kitchen and cleaned up the mess from breakfast. Working in his kitchen, she had a funny feeling. Ever since the woman had called, Dana had felt less special, as though for him last night might even have been routine. Of course, she had no reason to think he'd been celibate. If he was a normal healthy adult male it was to be expected he'd have a lady friend or two or three. God, she hoped it wasn't somebody different every night.

The telephone rang again. Dana dried her hands on a tea towel, then went to the front room to get it. She was a little wary of answering after the last call, but it could be for her, so she figured she'd better take it.

"Cross residence," she said, though even to her the purpose of the affectation wasn't clear.

"Dana? Is that you?" It was David.

"Oh, hi," she said, embarrassed.

"Who's Cross?" David had let his curiosity—perhaps jealousy—show, which was unusual for him. He almost never betrayed his emotions toward her, except annoyance.

"A friend. I'm visiting a friend."

"Oh." He was in control of his feelings again.

"How's Molly?" she asked.

"Fine, when I dropped her off at school."

"You'll be picking her up?"

"Yes, of course." He drew a breath. "Dana, I think you've got to rein yourself in a little. You'll drive yourself crazy if you don't get control."

"David," she said firmly, "I came within a hairbreadth of being raped by Ted O'Connell last night. If the police hadn't arrived when they did, I'd either be in the hospital or dead.''

There was a stunned silence. ''Jeez, Dana, I'm sorry. I had no idea.''

''So, you see why I'm anxious about Molly.''

''Forgive me.''

''That's not necessary,'' she said. ''Just take especially good care of her so I won't have to worry about that on top of everything else.''

''I will. You can count on it.'' David sounded duly chastened, but that wasn't what she cared about.

''I don't think there's any need to tell Molly what happened,'' she said. ''It'll just worry her unnecessarily.''

''I agree.''

''Well, that's really all I was calling about.''

''How long will you be gone?'' he asked.

''I'll probably be back this evening. Tomorrow at the latest.'' She wasn't quite sure why she'd added that—whether it was for David's benefit or her own. It was odd how she had a compulsion to be scrupulously honest with David. And it was odd how he still engendered feelings of guilt, too.

''There's nothing to worry about on this end,'' he said. ''But if anything comes up, I'll give you a jingle at this number.''

''Thanks. And please give my love to Molly.''

Hanging up, she returned to the kitchen. Out the window she saw Mitch leading his horse around the small barn. Dana wondered if he planned on going riding. She decided to go outside and find out.

The air was not warm, but it wasn't cold, either. Mitch watched her make her way toward him. His eyes were appreciative of what they saw. That made her feel good. She'd liked sleeping with him. And she'd rested surprisingly well, considering she wasn't used to another body being next to her in bed.

"My, my," he said, "don't you look scrubbed and clean."

"Soap can do that."

"How's the arm?"

"Okay," she said. She'd come up to where he stood with the horse.

Mitch was holding the cheek strap of the horse's bridle. "Won't be necessary to amputate, then?" he asked.

"Or put me down, either one," she said, glancing at the sorrel.

"Oh, forgive me," Mitch said. "Dana, this is Jake. Jake, meet Mrs. Kirk."

"Hi, Jake," she said, laughing.

"Do you ride?"

"Not for years. I had a friend in school who had horses. I rode with her some."

"Why don't we go for a little spin? I can show you my spread."

"Do you have another horse?"

"Jake doesn't mind two for a short jaunt. What's an extra hundred pounds?"

"Hardly, but thanks."

Mitch stepped back and looked her over. "A hundred and ten."

"No, but thanks again."

He stepped back a second time.

"That's close enough," she said. "I'll leave you with your illusions. And me with mine, for that matter."

"You don't have to worry about your figure, Dana. I can personally vouch for that."

"You could have gone all day without saying that."

"We're not exactly strangers, are we?"

"No, we're friends," she said, making her point.

Mitch studied her. "Is sleeping with me bothering you—in retrospect?"

"No, of course not. You know how appreciative I am. You're a gentleman, Mitch. I'll be forever grateful."

He stroked his chin. "Is it my imagination, or is there a reason why you sound like you found some lady's underclothes in my closet?"

She shook her head, smiling despite herself. "You know, it's kind of scary how perceptive you are."

"Don't tell me that's it," he said, looking slightly embarrassed.

"No."

Jake threw his head and whinnied. Mitch patted his nose. "Settle down there, big fella, I'm trying to divine this lady's mind."

Dana decided to be forthright. "You had a call a while ago. A lady friend, I believe, one who was a bit surprised to hear me answering the phone."

"Oh."

"I tried to be discreet. I offered to get you. She didn't want me to bother. And she didn't want to leave a message."

"I don't think it's basis for concern," he said.

"For whom?" Her tone was more pointed than she'd intended.

He tendered a smile. "Are we having our first spat?"

Dana blinked. "Spat?"

"You seem to be upset by the telephone call."

"I'm not upset."

"Then I'm mistaken, apparently."

"Look, Mitch, just because we slept in the same bed doesn't mean I've laid claim to you. I know you've got a girlfriend. If I was concerned about anybody it was about you and, for that matter, *her.*"

"I wasn't suggesting you were jealous—"

"Jealous? Why would I be jealous?" she asked incredulously. Then she laughed, shaking her head. "I hope you haven't gotten the wrong idea—what it means that I agreed to come here."

"Dana, I think we're having a communication problem," he said solemnly.

"Are we?"

"I think it's one of those man-woman things where people talk past each other."

"Oh, *that's* what it is." Dana didn't know why she'd gotten her dander up. It had started out as such a nice morning and he hadn't done anything all that horrible. Maybe she had misunderstood. Maybe she was being defensive. Maybe she *was* jealous!

Mitch looked like a chastened schoolboy. A sad one. Dana sighed woefully.

"I'm being snappish," she said. "I'm sorry. Maybe all the pressure I'm under is getting to me."

He brushed her cheek with the backs of his fingers. "You're entitled."

"I'm not entitled to take it out on you. Forgive me."

"Forget it. I wasn't as understanding as I should be. What say we go for a ride? Air and exercise will clear both our heads."

Dana was happy to move on. "Fine," she said.

"Do you mind riding behind?"

"No, I'd prefer you drive."

Mitch mounted the horse. Then he slipped his boot out of the stirrup so that she could use it to get a leg up. Taking her hand, he pulled her up behind him.

Jake was a little skittish and took a couple of abrupt steps. Dana threw her arms around Mitch, hanging on for dear life. She didn't feel very secure without a saddle.

"You all right?" he asked, glancing over his shoulder.

"I'll be fine until I fall off."

"Jake's not much of a bucker," he said, "though occasionally he runs across a perfume he doesn't care for and gets a little antsy."

"Is that what happened to your lady friend? Jake bucked her off?"

Mitch reached back and pinched her nose. Then, clicking, he gave the horse a gentle kick with his heels. Jake took off smartly. Dana clung to him even tighter, but Mitch didn't complain.

Kentfield

At three in the afternoon Lane Cedrick, red-faced, walked out the front door of the office building, past the Cedrick & Betts sign, to the sidewalk. He turned and moved swiftly up the street, his anger growing with each step.

The Village Lounge was half a block up, on the same side of the street. It used to be that he and Frank would walk up in the evening after work for a drink before heading home. Over the past year Frank had made it his office away from the office, and seemed to be spending as much time with his belly to the bar as he did sitting at his desk.

Lane pushed the front door open and stepped inside. It took a moment for his eyes to adjust to the darkness. Then he saw him at the far end of the bar, talking to Tina Bazooms, as Frank called her, the barmaid with the triple-D-cup tits.

A man and a woman sat at the near end of the bar. A couple of guys were at a table. Otherwise the place was empty. Seeing him, Frank straightened, but then he slumped in resignation. He drained the martini and gave Lane a dismal look.

"Well," Lane said, sitting on the adjacent barstool, "I knew I'd find you in conference."

Frank glanced woefully at the barmaid. "Will you excuse us, honey?"

She went off and Lane sat seething, staring straight ahead. He waited until he had full control before he spoke. "I spent the morning patting the asses you're supposed to be patting. I had lunch with Adrianne Stevens and Judy Povich, doing everything I could but kiss Judy's ass to get her back in the fold. I come back to the office only to discover you haven't been seen since eleven-thirty this morning. What the fuck are you doing, Frank, trying to drink us into insolvency?"

"I just couldn't sit at that desk," Frank said, dropping his head.

"Obviously the news from last night is not good. What the fuck happened?"

Frank gave him a rundown on his negotiation. "The bottom line is she's got us by the balls," he said, "and she knows it. I couldn't get her to commit. She wants to think about it."

"How long?"

"A week, two weeks, a month, who knows? She wouldn't say."

"Well, it's got to be in the next couple of days and the answer has got to be that she'll sell. I had a call from Stan Bishop. He's scheduled a meeting of the loan committee for next Monday morning."

"Oh, shit."

"Exactly. We have to get her off the board by Friday somehow, some way, period."

"But how?" Frank lamented. "I did everything I could. I offered her everything we've got to give."

"What will it take?"

"She'd probably settle for a hundred and twenty-five or so, seventy-five to a hundred in cash."

"Then we'll have to give it to her," Lane said.

"How? We don't have it."

"I'll throw in twenty-five cash. You come up with the rest. I don't care how you get it. Rob a fucking bank, if you have to. In the meantime, I'm taking over the negotiation. I'll sit down with Dana tomorrow and tell her to put her stock in escrow and that we'll close by Friday, so you better sober up and start hustling cash, Frank."

"What if I can't do it?"

"Then you'd better plan on trading in your condo for a cell at San Quentin."

Forestville, Sonoma County

Dana stood at the kitchen sink, tearing lettuce into the wooden salad bowl. The sky beyond the orchard was a rainbow of yellows, pinks and mauves. It was beautiful and it took her back to her years in Napa County as a girl. She remembered evenings when her father and she would go for a walk. It was one thing they enjoyed doing together. Sometimes he'd be half drunk, but it didn't stop him from savoring the evening air, at least not until his arthritis got so bad that he couldn't walk much farther than to the mailbox.

The back door opened and Mitch came in, bringing the smell of barbecue with him. "Two or three more minutes and the steaks will be done," he said. "How's the salad coming?"

"Two or three minutes is just right."

"Hey, we're a team, Dana. Perfect synchronization." Giving her a wink, he went back outside.

She smiled at his boyish affability. He'd been playful and in good spirits all afternoon, and so had she. He refused to let her stay in a peevish mood. Their ride hadn't taken long because his place was small. But they'd ridden through the surrounding orchards and along a trail that followed a creek. When they got back Mitch had taken a shower and then they'd driven to a little market up the road to buy some steaks and a bottle of wine for dinner.

Mitch had joked with the woman in the store. She was older, but her affection for him was obvious. He was well liked, Dana could see that.

"You have a way with women, don't you?" she'd said on the drive back.

"Truth be known, they have a way with me."

"What does that mean?"

"I'm a sucker for a pretty face."

"Any pretty face?"

"No," he'd replied. "I've gotten more discriminating in my old age."

She finished with the lettuce and dumped the chopped tomatoes and mushrooms into the bowl. Then she poured in some of the bottled dressing she'd found in the refrigerator. She was tossing the salad when Mitch came in with the steaks.

"Done to perfection," he said, putting the plate of meat on the counter.

"Smells good."

She put the salad bowl on the table, which she'd already set. Mitch had opened the bottle of Cabernet to let it breathe. While she scooped the rice from the pot on the stove into a bowl, he got a candle from the cupboard.

"If we're going to put on the dog, let's do it right," he said.

She sat down while he lit the candle and put it on a saucer between them. He turned off the overhead light and joined her.

"Not bad for a couple of kitchen klutzes," she said.

Mitch poured the wine. "I think we should drink to that."

They touched glasses. "To a better day than yesterday," he said.

"True," she said, after sipping her wine, "but yesterday didn't end so badly."

"Technically that was today," he said.

"Then it has been a good day."

They ate happily for a few minutes. She had developed an appetite after all the fresh air and exercise. Mitch was eating with gusto. He seemed as happy as she felt.

"This has been like a week in Hawaii," she said. "I'm really grateful for the respite you've given me."

"Hey, anything for a buddy." He chomped on some salad, looking especially handsome in the candlelight.

"Mitch, what sort of relationship do you have with that woman who called this morning? I know it's none of my business, but I won't feel comfortable around you until I know what's going on."

He'd just taken a bite of salad and chewed lustily as he pointed to his mouth, indicating it was full. Not waiting, she nervously rattled on.

"To be honest, I've felt uneasy ever since she called—like an interloper, a person who's invaded somebody else's territory. It's not a comfortable feeling."

He swallowed. "I told you I'm not seriously involved with anyone, Dana."

"*Serious* is one of those words that can get sort of fuzzy."

He nodded. "Okay. Her name is Carole. I've been seeing her for a few months on a nonexclusive basis. Over the weekend I broke it off."

"Why?"

He sighed. "The time had come."

"You mean you looked at the calendar and decided that was enough?"

He gave her a look of consternation.

"I'm trying to understand you, Mitch. The kind of person you are," she said defensively.

"If you must know, I broke it off because of you."

"Because of *me?*"

"If there's one thing I hate, it's hypocrisy. If I'm with one woman, I prefer not to be thinking of another."

"I see." Dana lowered her eyes. She picked up her fork and pushed some rice around on her plate.

"If it makes you feel any better, Carole said she was getting ready to move on, too. She wasn't crushed or anything."

"Is that true?"

"Cross my heart and hope to die."

She gave him a skeptical look. "Why'd she call this morning, then?"

"I don't know. Maybe it wasn't even her."

Dana arched a brow. "Then who else could it have been?"

"Somebody from my dark and *distant* past, obviously."

They both drank some wine at the same time.

"I'm sounding like a jealous lover, aren't I?" she said.

"Friends do that sometimes."

"I've thought about you a lot the last few days, too, Mitch."

He gave her an appraising look. "These are good signs."

"Are they?"

"Better than sitting here wishing you were somewhere else, with someone else."

"You've got a point," she confessed.

Mitch took another big bite of salad. She watched him chew. She wondered if they would have an affair and how long it would last if they did. The notion seemed as insane as it seemed inevitable.

"Good salad, Dana," he said. "You're not a total klutz in the kitchen."

"My moments of competence are brief and illusory. I am not at all domestic," she said.

"That's usually not the sort of thing women say to guys."

She gave him a long, hard look. "Mitch, you've got one foot in the Stone Age."

"That," he said, wagging a finger at her, "was not a compliment."

"You might like women, you may even treat them well, but you see them through a sexist veil. Your male ego keeps you from being truly enlightened."

"What are you saying, that I'm a cowboy?"

"Yes, I suppose you could put it that way."

"Now *that* is a compliment."

"You see! That's what I mean."

Mitch cut off a piece of steak. Dana watched him, then cut a bite of her own. Again they drank wine simultaneously. "Our chemistry is kind of delicate," he said, "isn't it?"

"Is that a polite way of saying I'm difficult?"

He shrugged. "This is not exactly a tranquil period of your life."

"You can say that again."

Mitch took a long drink of wine. He put his glass down carefully. "All right, the honest truth is I worry a little that whatever feelings you have for me are a product of the circumstances. Needy people are fragile, emotionally."

She was genuinely surprised by his frankness. "In other words, you aren't sure you're dealing with the real me."

"In other words."

"I can understand that," she said thoughtfully. She stared at the wobbling flame of the candle. "I'd like to say you're wrong—that this is me sitting here. But if I'm completely honest, I can't be sure of that myself."

"So we have a dilemma."

"How do you define our dilemma?" she asked.

"Where we go from here, I suppose."

"Where do you *want* to go?"

He gave her a faint smile, his eyes dark in the candle-light.

She fingered the stem of her wineglass. "Are you going to try to seduce me, Mitch?" she said, marveling that she actually had the courage to say the words.

He reached across the table and put his hand on hers. "The thought crossed my mind. But I'm concerned about what you went through last night," he said, his voice husky with emotion. "Something like that isn't so easy on a person's psyche. To put it mildly."

"That's true," she said. "But it also helped me focus my feelings for you. I can't tell you how good it felt coming here. How safe I felt sleeping in your arms. And how wonderful this day's been. It's almost as if all those things last night can't harm me now."

"I want that for you...and more," he said, toying with her fingers, "but I'm still not sure about the timing."

Her lips bent into a bemused smile. "If it feels okay to me, it should feel okay to you. All I can tell you is, being with you seems right. Safe."

"You're getting dangerously close to telling me you want me," he said with a wink.

"We seem to be headed down the same trail, cowboy, so yes, I guess that's what I am telling you."

"There are certain things a man shouldn't be asked twice, damn it, and this is one." He got to his feet. "Come on, woman."

She smiled. "Being dragged off by the hair isn't what I had in mind."

"Then I'll carry you. Nicely."

"Nobody's ever carried me to bed before," she said, looking up at his shadowed face. "Not even in my fantasies."

He stepped around the table and helped her to her feet. He handed her the candle, then lifted her into his arms with amazing ease.

"No cracks about my weight," she teased.

"Honey, you're just a slip of a girl."

His eyes glistened and he kissed her. She kissed him back. Then he carried her off to the bedroom like he was Rhett Butler and she was Scarlett O'Hara.

Mitch lay on his back with his eyes closed, perfectly contented. Dana rolled onto her side and backed her derriere against him. She was asleep, but instinctively sought the warmth of his body. He pulled the sheet up over them and wrapped his arm around her. Dana mumbled something but he couldn't make it out.

Her openness about sex had taken him by surprise. He'd figured she'd be shy, especially considering they'd never been intimate before. But she hadn't been. She'd been passive at first, watching as he slowly undressed her.

And when they were naked, he'd lightly caressed her skin, turning her tentativeness into slowly building confidence. The more aroused she'd become, the more she got involved, initiating kisses, touching his body as he'd touched hers.

Once she was on fire, there was no stopping her. Within seconds of his first intimate touch they were a jumble of limbs. She might even have been hungrier for him than he was for her, which was saying a lot. He'd been in a state of arousal to one degree or another the entire day. Evidently she had been, too.

She was moaning even before he was in her. When he did slip into her she arched hard against him, then squeezed and clutched at his flesh. "Oh, Mitch...oh, Mitch..." she kept saying. The more excited she got, the more aroused he became. There was a frenzied desperation in their love-making. Most surprising of all, they came at the same time, in perfect unison, like two longtime lovers equally lost in the moment.

As he lay on her afterward, he'd felt her heart pounding and he'd wanted to tell her how special and wonderful it had been, how moved he was. But instead he listened to her labored breathing as she struggled to get control of her body and settle back down to earth.

When she could finally talk she'd said, "My God," and swallowed hard. "Did you do that, or did I?"

He'd kissed her moist temple. "I think we both did."

Holding the sleeping woman in his arms, he felt protective of her. After Carole she seemed small and delicate, despite the fire in her lovemaking. He liked her size, her smell, and the cool, velvety feel of her skin.

He dug his face into her hair and inhaled the scent. When he exhaled his warm breath on her neck she moaned. He kissed her shoulder and she shimmied her butt against him. Mitch cupped one breast in his palm and felt himself harden.

Dana could feel her desire rising out of the depths of her slumber. Her yearning seemed to be pulling her from sleep. It was as if her body had taken a catnap and, having been refreshed, was ready for more. He was lightly rubbing his thumb over the tip of her nipple, making it hard, so hard it hurt. Her orgasm had been unusually intense, but it hadn't completely eradicated her need for him. She wanted something different this time, though. Before, she'd wanted him in her and she hadn't been willing to wait to discover him.

The candle was still flickering, though it had burned down to a stub. She watched the flame as Mitch began moving his hand over her body. Soon the skin of her stomach and thighs began to tingle. Mitch propped himself up on his elbow and ran his hand over her hip and down her leg. Dana rolled onto her back. She looked into his eyes and he into hers.

"You've done this before," she said.

"About an hour ago."

"Your first time?"

He shrugged.

"You're precocious, Mitch."

"No, you're inspiring." He leaned over and kissed her breasts, swirling his tongue around her nipples.

She began to tingle all over. When Mitch drew his tongue down her belly, the sensation grew more intense. He parted her plump folds and began kissing her cleft, running his tongue along the edges before dipping into her, lightly at first and then more forcefully. She dug her fingers into his thick hair, holding his face hard against her. Her excitement rose sharply. In seconds she was on the verge of orgasm.

"Oh, God, Mitch, the things you do. I don't believe this, I really don't."

He drew his tongue over her nub, sending a jolt through her. Her hips rocked and she came.

Mitch moved back from her and kissed her belly, preparing to enter her. He moved between her legs, his penis brushing against her before he slipped inside her again.

He moved slowly this time, gently rocking against her as he kissed her neck and shoulders, deliberately controlling the pace.

It was an exquisite dance, slow and tender and titillating. Her orgasm was more profound and consuming than before. After he came, Mitch collapsed onto her. She held him against her breast, incredulous that for a second time it had been so good. She hadn't even been sure she could relax enough to enjoy it at all, and she'd ended up having the best sex of her life.

"None of this is happening, is it?" she murmured.

"No, it's all a figment of your imagination."

"Does that mean at breakfast I don't have to feel shy and embarrassed?"

"Exactly right," he said. "I didn't see a thing."

A moment later the candle flickered out, plunging the room into darkness. She laughed. "Your timing's a little off, Mitch."

"No, my eyes were closed the entire time."

He kissed her chin and lips. Then he rolled off her. But he took her hand, interlacing his fingers with hers. They lay side by side that way.

"Would your ego rise off the scale if I gave you a compliment?" she asked.

"Cops are notorious for having low self-esteem, so you probably don't have to worry."

"That was the best sex I've ever had in my life, bar none."

"Does this mean we've got a relationship?" he asked.

"I think those kinds of questions are best answered by light of day."

"Why's that?"

"I don't know," she said, "but I think it has something to do with reality."

"What you're saying is, this might be a dream, after all."

Dana didn't answer—mainly because she didn't know.

Seven

Dana could see that Mitch wasn't kidding when he'd told her that they'd be in Marin before daylight. The sky over the doughnut shop was still dark as pitch and the light coming from inside the building so bright that it hurt her eyes.

She was enjoying watching him, though. He was flirting outrageously with the counter girl. She was just a teenager, but Dana could see they were having fun. It wouldn't have surprised her if his arrival each morning wasn't the highlight of the girl's workday. It would have been the highlight of hers at that age.

When he'd shaken her awake at five and said, "Rise and shine, bus leaves in thirty-five minutes," she could have punched out his lights. If there was anything she hated, it was early-morning cheerfulness.

"Go away and let me die," she'd groaned.

Mitch had pulled back the sheet and run his finger down her spine, letting it bump over each vertebra. "Come on, sweet pea, you've had your beauty sleep. Time to get up."

"Let me have ten more minutes."

"I've already had my shower. As soon as I'm dressed I'll be ready to go."

"I'll recommend you for the Congressional Medal of Honor," she'd grumbled. "Now, go away."

"I've got to be at my desk at seven," he'd said. "You can go with me or spend the day here. The choice is yours. And don't forget I've got to drive you to Corte Madera to pick up your car."

She had rolled over on her back, squinting up at him. "Why do I get involved with men who like getting up so goddamned early? I actually married one, which, now that I think about it, I can't believe."

It was the fastest she'd ever gotten ready in the morning. She'd done a half-assed job on her hair, partly because she was rushing, partly because he'd stood at the door of the bathroom, watching. Her makeup job had been less than sterling, as well. The place where Ted had hit her had really started to color and she wasn't able to cover it completely.

Finally she'd shut the door in Mitch's face, telling him voyeurs were loathsome perverts. There hadn't been time for breakfast, so he'd told her they'd stop at his favorite doughnut shop and have something in the car, which he did practically every workday morning anyway.

As they'd driven down the dark road toward Sebastopol she'd told him she wasn't human before the sun came up.

"No kidding," he'd rejoined.

Dana had whacked him, then apologized for being so testy. "I'll be better after a cup of coffee."

The girl in the doughnut shop was getting the coffees now. Dana could see her pouring it into two large disposable cups. She was looking over her shoulder at Mitch, smiling sweetly as only a girl of eighteen could.

Although technically the light of day hadn't come, as Dana waited for him to return, she was already thinking about the future and wondering what in the hell could possibly come of this. Mitch came out of the doughnut shop with a white sack in his hand. He climbed into the driver's seat and handed her the bag. "Food for the soul," he said.

"Fat for my thighs is more like it."

He leaned over and kissed her lips. "Your thighs are just fine, Mrs. Kirk, thank you very much. Take it from someone who knows." He checked his watch and then started the Bronco. "I've got ten or fifteen minutes to make up, so hang on, baby."

They took off and Dana peeked into the sack. She never ate doughnuts as a rule, but in light of the night she'd had, she felt sufficiently decadent to partake of unwholesome food. She took the lids off the coffees and handed Mitch one. She gave him a doughnut, had some of her own coffee, then started munching on a pastry.

"If I lived like you do, Mitch, I'd weigh two hundred pounds inside a year."

"The secret is short nights. Sleep is what puts on pounds."

"No wonder you're such a stud. How much sleep do you average? Three hours?"

"I'd have gotten my quota last night if the lady I went to bed with was more of a lady."

She whacked his arm again, nearly splashing coffee all over him.

"Hey!" he protested.

"Serves you right, impugning my morals."

"It's not your morals I was commenting on, it was your libido."

"Are you complaining?"

"Not unless I fall asleep at my desk."

"Don't worry, it won't happen again. The way my life's been going, I got a year's quota of sex last night."

"Maybe next time we should go to bed after lunch instead of after dinner."

"The jury's still out on the future," she said rather soberly.

He glanced over at her. "Does that tone mean it's time to stop joking around?"

She pointed up the road. "We're headed back to the real world, Mitch."

"Yeah, so it seems."

She rubbed his arm affectionately and they fell into a companionable silence, eating their doughnuts and drinking coffee. The caffeine woke her up, but unfortunately the effect was to turn her thoughts to her worries.

Mitch finally broke the silence. "You know, we managed to spend all day yesterday without once discussing the case."

"I know. Wonderful, wasn't it?"

"Yes, but I'm curious what happened with Betts. Anything come up I should know about?"

"Good Lord, in all the excitement I forgot about Frank."

"It wasn't memorable, then."

"It was strange, Mitch. The purpose of the meeting was to offer to buy out my interest in the bank."

"What bank?"

"Marin Pacific Savings. Haven't I told you about that?"

Mitch shook his head. "No, but I think you'd better."

She gave him a rundown of her history with the bank. "It doesn't surprise me that Frank and Lane would want me out of there, but the urgency has me confused."

"No idea why?"

"None."

"Anything unusual happen at the bank?" he asked.

"Not that I know of."

"I think it bears watching." He lightly drummed his fingers on the steering wheel. "What do you plan to do about their offer?"

"I don't know. I'd like to get as much for it as I can, the same as any other seller. Right now I've got the whip hand. The smart thing is to let their desperation work for me."

"That's the business mind, I guess."

She glanced at him, knowing it was an editorial comment. Because of the day they'd shared, she chose not to respond and make an issue of it.

After a moment he reached over and took her hand. "In saying that, I didn't mean to be critical of you."

She gave him a smile. "I didn't take it that way."

It was true she wasn't upset, and his concern was appreciated, but the comment was a reminder that they came from two very different worlds. What they had in common was rapport and a capacity for great sex.

Larkspur

One of the axioms of the world of small business was that if you went away for a while, the shit tended to hit the fan. Dana arrived at her office to discover her company was on the brink of collapse. Sylvia was waiting with the bad news.

Judy Povich had decided to return to C&B. Bev O'Connell had called that morning before checking out of the hospital. She was going to stay with her sister in Los Angeles for a while. She'd be in touch. That left Sylvia, Helene and Lucille. Sylvia told her that if it hadn't been for her new listing, Lucille would already have gone back to C&B.

"Don't be surprised if she doesn't ask you to release her license," Sylvia said. She shook her head. "I'm so sorry, Dana. You don't deserve this."

Sylvia had stared at her cheek as she spoke, but she hadn't asked any questions. Dana was grateful for the discretion.

"It's a new starting point, that's all," she said.

Sylvia went off, leaving her alone in her office to ponder her fate. The older black security guard, James, was on duty. It almost seemed like he was guarding an empty house. Chiara acted a little depressed, too. Dana had taken the girl under her wing and felt a special responsibility toward her although, like everything else, she'd been neglected of late.

Dana closed her eyes, wondering whether it was worth it. When she'd been one of Frank's minions she hadn't had to worry about anything but her clients. Now it felt like the whole world was on her shoulders.

Fleeting recollections of the day before went through her mind. Riding with Mitch, fixing dinner together, making love. It had been the happiest day she'd had in months, maybe years. She couldn't help but wonder if, in living the life she led, she was barking up the wrong tree.

The thought of surrender entered her mind. If she walked away from it all, she could probably salvage her house. It would mean immediately getting on the sales fast track. She could do that. She'd done it before. But the notion of failure cut into her soul. Could she really allow herself to be defeated?

Dana knew she had to pull herself up by the bootstraps. But she needed some moral support. She realized what she needed was Robin.

When Mitch had dropped her off to get her car, she'd rung Robin's doorbell, but there was no answer. On her way to the office, she'd called Robin at C&B, but she wasn't in. Dana could only hope she wasn't upset with her. After the disaster with Ted, Dana had let a whole day pass without touching base, and that had been inconsiderate if nothing else.

Ironically, in the middle of her lament, what should appear out front but Robin's Lexus. The sight of it brought a big smile to her face. Dana went out into the reception area and greeted Robin, embracing her the second she stepped in the door.

"Whoa," Robin said, "don't tell me the word's gotten here already."

"What word?"

Robin smiled. "Oh, you're just happy to see me."

"Of course, I'm happy to see you! I've had visions you were pissed at me."

"Why? Because Ted O'Connell broke—"

Dana cut her off, bringing her finger to her lips. "It's not common knowledge," she said under her breath.

"Oh." Robin took her arm. "Well, I do have news, so let's confer." They headed back to Dana's office. Robin greeted Chiara cheerfully as they passed the reception desk.

No sooner was Dana installed behind her desk than Robin reached over and deposited a piece of paper on her desk. Dana picked it up.

"What's this?"

"My license."

Dana could see that it was her real-estate license. "Robin..."

"I thought I'd join up, if you'll have me. As soon as I heard about Judy Povich, I thought, shit, Dana needs to score a point. I know I'm no Judy Povich or Nancy Tong, but I figured it could give the office a lift if you picked up a new agent."

Dana went around the desk and they hugged. "Robin, you are a friend in the truest sense of the word." She stepped back to look at her. "But I don't want you to sacrifice. A move only makes sense if it's good for you."

"I've been thinking about it for a couple of months. I want to do it, Dana, and this seemed like the right time."

They hugged again and Dana returned to her chair, feeling buoyed. It was the shot in the arm she needed. Robin leaned back in her chair, beaming.

"Feel free to ask me about the glow on my cheeks."

Dana gave her a questioning look. "Morton?"

Robin nodded, her mouth bending into a huge smile.

Dana pointed to her own cheek. "You might see a little color here, too. And I'm not referring to the bruise."

"The cop?" Robin said, her brows rising in surprise.

Dana nodded, smiling broadly herself.

Robin leaned forward eagerly in her chair. "Is our work schedule so full that we can't take half an hour to exchange stories?"

"I think we can spare the time," Dana replied, as she pretended to look at her calendar. "I don't know about you, but in my case half an hour may not be nearly enough."

"Hot damn," Robin said, rubbing her hands together, "I love girl talk."

San Rafael

David Kirk handed Sue Kaufmann another tissue and glanced at the clock on the wall behind her.

"I know," she said, wiping her eyes, "my time's up." She sniffed. "Why is it I always start crying when it's time to go home?" She was a thirty-two-year-old divorcée, pretty in a fragile sort of way.

"Because we get to the point where we uncover what you have to work on until our next session."

"Somehow that seems too convenient," she said, getting up. "Do you plan it that way?"

David rose, as well. "I try to help you, Sue. That means touching raw nerves."

She smiled through her tears. "We certainly do a lot of that."

She grabbed her coat and they went to the door. He opened it for her, saying goodbye. As Sue Kaufmann walked across the waiting room, David saw Nola Betts. She was sitting waiting, her legs crossed, a coquettish smile on her face. He was surprised to see her. Once Sue had gone, David stepped out into the reception area. "Nola, what are you doing here?"

"Does that mean you're glad to see me, or not glad to see me?" She stood, as if to present herself. She had on a tight skirt and a tight, scoop-necked sweater.

"Glad, but I didn't expect you," he said.

"We don't have an appointment, but I was in the neighborhood and thought I'd drop by. Are you free?"

"No, I'm expecting a client any minute."

"Damn," she said, pouting like a spoiled child.

"Why, what's wrong?"

Nola contemplated him. "The truth is I thought I'd come over and see what it would be like to make love on your couch. Since I'm not a patient, that'd be all right, wouldn't it?" She closed the distance between them and reached out to touch his cheek. "I've always wanted to get laid on a shrink's couch. It seems so Freudian!" she said with a laugh.

He felt a wrench of desire, even though he was holding himself in check. He'd fantasized about this sort of thing happening countless times, though he'd never seriously entertained the notion of having sex with a client. This was different, of course, but the situation was all wrong. There were still dangers.

"It sounds tempting, Nola," he said, "but I can't. At least not now."

"Later, maybe?"

"You're a temptress, aren't you?" He grinned, liking her boldness in spite of himself.

"If you must know, David, since you came over the other night, all I've been thinking about is sex. I dream about you. I fantasize about you, too. It seems to me if that's what's in my subconscious, it ought to be what I'm do-ing."

"Interesting theory."

"Well . . . if you're too busy."

She turned to grab her coat. He reached out to stop her.

"I have a couple of hours at lunchtime," he said.

A look of delight returned to Nola's face. "Oh? Shall I come back?"

"No, I don't think we should do it here, but we could go to my place. It's not far."

Nola pursed her lips. "Mmm, that sounds delicious. I'm getting wet just thinking about it."

He smiled, aware of the tingle in his genitals. "Yes, it does sound good, doesn't it?"

"What time shall I be there?"

"How about twelve-thirty?" He wrote his address on a business card and handed it to her.

Nola took it, then reached over and gave him a light kiss on his lips. She grabbed her coat and went to the door. "Want to know a little secret?"

"What?"

"I don't have on any underwear!" Then, giving him a devilish smile, she opened the door. "Be thinking about that, Dr. Love."

She went out, leaving David with a cold sweat on his brow and an erection.

San Rafael

Mitch was trying to study the lab reports on Dana's case, but he wasn't concentrating very well. He kept thinking about their night of lovemaking. When he glanced up, Corinne Smith walked past his open door, disappearing from sight. Then she backed up, reappearing, so that she could look in at him.

"Hi," she said.

"Hi, Corinne."

Her look turned inquiring. "Am I imagining things, honey, or is that a happy expression I see on your face?"

"Don't tell me it shows?"

"Lordy, is this somethin' you're going to talk about, or is it none of my damned business?"

"Yesterday was my day off."

"And the culture shock of bein' back at work hasn't hit yet, is that it?"

"Something like that."

Corinne stepped toward his desk and sat in the visitor's chair. "I see your boy O'Connell is still on the loose," she said.

"Yeah, the guy's elusiveness is beginning to get to me."

"Not so much as it gets to Ms. Kirk, I imagine."

"True."

"Maybe he flew the coop, headed for Chicago or someplace."

"I'd like to think so, but I'm not counting on it. The sonovabitch really has it in for Dana."

"I heard what happened. Congratulations, by the way. Seems like you got your timing down pretty good. Were you moonlighting as a security guard, or what?"

"Just happened to be in the neighborhood."

Corinne smiled. "Love and police work are a dangerous combination, honey, but I guess you already know that."

"Who said anything about love?"

"Your face, Mitch. Don't you know there's a reason they got me doin' domestic disputes? Lord, Dr. Ruth don't got nothin' on me."

"I appreciate the warning."

The phone rang and he picked it up.

"Mitch, it's me, Dana. Do you have a minute?"

"Oh, hi, Dana," he said, leaning back in his chair. "Sure, I've got a minute. Several, actually." He gave Corinne a wink. She winked back, got up and left his office.

"A couple of things happened this morning I thought you ought to know about," she said.

There wasn't any particular alarm in her voice, but Mitch's heart jumped a beat just the same. "What happened?"

"First I got a call from Stanley Bishop, the new president at Marin Pacific Savings. He's asked for a special meeting to review the bank's loan portfolio. He wants the loan committee to get together early next week, and he's sending over a package of documents for everyone to look over."

"So?"

"Well, it's a bit unusual to call a special meeting, but Stan said that since he's new he wanted to get up to speed. Said he'd been talking to Lane Cedrick about it and finally decided to get the meeting on the calendar."

"I'm not sure I understand the significance," Mitch said.

"Well, I didn't see any myself until Lane called me about twenty minutes later. He said he's taking over negotiations to buy me out and asked if I'd meet with him tonight. I told him I was tired and didn't think I had the energy. He said he'd be glad to come by my place."

"He sounds anxious."

"That's what I thought, too. Especially coming on the heels of my dinner with Frank. They're both pressing yet trying to sound casual about it."

"So, did you agree to meet with him?"

"Yes, he's coming by at seven-thirty."

Mitch thought for a second. "I'm not so sure I like the idea of you being there alone."

"I've decided to move back into my own place, Mitch. I can't impose on Robin again. Next time Ted comes for me, her place is likely to get torched or something."

"You can come home with me."

"No, Mitch. That's not fair to you. Besides, if I have to get up at five again I'm likely to melt like the Wicked Witch."

He laughed. "You were the perfect houseguest."

"Yes, perfect for a bachelor. But I don't think it's a situation either of us should get too attached to."

"The sex was secondary."

She laughed, though not cruelly. "That would go well on your tombstone, Mitch."

"Are you being critical or defensive?" he asked.

There was a long pause. "Defensive," she said softly.

"Then maybe we'd better stick to the issue at hand. I'll be at your place tonight when Cedrick arrives. I'll meet you there after work. After Cedrick's gone we can order takeout food and discuss this further. I like Chinese, by the way. Do you?"

"Yes."

"Well, there you are. We're compatible enough to eat the same food while arguing about security arrangements."

"*Security arrangements?*" she echoed. "That's the damnedest euphemism I've ever heard."

"Okay, sleeping arrangements," he said. "Do you like that term better?"

"No, but at least it's more honest."

"I'm nothing, Dana, if not honest."

"You're something else, Detective Cross, I assure you. I discovered it last night. So, shall we meet at my place at seven?"

"Sounds good."

"See you then," she said. "Bye."

Mitch hung up, feeling a grin spread across his face. Damn, if that woman didn't make him feel good. Maybe even happy.

San Rafael

Molly Kirk climbed out of the back seat of the BMW. "Bye, Tiffany," she said to her friend. "Bye, Mrs. Marks. Thanks for the ride."

"You're sure your father won't mind me bringing you home?" the woman asked.

"No, he'll be glad he didn't have to make a last-minute trip. Anyway, he's here," she said, pointing to the car parked in the street. "He must have come home for lunch."

"We'll wait until you get inside," Mrs. Marks said.

"Okay." Molly waved, slung her book bag onto her shoulder and went up the walk.

She'd been a little more casual about accepting the ride than she should have been, but she couldn't get hold of her father at his office and didn't want to be stuck at school all afternoon. It was her fault for forgetting that they had only half a day because of a teachers' conference, and she was sure she would hear about it.

When she got to the door she unlocked it, turned and waved to Tiffany and her mom. She stepped inside and was about to call out to her father when she heard a funny shriek coming from the back of the house. It was a woman's voice and she sounded all excited.

"Oh . . . oh . . ." the woman cried. "Harder, David. Harder."

Molly wondered if her father was in bed with some woman. Right here and in the middle of the afternoon! The cries of pleasure continued and, if she listened real carefully, she could hear the bedsprings creaking. "Oh, my

God," she said half aloud, covering her mouth with her hand.

Her friends sometimes talked about hearing their parents "doing it," but Molly had never had the experience. Her curiosity getting the best of her, she tiptoed through the front room and into the back hall.

"Fuck me, you sonovabitch," the woman cried. "Fuck me hard! Yes, David, yes."

Molly blanched. The bedsprings kept creaking. The sound was getting louder and louder. She slipped her book bag off her shoulder and tiptoed closer.

"Jesus Christ!" the woman screamed. "I'm almost there!"

Molly peeked around the doorframe of the master bedroom and saw her father on top of a naked redheaded woman whose arms and legs were tied to the bedposts. Molly was so stunned that for a moment she just stared at her father, humping away, grunting and heaving, his bare butt going up and down.

When she finally got control of herself she backed away, her face flushing with embarrassment. As she recoiled, her book bag slipped from her hand and fell to the floor with a thud. The creaking and panting and crying stopped. Molly snatched up the book bag and tiptoed away as fast as she could.

"David," she heard the woman say, "what was that? Is someone in the house?"

"God, I don't know."

"Well, for chrissake, untie me! Hurry!"

Molly ran to the front room and dropped onto the sofa, beet red. The only thing she could think to do was to pretend nothing had happened. It wouldn't be easy. What could she say?

* * *

Strawberry Manor

Chiara Fiolli sat at the back of the bus, staring straight ahead, oblivious to everything. Ever since she'd eavesdropped on Dana's call from Mitchell Cross that morning she'd been a zombie. She didn't know why she was so surprised that Dana had slept with him but she was. He was the only man she'd felt a serious attraction for since she'd come to San Francisco—and now Dana had him. Not that Chiara had truly expected anything to come of her crush, of course, but it was the idea of Dana winning again while she lost out. It was so unfair.

The bus had been sitting motionless for a minute and it wasn't until the doors closed that she realized they were at Town & Country Village. Her stop!

"*Si fermi!* Wait, stop! I'm getting off!" she called out as she ran toward the door.

The bus started to move, then lurched to a stop.

"Wake up, back there!" the driver shouted irritably.

Chiara gave him the Italian salute and banged on the door. It opened and she stepped down, grumbling obscenities in Italian. The bus took off and she turned on her heel, headed for home with tears in her eyes.

By the time she neared her apartment complex, she was in a dismal state of mind. Chiara hated her life. She hated the fact that she wasn't happy or rich or successful. And at the moment she hated both Dana Kirk and Mitchell Cross.

Looking up, she saw a silver Rolls parked across the street from her building. She loved beautiful expensive automobiles. One of her fantasies was being in the back seat of a Rolls or a Bentley with a very rich man and having him beg her to marry him.

As she drew closer, Chiara saw that there was somebody behind the wheel. She wondered why anyone in a Rolls would be parked in her neighborhood. To her surprise, the driver seemed to be staring at her. It was still light enough that she could see his face. He looked to be about forty or so. He had blond hair and was good-looking. As she started to turn up the walk to her building, the window slid down.

"Chiara," he called to her.

She stared across the street, wondering who driving a Rolls could possibly know her name. The man curled his finger, beckoning her. "Can we talk?"

She cautiously went to the curb. "Do I know you?"

"We haven't met. I'd like to discuss a business proposition with you. A very important one."

Chiara was skeptical, but she was also curious. Rapists didn't drive around in Rolls-Royces, and there had to be a reason why he knew her name. Glancing in each direction to make sure the street was clear, she warily approached the car.

The man smiled. He was older than she'd thought at first, perhaps five or ten years older than the initial impression. But he was nice looking in a smooth sort of way. He was checking her out, but not in the way men usually did. It was more like he was curious about her clothes. Taking a business card from his breast pocket, he handed it to her.

Chiara read the name: Lane Cedrick, Chairman, Cedrick & Betts. Her mouth sagged open. "You're . . ."

"Yes," he said, "one at those bad guys over at C&B."

This was no accidental encounter. What could he possibly want with her? "How do you know my name?" she asked.

"I make a point of knowing everybody in this business," he said easily.

"So, what do you want?"

"I'd like for us to get better acquainted. It's always easier to talk business with someone you know."

"Tell me what you've got in mind," she said, forcing herself to be cautious.

"I'd like to take you to dinner. A very expensive dinner on me."

She turned and glanced toward her building. Her mother wasn't there, waiting for her. Neither was Rossella or, for that matter, Dana Kirk. Nobody. She was free to do as she pleased. "All right," she said, "why not? When do you want to go?"

"How about right now?"

"Okay."

She went around to the passenger side and climbed in next to the man. The supple leather received her body as if it was made for her. She glanced over at her smiling companion. Funny, she didn't feel the slightest sexual threat from him. And yet she sensed his eagerness to take her to dinner. For some reason, in some way, he really wanted her.

Ross

Dana was relieved to see Mitch's Bronco in the drive when she arrived home at ten after seven. They waved at each other as she drove past and entered the garage. Mitch was at the car door as she climbed out of the Mercedes, dragging her briefcase behind her.

She smiled at him, feeling a little shy. She wasn't sure if she should act like a lover or a friend. He made the choice easy. He reached out to take her into his arms.

"You look like you could use a hug," he said.

Dana relaxed into his embrace, slipping her free arm around his waist. "You got that right, Detective Cross."

He bussed her on the cheek. "Shitty day, huh?"

"Mostly. How was yours?"

They parted and moved toward the door accessing the stairs to the house. Mitch pushed the button, lowering the garage door.

"Not too eventful," he said. "I did run down to the stone engraver's place."

"Stone engraver?"

"Yep. Ordered a tombstone. Wanted to get The Sex Was Secondary copyrighted before somebody else beat me to it."

Dana laughed. "You're crazy, Mitch. I knew cops were supposed to be odd, but I didn't know it was this way."

"You're seeing the terminal stages."

They climbed the stairs. The house was cold and Dana turned on the heat. The answering machine was lit up like a Christmas tree. She pushed the message button as she took off her coat. There had been a variety of calls—Bev O'Connell; Judy Povich twice, the second time saying she wanted to pick up her license; Anita Gomez, the housekeeper; then a voice that made her blood turn to ice.

"You were lucky, bitch. Next time I'll beat the shit out of you before I fuck you." The slurred, drunken voice of Ted O'Connell was unmistakable.

"Oh, God," she murmured, as she turned into Mitch's arms.

He held her tightly, but said nothing immediately. After several moments he told her, "You're coming home with me tonight."

"No," she replied. "I can't constantly run and hide. I've got a good alarm system, and my gun. I'll be all right." She didn't say it with a lot of conviction, but she wanted to believe it.

"Then I'm staying here with you," he said. "O'Connell's bound to be picked up in the next few days. In the meantime I don't want to take a chance."

She didn't protest—the thought of his company was too comforting. But in the back of her mind, she knew they were ignoring the larger question of where it was all leading. And yet she was at the point where she didn't want to think anymore. All she wanted was a respite from her fear.

It was hardly a time to put her head in the sand, however. The situation at the office was critical. She had Frank, and now Lane Cedrick, to deal with. And there'd been that disturbing call from David just before she'd left the office. She wasn't sure what to make of it. David had seemed confused—which was unlike him.

The next thing she knew Mitch was holding her face in his hands, trying to look past her blank expression and into her eyes. "Hey," he said, giving her a gentle shake, "I know at a certain point in every relationship boredom becomes a problem, but isn't this a little early?"

"Huh?" Then she realized she'd been off somewhere, lost in her thoughts. "I'm sorry, Mitch, I was thinking about David."

"Your ex?" He shook his head. "Not a good sign. I normally don't have that effect on women."

She laughed. "No, it's not you." She took him by the hand and led him to the sofa. There was still a chill in the room and she put his arm around her shoulder, snuggling close to him for warmth. "David called earlier. He told me Molly came home early from school and caught him in bed with some woman. Apparently the experience upset both of them and he felt I ought to know about it."

"Embarrassing, I would understand. Why upsetting? She's old enough to understand adult sex, isn't she?"

"It seems David and his lady friend were practicing a little bondage."

She saw a smile creep across Mitch's face. "Imaginative fellow. Was he always that way?"

Dana gave him a look. "Well, he never tied me up, if that's what you're asking. Lord, to be honest, I was shocked when he told me."

"Some guys are late bloomers."

Dana shook her head with dismay.

"Strange thing to admit to one's former wife, though, isn't it?" he said.

"I imagine he was afraid I'd hear it from Molly and wanted to preempt trouble. He admitted she might ask to move back here but asked me to give him a few days to work things out with her. I told him my only concern was for her welfare and he said his was, too. The trouble is, taking her back would be like bringing her into a war zone." She sighed woefully. "I don't know what to do."

"I suppose you ought to take your cue from her."

"You're probably right," she said after a moment's reflection. "Molly's not a child any longer. She's not an adult, either. Still, sometimes I forget she's no longer a little girl."

Mitch gave her shoulders a squeeze. She put her hand on his knee. Despite the tension of the day, she'd thought about him a lot. But it was only now that she began appreciating the comfort of his physical presence. And not only because of the vulnerability she felt. Mitch was fun to be with. His companionship made her happy.

"I thought about you today," he said.

"Did you?"

"Yeah. I liked yesterday."

"So did I, Mitch."

He put his hand on hers, then drew it to his mouth and kissed her fingers. She turned toward him and he kissed her on the lips. All the good, warm and exciting sensations of the night before came flooding back. But it wasn't the right time to get romantic. Lane Cedrick was due at any time.

"I've got to freshen up before Lane gets here," she said, scooting to the edge of her seat.

"How are we going to handle this?" he asked. "Should I be out in the open or eavesdrop from another room?"

"I'd say eavesdrop," she replied. "Lane might be inhibited by someone else's presence. And if he wants to come to my house, he's going to have to risk having the cops listen in." She got to her feet.

"You have a devious mind," he said. "I admire that in a woman. That, and salaciousness."

She arched a brow as he grinned up at her. "You into bondage, too, Mitch?"

"Do you ask hopefully?"

She kicked his shin and headed for her bedroom.

"What do you say I put my vehicle in your garage?" he called after her. "No sense advertising my presence."

She stopped at the door and looked back at him. "You're the expert," she said. "And evidently the pervert, as well."

"Don't knock it unless you've tried it," he retorted, laughing as she disappeared from sight.

Dana smiled. It was good to have a man in the house.

The doorbell rang at seven-thirty. Dana went to answer it while Mitch remained in the family room. She'd opted for the disarming look and had changed into her light blue velour jogging suit. The plan was to sit with Lane in the front room so that Mitch could easily hear.

Lane was looking dapper when she opened the door. He was in a brown suit with a beige tie and matching handkerchief. His icy blue eyes belied the polite smile.

"Good evening, Dana."

"Hi, Lane. Come on in."

He stepped inside. As Dana closed the door she noticed his Rolls. Lane's pretentiousness was legendary. Ironically, in all her years with the company, she'd had only a few one-on-one conversations with him, and never a private meeting. That made this a unique occasion—a fact that struck her only now.

"Nice place you've got," he said, as they went into the front room.

"Thanks. It's been a project."

He sat on a sofa, she took a chair. Lane crossed his legs and continued to look around as if he was considering buying the place. Habit, evidently.

"Can I offer you something to drink? Coffee? Juice? Mineral water?" He wasn't much of a drinker, especially in comparison to Frank—that much she knew about him. It was surprising how little else she knew. Common lore about Lane Cedrick was limited.

"No, thanks. I know I'm imposing. I imagine you'd appreciate getting right down to business."

"You apparently didn't like the answer I gave Frank, otherwise you wouldn't be here," she said.

"I want a deal. Tell me what it will take to buy your stock."

"Lots of money, obviously."

"How much?"

"A hundred and fifty thousand."

"Frank offered seventy-five. Can we agree the extremes have been defined?"

"Define things the way you want, Lane. You asked what I want. I just gave you my answer."

"A dollar figure is one thing. Terms and collateral issues are another."

"Do you have an offer you'd like to make?" she asked.

"Let's discuss the essentials first," he said. "On my side it's time. Any deal we make has to close by Friday. Unless you're willing to do that, I may as well leave."

"If the price is right, you can have the stock on Friday."

Lane had remained in a relaxed attitude and seemed to relax even more. He clasped his hands and rested them on his lap. "You want more cash than we have available," he said. "I believe that's going to be the sticky point."

"Money can be a deal breaker," she said sardonically.

Cedrick's eyes were hard and unsympathetic. The skin on his brow remained smooth, his expression implacable. "Let's say I'm able to scrape together seventy-five in cash. Will you take another twenty-five in paper?"

"That's better than what Frank offered but not good enough."

"How about if I throw in a pledge to help you keep Kirk & Company in business? I assume your company is worth something to you."

"How do you propose to do that?" she asked.

"I can't guarantee you won't lose your agents, but I can guarantee C&B won't take them back. That's got to be worth quite a bit to you."

"No offense, Lane. I'd rather your money than your promise."

His mouth widened into a bitter smile. "I'll save us both the pain of prolonging this. One hundred thousand, cash. Period. Bottom line. Final offer."

Dana studied him, wondering if it was so. Lane was not easy to read. Yet the offer seemed to have a feel of finality to it. She suspected that if she wanted to deal, this would be her chance. The money could buy her several more months to build up her sales force. And it might well get Frank and Lane out of her hair.

"I'll have my shares in escrow at the Larkspur branch of Bank of America tomorrow morning with instructions to transfer them as soon as you've deposited a hundred thousand cash, provided it's delivered by noon, Friday."

"Done."

Lane Cedrick allowed himself to look pleased. He got to his feet and Dana did, as well. He offered his hand, she took it.

"Frank is either tougher than you are, Lane, or you have more money," she said.

"It was his money I just spent, my dear, not mine."

"Why the desperation, if you don't mind me asking?"

"I never discuss my motives in a negotiation, Dana, just like I never show a losing hand in poker. It separates the amateur from the professional."

They started for the door.

"Does Frank have a hundred thousand dollars to close this deal?" she asked. "Or is this just a hope and a promise on your part?"

"We'll know by Friday noon, at the latest, won't we?"

They stood in the entry hall.

"I hope he's as pleased as you are," she said.

"Frank, as you well know, tends to think with his balls." He chuckled. "I'll let you in on a little secret. I understand the female mind better than he does."

She nodded. "You know, that wouldn't surprise me at all."

After locking the door behind him, she returned to the front room where she found Mitch standing with his hands in his pockets, a pensive look on his face.

"Sounds to me like I'd better pay a visit to Marin Pacific Savings," he said.

"I can't imagine why they're so desperate," she said.

"It must have something to do with that meeting you've got next week."

She nodded. "But if I sell the stock Friday, I'll be off the board."

"And you won't be attending the meeting."

"Right. That has to be why Lane was so eager to give me a hundred grand. If he'd fought a little harder I might have come down to seventy-five."

Mitch twitched his brows. "Not afraid to expose your negotiating strategy to me, eh?"

She gave him a dry look. "You got it for free, Mitch. What's to negotiate?"

He chuckled. "I like the way you handled Cedrick, by the way. You're good. Not that my opinion in such matters means anything."

"Thanks, anyway."

They headed back to the family room. Sitting next to one of the chairs was a small duffel bag. She noticed it for the first time.

"Hey, where did that come from?"

"It's mine. I got it out of my vehicle when I put it in the garage. Shaving kit, change of underwear and a fresh shirt and an extra tie."

"You brought it with you this morning?"

"Yeah, put it in the car while you were taking your shower."

"Plan ahead, don't you, Mitch?"

"You never know when and where you're going to have to slay a dragon," he said.

"Heaven forbid doing battle without fresh underwear."

"The dragon wouldn't care. Some damsels, though, get pretty finicky."

She shook her head. "What is it with men and sex?"

"I don't know," he said. "Some kind of obsession, maybe."

"That's what you call it?"

"You like mania better?"

She rolled her eyes. "Why don't you make yourself useful and order some Chinese food?" she suggested. "There's a take-out menu in the drawer under the telephone."

"Roger." He dutifully went over to check out the menu. "Anything you're particularly hungry for?"

"Whatever you want is fine, Mitch. You pick."

"I think I've discovered the key to your feminine soul."

"Really? What's that?"

"Food. As I recall, last night we didn't quite finish dinner." He paused to smile. "I guess my barbecue really turned you on."

"Bastard!"

He started laughing so hard it was a minute before he stopped. Tears were flowing down his cheeks.

"Know what you need?" she said.

He wiped his cheeks. "What?"

"A crash diet!"

Mitch watched Dana expertly eating her Chinese noodles with her chopsticks. He shook his head with amazement. She was even eating the rice with them, for chrissake.

"Tell me something," he said. "Since despite the designer clothes and million-dollar home, we now know you're really poor white trash, where did you learn to eat with chopsticks? It wasn't at finishing school."

"It was in Chinese restaurants, cowboy, where everybody else learns."

"Every Chinese restaurant I've ever eaten in has knives and forks. Stabbing egg rolls with a wooden darning needle always struck me as affected—unless you're Chinese, of course."

"Well, I guess I'm *affected* poor white trash."

Mitch took a bite of sweet-and-sour pork. "Suppose you and I will ever get past class hatred?" he asked, chomping his food.

"Whose class and whose hatred?"

He nodded, pushing around a big black mushroom with his fork. "You know, I've been giving my prejudices a lot of thought."

"And?"

"I've decided you're a traitor to your class, but that you've still got a heart of gold—worthy of Ma Joad."

"Am I supposed to feel complimented, Mitch?"

"I'm trying to be self-effacing and friendly at the same time."

"Maybe you should just admit that people shouldn't be judged by their bank accounts instead of the way they live their lives."

"All right, I'll admit it," he said. "But I want to know something. It's a serious question. Do you feel better about yourself because you've got money?" He watched her pick up a peapod and slip it into her mouth.

"You've asked me that before."

"Yeah, but you never really answered it."

Dana sighed and looked off thoughtfully. "Let me put it this way. I don't look down on anybody, but I like knowing nobody can really look down on me."

"Money's the difference?"

"It's an important measuring stick in our society."

"I don't romanticize poverty," he said. "As long as I've got food and shelter and a little piece of land, all I need is my freedom to be myself. You can have your Mercedes."

Dana put down her chopsticks. "I've got something to show you," she said, getting up. "And a question to go with it."

She went to the kitchen counter and got her purse. Opening it, she took out a piece of paper. Returning to the table, she unfolded it.

"Who's the guy?" she asked, handing him the paper. He looked at the picture, a surge of recognition going through him. He glanced at the caption.

"Bill Cross," he said.

"Any relation?"

Mitch put down the clipping and picked up his fork. "My father."

"So, you're heir to a fortune that makes my humble little abode look like a shack in a pea patch."

"I hope this isn't what makes me worthy," he said, stabbing the paper, "because I've been disinherited, and even if I wasn't, I wouldn't have his money." He watched her assessing him.

"Still angry after all these years, aren't you?"

"Yes, maybe, but there's no profit in this subject, Dana."

"I'm not looking for profit," she said, "but this money thing is standing between us like a sumo wrestler."

"No, it's not. I'm making a genuine effort to see you as a person, not just a financial statement. I've already learned my prejudices are invalid and the stereotypes don't apply in this case."

She looked like she wasn't sure that was enough. He could see she was questioning, trying to decide how she felt. Then, after a minute, an ironic grin filled her face.

"Hard to believe a second date has turned into such an intense metaphysical discourse, isn't it?"

"Hey," he said, "where did a broad who never even graduated from college pick up words like that?"

"Pretension," she said. "It comes with the money."

"Does one of those fancy tubs that make all the bubbles come with money, too?"

"Are you asking if I have a spa in my bathroom?"

"Yeah."

She nodded. "I do. Why?"

"How about if you and I go skinny-dipping?"

"Mitch, we haven't even finished dinner."

"Why break the pattern?"

She reached over and put her hand on his. "We've got a relationship, don't we?"

Mitch let his recollections of the previous evening and his expectations for the present one tumble pleasantly through his mind. They were at the point he'd wanted to be from the moment he walked in the door. "Either that," he said, "or food has the same lascivious effect on both of us."

"Oh, you college graduates with your big words think you're so clever and sexy."

"That's it," he said, rising from the table. "Time for your bath." He pulled her to her feet. "Come on."

"Tell me, Mitch, does always trying to run things and be in charge come with having balls?"

"Watch it, Mrs. Kirk," he said, slipping his arm around her and leading her toward the bedroom. "It may be your mouth that gets washed out first."

"I love it when you talk dirty," she chortled.

"Baby, you ain't seen nothing yet."

Eight

The ringing pierced Frank Betts's brain like a hot poker. He rolled over, lifted his head from the pillow, and glared at the telephone. It continued to ring. He crawled over and lifted the receiver from the cradle.

"Yes?" he managed.

"Frank, where in the hell were you last night?" It was Lane and he was in one of his pissy moods.

"I was out getting drunk with a woman. And no, by the time I got her in bed I couldn't get it up. Any more questions?" He groaned. Just getting a little hot under the collar made his head throb.

"Listen to me, you drunken jackass," Lane said, "and listen good because your fucking future may depend on it. I made a deal with Dana last night. She's agreed to sell her stock and we've got until noon tomorrow to close the deal."

Frank kept blinking his eyes, trying to make them focus. "How much?"

"A hundred thousand, cash."

"Christ, Lane, where are we going to come up with that kind of money?"

"I've arranged to call in a couple of markers. I'll put in forty myself. That means you only have to come up with sixty."

"Where am I going to get sixty grand in twenty-four hours? Twenty-five might be possible, but sixty...no way."

"Well, you'd better find a way. So, get out of bed and get to work on it. I, meanwhile, have to take care of another dagger at our throats."

"What?"

"I had breakfast with Stan Bishop. Told him we planned to buy Dana out so she'd be off the board. I was hoping he hadn't sent the package of loan documents to her but he already had. And what's worse, the Oak Meadow Partners loan and the forged documents are in the package. Dana should be getting hers today."

"Oh, shit. If she looks at the stuff, we're dead."

"That's right. She may not bother, considering we're buying her out. Still, we can't count on that. So I'm working on another approach."

"What do you mean, another approach?"

"The details don't matter, Frank. Leave that part to me. You've got enough to worry about, getting the sixty thousand. Just remember, your ass is hanging in the balance. You've got to get the money. And for God's sake, let me know as soon as you do."

Frank put the receiver back and groaned, rubbing his head. Where the fuck was he going to get sixty grand? He started running through the possibilities in his mind—every person he'd ever known who owed him a favor.

Under certain circumstances he could get a few thousand here, a few thousand there, but who would be willing and able to sit down and write out a big fat check in exchange for a wish and a promise? Who cared enough about him to risk that kind of money to save his ass?

The more he thought about it, the more it became clear that there was only one person who might do it. Nola.

Mill Valley

Mitch watched Stanley Bishop, in banker's gray, put his coffee cup down on the table. He smoothed his neatly trimmed mustache and looked at him pensively.

"Let me make sure I understand, Detective Cross. Is this a criminal investigation? Are you suggesting there are banking irregularities?"

"No, the case I'm working on involves death threats against Mrs. Kirk. We're investigating all aspects of her business activities. Her role with the bank is just one of several."

"I'm relatively new here, as I told you," Bishop said, "but I can't believe anyone connected to the bank would want to do Mrs. Kirk any harm."

"What about this loan-committee meeting next week? Is there any reason why any of the staff or directors wouldn't want her to participate in that meeting?"

They were in the seating group in the corner of his office. Bishop leaned back on the sofa, scratching his short-cropped gray hair. "Not that I know of."

"What's on the agenda that might be controversial? Anything?"

"No, that's the point. We're simply going to be reviewing existing loans. The exercise is mostly for my benefit. Mrs. Kirk participated in earlier committee meetings where the loans in question were reviewed and approved. There won't be anything on the agenda she isn't already familiar with. She'll have all the documents today. I've sent her everything by courier."

"Have Lane Cedrick and Frank Betts said anything to you that would indicate why they're so eager to get rid of Mrs. Kirk?"

"No, Detective Cross, nothing other than the fact that they consider her a competitor in the brokerage business. But there is nothing unusual or nefarious about that."

Mitch sighed. He wasn't getting anywhere, but he had no reason to believe Bishop was holding back. The guy seemed straight. Chances were he was ignorant of whatever was motivating Frank and Lane.

"Well, I won't take any more of your time, Mr. Bishop. Here's my card. If you get an inkling of anything I should know about, please give me a call."

"Certainly."

They shook hands and Mitch left the office.

Larkspur

Chiara checked the bottom drawer of her desk where she kept her own supplies. There were two boxes of staples. She slipped them into her purse and glanced in toward the bull pen where Dana stood talking to Robin and Helene. Dana was all smiles today. Chiara knew why. She was sleeping with Mitchell Cross.

Chiara didn't care anymore. The hell with Mitchell Cross. He was just a flirt. He was probably only out for what he could get. And if Dana was too stupid to see that, too bad for her.

No, she had more important things to think about. She checked the clock. In five minutes she had to be there, which meant she had to hurry.

"Kind of early to be lookin' at the clock, ain't it?" the security guard said.

Chiara gave him a look. It was Shawn—the young, annoying one. He'd been making remarks all morning. She hadn't given him any encouragement and he was starting to get obnoxious. She was tempted to tell Dana he was pestering her and let her deal with it, but it was hardly worth the trouble. Grabbing her purse, Chiara went to the closet and got her coat. She draped it over her arm and went into the bull pen to speak to Dana.

"Excuse me," she said, interrupting the gossiping.

The three of them looked at her.

"I'm out of staples and I thought I'd run over to the stationery store to pick some up. Could one of you watch the phones?"

"Sure, we'll cover," Dana said, "but why make a special trip? We're due to order a bunch of things anyway, aren't we?"

"Yes, but I need them and I felt like getting some air."

"Suit yourself."

Chiara nodded and left the sales floor, slipping on her coat as she went.

"Early lunch?" the guard said as she passed him.

She gave him a withering look. "No. Early retirement."

He didn't laugh because he didn't understand. What a jerk.

She stepped outside into the crisp morning air. She moved quickly along the sidewalk and started searching the parking lot for the Rolls-Royce. She hoped he wouldn't be late because she couldn't be gone long. Finally she spotted it, tucked behind a panel truck. She skipped along even faster.

Entering the coffee shop, she found Lane Cedrick sitting in a table in back. He had a cup of coffee in front of him.

"Am I late?" Chiara said, taking off her coat.

"No, I was early."

She sat down. "I had to make up a story to get out of the office."

"I'm sorry to make you sneak out. But I have a very important job for you."

She looked at his red face. He wasn't as calm as he'd been the previous evening when he'd given her the check. If anything, he seemed upset. "What sort of job?"

"Has a courier brought Dana a large envelope from Marin Pacific Savings yet this morning?"

"No, a courier hasn't come at all."

"Good. One should be arriving anytime. And I want you to intercept the package. You'll get another thousand dollars if you're able to keep it from Dana and put it in my hands."

She looked into his eyes. There was a quiet desperation hidden beneath the cool veneer. She sensed he was very nervous.

"Dana might see the deliveryman arrive," she said. "I may not be able to hide it. And if I get caught, she might fire me."

Lane Cedrick swallowed hard. He continued to gaze at her intently, almost angrily.

"Three thousand," he said. "Three thousand for the package. But you have to put it in my hands. That's more than you make in a month. Even if she catches you and you're fired, you'll have the money and the job at C&B. I've already promised you that."

Chiara felt a tremor go down her spine as they stared at each other. A strange feeling of power rose from deep within her. For one of the very few times in her life she felt in control of a situation, felt power over a man—an important but desperate man.

"Five thousand," she stammered, amazed to actually hear the words on her lips.

"*Five?*"

"You're asking a lot, Mr. Cedrick," she said. "You're asking me to take a very big chance. And what can I really trust? Only money in my hand, it seems to me."

Cedrick shook his head, but he managed a sardonic smile. "I've created a monster."

Chiara didn't care what he thought. For once, all that mattered was what *she* wanted. To his credit, he seemed to understand that.

"All right," he said. "Five thousand. One now and four when you put the package in my hands."

"You're making me risk getting caught."

"You've got to earn your money, Chiara, the same as everybody else."

"Okay, then. Where do I bring the package?"

"Call me when you have it and we'll make arrangements to meet."

"Give me the first thousand," she said.

Cedrick took his checkbook from his inside pocket. "The goddamn thing might be being delivered while we're sitting here bickering," he groused.

"I hope not," she said. "For both our sakes."

He glanced up as he filled out the check. "You've got that right, sweetie."

Sausalito

Nola sat alone in her spa with the water boiling around her. It was more enervating than relaxing. Everything felt empty to her now, just like it had before David had come into her life. She cringed with regret at the thought of him, hoping, praying as she had a hundred other times the past few days, that he didn't blame her for what had happened.

True, she was the one who'd suggested he tie her up, but he didn't have to if he didn't want to. And it was hardly her fault that that little bitch of a daughter came home when she did. The incident had really upset him. She'd tried her best to make amends; she'd even apologized. But all he wanted was for her to leave so he could talk to his kid. When he'd seen her to the door, he'd said he'd call. He'd given her a perfunctory kiss on the cheek—the sort a man gave to his maiden aunt—then ushered her out of the house.

Nola had waited and waited, thinking he'd at least call out of politeness. But nothing. She'd picked up the phone several times to call him, but she knew she shouldn't be overeager. Men hated that. Only if you were indifferent, did they want you. And if they thought another man was hot for your body, they'd trip all over themselves to steal you away. Men! What stupid, fucking bastards they could be!

And yet, she wanted him so much. The anxiety was killing her. Twice she'd decided to go to the liquor store. Once, she'd gotten as far as the garage. But she'd stopped herself, reasoning that she couldn't give up hope. Not yet. David Kirk wouldn't want a drunk on his hands. That was absolutely certain. It could all blow over and they could pick up where they'd left off.

She heard the doorbell ring and her hopes soared. She was certain it was David. Probably with a bouquet of flowers. After all, she'd been humiliated, too.

Nola hurriedly got out of the spa and dried herself with the towel. The doorbell rang again as she slipped on her big terry robe. Pausing only an instant to check her face in the dresser mirror, Nola dashed through the house. "Coming! Coming!" she cried.

Throwing the door open, she was shocked to find it wasn't David at all. It was Frank. Her heart sank. Then, in just the passing of an instant, she grew angry.

"Jesus," she growled, "what are you doing here?"

He blinked, startled by her reaction. "Nola, I need to talk to you. Can you give me a few minutes?"

She looked heavenward, wondering, Why now? When he saw she wasn't pleased, his shoulders drooped, he seemed to sag. Nola studied his face. The bags under his eyes were so dark they seemed almost purple.

"You look like hell, Frank."

"This is not one of the better days of my life," he lamented.

She sighed and looked past him, as though she expected David to come driving up at any moment. Then she realized he hadn't said he was coming, she'd only been hoping he would.

"Well, I guess you can come in," she said. "You can't stay for long."

"Are you expecting somebody?" he asked, crossing the threshold.

"What do you think? My life ended when you walked out?"

He turned to her apologetically. "I wasn't suggesting anything. I was just hoping you weren't, that's all."

"I have no intention of discussing my social life with you."

They went into her cozy sitting room and Nola motioned for him to sit. Because her robe was damp, she pulled up a straight chair. Frank looked at her, checking out the knee poking through the opening in her robe. She covered her leg. He managed a little smile.

"Were you in the shower?"

"No, the spa."

"Ah," he said wistfully. "The spa. Remember when we used to get in the hot tub and split a bottle of wine, fuck our brains out, drag ourselves to bed and fuck our brains out some more?"

He shook his head sadly, looking almost as though he were on the verge of tears. Nola stared, realizing this wasn't the Frank Betts she'd lusted after for a good part of her adult life. This was the defeated shell of the man who'd broken her heart.

"Don't you have fond memories of those days?" he asked.

"The world has changed, Frank. I don't drink anymore and I don't fuck you."

He stared at her blankly, not with the surprise she'd expected. Then his brow furrowed and he looked confused. "What happened, Nola? Have you changed? Only a few days ago you still had a soft spot for me. You've hated me for months, I know. Still, you felt something for me underneath. Don't you anymore?"

His tone was pleading.

"I don't want to talk about you and me. I have other things to worry about. If there's something you want to say, spit it out."

"Where's your compassion? You don't sound like yourself."

"What do you want, Frank?"

He drew himself up and looked her in the eye. "Honey, I gotta borrow some money from you. A lot of money."

She blinked. "Are you stoned, or have you flipped out?"

"I'm serious, babe, dead serious. It's a matter of life and death."

"Frank, I think you need to see a doctor."

He shook his head. "Nola, I'm in trouble. I need sixty thousand cash and I need it by *tomorrow!*" His voice rose in volume as he spoke, his desperation evident.

"You're serious."

"I'm dead serious," he said, pleadingly. "I desperately need your help."

"What kind of trouble are you in? Is it a Mafia thing? Have you been gambling? What have you done?"

He rubbed his hands together nervously. "Lane and I have to buy Dana out of the bank. He's putting up half the money and I have to come up with the other half. We have till noon tomorrow to close the deal. Sixty thousand is what I need," he said. "I'll pay you back in a few months."

Nola felt the blood rise in her face. "So, the money's for *her!*"

"It's not *for* her. It's to pay her off, to get her off our backs and out of our lives, once and for all!" Emotion welled in him and he looked like he was about to cry.

"I'm not going to loan you money to give to that bitch."

"Nola, she's not the issue. The point is if we don't get rid of her we could go to jail, lose everything. We could go under, Nola. That would mean no more alimony checks, no more nothing! I'll be dead! You've got to help." He bit his lip to keep from sobbing.

"What do you mean, *jail?* What have you done?" She walked over and stood in front of him, her arms folded across her chest. "If you expect me to help you, tell me what's happened, what you've done."

"I can't," he replied. "It's better for your sake that you don't know. You just have to trust me. I swear, everything will be all right. If I can just have the money, please, Nola."

His desperation was as shocking as the request itself. She didn't know what to make of it. And she was deeply suspicious. "Why don't you borrow what you need from the bank?"

"We can't. We're stretched to the limit. Lane had an investment deal a while back. It went bad and we've scraped and borrowed and pulled money from every place we possibly could. If we used operating funds and couldn't make payroll the company could collapse. We've already siphoned off more than we can afford."

"And you expect me to give you more?"

"This will turn it around. Once Dana's out of the picture we'll be all right. It's just a matter of time. Her agents are leaving her, we're about to turn the corner. We'll be home free if you'll just help."

Nola sat down again. "Even if I wanted to give you the money, which I don't, I couldn't come up with that much. I don't keep sixty thousand lying around and you know it. I don't know why you even came here."

"Nola, you've got an open-ended loan on this place. Don't forget I set up the loan for you. You can draw out a hundred and fifty thousand, if you want to."

"This house is my nest egg, my retirement. This is all I got out of the marriage. This is it!"

"But I'll pay you back! I swear it!"

"What if you're in jail? How'll I make the house payments?"

"For chrissake, Nola, we're only talking a few hundred a month, worst case. And if I do go under, then where will you be?"

"I'll have my house!"

Frank dropped to his knees in front of her. Tears started streaming down his cheeks. "I'm begging you. You've got to help me, honey."

"Listen to you, Frank Betts. It's 'honey' now. Whenever I called you up the last few months, wanting a little compassion and understanding, you told me to go fuck myself. Now that you're the one in need, it's suddenly 'honey' again."

"It's always been 'honey' and it always will be," he said through his tears. "I've tried not to give in to my feelings. That hasn't stopped me from loving you, Nola. Don't you think I haven't noticed that my life's gone to hell since we split? The biggest mistake of my life was leaving you and now I'm paying for it."

"And you want me to pay for it, too."

"Please don't hate me on top of everything else," he sobbed. "If you won't help, that's one thing, but don't hate me. Please, don't." He dropped his head down on her knees and wept, holding on to her like a child would its mother. Nola's eyes filled, too. Yet she resisted the temptation to comfort him. She sat rigidly, trying not to think of him as her husband. This was the man who'd used her and thrown her out like an old shoe.

After a while Frank got control of himself and looked up at her. He wiped his eyes. "You won't do it, will you?" he said.

"I want to see how you're going to treat me when you don't need money, Frank. It's a lot fairer test, don't you think?"

"I'm not kidding you, Nola, this thing is going to do me in."

"Maybe it will. Maybe I'll regret it but I refuse to be used, and I think that's what you want to do—use me."

Frank struggled to his feet. He went slowly to the door where he stopped. He turned to face her. "The ironic thing is I do love you, Nola. I really do."

He left then. He left her sitting on a straight chair in her living room, all alone.

Larkspur

Chiara sat at her desk, pasting ads from the I-J into the ad book and doing her best to eavesdrop on Dana and Mitchell Cross's conversation. Dana hadn't closed the door to her office. Mitch had arrived a few minutes earlier. One of the first things he'd asked was if Dana had gotten the documents from the bank.

"I haven't figured out why," Chiara heard Mitch say, "but that meeting next week has to be the key. Somebody doesn't want you to attend."

"Maybe," Dana replied, "but it doesn't make much sense. If we were going to consider new business, it might be understandable."

"Too bad the documents haven't arrived. I was hoping to review them with you so I could go over and have a chat with Cedrick and Betts."

"Chances are there won't be anything in the package that's very interesting. Whatever Frank and Lane are up to might not have anything to do with the meeting," Dana said. "And if they buy my stock tomorrow, like they say they will, we may never know."

"That's the part that concerns me."

"Couldn't you just go and get whatever you need from Stan Bishop?" Dana asked.

"Not without a court order. And for that I need probable cause. I'd be fishing and the courts don't like that."

"I see."

Chiara glanced into Dana's office and happened to catch her eye. Apparently deciding the conversation was too private for others to hear, Dana got up and stepped over to close the door. Chiara acted as though she didn't notice, but she was annoyed at having been excluded. This package from the bank seemed to have gotten everybody real excited. She wondered what could be in it that was so interesting.

The security guard had just eaten a candy bar and was licking his fingers and smacking his lips. Chiara looked over at him with disgust. He gave her a sappy grin. Then she noticed a large brown envelope on the floor next to his chair.

"What's that package next to you?"

"Oh, jeez," he said, looking down, "I forgot. The courier come while you was gone." He picked it up. "The other ladies was busy so I was goin' to give it to you. Sorry."

Chiara sneaked a glance in at Dana. She was laughing and joking with Mitch.

"Hand it to me, will you?"

The guard lumbered over and gave her the envelope. "Thanks."

Another quick peek at Dana told her the transaction hadn't been noticed. She slipped the package into the bottom drawer of her desk. The guard stood there, looking at her dumbly.

"You can go back and sit now," she said.

He frowned and returned to his chair. The guy was so dense, Chiara wondered if he could possibly be any good in an emergency. His only virtue seemed to be his size.

After a glance toward the sales floor to make sure nobody but bozo would hear, she picked up the phone and dialed C&B's administrative offices. "Mr. Cedrick, please," she said to the receptionist.

"I'm sorry, Mr. Cedrick isn't in. Would you like to speak to his secretary?"

Chiara started to say yes. It would be easy to leave an ambiguous message that he would understand, but doubt seized her. The matter was so sensitive that even the police were interested in this package. "No," she said, "I'll call back."

She hung up the phone and drummed her nails on the desk. The other four thousand was as good as hers now. All she had to do was put the package in Lane Cedrick's hands. She didn't know what this was about, but her instincts told her that whatever was going on, wasn't good for Dana.

San Rafael

Nola drove around the block for the third time. When she came to David's office again, she pulled up to the curb, parked, and stared at the sign in the lawn in front of the converted bungalow: David L. Kirk, M.F.C.C. It meant Master of Family and Child Counseling, but Mother Fucking Cruel Cocksucker was more descriptive. How could the son of a bitch be doing this to her?

She trembled with anger. She'd called David three times after Frank left. The first two times she'd gotten his goddamn machine. She'd left messages, pleading for him to call. The third time, he'd picked up the phone in the middle of her message and said, "Nola, I can't talk to you today, I'm really busy. I'll call this weekend. Now please don't bother me. I'm with a client." Then he'd hung up without so much as a "Sorry," or "How are you, anyway?" The bastard.

Nola knew that hard-ass tone. She knew what it meant. Frank had used it when he was kissing her off. And every time she'd wanted a little compassion from him he'd given her that cruel routine. It was different when he wanted pussy or money, like today. And David Kirk had been all sweetness and light when he'd wanted to fuck her in her spa and tie her to his bed. But if she needed compassion and understanding, he was suddenly "really busy."

She stared up at the building, her heart full of hatred. And yet, underneath it all, she still clung to a glimmer of hope. It had been that way with Frank, too. A part of her had believed he'd come back. She'd reserved forgiveness for him in her heart. And now, true to form, that side of her nature was making apologies for David, too.

Understandably, it had been traumatic for him to have his child discover them that way. He needed to sort things out, get everything into perspective. It could be that he cared for her deeply, but just needed time and space.

Nola started banging her fist on the steering wheel with a steady beat. Well, if that was true, he could damned well say so. He might be busy, but this was her life, for chrissake. All she wanted was a little respect. And some affection. Was that too much to ask?

Nola got out of the BMW and went to the door. She found the reception area empty, and the door to David's office was closed. She didn't know whether he was alone or not. There was only one way to find out. She went over and knocked. A few moments later he opened it. A smirk crossed his face at the sight of her.

"Nola, what are you doing here?" he said. "I told you I was busy today."

"I have to talk to you, David. It's important."

"I can't. I'm with a client." He half glanced over his shoulder.

She could see a couple seated facing his desk. "Just for a minute," she said.

David sighed with exasperation. He turned to the couple, excused himself and stepped out into the reception area, closing the door behind him.

"What is it? What do you want?" he demanded impatiently.

She saw the cold indifference in his eyes. The boyish lustfulness was gone. This was not the man who'd worshiped her body to the point of idolatry. "You haven't called or said one word to me," she lamented. "I've been sitting at home mortified about what happened. And you haven't so much as asked if I'm all right."

"Look," he said, sounding annoyed, "I'm as sorry about it as you are. It's created a terrible problem for me with my daughter. Imagine what it's like to be in my shoes!"

"I feel badly about that but it was not my fault."

"I know," he said with a sigh. He glanced away, unable to look into her eyes.

"Horrible as it was, though, it wasn't the end of the world," she said. "We can put it behind us, can't we? We just have to be more careful."

He looked down at his feet and cleared his throat. "Nola, I'm not so sure this is a good situation we're in . . . if we're doing the right thing."

"What do you mean?"

"Well, we had a fling, we had a good time, but . . ."

A sick feeling went through her. "But what?"

"I've given our relationship a great deal of thought. I've decided maybe it isn't as healthy as it should be. I'm thinking we should end it before any serious harm is done."

"Serious harm?" she asked, raising her voice. "What the fuck does that mean?"

"Please," he said, glancing back at the door to his office.

"No, goddamn it, I want to know what you're saying. You're through with me, is that it? We've fucked a few times and you got your rocks off, played out your shrink fantasies, and now you want to pretend it never happened? Is that what you mean?"

"No, of course not," he said in a low, firm voice.

"Then, what?"

"Nola, even though you're not my patient, I'm certain this isn't a healthy situation for you. It would be irresponsible of me to continue the relationship. You're vulnerable. I didn't fully appreciate that at first, but I see now that—"

"Oh, don't give me that horseshit, David. You got what you wanted and now I've become inconvenient. Why not be man enough to admit it?"

"That isn't it at all. What happened with my daughter woke me up."

"So you feel guilty."

"Yes, I feel guilty," he said.

"And the simple solution is to get rid of me." Her voice quavered.

"You told me you'd been seeing a therapist," he said. "I think it would be a good idea if you worked this out with him."

"Oh, you do? You've shit in my hat, and now you want me to carry it to somebody else and let it be their problem, while I pay the hundred and a quarter an hour to get you off the hook. Very professional, David. Very professional, indeed. Christ Almighty."

"Nola, we aren't getting anywhere. Maybe we can meet later to discuss this."

Her eyes filled with tears. She was looking at David Kirk but she was seeing Frank Betts—the expression on Frank's face when he'd told her he wanted a divorce. The love he'd felt for her had died. It had been so obvious, just as David's change of heart was obvious, now.

"I was never anything to you but a piece of ass, was I?" she accused, holding back her tears.

"We only met last Saturday," he said. "Everything happened too fast. That was the problem."

"No," she replied in a small voice, "that's not the problem. The problem is I trusted you."

He looked down at his feet again.

"That's all right," she said, wiping away a tear. "At least we didn't waste much time. Like you say, we had some fun." She forced a smile. "Perhaps I'll see you at another workshop the next time my self-image needs an overhaul." With that, she turned on her heel and walked out the door.

Larkspur

Chiara looked at herself in the mirror behind the cash register. It was like looking at Dana. The hairstyle was a perfect copy. And who better to do it than Dana's own stylist, Hiroshi himself?

Hiroshi Yoshitomi, all five feet one inch of him, grinned his self-satisfied grin and nodded proudly as he looked back at her. "With your new hair, maybe you should go into real estate, too, and become a millionaire."

"I think it takes more than a hairdo, Hiroshi," she said. She took a ten from the change he handed her and gave it back. "Thanks."

"Thank *you*, so much," he said, bowing, his spiked hair pointing at her like the quills of a porcupine. "We see you again, I hope."

"I hope so, too."

"Good luck with new portfolio," he called to her as she went to the door.

"Thanks, I need it."

Chiara went out into the bright sunshine. It wasn't far to the office, just across the complex. She walked briskly, though. Her lunch hour had already stretched to an hour and a half. But when she'd called and discovered Hiroshi had a cancellation, she'd figured what the hell. Dana had told her she could have extra time if she stayed later, and Sylvia had agreed to watch the phones.

There was a definite bounce in her step. Before going to the salon, she'd gone to the bank and deposited Lane Cedrick's check. One thousand dollars, with another four on the way! She felt positively rich!

Chiara had given it some thought and decided to make one last push in the modeling business. She'd called her agent and said she wanted to do a new portfolio, really go for it. Camille was pleased because she'd been saying for months it was time to either give it her all or kiss it off. Chiara had made her decision. This was it. Do or die.

Camille had set up the photo shoot for the beginning of the week. She had told her to get her hair cut and skip milk shakes for a few days. The time off was easy enough to arrange. Dana owed her a day or two, anyway.

But her immediate problem was to get that package of documents to Lane Cedrick. A second call just before lunch had been unsuccessful. If he wasn't there when she got back to the office, Chiara decided she'd leave a message with his secretary.

She skipped along the sidewalk, feeling like a girl again. It was a glorious early-spring day. Maybe the winter of her life was behind her, as well.

When she entered the office the security guard was stuffing a submarine sandwich into his mouth. Chiara gave him a sideward glance as she walked past. His mouth was so full he couldn't talk, but he managed a grunt.

She hung up her coat in the closet, then opened the bottom drawer of her desk to drop in her purse. The drawer was empty. The bank envelope was gone.

She looked at the guard, her heart beginning to race. He was hunched over, his elbows on his knees, chomping away. She glanced into Dana's office. It was unoccupied. The only one in the bull pen was Sylvia Hansen, and she was on the phone.

"Where is that package?" she demanded, panic rising in her voice. The implications hit her hard. It was as if four thousand dollars had suddenly vanished.

The guard looked her way, swallowed hard and tried to speak. "The one I gave you this morning?" he asked. He wiped a smudge of mayonnaise off his lip with the back of his hand.

"Yes, do you know what happened to it?"

He swallowed again and nodded. "Yep, the boss has it. Mrs. Kirk."

"Dana? How did she get it?"

"She came in while you were at lunch and said she called the courier to find out where her package was and they said that they already delivered it. So she asked me if I seen it and I told her I gave it to you and that it was in your drawer.''

"Why did you do that, you idiot?" she snapped. Her anger flared. She felt like going over and wringing his neck.

"She's the boss, ain't she? She asked me and I told her. What's wrong with that?"

"*I* wanted to give it to her," Chiara said disingenuously.

"Well, you weren't here and she wanted it."

She looked anxiously toward Dana's office. "Where is she now?"

"She went to lunch with the other lady."

"Did she take the envelope with her?"

The guard shook his head. "No, I saw her take it into her office and she put it in her bottom drawer, just like you done." He gave her an oafish grin. "I watch things that happen, see? It's part of being a good security guard."

Chiara groaned miserably. She felt like she was going to be sick. This idiot had saved her butt earlier, then he'd turned around and handed over the package to Dana. It had probably cost her four thousand dollars!

She tried to figure out what to do. She couldn't walk in and take the envelope from Dana's drawer. The guard would see her and he would tell. Her only hope was that Dana wouldn't open it, that she'd leave it in the drawer until night.

But what should she do about Lane Cedrick? The best thing was probably to tell him that Dana had the package locked away, but that she hadn't looked at it yet. Maybe he could find a way to distract her for the rest of the day, lure her out of the office. Then, that evening after Dana and everyone else was gone, she could come back and retrieve the envelope. That was probably their best chance, but she'd have to call Lane immediately.

God, what if he wasn't there? She was sick at the thought that four thousand dollars could be slipping through her fingers! Holy Mother, how could this be happening? God or somebody had it in for her.

Sausalito

Nola stood at the railing on her deck, staring through her tears at the skyline of San Francisco and the wispy tongues of fog that had begun working their way through the Golden Gate. She lifted the bottle of champagne to her lips and guzzled down a bunch more of the bubbly, savoring the burn of the effervescence as the alcohol went down her throat.

The more she drank, the harder she cried. She hated herself for what she was doing, but getting fucked over twice in one day by two different men was about as bad as it got. She just didn't give a damn anymore.

She couldn't decide which of them she hated more. Both were selfish—Frank out of weakness and desperation, David out of fear and insensitivity. A couple of assholes, that's what they were.

She quaffed more champagne. Why was it these things always happened to her? Did she ask for it somehow? Maybe men looked at her and saw a sign around her neck that said Fuck Me.

Ironically, the bitch had been involved with the same two jerks. But Dana had come out a lot better than she had. Dana had dumped David and then used Frank. Just the opposite of what had happened to her. Either Dana was a hell of a lot smarter, or a hell of a lot meaner. Nola wondered if maybe that wasn't her problem. Maybe she was too goddamn nice, too willing to give a guy what he wanted. Maybe that was the lesson. Fuck them before they fuck you.

What a crazy world it was. Dana shits on David and Frank; David and Frank turn around and shit on her. "Thank you, Dana Kirk!" she cried, lifting the bottle of champagne in salute. "Thanks for ruining my life!"

Draining the last of the wine, she flung the bottle down the hillside, into the trees. She listened to it crash harmlessly into the undergrowth, then turned and staggered into the house. Taking off her clothes as she went, Nola made her way to her bedroom. She intended to throw herself onto the bed and have a good cry. But seeing the answering-machine light flashing, she went to it instead and pushed the Playback button.

"Nola," Frank said, after the beep, "I'm sorry you aren't home because I wanted to apologize to a person, not a machine. But maybe it's just as well. If you listen to this twice, you might accept that what I'm trying to say is true.

"I'm sorry about this morning, honey. I truly am. I'm sorry I put you through that. I don't want you to remember me begging for money, so please forget it happened. Try to remember me as I was before my life started going to hell. How I want to stay in your heart is the way I feel about you now, at this moment. I love you, Nola. When I told you that this morning I wasn't saying it just to get your money. It's how I feel. I guess I've realized it kind of late, haven't I? Well, like they say, better late than never. As far as the money is concerned, forget it. I'm sorry I even asked. It's probably better that you didn't give it to me. The truth is, it wouldn't have saved me. I'm dead already, Nola. I started dying the day I left you. That shows what a jackass I am. You deserve better than me. I hope the new guy in your life does better by you than I did. You're a jewel, babe. You truly are."

The recording clicked off then. Frank had used up his time. Nola had stopped crying while she listened, but she began weeping in earnest now. "Frank, oh, Frank," she cried as she fell onto the bed, burying her face in the comforter.

After a while she pulled herself together. She had to talk to him. She couldn't let it end on a note like that. He sounded so despondent, so defeated. If it was a cry for help, then she'd answer. The hell with pride. The hell with justice. She didn't care anymore.

She dialed his number. The phone rang and rang and rang, but nobody answered.

Larkspur

It was dusk when Dana pulled her Mercedes up next to Robin's Lexus and turned off the engine. They were in the parking lot at her office. She glanced at Robin. "Do you feel like you've been on the biggest wild-goose chase of your life?"

"That *was* strange," Robin said. "Frank's been weird for weeks, even months, but I've never seen Lane act so bizarre."

"If you want to know the truth, I was scared. I started getting the feeling Lane had lured us over there for some reason other than to discuss your escrows and listings. On the phone he made it sound like a lawsuit would be coming down on our heads at any moment, but it was a tempest in a teapot.

"Then I started wondering why he would want us there. In my paranoia I started thinking maybe it was a trap. When we walked out the door, I half expected Ted O'Connell to be lying in wait, ready to shoot me or something."

"Maybe Lane is losing it like Frank did. Maybe the pressure has finally gotten to him."

Dana shook her head. "I don't know what to make of it, I really don't."

"There's something going on with Frank that had Lane worried, too. Did you notice he buzzed his secretary twice to see if Frank had showed up or called in?"

"I assumed he expected him to join us," Dana said. "In fact I thought maybe they wanted to talk to me about my shares in the bank—renegotiate the deal or whatever. But Lane didn't bring it up. To the contrary, when I told him I'd put the stock certificate in escrow he kind of blanched. Did you notice that?"

"Maybe he didn't want to talk about it in front of me," Robin said.

Dana shook her head. "I don't think so. I can't explain it, but I know something's going on over there."

Robin looked at her watch. "Well, it's a cinch we won't be able to figure it out tonight. Let's shift to a more lurid and licentious subject. What are your plans for the evening? More fun and games with Dick Tracy?"

Dana smiled. "Mitch wants me to go home with him tonight. Said he'll be going in later in the morning, so we don't have to get up so early. We can sleep till seven."

"Whoopie!"

"Beats the hell out of five."

Robin shook her head. "I advise against marriage until you get the business with waking and sleeping hours worked out. Men who want to go to sleep at nine and screw at five in the morning would be hung by the balls in my universe."

"Mitch isn't particular about when he makes love. So far, it's been entirely mutual. Anyway, talk of marriage is a bit premature. Our first week's anniversary isn't until day after tomorrow."

"Time certainly flies when you're having fun."

Dana stared off and sighed. "I've been as amazed at what's happened the last several days as anyone. I keep thinking, 'No, this doesn't make any sense. It's a balloon and it's going to pop.'" She looked at Robin. "I've never done anything that seemed so irrational on the surface but felt so good underneath."

"A man with firm loins will do that to a girl."

"Really, Robin. I think there's more to it than that."

"What can I say? Opposites attract."

"That's the funny thing," Dana said. "Mitch doesn't seem like an opposite. It's like I've—"

"Known him all your life?" Robin shook her head. "When you sink to the level of petty clichés, it's definitely love, kiddo."

"No, I'm not prepared to go that far. Mitch and I are in like and in lust."

"You sound like you're describing a week you'd just spent with Mr. Adonis at Club Med."

"Maybe that's all it is."

"Well, my philosophy is, if it's free, don't knock it."

"I'm not rushing to any conclusions, believe me. I'm sort of riding the tide to see where it takes me. It beats sitting at home alone, waiting for threatening letters, anonymous phone calls and Ted O'Connell's heavy feet, I'll tell you that." Dana glanced around at the falling darkness. "Speaking of which, we shouldn't be sitting here like this. Mitch said always to be moving when I'm in the car. You coming into the office, or going right home?"

"I think I'll head for home and sit by the phone with a fainting heart, waiting for Morton to call."

"You haven't exactly spent the week in a convent, Robin."

"No, and we're really getting racy tomorrow night. We're going to the movies."

"How sweet."

"Yeah, I told Morton my rule was a kiss on the second date only if the movie was romantic and the sundae was extra large."

"But you slept with him on your first date."

"Mom never said anything about the first date. She just said wait until the second date to kiss the guy."

Dana reached for her briefcase. "On that note, I think I'll go in and check my messages before I go find Mitch. I'm meeting him at his office and leaving my car there so that he doesn't have to drive me all the way down here in the morning."

"You two sound like a couple to me," Robin said, reaching for the door handle.

"No, dear, just lustful friends."

"I won't be taking my bridesmaid dress to the cleaners just yet, then."

"You wore the same one to all three of your sisters' weddings, didn't you?"

"They all wore Mom's wedding dress. You think I'd risk family harmony by lobbying for a bridesmaid's dress I actually liked? Besides, when you're the youngest you do what you're told."

"Except on first dates?" Dana teased, arching her brow.

Robin laughed. "Give my best to lover boy," she said, opening the door.

They both got out.

"I'm glad you got to meet him," Dana said, over the roof of the car. She locked the door.

"Mitch is a hunk, all right," Robin said. "I can see now why you fell off the wagon."

"It's early. I still regard it as a passing thing."

Robin opened the door to her Lexus. "Well, have a nice evening."

"You, too."

Robin got into her car and Dana, glancing up at the high fog, hurried toward the office. Alone outside with darkness falling she was again in the grip of the flight instinct.

It didn't matter that there was nobody suspicious lurking about. She felt at any moment the wolf might leap.

Chiara saw Dana coming toward the door and glanced over at the security guard who was in the middle of a yawn. She'd been sitting there all afternoon, dying a thousand deaths. Lane had gotten Dana out of the office, but what was going to happen now?

Dana breezed in the door like she'd just run a race. "Hi," she said. "You two the last of the Mohicans?"

"Lucille was in for a while," Chiara said. "She left a few minutes ago."

"There's no reason for you to stay," Dana said, glancing at the clock. "Shawn and I will lock up."

Chiara glanced at the oaf. She'd come to detest him, even though he'd eased up on his flirting, if that's what it could be called. Somehow she blamed him for her troubles, even though it was more likely God's doing. The blasphemy caused a pang of guilt and she mentally crossed herself. "Okay," she said, opening her bottom drawer to get her purse.

Dana was looking through the phone messages. Chiara had only taken one of consequence—from Mitchell Cross. He'd said, "Please remind Dana to bring the bank documents with her." Chiara had said she would, but, of course she hadn't put that on the message slip. The oversight could put four thousand dollars in her bank account—unless, of course, Dana decided to take the documents with her when she left. Again, she mentally crossed herself.

The smile on Dana's lips told Chiara she was reading the message from Mitch. She'd written, "See you around seven."

Dana looked up at her as Chiara fiddled with her purse. "Mitch didn't want me to call?"

"No, he just said he'd see you later."

Another smile. Chiara felt her stomach turn. And her heart ached for Dana to leave. Please, God. She got up and went to get her coat. The security guard was standing now, stretching his big, lumbering body.

"How long do you think, Mrs. Kirk, before you want to go?" he asked.

"You've had a long day, haven't you?"

"Well, I'm earning overtime, but there's a Warriors game tonight, you know."

Dana nodded politely. "I'll just be a few minutes, Shawn. I need to take care of a few things, then we can go."

Chiara moved tentatively toward the door, her heart pounding, her mind reeling with prayer. "Good night, Dana," she called.

"Night, Chiara. See you in the morning."

Dana went into her office and Chiara went out the door. She headed across the parking lot, toward the bus stop as she usually did. Once she got beyond the envelope of light from the building, she moved into the shadows. Finding a spot behind a parked car, she turned to watch.

The fog was thickening. However, the bright light inside enabled her to see Dana clearly through the windows of her office. She was at her desk, and looked to be organizing things for the next day. Chiara wondered if she could have forgotten the envelope in her bottom drawer. She waited, shivering in the cold wind, half hidden behind a car, as four thousand dollars hung in the balance. Just when she was beginning to hope that Dana had forgotten, she opened the drawer and lifted the package onto the top of her desk. Chiara's heart sank. When she saw Dana open the envelope, she just about died. Damn her anyway! Everything was coming unraveled before her eyes.

Inside, Dana was looking over the top sheet in the bundle of documents. Then, to Chiara's relief, she put the rest of the documents back in the envelope and returned them to the drawer. Taking the paper she'd been looking at, Dana slipped it into her purse and got to her feet. Chiara's hopes soared. Unless the piece of paper she'd taken was the one Lane Cedrick was concerned about, the day might not be lost, after all!

She watched as Dana went to the reception area. It looked as though they were about to leave. Once they were gone, Chiara figured she could go back in and get the package and trade it to Lane Cedrick for her money.

Just as Dana and the guard were at the door, a car with three people in it drove up and parked directly in front of the building. Sylvia Hansen and the buyers she'd been working with earlier got out. If they were returning to the office at this hour, chances were it was to write an offer. That meant they could be there for hours. What was she going to do now?

She watched miserably as Dana and Sylvia paused to exchange pleasantries. Shawn walked Dana to her car as Sylvia took her buyers into the office. Damn.

A few moments later Dana was driving off and the guard was climbing into his car. Chiara stared at the brightly lit office, now occupied by Sylvia and her clients. Shivering in the damp air, she folded the lapels of her coat over her chest and walked off. She needed to get to a pay phone and call Lane Cedrick.

Kentfield

Lane Cedrick reached for the phone and dialed Frank's home number for the sixth time since Dana had left. Still no answer. Why hadn't the bastard put on his goddamn machine? He'd tried to reach Frank on his car phone, too. Same result. Was the son of a bitch hiding out?

The news clearly wasn't good. Frank probably hadn't been able to come up with the money and chances were he was sitting in a bar someplace, up to his gills in martinis. Lane knew he could be wrong, though. Occasionally Frank surprised him. It was still possible he'd come rolling in with the sixty grand in his pocket and a smile on his face. But Lane wasn't sure how long he could afford to wait. That was the problem.

The other sword hanging over his head was the package of loan documents. It was hard to tell whether Chiara would come through or not. Probably it depended more on what Dana did than what the girl did. He'd need a couple of lucky rolls of the dice to survive this ordeal. Too damn bad. He'd tried to solve the problem for weeks now; he'd taken serious risks and it had come down to whether his drunken partner could hold himself together, and whether a postpubescent little bitch answering phones in a real-estate office could steal a few documents for him. What a sorry state of affairs.

The phone rang. He glanced at the instrument and saw that the call wasn't coming in on his private line. That meant that if it was for him, it was likely the girl. Everybody else had gone home. He picked up the receiver.

"Cedrick & Betts."

"Mr. Cedrick?"

"Yes?"

"It's me, Chiara."

Lane drew an uneasy breath. "Well, what's the story?"

She related what had happened, the fact that the package was sitting in Dana's desk drawer and that she'd seen Dana open the envelope and remove the sheet of paper.

"Are you sure it was only one piece of paper and that it was on the top?"

"Yes, Mr. Cedrick. I watched from outside until she left the office."

"Chances are it was the agenda for the meeting. That's not too bad." Lane stroked his chin. "Listen, Chiara, wait a few hours to make sure no one is there, then return to the office. Since the envelope has already been opened, it won't be necessary for you to take the whole thing. In fact, it's better that you don't. Just remove the documents with Dana's signature on them that concern the Oak Meadow Partners loan. Got that? The Oak Meadow Partners.''

''Yes, Oak Meadow Partners. I understand.''

''Leave anything that doesn't have Dana's signature on it.''

''Okay. What do I do with them once I have them?''

''Call me. I'll be at home. You have the number. Then I'll meet you to pick up the documents. I can give you a lift home if you like.''

''Yes, fine. You'll remember the check, won't you, Mr. Cedrick?''

''Yes, you'll get your money, Chiara.''

''Okay, I'll call you,'' she said, and hung up.

Lane leaned back in his chair. Maybe he'd pull this off, after all. Of course, he still needed to close the purchase of Dana's stock. If Frank had pooped out on him, he had to know.

He got up from his desk and headed down the hall toward the controller's office. If Frank didn't produce, Lane figured he'd better know exactly how much money was lying around. That done, he'd go looking for his rummy partner.

Kentfield

Nola stood at Frank's door, ringing the bell. Why didn't he answer? His car was out front, so he was home. She shivered. The fog was so cold and damp that Nola could almost taste it when she inhaled. It had been a bitch trying to drive over. She'd almost run into a truck on the freeway. The scare had sobered her up momentarily. She was in no condition to drive, but she desperately had to see him.

Tired of ringing the bell, she tried the doorknob. To her utter amazement, the door swung open.

"Frank?" she hesitantly called. No response. "Frank, are you home?" Still no answer. She stepped inside and closed the door behind her.

A lamp in the corner of the front room was on and she could see a soft glow coming from the back of the condo. It looked like it was coming from the master suite. Nola moved toward the rear hallway, listening for a sound.

She stopped at the entrance to the hall. "Frank?" Still nothing. She had a bad feeling. All afternoon, ever since she'd listened to Frank's message on her machine, her emotions had vacillated between dread and desperation. Frank had not been himself. Something was terribly wrong. Coming to the bedroom door, her heart tripping with fear, she peeked around the corner. In the soft glow of the bedside lamp, she saw him lying on the bed. He was fully dressed and even had on his shoes. For an instant she thought he'd passed out but there was an odd cant to his head.

Nola took a couple of steps into the room before she noticed a deep crimson spot on the pillow, beside his head. She gasped, her throat clutching when she saw the gun in his hand, the pencil-size hole in his temple, the lifeless clench of his jaw.

She dropped to her knees. The sound welling from deep within her was half wail, half scream, and it was filled with utter horror.

Novato

The fog spilling over Mount Tamalpais and streaming through the Golden Gate had blanketed lower Marin, but it hadn't extended to the northern reaches of the county. Once they'd passed Lucas Valley Road the mists thinned considerably, enabling the late-evening traffic to move at near-normal speed.

Dana had volunteered to drive since she couldn't very well leave the Mercedes on the street overnight. Mitch's Bronco was secure in the departmental lot, and he'd told her he didn't mind riding shotgun for a change.

She glanced over at him, feeling secure in his company after that lonely drive in the fog up from Larkspur. He'd been waiting for her in the reception area since the outer door of the police department had already been locked. "I was afraid maybe you'd gotten lost in the fog," he'd said, folding her into his arms.

After they'd kissed, she'd told him about her strange visit to Cedrick & Betts's administrative offices, and Lane's bizarre behavior.

"I don't know what it means," Mitch had said, "but maybe it's time to put a little heat on those two fellas. There's been a smell there from the start, but it's turning into a stench."

He'd asked her about Marin Pacific Savings, whether she'd brought the committee documents with her.

"No, I left them in my office."

He'd grimaced. "Didn't Chiara give you my message? I told her to tell you to bring everything, so that we could review it this evening."

Dana had shaken her head. "No, she just told me to meet you here."

"I suppose we can drive back and get the package. It's not all that far."

"That's not necessary, Mitch. I know what's in it. I brought the agenda."

"Maybe that's all we need, then."

They'd sat down to look it over. It was a neatly typed schedule listing the loans the committee was to review. Included were dates of approval and funding, loan amounts and, in the case of construction loans, the amounts drawn.

"Anything strike your eye?" Mitch had asked.

Dana had run down the list. "No, these are just a select group of loans the committee approved over the past year or so."

"Nothing unusual?"

She'd shaken her head. "To be honest, I don't remember them all. A few I recall clearly, like this strip shopping center in Walnut Creek. The developer didn't want to guarantee the loan personally, but we made it a condition." She continued to study the list. "A couple of these were before my time, Mitch. I don't know a thing about them."

"I wonder if there was something Frank or Lane didn't want you to know about in the old ones—some irregularity, maybe."

"I don't see why they'd be particularly concerned about me. If they'd done something shady, they'd be more worried about Stan Bishop catching on than me. As president he's responsible for managing the portfolio. Besides, what are the chances I'd even notice an irregularity, assuming there was one? They'd have to be pretty paranoid to worry about that."

Mitch had shrugged. "Just a thought."

"Wait a second," she'd said, noticing an entry near the bottom of the list. "This one's odd." She'd pointed with her finger.

"Oak Meadow Partners?"

"Yes, it's an apartment complex in Novato. A fourmillion-dollar construction loan," she said, reading the entry.

"What's strange?" Mitch had asked.

"The date more than anything. The loan was approved during my tenure on the committee. Yet I don't remember it. And I can't imagine forgetting one this large, especially a project nearby."

"Who are Oak Meadow Partners?" he'd asked.

"It's probably a limited partnership. I have no idea who the principals are."

"Would you be able to tell from the documents?"

"Probably. The general partners would have signed individually."

"Is the stench getting stronger?" he'd asked.

"You're the expert on stench, Mitch."

"I think we should check out those documents first thing in the morning."

"According to this, the partnership has drawn half a million dollars on the loan," she'd said. "That means the buildings have been framed, at least."

"If you say so."

"Funny I'd have forgotten a project this large. It might be interesting to see it. Four million's not peanuts."

"Novato's on our way home."

"Would you mind terribly if we stopped by?"

"Is the pope Catholic? Don't forget, you're working with the expert on stench. Let's go!"

They were nearing the Novato Boulevard exit and Dana slowed, pulling into the right lane. After exiting, and crossing over the freeway, they followed the road into town.

Passing through the pools of light under each lamppost, Dana started getting a strange feeling—the same sort of feeling she'd had leaving Lane's office that afternoon.

"We just might be on to something, Mitch," she said. "I still don't know how it all fits together, but I think you're right about the stench. A few years ago there was a lot of talk around C&B that Frank and Lane were going to start up a development company, but in recent months I haven't heard much about it."

"Do you think this Oak Meadow Partners could be connected to them?" he asked.

"That's what I'm wondering."

The construction site was two blocks off Novato Boulevard, at the far edge of town. It was an open field. Dana pulled the Mercedes up to the curb. They got out.

Though it was dark, they could see that the job consisted of little more than a hole in the ground.

"Pretty primitive accommodations," Mitch observed.

"That's a few thousand dollars of earthwork out there," she said. "And nothing more."

"Where's the rest of the money that's been drawn on the loan?" he asked.

"My guess is, that's probably something Oak Meadow Partners would prefer not to discuss."

"You know what?" Mitch said. "I'm wondering if there's a reason you don't remember this project."

Dana slowly nodded. "Chilling thought, isn't it?"

"Could the committee have met without you to approve a loan?"

"Yes, but I would have to have gotten notice that a meeting was being held. I went to every board and committee meeting I was told about."

"It'll be very interesting to see those documents," he said.

"I should have brought them. I'm sorry."

"Your girl has to improve on her message taking."

"Yes, Chiara hasn't been herself lately. She's been moody and distracted."

"She probably has a boyfriend."

Dana laughed. "Honestly, I don't understand how men can be so naive."

"Why do you say that?"

"Mitch, Chiara has a crush on *you*."

"On me?"

"Yes, didn't you notice?" She looked at him in the light of a distant lamppost. "Of course you noticed. You're just being modest."

"I teased her a little, that's all."

"Maybe you're so used to women fawning over you that you don't see it for what it is."

"Is that a criticism or a compliment, Ms. Kirk?"

"Both." She laughed. "You don't think I'm going to make it easy for you, do you?"

She shivered and Mitch put his arm around her. They looked out at the dark field.

"Do you suppose this is what it's all been about? The letters, the phone calls, the armless dolls?"

"That's something I intend to find out in the morning. At least now I have something to discuss with Messieurs Cedrick and Betts."

Dana turned to him, slipping her arms around his waist. "You're an odd duck, Mitchell Cross, you know that?"

"And what, pray tell, does that mean?"

"You're an eccentric cowboy. And you're also more than you like to admit."

He kissed the middle of her forehead. "Are these sweet nothings I'm hearing?"

She grinned. "Something like that."

"Since the mood seems to be getting all romantic, how about if I take you to a Basque restaurant that's a special favorite of mine? It's one of those fancy places with table-cloths and candles."

Dana laughed. "You *are* a romantic, aren't you?"

He took her by the arm and they headed back toward her car. "Baby, you ain't seen nothing yet."

* * *

Kentfield

Lane Cedrick pulled up in front of Frank's condo. The bastard's car was there, so that meant he was probably home. It was about goddamn time.

He got out of the Rolls and, as he made his way toward the unit, he noticed the front door was ajar. Had Frank staggered home so drunk he hadn't had the presence of mind to close his own goddamn door? Lane shook his head in disgust. It was obvious to him that Frank hadn't gotten the money. Now he'd be forced to go to plan *B*.

It was probably a wasted day, all the shit he'd gone through with Chiara. But he'd wanted to give it every chance. Narrow as the odds had been, it was possible Frank would have come through. All that remained was to confirm the worst.

Arriving on the porch he rang the bell, though he knew it was probably a futile gesture. After waiting several moments, he pushed the door open.

"Frank?" he called loudly. When there was no answer, he boldly walked in, glancing around. "Frank, it's me! Where the hell are you? Let's get this settled."

He listened, but didn't hear a sound. He started toward the bedroom, figuring the bastard had probably drunk himself into a stupor. What else could he reasonably expect under the circumstances?

San Rafael

Corinne Smith walked wearily down the corridor toward her office. She looked up and saw Al Bensen coming the other way.

"What are you doing here at this hour, Corinne?" he asked.

"I been out rapping knuckles with my ruler, Lieutenant. Some crazy S.O.B. got an idea that by beatin' on his woman she was going to love him more. Can you imagine that?"

He gave her his characteristic grin and hitched up his pants. "I take it you straightened him out."

"Oh, yes, sir. He won't be beatin' on that woman again until the next time he does." She shook her head. "It's always the same."

"It might seem like a lost cause, but who do these women have to turn to if it's not us?" he said. "And you're the best we've got at handling these situations, Corinne."

"Thanks, Al."

"Listen, have you seen your buddy, Cross, recently?"

"He's up to his eyeballs with that real-estate broker case. Why?"

Bensen laughed. "Up to his eyeballs, eh? Knowing Cross, I'd say up to something else."

She gave him a look. "I don't make that stuff any of my business, Lieutenant."

"I'm glad I've got one detective with moral fiber."

"I'll tell my husband you said that."

He chuckled. "Listen, will you do me a favor? And maybe a favor for Cross. The dispatcher just buzzed me. The Ross P.D. called a few minutes ago asking for Mitch. Seems like they've got something of interest regarding his case. They want a detective to get back to them and I'm on my way to a counsel meeting with the chief. Will you check it out?"

"Sure, why not?"

Corinne went to her office, glancing at her watch, wondering. Anybody but Mitch, she'd make it wait until tomorrow. After checking her Rolodex, she dialed the Ross P.D.

"This is Detective Smith in San Rafael," she said. "You got something you want me to pass on to Mitch Cross?"

"Patrolman Savic has something for you. Hang on."

Corinne waited and after a few seconds the officer came on the line. "Hello, ma'am, this is Savic," he said. "I answered a call this evening that Detective Brockmeyer said Detective Cross would probably want to know about."

"Yeah, what's that?"

"We had a house alarm at the Kirk residence. I checked it out. Somebody had broken a window by the door. They didn't gain access. The alarm must have scared the intruder off. Whoever it was also knocked down the mailbox at the entrance to the drive. You can see the tire marks where they made what must have been a fast getaway. We couldn't locate Mrs. Kirk, but we went ahead and boarded up the window.

"I wouldn't have bothered calling on a thing like this except that Lieutenant Brockmeyer said it could be important."

"Thanks, Officer Savic, I'll pass this on."

"Good night."

Corinne hung up. She thought for a moment, trying to decide if it was worth bothering Mitch. She had an inkling he might be with Dana Kirk. If so, passing on this tidbit wasn't going to help them enjoy the evening. She decided instead to leave word with the dispatcher in case he called in. She also decided to jot out a note and leave it on his desk.

Forestville, Sonoma County

They lay side by side in his bed, holding hands, the contentment of their lovemaking enveloping them like the warm air of a sensuous summer night. She could feel the heat of his body and smell its pungent masculine tang. She was starting to get the feeling that sex with Mitchell Cross was more than just a random coupling. It was starting to feel like a mating, though for that to be true in a meaningful way she knew a lot more ground had to be covered. Feelings had to be explored. And Dana didn't know with certainty how *she* felt about it, let alone him.

He rubbed the back of her hand with his thumb. "So tell me what you're thinking," he said.

"Pervert."

"No, it's a serious question."

"It's impolite to probe, Mitch."

"I'm not afraid to say this feels good to me."

"Men tend to feel the same way about sex all the time, don't they? It makes you feel good."

"What's critical isn't the sensation at the moment of orgasm. It's the way you feel afterward."

She rolled her head toward him. "That's a very nice sentiment." Dana rubbed his hand against her cheek.

"You never answered my question," he said. "What were you thinking?"

"I was thinking how nice it is here in the country. I'm sort of a refugee from this, you know."

"Yes, you were a sharecropper's daughter who went to the city to make her fortune. And succeeded magnificently, I might add."

"At the risk of flattering you unduly, Mitch, this place of yours feels good to me in much the same way you do. Maybe it's because it's been a place of refuge from the storm—I don't know for sure. But I like being here. That much I do know." She sighed. "Does that answer your question?"

Mitch rolled onto his side, facing her. Pushing her hair back off her ear, he lightly kissed the shell, letting his warm breath caress her skin. He gently cupped her breast, lowered his face and kissed it. Then he lay back on his pillow. She looked at him. He was watching her.

"What?" she said, uncertain what his kisses and the silence meant.

"What happens when I catch the bad guy and you don't need a place of refuge anymore?" he asked.

"I don't know."

"It's crossed my mind. Has it crossed yours?"

"Sure."

He didn't say anything.

"Maybe you'll go on to your next damsel in distress," she said. "It's a big bad world with other victims awaiting your protection, Mitch."

"The fair damsels are few and far between in this business."

"So, I'm an anomaly."

"Yeah, you're an anomaly, all right."

"I think I like that," she said.

"You like keeping all the fun to yourself?"

She smiled in the near darkness of his room. "It's okay to think of it that way for now, isn't it?"

"You're asking me?"

"It *is* all right," she said. "It's all right because I like you, Mitch."

He kissed her then, and they embraced, his warm skin pressing against her cool flesh. In only seconds she became aroused and could tell he was, too.

And then the phone rang.

"Damn," he said.

"Yes, damn." She glanced at the clock. It was almost midnight.

Mitch reached for the receiver. Dana's first thought was that it was Carole.

"Yeah?" he said into the phone, propping himself on his elbow. He listened for a few seconds and then sat up on the edge of the bed. "When was this...? They're on the scene now...? I see. Okay, I'll drive down. Tell the Larkspur P.D.

I should be there in about forty-five minutes, will you, Lynn? ... Right. Thanks.'' He hung up the phone and turned on the bedside lamp.

"Mitch, what happened?"

"More bad news, I'm afraid. That was my dispatcher. Chiara has been murdered."

An icy horror went through her. "Chiara?"

"Dana, she was shot in the office, sitting at your desk."

"Oh, my God." She clutched her hands to her mouth.

He reached out and took her hand. "Will you be all right here alone?"

She got up from the bed. "No, Mitch, I'm coming with you."

Nine

Dana sat in the reception area, feeling more like a visitor from outer space than the owner of the company. Police were all over the place and she kept hearing the crackling of the radios they carried on their belts. Brightly lit in the middle of the night, and full of strangers, her office had an eerie, surrealistic feel.

She chanced another look through the blinds into her office. Chiara still lay slumped across her desk like a rag doll. The officers were going about their business almost as if she were a piece of furniture. Mitch was off in the corner, talking to the Larkspur detective. He'd left her on the love seat when they'd arrived, and he'd been inspecting the murder scene for the past ten minutes or so.

Dana again looked at Chiara. She couldn't see her face, only her shiny black hair and limp shoulders. Her heart ached, knowing that the girl was dead. Who would want to kill her? And what had she been doing in the office in the middle of the night, anyway?

During the drive down to Marin in the fog she and Mitch had done a lot of speculating. Could Chiara's death somehow be related to what had been going on, or was it an act of senseless violence? They wouldn't know, Mitch had said, until they got there, and maybe not then.

Dana knew nothing more now than when they'd first arrived. Mitch hadn't come back out yet, so she could only speculate, but by all appearances Chiara hadn't fled to her office, she'd gone there purposefully. She'd been shot while sitting at the desk but, from her present vantage point, Dana had no idea where the bullet had struck Chiara—and she didn't think she wanted to know, either.

Mitch came out to the reception area just then, having finished his conversation with the other detective. His expression was grim.

"Have you figured out what happened?" she asked, as he sat next to her.

"The bullet came through that side window and struck her in the back of the head as she sat at the desk. Chances are she had no idea anyone was there."

Dana closed her eyes as the weightiness of the words sank in. She shook her head, wishing she could escape from the terrible image Mitch had painted.

"Dana, we're wondering if Chiara was the intended victim, or if maybe the gunman wasn't really after you."

"Me?"

He took her hand, as if to soften his words. "You have virtually identical hairstyles and are roughly the same size and build. Unless the killer approached along the front window, he probably never saw Chiara's face. She was in your chair. From behind, it would have been easy enough to assume it was you."

"Oh, my God," she mumbled, as the implications became clear.

"We won't know for sure unless and until we make an arrest," he said.

Dana glanced into her office, staring at the lifeless body. "Do you think it was Ted?"

"He certainly is a prime suspect."

"But there's no way to be sure?"

"Not yet. We'll have more to go on when we get the lab report."

She shivered.

"And there's something else in there we need to discuss. When Chiara was shot, she was paging through that package of documents from the bank. The Oak Meadow Partners papers were set aside. It appears she was in the process of removing them from the pack when she was killed."

She shook her head. "Why would Chiara do that?"

"I don't know, I was wondering if you might have an idea."

Dana tried to think, but it was difficult to unscramble her brain. The excitement, high emotion and late hour all conspired against her. "Mitch, I'm not sure if Chiara was even aware of my connection with Marin Pacific Savings, so how would she have known about Oak Meadow Partners? It doesn't make any sense."

"Well, this didn't happen by accident. Chiara was going through those documents for a reason. It was either at her own initiative or someone else's."

"It would have to be either Frank or Lane."

"That's what I'm thinking," he said. "She had some objective in mind and I realize now that she was very intent on getting to those documents. Remember, I asked her to remind you to bring the package home and she omitted that from the message?"

"That's right! She must not have wanted me to take them before she had a chance to go through them herself."

"The question is, why? What's so interesting about those documents?" He shifted uncomfortably. "I really think we need to know, Dana."

"You want me to go in and look at them, don't you?"

"We've got everything in there sealed off until the lab guys do their job. We haven't touched anything, but several of the documents are easy enough to see as they lie there. You could have a look at them without disturbing anything. It would mean—"

"Going in there with her."

Mitch nodded. "Some people are pretty squeamish."

Dana drew a fortifying breath. "I've never had to do anything like this before, but I'll do my best."

"There's a lot of blood. I don't know if the smell bothers you."

She swallowed hard. "Let's just go do it."

Mitch took her arm and they went to the door. A policeman stepped aside to let her enter. From this new angle, she was able to see that Chiara's eyes were open. She looked stunned. Dana felt a wave of nausea.

Somehow it seemed that it ought to be a terrible joke, that Chiara would sit up and everybody would laugh. However the pool of blood was real and, as she drew close, she did notice a distinctive smell.

"Try not to touch anything," Mitch said, as she moved around the desk.

Passing behind the chair she noticed the hole in the side corner window. She winced at seeing so graphically how it had happened. Once she was on the other side of Chiara, where the documents had been stacked, she leaned down for a closer look. In doing so, she caught a whiff of Chiara's perfume. She tried not to look at the body, but the odor of blood, mixed with Chiara's unique scent, made it impossible not to. She sneaked a peek, but the wound was not obvious in the mat of blood-soaked hair.

An image of Chiara as she'd been that afternoon came to mind. After returning from Hiroshi's, she'd shown off her new hairdo to Helene and Robin. Dana had a vivid recollection of her striding up and down like a runway model, turning a couple of times and letting her hair swing. The memory made her want to cry.

Dana glanced up at Mitch, braced herself, and turned her attention to the documents. There were three or four. Only the nearest to the body was spattered with blood. For the most part they were the signature pages of various bank and committee forms. There didn't appear to be anything unusual about them until she noticed her own signature. Her mouth sagged.

"What is it?" Mitch said.

She looked at him. "Somebody's signed my name here, Mitch, but it's a forgery."

"Are you sure?"

"Yes, it's an attempt to copy my signature, a clumsy one."

Mitch exhaled slowly. "That probably explains what was going on here."

She wasn't sure she understood. "You think Frank and Lane are responsible?"

"It could be that they forged your signature, or were aware it had been forged, and then panicked when they thought you'd be getting copies of the documents. They probably enlisted Chiara's support to remove them. She must have been killed in the process."

"By whom?"

"That's the question. We can't even be sure there was a connection between the documents and the shooting. Not if O'Connell's our man, anyway."

Mitch signaled for her to come back around the desk. She returned to his side and he put his arm around her shoulders. They went back into the reception area.

"It's time we picked up brothers Betts and Cedrick," he said. "I'm not going to wait until morning."

Dana sat in the love seat and dropped her face into her hands. Her entire world seemed to be coming unhinged. Mitch massaged the back of her neck.

"I think you should probably get some rest," he said. "Do you want me to drop you off at a motel?"

"What about you?"

"I've got a lot yet to do tonight. Generally speaking, murderers don't wait until business hours to accommodate the police."

Dana shook her head. "I feel so confused. None of this makes any sense."

"We'll sort it out." He drew a long breath. "Can you give me a few minutes? Then I'll drive you to a motel."

She nodded and he went off to confer with the other detective. She watched him. Mitch was calm, quietly in control. He was very good at what he did, she could tell that. Nonetheless, these were horrible circumstances under which to discover it.

For the next several minutes she sat numbly, waiting for him to return. In her heart, she began to grieve for Chiara. When he came back, Mitch handed her a handkerchief. She looked up at him questioningly. She hadn't realized it until then, but tears were streaming down her cheeks.

Strawberry Manor

It was barely light when she heard a key in the lock. Lifting her head from the pillow, Dana saw the door open, then Mitch's silhouette in the doorway. Behind him she could see the thick fog and she could hear the sound of the early rush-hour traffic on the freeway.

Dana sat up and Mitch turned on the light.

"Did I wake you?" he asked, coming over to the bed.

She'd slept in her blouse, as a sort of makeshift nightshirt. She pulled the covers up to her waist and fluffed a pillow behind her. "I was sort of half dozing," she replied. "I didn't sleep very well. What's happened?"

He sat on the edge of the bed. "Quite a bit. O'Connell was arrested last night in Los Angeles, sometime before Chiara was killed."

"*Before* she was killed? Then he definitely couldn't have done it."

"No, he was over three hundred miles away when it happened."

Dana groaned. "I was so sure it was Ted."

"He was the obvious candidate. Still, he couldn't be in two different places at once. O'Connell's going to be facing other charges and won't be seeing the light of day for some time. However, that doesn't solve our problem here."

"I guess I should be glad," she said, rubbing her face, "but it almost seems anticlimactic."

"We've suspected all along there was more than one villain. This simply confirms it." He took her hand. "I have more news, Dana, and I'm afraid it's tragic."

She got that sick feeling again.

"Frank Betts is dead," he said. "We found him in his bed, shot in the head."

She gasped, stunned. For several seconds she struggled to fathom the reality of what he was saying. "Frank's dead?"

"Yes."

"Was he murdered, too?"

"We aren't sure yet. It could be a suicide. If it weren't for the fact that the weapon was missing, suicide would be the logical conclusion, considering the circumstances."

She shuddered. Images of Frank went through her head, bits and pieces of recollections from over the years. But the image that stood out most strongly was from that last night she'd seen him, the hurt look on his face when she wouldn't make the deal he wanted. At the time she'd assumed it was all part of his act, but in retrospect she saw how critically important that stock sale was to him. She'd had no idea his anxiety would lead to this. A tremor went through her.

"We think the same caliber weapon killed both Chiara and Frank," Mitch said. "If it turns out to be the same gun, then we've really got a conundrum."

"What are the implications?"

"One possible scenario would be that Frank was despondent over both his personal and business problems. Blaming you for his troubles, he decided to do you in. When he found Chiara in your office, he assumed it was you and shot her. Afterward, he went home and shot himself. The problem with that theory is there was no gun in his hand."

"Could someone have come and taken it?"

"We considered the possibility. It's feasible, considering the door to the condo was unlocked. Nothing else was missing as nearly as we can tell. If there was a burglary subsequent to the suicide, then the burglar took only the gun. Another problem is the timing. We aren't sure yet, but it seems Frank may have died prior to Chiara. I'll be getting a definitive answer on that soon. If it's true, then Frank couldn't have shot Chiara, either."

She shook her head incredulously. "I'd be shocked if Frank was the one. Shooting people is just not his style, whatever his motive or state of mind."

"What about suicide?" Mitch asked. "Could you buy that?"

Dana thought for a moment. "He seemed depressed that last night I saw him. I wasn't sure how much of it was an act, for effect. Frank was a man of extreme emotions. He was either up or down."

"We'll see how the lab report comes back," Mitch said.

"Well, if we assume it wasn't Frank, then could it have been Lane?" she asked.

"That's the next bit of news. He's disappeared. We went to his house in Mill Valley. He's cleared out. It appears he packed for a long trip, and in haste."

"Does that mean he could be the one?"

"He was fleeing something. That always makes you wonder. He had some of the same financial motives as Frank for wanting you dead—assuming you were the intended victim."

"Killing me wouldn't have solved his problem, Mitch."

"It's hard to say what he might have been thinking. The point is, he's gone, and we've got to wonder why."

Dana rubbed her throbbing temples. "It must have something to do with that hole in the ground we saw last night. I can't imagine what else."

"Yes, we'll be checking with the bank on that. And with regards to Chiara's connection, I've got a couple of men at her apartment, looking for clues, as we speak."

Dana sat in a daze, trying futilely to make sense of it all. "Ted's been arrested, Frank's dead, and Lane has disappeared," she said. "Does that mean that the danger is over, that I can safely relax?"

"I'll feel better when Lane's been picked up. We've put out an APB. He's probably fled the Bay Area, which means the immediate danger to you is probably over. But there have been so many surprises in this case, I'm not going to encourage you to take anything for granted."

She gave him a woebegone look. "What a night, huh?"

They exchanged long looks.

"You know, this bed looks damned good," he said. "And not just because you're in it."

"You poor thing. You must be bushed."

"It's been a long night."

"Why don't you lie down for a while?" she said. Giving him a little smile, she added, "I might even be persuaded to stay."

He leaned over and kissed her cheek. "I can't tell you how tempted I am. I've got a lot to do, though. There was another interesting development this morning that raises more questions."

Dana's shoulders sagged. "What now?"

"One of the lab fellas found a few tiny drops of blood on the sidewalk outside your office, close to the spot where the gun would have been fired."

"Blood?"

"It's strange, I know. But if it was the gunman's blood, then we've got physical evidence placing him at the scene of the crime. We'll be checking the blood type against Frank's, for starters. If nothing else, it should confirm that he's probably not our man."

"And what about Lane?" she asked.

"That would be rather interesting if it was Lane's blood, wouldn't it?"

"Oh, Mitch, I feel whipsawed. This is all coming at me so fast."

Mitch took her hand. "I haven't even told you all the little bullshit."

"There's more?"

"I had a message from the Ross Police Department. Last evening a window was broken up at your house. Your mailbox was knocked over, too. The intruder set off the alarm and apparently it scared whoever it was away. A patrolman investigated, but saw no sign of entry. They boarded up the place, so you'll have a window that needs to be replaced."

"A gnat on the nose compared to the rest of what's happened."

He pressed her hand to his cheek. "I figured you should know."

"Thanks."

He scooted closer and gathered her into his arms, giving her a big hug. For a minute or so they just stayed like that. She savored his warmth, his protective embrace, realizing how lucky she was. It could so easily have been her dead in the office, crumpled on the desk, not Chiara. She pulled back and looked Mitch in the face.

"You know what I'd like right now more than anything?" she said. "I'd like to go home."

"I won't tell you that you can't."

"What time is it, anyway?"

"A little after six."

"What's my office like?"

"The body's been removed, the technicians have finished and everything has been pretty much cleaned up. You'll have to straighten things and maybe have somebody in to take care of the carpet."

She shivered. Mitch kissed her hand.

"It's been a rough night, Dana, but I think the worst is behind you."

"I hope so."

She got out of the bed, straightening her blouse. Mitch watched as she slipped on her jeans and sweater.

"Can I buy you breakfast?" he asked.

"No, thanks. But if you want to come to my place, I'll fix you some."

"Wish I could. But duty calls. I'll drive you to your office so you can get your car."

"Come to think of it, I should make some calls while I'm there. I want to get a cleaning service in. And I also have to hire a temp to come in to answer phones." The thought of Chiara dead sent a tremor through her.

"I imagine there'll be a lot of questions once your agents start arriving."

"I'm not looking forward to that, believe me."

Dana stepped over and let him hug her again. It felt so good to be in his arms. "You've been the only positive in this whole thing," she said.

"No, Dana, you have, as well."

She squeezed him tightly. "You know, the first thing I'm going to do when I get home is call Molly. David's had plenty of time to make his peace with her. I want to see her. I think it's time she came home."

Mitch nodded. He seemed to understand the subtleties of her relationship with her daughter. That struck her as pretty enlightened for a man who'd been a bachelor his whole life.

"Will you come over and have dinner with us?" she asked. "I'd like for you to get to know Molly."

"No, I wouldn't want to interfere."

"I want you to come, Mitch."

"Well, let's see how the day goes. I've got crooks to catch."

Kentfield

"Oh, dear God!" Gloria Edwards said, when Mitch told her what had happened during the night.

The Cedrick & Betts comptroller was a tiny woman of forty-five, prim, yet with a good professional manner. Her large desk nearly swallowed her. Still, she gave the impression of being very much in command. The news clearly shocked her.

"I can't believe it," she said. "I simply can't believe it."

"The important thing at this point is for us to speak with Mr. Cedrick. Do you have any idea where he might have gone?"

She shook her head. "None whatsoever. Lane is a very private person. Outside the office his life was almost a total mystery."

"If you don't mind, I'd like to look around his office. There may be something there that would help us."

"Certainly." She got up from her chair.

Mitch rose, as well. "I'd also like to ask if the name Oak Meadow Partners means anything to you, Mrs. Edwards?"

"Yes, that's the name of Lane and Frank's limited partnership. They're developing an apartment complex in Novato."

"Do you handle the books on the project?"

She smirked. "No, Lane handled those personally. I don't know why—especially since I've done everything else—but he wanted to do that one himself for some reason."

"I see."

She led the way to Lane's office. It was neat, stylish, more formal than Frank's. Mitch glanced around.

"If you don't mind, Detective Cross, I'll get back to my desk. I should probably talk to my staff. The word will be spreading and I'm sort of left in charge now."

"Sure. I'll check back with you before I go."

Mitch went to Lane's desk and began going through the drawers systematically. There was nothing of interest in any of them until he came to the pencil drawer. In it he found a slip of paper with a name—Chiara Fiolli. There was also a phone number and an address. At the bottom of the slip a figure had been scrawled, "$1,000."

He put the slip in his pocket. Then he turned his attention to the credenza on the wall behind the desk. It contained mostly supplies and files, but in the bottom rear corner of the end cabinet he found a plastic sack from Toy World. Inside it, Mitch found a doll identical to the one left outside Molly's window. And, lying loose in the bottom of the sack, were six severed arms of missing dolls.

"Detective Cross," Gloria Edwards called from the door.

Mitch turned around.

"I've found something I think you should see."

He followed her to an office adjacent to the one where they'd met earlier. It was divided into three cubicles, two of which were occupied. They went to the empty one. The computer at the station was on and the monitor was filled with a ledger. Gloria Edwards pointed to the screen.

"Sometime last evening Lane generated three checks," she said. "He zeroed out the balances in the company operating account, the trust account and the reserve account."

"What kind of money are we talking about?"

"Close to half a million dollars, including payroll that was supposed to be paid today."

Mitch looked at her ashen face, aware as she was of the implications. "Can you contact your bank to see if the checks have been cashed?"

"Yes." She left the room.

Mitch looked at the screen, then at the stricken faces of the women in the other cubicles. He decided to go make his own calls in the privacy of Lane Cedrick's office.

Ross

Mitch called Dana and told her that what they'd suspected had now been confirmed—Oak Meadow Partners were Frank and Lane, and they had apparently embezzled funds from the project. He also told her about the doll and the severed arms he'd found in Lane's credenza, and the paper with Chiara's home number and address.

"So it *was* Lane," she said. "*He* was the one terrorizing me."

"It appears his motive was to weaken your resolve, probably force you to abandon your business and give up your interest in the bank. I suspect he was the one who sent the letters and made the calls. It all fits together.''

''Well, if his intent was to upset me, he did a damned good job.''

''I figure that loan-committee meeting threw him into a panic. He apparently enlisted Chiara's help with the documents because we found her checkbook showing that one thousand dollars was deposited in her account yesterday. Her notation indicated that Lane was the source of the funds.''

Dana was stunned. ''So Chiara *was* working for Lane.''

''That's the way it looks.''

''Seems odd that he could have killed her, under the mistaken belief it was me.''

''Yes, every time it feels like the cloud is lifting, something else happens that makes no sense. By the way, Frank can officially be eliminated as a suspect in the shooting of Chiara. I've gotten confirmation that he died before she did. Also, the blood on the sidewalk was neither his nor Chiara's. And the lab has informed me that they were both killed by the same weapon.''

''That's what you predicted, Mitch.''

''Yes, but it doesn't please me. It just confuses the situation.''

''So Ted didn't get involved until after that confrontation we had in my office, the day he came for Bev.''

''That's the way it looks, yes.''

''It all seems to be coming back to Lane, then,'' she said.

''Yes, it does. My guess is Frank Betts got swept up in the plot against you, but that Cedrick was the boy handling the dirty tricks. And there's been yet another interesting development I haven't mentioned. Before he took off, Lane cleaned out the till at Cedrick & Betts. That leads me to believe he's on a plane for South America or someplace. We're checking into that now.''

"By the way," Dana said, "you know the broken window up here?"

"Yeah."

"The police may not have noticed it in the dark last night, but I found drops of blood on the porch, possibly the blood of whoever broke the glass. Do you think there could be a connection with the blood found outside my office?"

"That's a very interesting question. I'm glad you noticed it and thought to ask. Whoever shot Chiara may have paid a visit to your place, as well. I'll send somebody up right away to gather a sample."

There was a silence on the line.

"Any further thoughts about coming to dinner tonight?" she asked.

"I'd like to, but give me a few more hours before I commit, if that's okay. Things on my end are moving fast and furious."

"I don't wish any hardship on you, Mitch, but I'm glad it's your problem now."

"It's my job to look out for the taxpayers."

"Maybe you're entitled to a bonus," she teased, "at least from one particularly grateful taxpayer, if you get my drift."

He chuckled. "I may hold you to that, sweetheart."

"I hope you do."

"Talk to you later," he said.

Dana hung up the phone, smiling. She looked over at the clock. Molly would be up for sure by now. She dialed David's number. Her daughter answered.

"Mom," the girl lamented, "where have you been? I must have left ten messages on your machine last night."

Dana pushed back her wet hair with her fingers. "I know, honey, I got home this morning and heard them. I had a pretty traumatic night but the good news is I think my ordeal is over." She told Molly what had happened in general terms.

"So it wasn't Frank," the girl said cavalierly. "I was sure it was him."

"Poor Frank," Dana said. "I certainly never would have wished that on him. But as between you and me, I'd rather think about the future."

"So would I, Mom. To be honest, I've been wanting to come home. Dad wanted me to stay until we've worked things out. I guess he doesn't understand that I don't care what he does with his girlfriends. It bothered him more than it did me. He said I'd have to stay here because of the stalker. If that's over with now, there's no reason I can't come home, is there?"

"No, honey, there isn't. Where is your father, anyway?"

"In the kitchen having breakfast."

"Will he be driving you to school?"

"Yes."

"Why don't you ask him to call me sometime today and he and I'll work out the arrangements."

"Can I have him take me back to your house after school?"

"Sure."

"Oh, good. This has been nice being here, but I'm really ready to go home."

Dana beamed. "Molly, I couldn't be happier. We're going to have to do some rethinking about how we live. I've been giving the subject a lot of thought."

"Me, too, Mom."

"I'll see you this evening after work. I'll try and be home early."

"Okay, see you then."

Dana felt lighthearted for the first time in weeks. She'd certainly had to wait a long time for her luck to change but it was beginning to appear that the wait was worth it. Dinner with Mitch and Molly was about the nicest thing she could imagine in the whole wide world.

Larkspur

Dana looked over at her desk and the bullet hole in the window behind it. "You know, I still haven't sat in my chair," she said.

"You're going to have to one of these days, kiddo," Robin replied. "Either that, or buy a new one."

"I may buy a new one. In fact, maybe I should get a whole new office."

Robin, in a red suit, crossed her legs. "The way the phones have been ringing the last couple of hours you could probably staff a fifty-desk office. I think every C&B agent in Marin has already called, wanting to go to work for you."

"It's a temporary reaction, the herding instinct," Dana said. "Once things settle down, most people will take a calmer look at the situation. Somebody is going to pick up the pieces over there."

"I think what people are saying, Dana, is that it ought to be you. The king is dead, long live the queen!"

"This has been a Shakespearean tragedy, all right, but I'm not quite ready to proclaim myself emperor." She recrossed her legs, smoothing her skirt. "In fact, if you can keep a secret, I'm thinking of cutting back to a normal workweek."

"Uh-oh," Robin said. "That's a sign."

"A sign of what?"

"Love, of course. Career women on the fast track don't cut back unless it's for a man."

"Or a child."

"A man *and* a child," Robin said. "An even deadlier combination."

Dana nodded, conceding the point. Sometimes she marveled at her friend's abilities to draw out her deepest thoughts. There was something about Robin that made her want to confess all whenever they talked, even though she often started out by denying it. Robin said it was the same way with her. Considering the week she'd had, Dana found the urge to test her feelings to be stronger than ever.

"If you must know, I've been thinking of moving to the country," she said. "Nothing way out, just upper Marin or Sonoma. A place within commute range would be nice."

"And horses, I bet. You've decided you want horses."

"No, I haven't!" Dana retorted. "I haven't given horses a thought. It's not what you're thinking."

"Yeah, sure, Kirk. Tell me another."

Dana paused to evaluate her feelings. "Spending time with Mitch at his place rekindled my love of the country, I admit. It kind of went hand in glove with this feeling that I should kick back a little, slow down and smell the roses. Plus, Molly would like it. She hasn't mentioned it for a while, but now that I think about it, she used to be very interested in horses."

"You sound to me like a woman in the bloom of early love. And it's long overdue, if you don't mind an editorial comment. I say, bravo, Dana! Good for you!"

"Well, I'm not prepared to go quite that far. But I am serious about slowing down," she said. "My private life won't change unless I make some adjustments in my professional life."

"Such as?"

"To be frank, I was thinking of making you my general manager, so I'd have a little more time for myself."

Robin laughed, shaking her head. "Thanks. I take that as a vote of confidence, and I'm grateful. But this kid is not about to assume those kinds of headaches. My evenings are for the Mortons of this world, and the occasional contract presentation. I don't want weeping agents calling me up when I'm in bed with Mr. Wonderful.''

"So much for that plan."

"It was a sweet thought, however."

There was a rap on the door and Dana turned around. Terry, the temp the agency had sent over, was standing in the open doorway.

"Excuse me, Mrs. Kirk," she said, "but there's an Adrianne Stevens from Cedrick & Betts on the line."

"Thanks, Terry, I'll take it." Dana got up from her chair.

"Now *there's* your general manager," Robin said, as Dana went to the desk. "The two of you could put together a couple of twenty-agent offices virtually overnight."

Dana's brows rose at the thought. She picked up the phone, standing at her desk. "Hi, Adrianne, long time no see."

As she listened, she gave Robin a wink. Robin smiled back.

"Listen," Dana said, "I've got a better idea. Rather than all of you traipsing over here, why don't I come by your office? Would that work for you...? Great, shall we say this afternoon...? How's two-thirty? Will that give you time to contact everybody...? Fine. Sounds good. Oh, and Adrianne, if I came a few minutes early, maybe you and I could chat for a while in private.... Super. See you then."

Dana returned to the chair next to Robin. She couldn't help a smile.

"You've got the blood of a robber baron in your veins, Dana Kirk," Robin said.

"No, I'm determined to proceed on a sensible basis from here on out. Frank—God rest his soul—always said the best job in the business world was managing managers. I always thought I was a number of years from that, but now I'm thinking maybe not. And if I can do it with a competent general manager dealing with the day-to-day problems, so much the better.''

"And what about Mitch? Is he too proud to be married to a successful businesswoman?"

"Robin! I've known the man exactly one week! I wish you'd get off this marriage business. Honestly, you'd think you were a younger sister who couldn't marry until I was gone."

"You've always been my mentor and moral guide."

"You take care of Morton and let me worry about Mitch. And leave morals out of it."

Robin hooted. "Now there's an idea I can live with!"

"Come on," Dana said, rising from her chair, "let's get out of here and have some lunch."

San Rafael

David was playing back the messages on his office answering machine when he heard the outside door open and close. A moment later the door to his office flew open and Nola stood there, her hair in her face, a wild look in her eyes. She was in a jogging suit and was breathing heavily, as though she'd run up to the building. Then he realized she was drunk.

"Nola."

"Well, congratulations, Dr. Kirk," she said, badly slurring her words, "you remember my name. It must be the professional training."

David noticed her hand was bandaged. The dressing was stained red. "What do you want?"

"I just thought I'd come by to compare notes, lover boy, now that we're both divorced *and* widowed."

He shook his head. "What are you talking about?"

She blinked. "Don't tell me you haven't heard. Dana and Frank are both dead! Christ, they must have found the bodies by now."

He screwed up his face. "Nola, Dana isn't dead."

"Yes, she is. She was killed last night. Shot."

He shook his head. "I'm afraid you're badly mistaken."

"David, she's *dead!*" Nola said angrily.

"If so, my daughter talked to her ghost on the phone this morning. And Dana's left two messages on my machine since ten o'clock. We've traded calls all morning. I tried to reach her a few minutes ago and they told me she's out to lunch."

Nola began shaking her head. "No, that's not true. She's dead. And so is Frank. They're both dead. I *know!*"

"When was the last time you slept and had something to eat?" he asked, walking toward her.

"Goddamn it, David, don't lie to me!" she screamed. "This isn't funny!"

"You've been drinking, Nola. Your mind's playing tricks on you. I think you need professional care."

"Shut the fuck up! Don't talk to me about that shit. I want to know. Is Dana alive or is she dead?"

"I told you, she's alive. Do you think I'd be sitting here if something had happened to her? I'd be with my daughter, if nothing else."

Nola shook her head with utter disbelief. "It's not possible. Not possible." She glared at him. "I don't trust you. You're a fucking liar! I wouldn't take your word on anything. I'm going to find out for myself!" With that, she turned and staggered out the door.

* * *

San Rafael

Mitch walked in the front door of the station, gave the clerk behind the window a high sign and proceeded back to the corridor leading to his office. Corinne Smith came out of her office, almost running into him.

"Well, look who the cat dragged in!" She drew back, looking him over. "Honey, pardon my French, but you look like hell!"

"Pardon my French, Corinne, but I feel like hell."

"Seems like we got no argument on that point." She grinned. "However, I have some news for you on your case."

"Yeah?"

"Before we get into that, you look like you could use a cup of coffee. Why don't you go sit at your desk and get all comfy and I'll bring you a cup?"

"Corinne, if you weren't already married, I'd marry you." He grinned and went to his office.

While he waited for her, he tried to calculate how long it had been since he'd slept. When he got past thirty hours, he gave up. Corinne came in, putting a steaming mug of coffee on the blotter in front of him. She sat down across from him and gave him one of her toothy grins.

"Now, about your case. You may need to go back to the drawing board, honey child," she said. "We got confirmation about twenty minutes ago that Lane Cedrick boarded a flight at San Francisco last night bound for Miami. As best they can tell he didn't make a connecting flight. The FBI and the local authorities are looking for him. With any luck they'll grab him before he skips the country."

"Corinne, what time did Cedrick's plane depart SFO?"

"That's the kicker. It left at ten-thirty, on schedule. And Mr. Cedrick was definitely aboard. I faxed his photo to airport security and both the ticket agent and the gate agent recognized him. I'd have known sooner, but they had to wait for the airline employees to show up for work this afternoon."

"Shit, that means Cedrick couldn't have shot Chiara, either."

"Not unless he's got blue tights, a red cape and flies faster than a speeding bullet."

Mitch sat dazed. "You just shot down my last suspect, Corinne. You realize that."

"You want that I phony up some evidence, honey? Cedrick's as good a fall guy as anybody. Or you got an old enemy you want to put in the tank instead?"

"Unfortunately it's no joking matter. I've got a killer on the loose, one who's bent on killing Dana, and I don't have the slightest idea who it is."

Corinne seemed to read by his expression that the time for lightheartedness was over. "None at all?"

Mitch shook his head. "O'Connell, Betts, and now Cedrick were either dead or out of the area when Chiara was shot."

Corinne snapped her fingers. "I almost forgot. The lab report came back on the blood outside the office and up at Mrs. Kirk's place."

"Yeah?"

"Same bleeder, Mitch."

"I could have guessed that."

"Well, now you know for sure."

Mitch rubbed his chin. He was beginning to regret he hadn't found the time earlier to grab a few winks in the back seat of the car. His brain was muddled and he wasn't likely to think any more clearly until he'd had some rest.

Corinne shook her finger. "Oh, another thing, Mitch. They went over Betts's body and the consensus is self-inflicted. They think the gun was probably removed from his hand hours after he shot himself."

"So our murderer was probably inside Betts's condo, took the gun, and went from there to Dana's. He cut himself on the glass, subsequently bleeding on the sidewalk outside Dana's office when he shot Chiara."

"Sounds to me like you got the when, the what and the how. All you need now is the who and the why."

"Very good, my dear Watson," he chided.

Corinne laughed. "So, what's next, Sherlock?"

"I'm getting out of here, Corinne. I'm going to brief Dana, then see if I can find this goddamn killer."

"You headed to the real-estate office?"

"Yeah."

"Give my regards to the lady."

"Thanks, I will."

"Oh, Mitch..."

"Yeah?"

"I'm sorry it wasn't Cedrick. Sorry to keep throwin' you curves."

"I obviously haven't been doing my job. That's the part that bothers me, Corinne."

"There's still time, honey."

"I hope so."

Ross

David Kirk stopped in front of Dana's garage, shut off the engine of his car and turned to his daughter. "Molly, I've said it all before. I want you to know I feel just terrible about what happened the other day."

"Dad, please. It's no big deal. Coming back has nothing to do with that. Mainly, I went to live with you because that's what you and Mom wanted. I'd have stayed here if it wasn't for that. I still want to see you weekends. In fact, I like it better. We have more fun that way."

David gave a begrudging nod. "You're probably right."

"Mom's not a bad mother," Molly said. "She's just real busy."

"I've probably been more critical of her than I should be."

They smiled at each other and David patted Molly's cheek.

"I'll carry your big suitcase up for you."

"Ugh. I hate the thought of unpacking."

David got out of the car and removed the bags from the trunk. He looked up at the sky. "Seems like the fog is finally starting to lift."

"It's been spooky for two days."

He grinned and carried the suitcase up the steps to the porch. Molly followed along behind.

"What happened?" she asked, seeing the boarded-up window.

"Probably a consequence of your mother's recent battles. I noticed the mailbox had been knocked over, too."

"Poor Mom."

"Looks like it's all behind her now."

Molly opened the door and David set the suitcases inside.

"Guess you can relax a little and not have to worry like you have been," he said. "You've had a pretty rough time, yourself."

"I'll be glad if things can get back to normal," she said. "If Mom's not so uptight, maybe she'll be happier."

"I hope so." David gave her a hug and a kiss, then went down the steps to his car. Sighing, he backed down the drive and into the road.

Two minutes later he'd come to Sir Francis Drake Boulevard and was waiting for a chance to make his left turn. He was so busy looking for a break in the traffic that he didn't see the red BMW convertible make the corner and continue up the street behind him, headed for Dana's place.

Larkspur

Robin Cohen pulled up in the parking lot opposite Kirk & Company at almost the same moment as Mitchell Cross arrived.

"Ms. Cohen," he said, giving her a lazy grin, "we meet again."

Robin closed and locked her door. "Yes, Detective Cross, how good to see you."

Dana had introduced them when he'd come by the office the day before, but they hadn't really talked. He'd apologized for trying to kick in her door, noting that it was good and strong.

"Were you coming to see Dana, or did you just get an overwhelming urge to buy a house?" she asked, as they walked toward the entrance. "If it's the latter, I'd be more than happy to assist you."

"Thanks, but Dana already warned me about poachers. She threatened certain unmentionable acts of violence if I ever bought real estate from anybody else."

"Dana is known for her ability to gain customer loyalty."

Mitch chuckled. "She said you had a sense of humor."

"Like we say in the business world, that and a buck will buy you a cup of coffee."

"Cops usually get their coffee free."

"Then it sounds like you're in the right line of work."

"You mean I shouldn't get my real-estate license?"

"Oh, God."

"It's what you do when you get a divorce or lose your job, isn't it?" he joked.

"You *do* have a mean streak."

"My reputation has spread."

Robin laughed. "I don't know if you're going to find Dana in. She had a meeting this afternoon with C&B's Kentfield office. She said something about maybe going home early to see her daughter, so she may not be coming back."

She peered into Dana's private office as they arrived at the entrance, then the other way toward the sales floor. It looked deserted. "No sign of her, but let's check with the receptionist."

Mitch opened the door and Robin stepped inside. The temp, Terry, came around to greet them. She had a distraught look on her face.

"I'm glad somebody came back," she said.

"What's wrong?" Robin asked.

"About twenty minutes ago the most horrible woman I've ever met in my life came in. She was drunk and abusive. I almost called the police."

"What did she want?"

"She wanted to know if Mrs. Kirk had been in today. I told her she'd been in this morning but that she was at a meeting now. She demanded to know where. I told her I didn't know." Terry shook her head with disgust.

"Who was she?" Robin asked.

"I don't know. She never said her name."

"What did she look like?" Mitch asked, starting to show considerable interest.

"She was about forty. Red hair. Good figure, but a sloppy, mean drunk."

Mitch turned to Robin. "Do you know who it could be?"

"Oh, I know, all right. It was Nola Betts."

"Frank's wife?"

"Former wife. She hates Dana with a passion. I imagine she flipped out when she learned what happened to Frank."

He had a look of consternation on his face as he turned to the receptionist. "Did Mrs. Betts say where she was headed?"

"No. I just wanted to get rid of her. I told her Mrs. Kirk would probably go directly home from her meeting. Then the woman left."

Mitch started looking rather agitated. "Terry, did you notice any injuries on Mrs. Betts? A cut or gash, for example? Hands, arms, anything like that?"

"Yes, she had a bandage on her hand. A bloody bandage."

"Jesus," Mitch said. He turned to Robin. "Listen, I think Nola may have been the one who shot Chiara last night, intending to kill Dana. I want you to get on the phone and track Dana down. Tell her not to go to her place under any circumstances. Nola is probably there, waiting for her. I'll notify the Ross police from my car. I'm headed up to her place now. Got that?"

Robin nodded. "Yes, I'll start with C&B. She may still be there."

"Good," Mitch said, as he raced for the door. "I just hope we're in time."

He ran out the door and Robin dashed to the nearest phone. What the hell was the number of the Kentfield office? Damn, what a time to draw a blank. She hastily dialed Information.

Ross

Dana sat at a light on Sir Francis Drake Boulevard and wondered if Molly would be home yet. Unless she had to go back to David's to pack, he already should have dropped her off by now. Dana was eager to see her. They both needed this reunion. She more, perhaps, than Molly.

The light changed and she moved on up the boulevard, switching to the center lane to make her left turn. Once she was on the side street, and approaching her hill, she began to relax. She'd missed her home as well as her daughter, though it would take a while to adjust to the fact that they weren't in danger anymore.

Even now, it was hard to believe that Lane had been the killer. She never would have guessed he'd go that far. But at least it was over and she could turn her attention to other things. Ironically, Frank's and Lane's demise had left her with a wonderful business opportunity. She and Robin had joked about two twenty-person offices, but the idea didn't seem at all far-fetched after talking with Adrianne and her people. If she could pull it off, and still have time for herself, she might well give it serious thought.

Before she plunged headlong into anything, though, she'd stop and catch her breath. Spending some time with Molly would be a top priority. It was a happy thought, and it felt awfully good to be having them again.

Dana was a quarter of the way up her hill when her car phone buzzed. She picked up the receiver. "Hello?"

"Dana, where are you?" It was Robin.

"On my way home, why?"

"Don't go! Stop. Nola's there!" Her voice was desperate.

"Robin, what are you talking about?"

"Mitch came in a few minutes ago. He said Nola was the one who killed Chiara. Dana, she's flipped out and she's dangerous. Mitch told me to tell you not to go home under any circumstances."

"Robin, Molly could be there!"

"Well, Mitch and the police will handle it. You can't go up there. Do you understand?"

"But, Robin . . ."

"Don't argue with me!"

Dana slowed the car, her mind spinning. "All right," she said numbly. "Don't worry." Then she hung up, pulling to the side of the road.

Her heart was pounding as she considered the possibilities. If Nola was crazed and bent on revenge, what would she do if she found Molly at the house? Was she so far gone that she might hurt her? With Nola, there was no telling.

Dana moaned in agony. She snatched the phone and dialed David's office. She had to know whether Molly was up there with Nola or not. He answered right away.

"David, where's Molly?" she said without ceremony.

"I dropped her off at your place half an hour ago. Why?"

"Oh, my God."

"Dana, what's the matter? Isn't she there?"

"Yes, I think so. Never mind, David, it's all right. I'll take care of it. Goodbye."

She slammed down the phone, hesitating for only the briefest instant before jamming the gearshift into Drive and pressing the gas pedal to the floor. The tires screeched as she sped up the hill. She couldn't let anything happen to her child, no matter what! Moments later she came to her drive. Nola's red BMW was sitting in front of the garage. Dana's pulse raced even harder. If Nola had hurt Molly, she'd kill the bitch with her bare hands!

She leapt from the car and ran up the stairs. The door wasn't locked. She flew in, arriving breathlessly at the entrance to the front room. And there she found them—Molly seated on a sofa, tears running down her cheeks, and Nola standing behind her, disheveled and looking like hell. A gun was in her hand.

"Well, dear," Nola said, "it looks like Mommy is home at last."

"Nola," Dana said between breaths, "what do you want?"

"What do I want? *What do I want?*" she screamed. "I want you to pay for what you've done, goddamn it!"

Molly sobbed quietly, biting her lip.

Seeing her child weeping, Dana's adrenaline surged. But she tried to calm herself, to stay in control. "Listen, Nola," she said, "our problems have nothing to do with Molly. Let her go. She hasn't done anything to you."

"She's your goddamn brat, isn't she? That's enough to make me detest her—along with David and everything else associated with you." Nola drew a ragged breath. "You killed Frank. You killed the only man I truly loved. You destroyed my marriage, my home, my life, and you have the *gall* to ask me to do something for you?"

Nola stepped around the sofa and moved toward Dana, the gun shaking in her hand. "You have no idea how I've loathed you, Dana Kirk, how I've hated you for what you've done. But it wasn't until I saw Frank lying dead, shot in the head because of you, that I knew I had to make you pay."

"If Frank killed himself, it had nothing to do with me."

"Oh, don't even *try,*" Nola said through her teeth. "Don't even try to give me that shit. You killed him! *You!* You ruined his life. And *mine!*"

"Nola, you aren't thinking clearly. This won't do you any good."

"There's only one thing I care about and that's seeing you dead." She moved closer. "I wish it didn't have to be suddenly. I'd rather you die slowly, the way I've been dying—day by day, hour by hour, knowing you're the one responsible for my suffering."

Dana braced herself. Faintly in the distance she heard the sound of sirens. Nola seemed oblivious. She was bent on murder. Dana's mind reeled. If only she could stall for a few more minutes.

"Maybe you're giving me too much credit, Nola. Maybe your problem with Frank had nothing to do with me."

"Don't give me that shit," Nola said, taking another step in her direction. "You didn't give a damn about me. You wanted to take Frank away from me. And when you got him, you used him and then tossed him out, just like you did David. You're nothing but a selfish bitch."

Dana saw Molly get to her feet. Nola was unaware because she was so preoccupied. She kept inching her way closer. The gun in her hand shook as she extended it, pointing it toward Dana's breast. The sirens were louder, but still seemed a million miles away.

"What good is it going to do to kill me?" Dana asked, her voice quavering. From the corner of her eye, she saw Molly pick up a large Chinese porcelain vase. "It's not worth sacrificing your own life, Nola," she pleaded.

"I've got no life. Seeing you dead is the only satisfaction I want."

Molly began creeping toward Nola. The police sirens were practically outside.

"Please," Dana said, "can't we talk, reason this out?"

Nola extended the gun, her hands trembling. Molly, only a few feet from Nola, lifted the vase. Dana tensed, expecting a bullet to come crashing into her body. Nola gritted her teeth in anticipation of the explosion, but before she could pull the trigger Molly brought the vase down on her head, shattering it as the gun went off. Nola collapsed under the blow and fell to the floor.

Dana stood frozen, the shot having struck the floor at her feet. Molly was stunned, her eyes widened with horror. After a second she shrieked hysterically, her hands clasped to her mouth. Dana rushed over and put her arms around her.

"Mom, oh, Mom!" Molly cried.

Dana stroked her head and kissed her. "Honey, you saved my life."

The sirens stopped and Dana could hear a commotion outside, the sound of vehicles and people running, shouts. Nola moaned. Dana bent over and took the gun from her hand as Molly went to the window.

"Mom, it's the police!"

Nola continued to groan. She opened her eyes, squinting up at Dana. Nola looked so pathetic, Dana couldn't hate her. She'd fallen about as far as a person could fall.

Molly went to the entry hall to let in the police. Two officers came rushing in, guns drawn.

"It's all right," Dana said sorrowfully, "she hasn't hurt anyone except herself."

Mitch was racing up the hill about as fast as he could safely go. The sirens had stopped a few moments earlier. He could only hope the officers responding had arrived in time.

Coming around the curve he saw the patrol cars at the foot of Dana's drive, their emergency lights flashing, doors open. It was an all-too-familiar sight.

He brought the car to a lurching halt behind the first patrol car and jumped out. He ran up the steep drive. The front door was open, but he couldn't see anyone. He took the steps two at a time. By the time he reached the porch his heart was chugging and his breathing was labored. A uniformed officer was standing in the entry, his radio in his hand, talking to the dispatcher. Mitch came up beside him and looked into the front room.

Another officer was bent over a woman lying on the floor. For an instant Mitch thought it was Dana, but then he saw the tangled red hair and the contorted face and knew it was Nola Betts. He showed the patrolman his badge.

"Where's Mrs. Kirk?"

He pointed toward the family room.

Mitch went back to where he found Dana and Molly huddled on a sofa. Dana had her arm around the girl. Molly had been crying, but seemed more dazed than anything. Dana gave him a bewildered look, yet there was relief on her face, as well.

He went over and sat on the edge of the cushion, next to her. "You all right?"

"Yes. We both are. Molly saved my life. Nola was about to shoot me when Molly clunked her."

"You're a brave girl," he said.

She looked at him through eyes bubbling with tears, but she couldn't speak.

"Well, it's over," he said.

"Really over?" Dana's expression was disbelieving. "I don't know if I could handle another surprise, Mitch. Just when I think things are going to be all right, something else happens."

"This is it, I promise." He patted her knee. "At least for this week." Then he grinned.

"Don't even joke about it."

"I think you two could use a few minutes to relax and gather yourselves. I'll step into the other room and help out. Will you be all right?"

Dana squeezed Molly's shoulders. "Yes, we're fine."

Mitch reached over and gave Molly's cheek a pinch. "Playing cops and robbers can get kind of rough, can't it?"

"I like watching it on television better."

"Want in on a secret?" he said leaning closer. "I do, too." He gave her a wink and got up. "I'll be back in a little while."

Half an hour later Mitch returned to the family room. Dana was in the kitchen and Molly was sitting at the counter, drinking a mug of hot chocolate.

"All done?" she asked, sounding in much better spirits than when he'd left.

"The officers are working on their report. Nola's been taken away. She has some lacerations and a big lump on her head. That's the least of her problems."

"Mitch, why did she come here like this? I thought Lane was the one who'd been harassing me."

"He was. Nola flipped out when she discovered Frank's body. She told me she blamed you for driving him to suicide and decided to take her revenge. She grabbed Frank's gun, got drunk and went looking for you."

"And she found Chiara instead."

"Yes."

"So Ted, Lane and Nola were after me independently, each with a different ax to grind."

"And all with tragic results."

"At least Ted and Nola have been arrested," Dana said.

"Lane also. I got word a short while ago that he'd been picked up trying to board a flight in Miami."

"Then it *is* over."

"Except for the shouting, yes." He glanced back and forth between them. "So, how's everybody here holding up?"

"Fine," Molly said, seeming not too much the worse for wear.

Mitch had been in these situations often enough to know that with younger people, particularly, a little humor sometimes helped. He stepped over to her and squeezed her biceps. "You're pretty strong, kid, fortunately for your mother. Are the girls doing boxing in P.E. these days?"

"No," she said with a laugh. "More like soccer and badminton."

"Did you learn to be a scrapper from your mother, then?"

Molly glanced at Dana and smiled. "I never saw her hit anybody," she said. "Actually she gets scared real easy. *She* screamed all through *Jurassic Park,* not me."

Mitch gave Dana a wry look. "You're more innocent than I thought, Mom."

"Where is this line of questioning leading, Detective Cross?" she asked. "Or are you just having a good time?"

"Oh, having a good time, by all means."

She narrowed her eyes in a mock glare, but couldn't repress the smile, or the blush, that followed. "You are an evil man, Mitch."

He noticed Molly's awareness of the word play between them. He could tell she was starting to notice that there was something going on. "Your mother feels free to talk to me that way because we've become friends," he explained. "Otherwise I'm sure she'd show me the respect due a peace officer."

Molly gave Dana a bemused look. Mitch could tell there were unspoken messages passing between them.

"I've invited Mitch to stay and have dinner with us," Dana said to her daughter.

"Maybe under the circumstances Molly would prefer to be alone with you," he said. "We can always do it another time."

The girl shook her head. "No, it's fine. I don't mind."

"Are you sure?" Mitch asked.

Molly nodded, looking perfectly content and more than a little intrigued. Dana went to the refrigerator. "Well, I'm having a beer. I need a drink after today. How about you, Mitch?"

"I think I could use one, considering I've pulled an eighteen-hour shift already. But first, maybe I should ask the boys if they'd take the statements from you two in the morning instead. Would you mind going down to the station first thing?"

"That would be much better than doing it now," Dana said.

He started for the front room to send the patrolmen on their way when Dana stopped him.

"I was thinking of calling out for Chinese," she said. "It's a favorite of Molly's and mine. Would you enjoy that?"

He considered the invitation. "Do you allow forks?"

"We make exceptions for our less sophisticated guests, yes."

"Mom!" Molly protested. "That's not very polite."

Mitch laughed. "Don't think a thing of it, honey," he said. "That's how ladies of a certain age let a gentleman know they want to be friendly."

"What a thing to say after I invite you to dinner!" Dana protested, her hands on her hips. "Some gentleman you are!"

"Part of being a cop is being brutally honest, my dear."

"Go, Mitch! And when you come back, you can open your own beer for being so rude."

Laughing, he left the room with a light step. He was having fun, but he knew he'd be paying for his remark for a good long while. For better or for worse, that's the way women were. But this time, he didn't mind at all.

He'd blown back into town like a

DUST DEVIL

REBECCA BRANDEWYNE

She was young and beautiful; he was the town's "Bad Boy." They shared one night of passion that turned Sarah Kincaid into a woman—and a mother. Yet Renzo Cassavettes never knew he had a child, because when blame for a murder fell on his shoulders, he vanished into thin air. Now Renzo is back, but his return sets off an explosive chain of events. Once again, there is a killer on the loose.

Is the man Sarah loves a cold-blooded murderer playing some diabolical game—or is he the only port in a seething storm of deception and desire?

Find out this March at your favorite retail outlet.

Now available for the first time in paperback!

SOMEBODY'S BABY

By *New York Times* bestselling author

CHARLOTTE VALE ALLEN

Snow Devane is devastated when her dying mother confesses that she stole Snow from a New York City supermarket thirty years ago. She is not Snow's mother. Snow is someone else's baby. With the help of friends and unexpected lovers, Snow begins to look for answers. Who was this woman who raised her? What happened to her "real" mother? And, most importantly, who is Snow Devane?

Find out this April at your favorite retail outlet.

In the public eye, nothing is kept sacred.

BARBARA BRETTON

STARFIRE

Sara Chance, the wealthy widow of celebrity
Maxwell Chance, is in the spotlight. And she
wants out.

Sam Berenger, an unforgotten love from Sara's past,
enters the scene. And he wants Sara.

Sara is desperate to change her life, especially when she
discovers that someone close to her is trying to destroy
her reputation and her wealth. But can Sam be trusted?
Because the enemy is often the one you least suspect....

Available this March at your favorite retail outlet.

LET BESTSELLING AUTHOR
ERICA SPINDLER

TEMPT YOU WITH

FORBIDDEN FRUIT

Beautiful and headstrong, Glory St. Germaine was born
into one of New Orleans's finest families. But good *and*
evil run through three generations of Glory's family. Her
mother, Hope, and grandmother, Lily, are trapped by
shame, secrets and circumstances. And Victor Santos, in
love with Glory, is trapped by his own past. Can Victor
and Glory find a way to put the past behind them? Or will
their love remain forbidden fruit?

Available this April at your favorite retail outlet.

 MIRA The brightest star in women's fiction

MESFF

If you love the exciting stories of

JANICE KAISER

Then order now to receive more passionate tales
by this popular MIRA author:

#66029	LOTUS MOON	$4.99 U.S.	☐
		$5.50 CAN.	☐
#66024	PRIVATE SINS	$4.99 U.S.	☐
		$5.50 CAN.	☐

(limited quantities available)

TOTAL AMOUNT $
POSTAGE & HANDLING $
($1.00 for one book, 50¢ for each additional)
APPLICABLE TAXES* $_____
TOTAL PAYABLE $_____
(check or money order—please do not send cash)

To order, complete this form and send it, along with a check or money order
for the total above, payable to MIRA Books, to: **In the U.S.:** 3010 Walden
Avenue, P.O. Box 9077, Buffalo, NY 14269-9077; **In Canada:** P.O. Box 636,
Fort Erie, Ontario, L2A 5X3.

Name:_____
Address: _____City:_____
State/Prov.:_____ Zip/Postal Code:_____

*New York residents remit applicable sales taxes.
  Canadian residents remit applicable GST and provincial taxes.   MJKBL2

MIRA